GASLIGHT GHOULS

UNEASY TALES OF SHERLOCK HOLMES, MONSTERS AND MADMEN

CVP '02

GASLIGHT GHOULS

UNEASY TALES OF SHERLOCK HOLMES, MONSTERS AND MADMEN

EDITED BY J.R. CAMPBELL AND CHARLES PREPOLEC

Belanger Books
2022

For information contact:
Belanger Books, LLC
61 Theresa Ct.
Manchester, NH 03103

derrick@belangerbooks.com
www.belangerbooks.com

Cover Art by Dave Elsey©2022
Cover and Design by Brian Belanger
www.belangerbooks.com and *www.redbubble.com/people/zhahadun*

Table of Contents

COPYRIGHT INFORMATION

"The very horror of my situation lies in the fact
that my fears are so vague———"

DEEDS OF HELLISH CRUELTY AND HIDDEN WICKEDNESS: It's in the trees! It's coming!

A brief introduction by Charles Prepolec

"You look at these scattered houses, and you are impressed by their beauty. I look at them, and the only thought which comes to me is a feeling of their isolation and of the impunity with which crime may be committed there...

...They always fill me with a certain horror. It is my belief, Watson, founded upon my experience, that the lowest and vilest alleys in London do not present a more dreadful record of sin than does the smiling and beautiful countryside."

"You horrify me!"

"...look at these lonely houses, each in its own fields, filled for the most part with poor ignorant folk who know little of the law. Think of the deeds of hellish cruelty, the hidden wickedness which may go on, year in, year out, in such places, and none the wiser."

–The Adventure of the Copper Beeches

Welcome, dear reader, to *Gaslight Ghouls: Uneasy Tales of Sherlock Holmes, Monsters and Madmen*, the fifth in our 'Gaslight Sherlock Holmes' series of anthologies pitting the supreme rationalist, Sherlock Holmes, against the weird, the supernatural and even the otherworldly. In previous volumes our general themes have explored the outright fantastic, the nightmarish, the uncanny and the gothic, but this time out we take our thematic cues from no less a personage than Sherlock Holmes himself, and, of course, these being horror-oriented stories, at least a couple key films, as well.

The quotations above come as Holmes and Watson are aboard a train on their way to "Hampshire. Charming rural place. The Copper Beeches, five miles on the far side of Winchester" at the request of Miss Violet Hunter, a governess who has found herself in the most gothic of situations. Watson casually remarks on the charm and appeal of the passing rural scenery, prompting the frankly horrifying, but incredibly insightful response by Holmes given above. In short, in one little sidelight of observation he not only sets our stage by suggesting stories around themes of sin, hellish cruelty and hidden wickedness, but provides an explanation for why they can occur with such frequency with the two factors of isolation and impunity that are a simple part of life away from the bright lights and ever-present observation of neighbors found in urban landscapes. Holmes makes it clear that the countryside may be a very dangerous place, indeed, so we have the first half of our theme, or at least a strong sense of setting, but obviously tales of murderous farmers will only carry us so far, and this being one in our 'Gaslight Sherlock Holmes' series, we needed a suitable infusion of the weird or supernatural to make good on our remit.

So, what comes to mind when you think of evil and hidden wickedness in lonely places set in rural Britain? Why, folk horror, of course! A subgenre of horror that is currently undergoing something of a revival in film —see *Kill List* (2011), *A Field in England* (2013), *The Witch* (2015), *Apostle* (2018), *Midsommar* (2019), and *Lamb* (2021) — and to a lesser degree literature (*The Fiends in the Furrows: An Anthology of*

Folk Horror (2018), *Damnable Tales: A Folk Horror Anthology* 2021, etc…). The classics in the field, however, remain *Witchfinder General* (1968), *The Blood on Satan's Claw* (1971) and arguably the most influential of them all, *The Wicker Man* (1973), which deals with a strait-laced Catholic policeman (Edward Woodward) visiting a remote Scottish island in search of a missing child, only to find the entire population has reverted to paganism under the charismatic rule of Lord Summerisle (Christopher Lee) and are engaged in ritual sacrifice to ensure a bountiful harvest (It's curiously fun watching two actors who have both played Sherlock Holmes face off against each other). *Witchfinder General* deals with the paranoia during 17th century witch trials and *The Blood on Satan's Claw* sees a malign presence taking hold in a community when a curiously shaped skull is found in a farmer's field. This latter concept of evil spreading from an unearthed ancient object also powers much of the writing of M. R. James ('Oh, Whistle, and I'll Come to You, My Lad') and the remarkable 1957 Jacques Tourneur film adaptation of 'Casting the Runes' - *Night of the Demon*. Here we have a scientific paranormal investigator (Dana Andrews) looking into the activities of a powerful cult-leader, Julian Karswell (Niall MacGinnis), who is utilizing a runic parchment to set a demon on his critics. The séance scene featuring Reginald Beckwith as a manic medium, provides us with the memorable, and oh so suitable, line given our cover art, "It's in the trees! It's coming!" So memorable, in fact, that Kate Bush sampled it for her 1986 single 'Hounds of Love'. In any case, it isn't just location that feeds into folk horror.

Folk horror, at its loosest definition, is simply the use of folklore elements to create a sense of fear or horror. More pointedly, as folk horror student Adam Scovell put it in an article for the BFI, scenarios that place "emphasis on landscape which subsequently isolates its communities and individuals, skewing the dominant moral and theological systems enough to cause violence, human sacrifices, torture and even demonic and supernatural summonings." Now, that definitely seems to fit our remit. And when you add in that often the sinister elements in folk horror stem from the behaviors and in-bred traditions of people in lonely places (think Shirley Jackson's *The Lottery* and Robin Hardy's *The Wicker Man*), instead of just the overtly supernatural, we had all the elements in place for our theme of 'uneasy' Sherlock Holmes stories.

As a result, the guidelines sent to our selected list of talented authors requested stories along these two tracks:

1. A focus on horrifyingly driven, possibly charismatic, influential cult of personality villain types. Those so obsessed with their goals, beliefs, plans, desires, needs, etc… that they have no moral guides and care not a jot about anyone or anything that does not support their obsessions, placing them outside the normal values of a decent or civilized society. Scientists, cult leaders, necromancers, politicians, etc… these individuals may play either a direct role in events (Squire Hamilton in Hammer's *Plague of the Zombies* or Lord Summerisle in *The Wicker Man*, for example) or their legacy must influence that action (via cursed objects, superstition, revived pagan or occult practices or buildings, think Emeric Belasco in *The Legend of Hell House* or Julian Karswell in *Night of the Demon*). Focus on the evil that men do, or can convince others to do in their name or for a shared belief, whether from some supernatural influence or simply cruel perverse obsession.

2.   We would like to see the above played out in, to quote Adam Scovell's point about folk horror films, scenarios that place "emphasis on landscape which subsequently isolates its communities and individuals" although in our view these need not specifically be country locations, but simply underground, or somehow closed or hidden communities, families, societies, organizations and the like. After all, urban legends are simply folk tales within an urban setting, and the UK certainly has enough hidden history, buried under a couple thousand years of progress built over earlier layers, to make this a rich vein for possible story ideas.

Needless to say, our talented writers rose to the occasion with skill and enthusiasm. The fruit of their labors lie in the pages ahead, and it's a bountiful and rich harvest, to be sure. Now turn the page and prepare for a journey to the smiling countryside, alongside Sherlock Holmes, where you will uncover 'the deeds of hellish cruelty, the hidden wickedness which may go on, year in, year out, in such places' for yourself!

Charles Prepolec
Calgary, 2022

THE ADVENTURE OF THE GHASTLY REVENANT

Jonathan Maberry

"Tell me, gentlemen," said the visitor, "do you believe in life beyond death?"

We were all arranged around a comfortable fire in our sitting room at 221B Baker Street. My friend, Mr. Sherlock Holmes, was curled into his own chair, legs crossed Indian fashion beneath a brocade rug, dark eyes glittering with interest. I sat across from him, my notebook opened on my lap.

The speaker was a short and portly man, with a lugubrious face that was very much in keeping with his trade as a country undertaker. He perched on the edge of the couch, his thick fingers slowly turning a hat which he held by the wide, flat brim.

"That would depend," drawled Holmes, "on whether this is a religious or medical question. If the latter, then Watson is your man, for there is a riot of life even in a cooling corpse. Bacteria and such. If the former, then I fear you have made a long journey in vain."

The undertaker, whose name was Japhet Tobias Renner, nodded and sat for a long moment, lips pursed in thought.

"Perhaps it is both, gentlemen," he said.

"Ah," said Holmes, looking a bit disappointed. And in this I could sympathize. Of late the cases that brought a stream of hopeful visitors to our rooms were of the kind Holmes uncharitably called 'unbearably mundane wastes of human breath.' Or worse; and as his small store of patience dwindled, he began to say as much to the faces of the people who occupied Mr. Renner's place. Some went away with a flea in their ear, some snarled replies that ranged from apologetic to crushingly disappointed.

While I could sympathize, I was perhaps less inclined to dismiss outright any claims that suggested a connection to matters of the spiritual. And, on the other hand, I occasionally reminded Holmes that we had taken cases that were brought to us as supernatural mysteries and yet turned out to be grounded very much in this world, and particularly in Holmes's purview. The Adventure of the Sussex Vampire comes to mind, and of course the recent and quite grotesque matter of the Hound of the Baskervilles.

The greatest number of such cases turned out to be not only mundane but trivial. Just in the last fortnight we had listened to tales of missing cats, straying husbands, minor thefts of such little importance that I could hear Holmes grind his teeth. However, sprinkled among them were all manner of wild claims of witchcraft, hauntings, and even demonic possession.

Not a single case of merit had come to Holmes in so long I was concerned for his state of mind. Inaction is anathema to him, and the commonplace a plague.

"Pray sir," said Holmes abruptly, "make a decision and by all means consult someone whose profession is more appropriately suited to—"

17

"If you please, Mr. Holmes," interrupted the undertaker, "I am well aware of how my comments and questions sound. Just as I am aware of your reputation and your intolerance for nonsense."

"Indeed?" asked Holmes, raising one eyebrow.

"I did not pick your name at random, sir," said Renner. "And, despite my occupation, I am not prone to deep beliefs in the fantastical. I blush to admit that even my faith in the Creator is not what it should be, and I have been taken to task about this by the vicar of our parish more than once. I do not dare call myself an agnostic, you understand, but between us I will admit freely that I am more devoted to texts on natural philosophy than to holy scriptures. It may be said fairly of me that I possess as little of what is called 'fancy' as anyone you might care to meet. If it cannot be weighed or measured or described in a taxonomical way, then my attention wanes quickly." He paused. "I believe that you, too, share a similar empirical view of the world."

I saw Holmes's eyes grow a bit brighter with interest at these words.

"Perhaps," he said dryly. "Whereas, my friend and colleague, Dr. Watson embraces both the realities of science and the mysteries of faith with some vigor."

I inclined my head, though I was aware that there was more than a little mockery in what Holmes said. To Renner, I said, "Your views are not common for an undertaker, I take it?"

"Not at all," said Renner. "Most of my colleagues are quite deeply religious and many are equally superstitious. I suppose it is an occupational hazard when one works among the dead. To say nothing of the constant atmosphere of grief and loss exuded by the mourners and enduring sadness from those who visit graves on anniversaries of birth, marriage, and so forth. Ours is not a happy profession."

"What, then, brings you here to raise the question of life *beyond* death?" asked Holmes. He opened a cigarette case; when our guest declined, Holmes took one and fished for a match.

"Before I answer that, Mr. Holmes," said Renner, "let me ask one more question." He took what appeared to be a steadying breath. "Do you believe in the 'larger world'?"

"I beg your pardon," said Holmes, his match pausing an inch from the cigarette. "'Larger world?' Should I infer from this that you are asking about beliefs in the supernatural?"

"I am, sir."

"I am under the impression that we have already touched upon that subject and you rightly guess that I do not. However, it seems clear you do." Holmes lit his cigarette, and I saw his eyes narrow as he reappraised our guest. "You are not a theosophist, I perceive. You display none of the charms or trinkets so common among that lot. Nor, I daresay, their hauteur. And you are a rural practitioner of your trade. Out where nights are long and dark and it is, perhaps, easier to believe in ghosts and goblins, werewolves and vampires."

"Perhaps that is true, sir," said Renner, taking no obvious offense. "But it is none of those that troubles me."

"What then?" asked Holmes.

"Are you familiar with the phenomenon known as a revenant? A walking corpse?"

Holmes blew pearlescent smoke into the air. "If you hurry, you can catch the 10:30 train. It should have you home by this evening."

Renner sighed and looked down at his hat, turning it slowly.

Without looking up he said, "I know how it sounds, and I feel half a fool for even bringing this to you. Had I not seen him with my own eyes I would not have even considered coming here to seek your advice."

19

"Seen...*whom*...?" asked Holmes.

"My brother, Ian."

Holmes and I looked at him.

"My *dead* brother," said Renner. "The brother I buried with my own hands in the churchyard not four days ago."

*

"I beg your pardon?" said Holmes after a long moment. "Your *dead* brother...?"

"Yes, sir," said Renner, and his dour expression became even more grave.

"Are you claiming to have seen his ghost?"

"No, sir," said the undertaker, "I am not."

"Then...?"

"Ian showed up at my very door," said Renner, his face growing pale at the memory. Small beads of sweat appeared on his brow. "In the flesh, gentlemen, for in my shock I embraced him. He was quite real...and quite cold. Cold as the grave in the truest sense of that expression. His clothes were the ones in which he was buried, and although they were quite ragged and torn, I recognized them. And...they were clotted with the very dirt I had shoveled onto his coffin."

I leaned forward. "I must ask, Mr. Renner, but how surely can you rely on the doctor who examined him following his death? There are a number of medical conditions, narcolepsy among them, that might be factors here."

"Excellent, Watson," said Holmes quietly.

But Renner shook his head. "Doctor Oldkirk examined him. Perhaps you have heard of him?"

"Jonas Oldkirk?" asked Holmes, showing a renewed spark of interest. "The author of the excellent paper disputing the prevailing belief that phlebitis was the cause of most diseases. I found that particularly useful in the case of the jeweler's ring finger. Do you recall that one, Watson? No? Ah well, it was before your time, I suppose." To Renner he said. "Dr. Oldkirk examined your brother upon his death?"

"He did, sir," said the undertaker, "and pronounced him dead of a cirrhotic liver. Alas, my brother was overly fond of the bottle."

I asked, "An autopsy performed…?"

Renner gave me a bleak stare. "It was, sir, and through those torn clothes I could see the signs of it. His chest was partly exposed, and I could see the big incision which was but lightly stitched for burial purposes."

"Dear lord," I gasped. When I turned to Holmes, I found him studying Renner with the sharpness of a falcon.

"You interest me, Mr. Renner," he said slowly.

"What we mean," I said hastily, "is that you have our deepest sympathies and—"

Holmes cut in. "Watson, please. Mr. Renner, you said you embraced your brother? What did he say? What happened after that? Tell me all and leave nothing out."

Renner kept turning his hat along the brim. His face, which had been pale, grew paler still, and there was in his eyes a look of profound sadness mingled with something else that I can only describe as horror.

When he spoke, his tone was faint and ghostly. "Yes, gentlemen, I did embrace my brother. How could I not, for here he was alive again. In such a moment as that reason lags behind emotion, and there had been great love between us. We were orphaned at a young age and raised by an aunt who clearly regarded us as a burden. She lived in a remote old house far from anyone of our own ages. So, Ian and I were best friends to one another. We were of an age, he being my elder by a year. We made of our rooms a tower under siege or a ship at sea or anything that would provide us joy. We ran wild in the surrounding forests and were happy in our way. When we were of age, he went to sea and sailed the world, and I entered into apprenticeship in what had been our family business before our parents' death. There was some money put aside for this education, and I embraced it with enthusiasm. My devotion to natural philosophy was born in the fields and forests, and by studying even the rats in our aunt's old house."

I got up and poured him a knock of scotch. Renner sipped gratefully and continued his narrative.

"My brother met Dr. Oldkirk during his travels. Ian's ship put into Haiti, a small and impoverished country located on the island of Hispaniola in the Greater Antilles archipelago of the Caribbean Sea. The doctor was there to study a species of tree frog in hopes that its skin secretions might have some medical benefits, as the locals claimed. He owned a farm there in which he grew a great variety of herbs and special plants from all over the world. Oldkirk believed that the cures to many of the world's ills could be found in medicines based on plants. He was selling some of his cures via mail order to customers around the world."

"I have seen his tinctures and decoctions in the apothecary," I said.

Holmes pursed his lips in thought, then indicated that Renner should continue.

"There was some trouble on the island," said the undertaker. "There was an outbreak of some kind among the townsfolk. A virulent disease that killed many. Lucky for the rest that Dr. Oldkirk was there for he used his plant medicines to cure. Naturally these families were grateful to him and became very loyal. The same disease seemed to hit harder on other farms in the area, and it was quite terrible, as Ian wrote in his letters. However, those people who used Oldkirk's cures, even those sick unto the point of death, recovered. In fact, no one who went to Oldkirk for treatment died."

"Remarkable," I said.

"Quite," said Holmes quietly.

"The plague continued to spread, and Dr. Oldkirk offered his services to some of the surrounding farms, but the owners did not allow their people to accept his help."

"Whyever not?" I demanded.

Renner sighed. "Because they said he was a witch who farmed the devil's acres. Ian said that this was jealousy because their local *bokors*—witch doctors—were unable to cure their own sick. The plague petered out on Oldkirk's farm but continued to claim lives on the surrounding farms. You can probably guess the rest. One night the other farmers rose up and burned Oldkirk's fields and killed many of his servants. Cut their heads off like barbarians. Dr. Oldkirk escaped with his life and the clothes on his back and was fortunate to take refuge among British merchants on the island, which is where he and Ian became friends. Ian was a seed and grain broker, you see, representing many of the farms here in this part of England, as well as many in Scotland."

"How fortunate for Dr. Oldkirk to have found refuge," said Holmes, gazing at Renner through the slowly rising veil of blue smoke.

"Fortunate indeed, gentlemen," said Renner. "For around that time, Ian fell sick and was fortunate that the doctor was there."

"What lucky timing," said Holmes.

"Dr. Oldkirk cared for my brother and restored him to health," said Renner. "Or, at least somewhat, because it was clear Ian had contracted some kind of tropical sickness. Malaria, or something like it. The kind that can be controlled but which tends to spring up again. The doctor —good hearted man that he is—prepared various medicines for my brother. But alas, as can happen with tropical diseases, Ian never quite recovered full vigor, and so he came home to England and settled in my house. By then I had had some small success in my profession, having bought the firm from my uncle shortly before his death. A success I say, though sadly at the expense of any neighbors for that region has suffered its own full share of diseases."

Holmes glanced at me, eyebrows raised in enquiry.

"Without a doubt," I said. "There have been several articles in *The Lancet* about the persistence of pernicious diseases throughout that part of the Cheviot Hills. Written, I believe, by Dr. Oldkirk himself."

"So, the doctor returned to England with your brother?" asked Holmes.

"He did, God bless him," said Renner. "Ian was far too frail to risk a long sea voyage without care, and so Dr. Oldkirk accompanied him as physician and companion. And I tell you, Mr. Holmes, despite my not having a great deal of faith in such things, I swear that his joining our community was a miracle. Many called it a godsend. An illness began attacking workers on one of our local farms. One of good size. There were a number of deaths, including—sadly—every member of the farmer's family. However, Dr. Oldkirk was able to save the lives of nearly all the field hands and even some of the house staff, some of whom were at death's very doorstep."

"And the owners of that farm?"

"Oh, alas, they were among the first to succumb."

"I see."

"Their deaths were a blow to the community," said Renner. "And sadder still that they had no heirs. The estate was left in a kind of legal limbo, with some back taxes owed. It looked like it would be sold and broken up—and that would have been quite a blow, since it was one of the largest farms in the area and employed many locals to work the house and the fields. But, again, Oldkirk was the hero we needed. He was upset by the impending poverty from the loss of a farm that employed so many...and so bought the place. Not only did he keep the workers, but over time took on many more."

"Bought it?" asked Holmes. "Having fled Haiti with only the clothes on his back."

"Well, perhaps I over-dramatized that. He did have money in a bank in Port-au-Prince and the bulk of his wealth in good banks in London and Edinburgh."

"I take it Dr. Oldkirk has thrived up there in the Cheviot Hills?"

"Indeed, Mr. Holmes. Dr. Oldkirk lives there still and has become the doctor to our village. He has repurposed the fields to grow the herbs and plants that he needs for his work and his many cures. He has quite a thriving medical practice as well, and let me tell you, gentlemen, there are times he has been the only thing standing between my neighbors and the hand of death itself. His remedies have brought many back from the brink. Many of his farm workers had been afflicted with a rare disease, and he cured them. He is a miracle worker and a saint."

"Do continue," said Holmes without comment. "You have given me quite a substantial picture of your friend and neighbor, but did you not come here about your brother?"

Renner looked abashed. "I...well...it is easier, I find, to talk about anything *save* my brother. Even now, as my mind recalls what happened I feel the cold fear, the mortal dread that has come to dominate my life."

"Then tell it plain and straight," said Holmes. "You have come here for help, so lay it all out before us."

"Alas, with his diminished health, Ian's business suffered. He cannot—I beg your pardon—*could* not travel to meet clients in England or abroad. His fortunes dwindled along with his health. He became a sad and broken man, and I suppose it was no great surprise that he took to drink. I tell you, Mr. Holmes, that it was more painful than I can describe to witness his slow dissolution. And although I was heartbroken, I was not surprised when he passed. He died in his sleep after a protracted battle with his liver, poor fellow." He swallowed the rest of the whiskey, and I refilled the glass with another generous knock. "Dr. Oldkirk was sitting with Ian up to the last, trying one decoction after another to try and save him, but it was impossible by then. I was there in the room when Ian breathed his last and I'm not ashamed to say that I wept, for he was the very last member of my family apart from me. It is a terrible thing, Mr. Holmes, to become aware that your entire family is one heartbeat away from extinction."

For a moment the only sound in the room was the crackling of the fire in the hearth.

"Dr. Oldkirk, being the only official doctor in the area, pronounced his death," said Renner. "He asked my permission to perform an autopsy. I was naturally alarmed since the cause of his death was obvious, but he explained to me that medical science was growing in its understanding of illness and perhaps by a study of my brother's internal organs some benefit might be drawn that could save other lives. Well, sirs, my profession is burying the dead and it is how I make my living…but it would be a blessing if that examination of my brother could prolong and improve the lives of the people in my town."

"You are a remarkably generous fellow," said Holmes. "And a practical one. I admire the latter quality as much or more than the former."

Renner merely grunted. "After the autopsy, Dr. Oldkirk in his great kindness prepared my brother for burial rather than leave such a task to me. I only assisted at the end with dressing

Ian for the viewing. And then, perhaps in penance for not having been a more faithful brother in our later years, particularly after he fell into heavy drink, I dug his grave with my own hands and buried him right and proper."

"And then," said Holmes, "you say your brother *returned* to you."

"He did, sir. Three days after I placed the headstone over him. And we embraced, as I said. I will admit that my joy at seeing him was born of shock. Then the reality…the *horror*…of it took hold of me and I shoved him away. He reached for me as if to embrace me again, and he…tried to speak. His mouth worked but he could not utter a word. Perhaps his lungs were still unable to draw breath. I don't know. I…I…well, sirs, you may think me weak, but I screamed."

"I daresay," I cried. "Who would not in such a circumstance?"

"What happened then?" Holmes asked.

"Dr. Oldkirk happened to be staying over that night as we had dined late together. He came running, as did my housekeeper and my assistant, Roger. We…were able to restrain Ian. That was yesterday, sir, and I came here on the first train."

"Wait," I cried, "but you left so much out. Where is your brother now? Is he still ambulatory?"

Renner's eyes were filled with ghosts. "We managed to lock him in an empty room in my house. Dr. Oldkirk spun a convincing story to keep the housekeeper and Roger quiet." He flicked a look at me. "Sleeping sickness."

"Ah," said Holmes. "And you say your brother—your *dead* brother—is still in that locked room?"

"He is," said Renner. "With Dr. Oldkirk watching over him."

Holmes was silent for a very long time, his eyes closed. But I watched the tightness of his mouth and the angle of his back. Renner accepted another glass of whiskey and gulped it down.

"Mr. Renner," said Holmes, "we will come at once, of course."

*

Mr. Renner left for his return to the Cheviot Hills, a remote place hard against the Scottish border. Holmes had a small matter to dispense with for Scotland Yard, but we promised to be at his doorstep by the following afternoon.

"What should I do while I wait?" asked Renner, his face clouded with a mixture of emotions. Hope warred with his fears of returning to the troubles left unresolved.

"Do nothing," said Holmes. "Keep everything in place. Take no significant action."

As soon as we were alone, Holmes turned to me. "I trust you can leave your surgery in good hands for a few days?"

"Of course," I said. "Things have been slow this last week and—"

He cut me off. "Excellent. And, Watson, be sure that you also bring your revolver."

"But why? Surely this is a medical issue and not a criminal one."

He studied me for several seconds, his eyes glittering in thought, although the nature of these were unreadable to me.

"It is certainly medical," he said slowly. "But we cannot rule out criminality. It is strikingly singular, and I feel that there is much more to learn than the unfortunate Mr. Renner believes."

"More than a man back from the grave?" I asked.

Holmes said nothing and instead threw on his coat and hat and went out. I did not see him again until it was time to take a cab to the railway station.

*

"This is a strange place," mused Holmes, as our conveyance rattled along a small road. Our journey had been a complicated one of trains and carriages, each taking us a certain way before handing us off like mail parcels to the next.

The farther north we went the bleaker the landscape. The Cheviot Hills are a highland range that for more than thirty miles marks the boundary between England and my native land of Scotland. The dozing ghost of a prehistoric volcano rises more than half a mile above rocky hills and farmland. Except in little villages where handfuls of homes huddled around small churches and businesses, the landscape was often empty. The autumn chill we felt down in London was nothing compared to the biting winds that whipped through passes and along the coach lanes. Even the hardy northern cows and sheep seemed threadbare and miserable. The few people we saw along the way wore layers of drab clothes, and their faces showed the marks of a life spent enduring that cold. Their eyes were lifeless and there was no welcoming smile anywhere to be seen.

The sky above was a featureless and sullen gray from which no promise of comfort could be detected. Ragged birds shivered in the trees and our own horses had the defeated look of animals who knew that no matter how far they traveled they would still be, essentially, *there*. Even the wild cattle we spotted held no joy at their freedom.

I had passed through the area twice before, once in summer and then again in spring, and although there is a certain kind of beauty in desolation, I never perceived the rural charm spoken of in travel articles on the subject.

29

When Holmes made his comment, I replied, "This weather is by no means a friend to joy."

"It is not the weather about which I comment," he said, but no amount of questioning from me could encourage him to enlarge on his remark.

The journey north through Northumberland devoured much of the day, and the landscape was so dreary that I often found myself nodding. Once, Holmes touched my arm and when I roused myself, I saw that there was a castle squatting within sight of the Cheviot Hills.

"What is that place?" I asked.

"Chillingham Castle," said Holmes. "A medieval stronghold. While you were dozing, Watson, we passed a town of the same name."

"It's not a welcoming sight," I said.

"Nor is it a happy place," said Holmes. "It was built as a monastery, Edward Longshanks relied on it for its obvious strategic location for defense against raids by William Wallace and his highland Scots. Edward III had Sir Thomas Grey further reinforce it. Some of its walls are a full ten feet thick, though there are stories that those walls are honeycombed with secret passages and hidden rooms."

"Have you ever visited it?" I asked. "You seem quite knowledgeable on the subject."

Holmes offered a small smile and waved a pamphlet at me. "I picked this up at the train station. Always useful to know some details about the area."

He told me a few other things, but as the castle faded into mist and gloom behind us Holmes settled back into his brooding silence. I seized that opportunity to ask him what he thought about Mr. Renner's extraordinary tale.

"Watson, come now," he said with mild reproof. "You know full well that I am loath to speculate in the absence of facts, and we are in no way in possession of enough of this story. Let us wait until we have seen this ghastly revenant, or whatever he is. And until we have had a chance to interview this paragon of virtue, Dr. Oldkirk."

*

A thick fog had invaded the region by the time we arrived at the house of Mr. Japhet Tobias Renner. His place was on a small hill around which were miles of fields belonging to local farmers.

It was an odd place that looked as if it had once been a cottage, but a line of subsequent tenants had added to it, often with no visible plan for either balance or aesthetics. The upper floors were clearly added later and there had been no attempt to homogenize the exterior paint—the ground floor being a faded gray and the two upper stories mottled like the flesh of mushrooms. Anemic ivy hung listlessly from the cracked walls. Two wings had been added but at unlikely angles, destroying any chance of at least the minimal grace of symmetry.

"Charming," was Holmes's only comment, and he said it for my ears alone.

The door opened to our knock and the woman who answered fair gave me a start. She was one of the thinnest people I had ever seen, and unusually tall. She was no less than an inch taller than Holmes, though less than half as wide. Her skin was the same unhealthy pallor as the paint on the upper floors. She had intensely black hair and equally black eyes and wore a black frock that, despite being cut for household staff, would not be out of place at a funeral.

She looked into our faces and I could see her struggle to maintain some level of composure, but that attempt failed and a mask of mingled grief and despair won out.

31

"You are the police," she said, not making it a question, but instead infusing those words with resignation. "You had better come in."

Holmes lingered on the doorstep. "For what reason are the police expected here?"

"Why," she said, "for the murder."

"Madam, I am Sherlock Holmes, and this is my associate, Dr. Watson."

Her eyes flew wide. "Oh, Mr. Holmes! Poor Mr. Renner was so excited because he said you were coming. But with all that's happened, I forgot. And now here you are and too late…oh, too late." Tears fell from her eyes and she wrung her hands as her tall frame swayed. "Too late…"

When her knees began to buckle Holmes caught her. Together we managed to get her inside and onto a couch in the front parlor. I ordered Holmes to fetch brandy while I checked her pulse and respiration.

"She is overcome by strong emotion," I said. The brandy helped revive her and we waited as she gathered the frayed ends of her composure. She tried to apologize, but Holmes waved it away.

"If you can, madam," he said urgently, "tell us what has happened. Who has been murdered?"

She looked at him blankly. "Why…Mr. Renner, sir."

And then she burst into hysterical tears.

*

It took some time to get Mrs. Cumber—for that was the name of the housekeeper—to calm down enough to tell us what happened. Once she was back in possession of herself, she turned out to be quite a strong woman. A widow who had buried a husband and both of their children over the last few years. She gathered both her wits and her dignity and answered every one of Holmes's many questions.

She said that Mr. Renner had returned from London with guarded hopes because he had enlisted the aid of the famous Sherlock Holmes. He told this to Dr. Oldkirk, who had been tending to the "ill Mr. Ian" while the master was away.

I noted that she referred to Ian as ill and not dead. Not a revenant.

"The doctor and Mr. Renner had argued about this," she said.

"Argued?" I said. "But why? Surely a man as learned as Dr. Oldkirk would welcome our help."

"Oh no, sir," said Mrs. Cumber. "The doctor was quite upset. He said that it was an insult to bring in an amateur to consult when an established medical expert was already involved. He and Mr. Renner got into quite a row about it. I was not privy to this, of course, but even through closed doors I heard them shouting."

"I see," said Holmes. "Did this come to actual blows?"

"Beg pardon, sir? Oh! No, sir…that was not how my poor master met his end."

She explained that the two men were still arguing—though in lower tones—as they left the parlor and went upstairs to the small room where Ian Renner was incarcerated. There was a time of silence, and then Mrs. Cumber heard Ian howling.

"It was truly awful," she said. "And I don't like to speak ill of my betters, but poor Mr. Ian howled like a dog. I went to London once and paid for the Bedlam tour, and the poor wretches there were like that. Howling fit to burst, and all of it awful to hear. Luckily there was only a maid and Mr. Renner's assistant, Roger. We all stood at the bottom of the stairs, hearing it all—and some more yelling from our master and the doctor. The upstairs door was closed, so we could not understand a word of it. We were so frightened and concerned, but we had not been called to help and so just stood there."

She paused and touched her throat.

"That's when we heard the door bang open and there was some shouting we *could* hear." She immediately hesitated.

"You are doing very well, Mrs. Cumber," encouraged Holmes. "If we are to be of any help you must tell me everything you saw and heard."

She took a steadying breath. "I heard Mr. Renner beg Dr. Oldkirk to do something, to *help* poor Mr. Ian. He said, 'This is your world, Oldkirk. This is what you do.'"

"Those were his precise words?" asked Holmes.

"Yes, sir. Dr. Oldkirk told him that he was a fool, and that Mr. Ian was alive, and wasn't that enough? And then it was Mr. Ian himself who cried out. 'Enough? Enough you say? You have not saved me, Oldkirk, you have damned me.' And then there was a struggle and Mr. Renner cried out. Suddenly Mr. Ian came blundering down the stairs, and he looked such a fright. His face was covered with blood, and more of it soaked the whole front of his shirt. Roger tried to restrain him, but as they wrestled on the landing, Mr. Ian *bit* the lad on the arm. A bad bite, too. Then Mr. Ian broke free and ran out the back door. The last I saw him, was him framed in the doorway with that fog behind him, looking like the damned thing he swore he was. He looked at the lad he'd bitten and then wiped at his mouth. The sight of all that blood made him scream, and he cried out in a voice of the lost, 'I'm damned. I am a monster.' And then he turned and vanished into the fog."

"Dear God," I cried.

After a moment, Holmes asked, "And Mr. Renner…?"

Her tears returned, but she kept herself from hysterics by force of will. "Oh, it was an awful sight, sir. Mr. Ian, in his madness, had torn his own brother's throat out."

She said that Dr. Oldkirk ran out after him and nothing had been heard of either since. After that pronouncement she lost her fight against the tears and dissolved into terrible sobs. We left her there sitting with her face in her hands. We found the maid, a young girl whose life, I knew, would forever be marked by the horrors she had witnessed. I bade her make tea for Mrs. Cumber and herself, and to sit with the housekeeper.

"Where is Mr. Renner's assistant?" asked Holmes. "The lad who was bitten?"

"Roger is in his room," she said in a small and fragile voice. "It's behind the scullery."

"Let us see him first," said Holmes, touching my arm, and we found the tiny room in which a lad of seventeen lay upon a narrow bed. His forearm was bandaged, but the dressing was already soaked through with red. I pushed past my friend, opened my medical bag, and quickly examined the unfortunate lad, who was unconscious.

"He must be in shock," I said quietly. "The bite itself is bad but not mortal."

"He is perspiring," observed Holmes. "From a bite received less than an hour ago? That seems remarkable to me."

"His pulse is rapid but thin, and his respiration is likewise quick and shallow."

"He has a fever?"

I stood up and drew Holmes into the hall. "That's the oddest part, Holmes. As you can see, he is bathed in sweat, but his skin is remarkably cool to the touch. Almost cold. I have seen bites in my time as an army surgeon and in private practice, and a fair few resulting in infections, but I have never once seen an infection this bad that had no fever."

"Perhaps we should consult Dr. Oldkirk," said Holmes, his face wooden and his tone bitter. "Perhaps he might be able to shed some light."

He turned away and I followed him back to the entrance hall. We stood at the bottom of the steps and I watched Holmes begin his examination. There were many bloodstains on the carpeted stairs and on the wall and banister. Holmes removed a small pocket magnifying glass and bent to study the markings while ascending the steps. He bade me follow but said to mark where he stepped and only walk thusly.

"Touch nothing, Watson," he warned.

"Do you fear something communicable?" I asked, recalling Renner's tales of widespread infection throughout the district.

"I do," he said.

"An infection of the blood?" I asked.

But he did not answer, and so I followed him to the second landing, often bending close to peer at the spots that so intrigued him. Upon doing so I saw that there were two kinds of bloodstains—those of the normal dark red hue, and others that were much darker still. Nearly black, in fact.

"That's very strange," I said.

Holmes turned at the top of the staircase and glanced down at me. "Tell me what you perceive."

"The darker blood…it looks and even smells different. Had it been somewhere else, at the morgue, perhaps, or at a place where a murder had been committed, and the body left undiscovered for a few days, I would even say it smelled like death. Like blood where the process of putrefaction was very far along."

"Yes," said Holmes. "Remarkable, isn't it?"

And yet, beyond that, he made no remark.

We went down a short hall, avoiding the blood spatter, and found ourselves at a doorway that opened into a small bedroom. The room was awash in blood. An abattoir could not have been more gruesome. The furniture was smashed to sticks, paintings askew or smashed on the floor, a washstand overturned and the basin in fragments, and the bed was half collapsed, with both legs at the head end buckled and broken. A lantern stood on a bureau, and it was about the only thing undamaged.

And there, sprawled half on and half off the bed, was our client, Japhet Tobias Renner.

Or, at least, what was left of him.

To say that he had been bitten was an understatement. His throat had been torn away and his head turned so severely to one side that surely his neck had been broken as well. There were smaller bites on his hands, and two fingers were missing. We looked for them but could find neither.

A Gladstone bag lay on the floor and Holmes crouched over this, using a pencil from his inner pocket to move the blood-smeared items so he could better examine them.

"Undoubtedly Oldkirk's," said Holmes. "What do you make of these? Remember, Watson, touch nothing with your unprotected skin."

I took a probe from my own bag to aid in my observations. "This is a rather odd collection of items for a medical man," I said. "A general practitioner such as myself would have things useful for the range of our trade, which might include anything needed to care for wounds, treat a fever, calm hysteria, extract teeth, and even deliver a baby. My own bag has scalpels, tweezers, razors, scissors, catgut for suturing, gauze bandages, a stethoscope, glass thermometer, splints for broken bones, and bloodletting instruments. And yet..."

"And yet," agreed Holmes.

Dr. Oldkirk's bag included very little of the common items. Instead, there were a great many jars of various powders, vials of unknown liquids, pots of strange-smelling creams, and other items whose purpose for being there I could not even guess.

"What do you make of these?" asked Holmes, indicating a spool of heavy twine, a pouch of salt, a bag of silver coins, long iron nails, and a hammer.

"I am at a loss," I confessed. "I cannot for the life of me imagine why a doctor—even a country practitioner—would have such items as these."

Holmes rose and stood for a moment studying the bag, and it seemed to hold more of his attention than did the dead man mere inches away.

"This is a dark business, Watson," he said. "Very dark. Perhaps the darkest we have ever investigated. I fear that things are going to get very much worse unless—"

And whatever else he might have said was erased by a terrible, piercing scream from downstairs.

*

"Watson, quick!" yelled Holmes as he ran for the stairs.

I hurried after, my bag in one hand and my other slapping my coat pocket to assure myself of the comforting weight of the .45-caliber Adams that had been a frequent companion since my army days in Afghanistan. A pistol that had been called to service more than once during my adventures with Sherlock Holmes.

We ran, this time ignoring the bloodstains on the stairs, for the screams were a woman's and they filled the old house.

"The scullery," barked Holmes and his long legs outran mine. He reached the kitchen door and swung it open, and I saw past him into one of Dante's rings of hell.

The young maid sat on the floor, her eyes wide with shock and terror, both of her hands clamped to her throat. Red blood pumped between her thin fingers and she sat in a widening pool of it. That alone would be awful, but a few feet away Mrs. Cumber was locked in a deadly struggle with Roger. Her black clothes were torn, and she bled from half a dozen bites, though none as mortal as the girl's.

Roger's eyes were wide but if there was any trace of humanity left in them, I could not see it. There was even less obvious intelligence or awareness than could be seen in the eyes of a rabid animal. Even though his mouth snarled and snapped as if driven to a state of utter rage, there was no expression at all in his eyes. They were as blank and lifeless as a doll's.

Holmes, heedless of his own safety, plunged into the fray. He grabbed Roger by the shoulder and spun him with prodigious force. The young man whirled away, his gray fingers still clutching a swatch of Mrs. Cumber's sleeve. He hit the side of the big preparation table, rebounded and dove straight at Holmes. There was no pause to acknowledge the force with which his lower back had struck that heavy wooden table. He did not even grunt. It was as if the table were a wall and he a rubber ball. In another circumstance it would have been comical. Not now. Not in that terrible moment.

He instantly grabbed Holmes by the wrist and lapel and thrust his head forward, teeth snapping at my friend's throat. The force of that grab sent Holmes backpedaling several steps, but then he twisted and suddenly Roger was flying.

Among his many talents, that include boxing and single-stick fighting, Holmes was an expert in Bartitsu, the combat science developed by the engineer Edward William Barton-Wright, who blended several styles of Japanese martial arts into a form very popular in England. I could make no sense of the complex yet subtle techniques, but Holmes was an adept.

Roger hit the wall hard enough to shake crockery off the shelves, but once more he was neither dazed nor slowed. He recovered at once and attacked again. This time neither Holmes nor Mrs. Cumber were closest to him, so Roger went for *me*.

He reached those pale hands toward me and I swatted them away with my left hand while being careful not to accidentally discharge the revolver. My effort barely turned Roger to one side, but it was enough so that his snapping teeth missed my cheek by an inch. Roger clawed at me and it was obvious he had the strength of the damned. I knew full well that crazed persons are enormously strong, but this was beyond my understanding. In my terror I hammered at him with the butt of the pistol, striking his arms and shoulders and even his face, but he kept coming. Undeterred and unbelievably ferocious, but with eyes that showed no trace of understanding or emotion.

"For God's sake, Watson," shouted Holmes. "Shoot him!"

"He is unarmed, Holmes," I cried. "He's not a criminal.... he's delirious."

"He is worse than that," roared Holmes, trying to find a way to lay useful hands upon Roger. But it was like trying to grab a nest of hissing vipers. "He will kill us all. Shoot him!"

It broke my heart to pull the trigger. This was a very sick young man driven beyond his reason. Had anyone but Holmes begged me to do so, I would have refused, but Holmes does not say what he does not mean.

As Roger rushed at me once more, I fired.

The bullet took him in the chest, staggering him backward toward the door that led out to the kitchen garden. Roger hit the door very hard and it burst outward, spilling him into the foggy evening. I ran across the kitchen and outside.

"Watson," yelled Holmes, "no!"

Then he caught up to me and we stood there, panting with the exertions, staring at the rows of neatly planted herbs and vegetables as the mist swirled around them.

"I...I don't...," I began but words failed me.

Roger was gone.

His footprints led off into the fog and I knew from a score of cases with Holmes the difference between a walking and running gait. Roger, with a bullet in his chest, had run away, and at a manic pace, for he was completely gone.

Holmes grabbed my arm. "Watson, your gun. Quick, man."

"But—"

"The women are badly hurt," he snapped. "See to them. I'll follow the lad."

He took the gun from me, whirled, and he, too, vanished into the milky fog.

*

I returned to the kitchen, but I knew that for the maid, at least, I was too late. As I re-entered the house, I saw that she had slumped over. Her eyes were wide open, her lips parted, but even before I pressed fingers to what was left of her throat the truth was apparent. She lay in a lake of blood.

Mrs. Cumber was alive and still on her feet, though she leaned weakly against the table. I fetched my bag from where I'd dropped it and spent several hasty moments cleaning and dressing her wounds. My heart was racing, though. From the fear and terror of that fight with Roger, from the air of pain and misery in Renner's house, concern for Holmes, and for what I saw as I bandaged Mrs. Cumber.

Her skin was already growing oddly cool. Like Roger's had been, though not as chilly yet. And there was a strange glaze in her eyes. She said very little, though she wept for the dead girl. Perhaps for all the death that surrounded her.

"I need to leave you here," I told her. "I must go help Mr. Holmes…"

Mrs. Cumber gave me the strangest look. Even with the veneer of trauma in her eyes, there was a kind of philosophic acceptance. She had tended to Roger and was perhaps wise

41

enough to make connections with what happened to him and what was now happening to her.

"Go," she said.

And it was all she said. In that single word, she conveyed to me a profound understanding and even a heartbreaking acceptance.

I touched her cheek. It was an oddly intimate thing to do, for we were total strangers. But she caught my hand and pressed it tightly against her clammy skin. Then she nodded and released me. I rose and headed toward the door.

I never saw her alive again.

*

The thick fog of that afternoon was becoming an impenetrable wall of milky white wherein few details could be discerned. I could follow Holmes's footprints but was only able to see a few steps ahead. It was nearly like being blind.

And I became acutely aware that Roger was out here somewhere, gunshot wound notwithstanding, and I was unarmed. I saw a scattering of fallen branches beyond the garden fence and snatched one up that had a comforting length and heft. Thus armed, I crept forward.

With no material landmarks to pick out, and fear dominating my mind, it was nearly impossible to determine how far I walked or for how long. Time and distance both lost their meaning to me. I had to bite back the urge to call out to Holmes; he might be crouched somewhere or sneaking up on Roger and my shout might startle him and expose his presence at just the wrong moment. And so, in silence, I went.

Then I realized to my horror that, somehow, I had lost the trail.

There was nothing for it but to try and backtrack and find those footprints.

But then that silence was shattered by a gunshot. I froze, trying to place the direction, but with a single report and then distorted echoes it was impossible. Then a second shot rang out and this time I saw a pulse of light off to my left. The muzzle flash, I was sure of it.

The flash had been some way off but higher, and as I hurried in that direction, makeshift club held in both hands, I realized that the ground angled upward. That explained the thinning fog, for mist is heavy and clings to the ground. Plus, there was a breeze up there, frigid and steady, that was tearing at the bank of white nothingness.

There was a third shot, and I wheeled, for I had moved too high and too fast and had passed it. As I spun, I saw that there were shapes in the mist. I crept forward, not wanting to blunder into a gun battle.

The mist was decidedly thinner and, as it swirled around me, I could see my friend standing with his legs braced wide and the revolver held out in front of him with both hands. He faced four men who seemed frozen in a grisly tableau. One was Roger, and the lad was on his back between orderly rows of what I perceived was echinacea—a potent healing herb. Two men dressed in the simple clothes of farmhands knelt to either side of him, pinioning his arms. The fourth man knelt at Roger's head and there was just enough light for me to see something so foul, so strange and hideous that it came close to unmanning me.

The fourth man—from his refined clothes and our placement amid fields of medicinal herbs—had to be Dr. Oldkirk. But the medical man, that paragon of virtue and benevolence, held a heavy needle in one hand, the eye threaded with twine identical to what had been in his bag. The twine hung pendulously between the needle in the doctor's hand and the mouth of the lad, Roger... it was clear that Oldkirk was in the process of *sewing the wounded man's mouth shut.*

The lad's jaws were held in place by one of the farmhands, but I could see a great quantity of what was clearly rock salt filling his mouth to overflowing. A sack of salt lay spilled beside Oldkirk.

Sherlock Holmes stood just outside of grabbing range, the pistol in his hands, but even his nerve had clearly been jolted, for his hands shook. Not in all my years of friendship, not in any of our adventures, had I witnessed Holmes in such a state. His face had gone wax white, his eyes were wide with comprehension and disgust, and tremors of fear rippled through him.

I moved into his line of sight before I spoke.

"I'm here," was all I said. Holmes flicked a momentary glance my way, but then his gaze returned to the horrific scene before him.

Oldkirk was also pale and frightened, but more than that he was furious. His eyes blazed. He was middle-aged, but looked fit, and wore a tweed country suit that was impeccably tailored.

"I see that you have brought your biographer," said Oldkirk with cold contempt. "The so-called *Doctor* Watson. As if someone trained in the army has any right to the title of 'doctor' when it should be reserved for those who have actual insight and understanding."

I said nothing, for this kind of haughty rebuke was not at all uncommon. Even Holmes has offered criticism of my level of medical skill now and then.

Holmes thumbed back the hammer of the pistol. "And here you are, *Doctor* Oldkirk," he said, giving the title the same weight of scorn, "in what is perhaps the most flagrant and detestable mockery of your Hippocratic Oath."

44

"You are a meddler and a fool," snarled Oldkirk. "You have no idea what is happening here, and if you interfere with my work then it is you who will be doing the greatest harm."

And with that Oldkirk bent down to sew another stich.

Holmes fired.

The blast was enormous, and the bullet punched through a narrow gap between Oldkirk and the struggling Roger. The two men restraining Roger flinched, but they did not let go their grip.

"Kill me and you will kill everyone in this town," said Oldkirk. "And bear in mind, Holmes, that you have only two bullets left. Yes, I can see the bullet wound in this boy's chest, and you have fired thrice out here."

"I only need one bullet to end your reign of terror," said Holmes calmly. "Trust that I know where to put my next bullet."

Oldkirk looked at the barrel of the gun and it was clear that Holmes now aimed it at Roger's head. I was shocked and nearly cried out to demand an explanation, but Holmes must have sensed what my reaction would be, and he gave me a small shake of his head.

"You say that I do not understand what is happening," he said to Oldkirk. "On that, as on many things, you are mistaken. Shall I tell you?"

Oldkirk looked both irritated and strangely amused. "Ah, the famous moment I have read of in the scribblings of your pet Boswell. The big reveal when you attempt to impress everyone with details that are obvious to even the meanest intelligence. Though, clearly not to Watson there. He thinks you are a magician." He shook his head, the needle still poised. "Go on then. Impress me."

"Ian Renner met you in Haiti, where you had a farm not unlike this one," began Holmes, as casually as if we were in our

45

sitting room at Baker Street. "Growing the herbs you need for—as you call it—your *work*. You made a great deal of money from those herbs and continue to do so throughout Europe and the Americas. And while these concoctions have inarguable health benefits, they are hardly the wonder cures of your advertisements. But that bit of fraud is of the least important kind. What matters more is that you create both a belief in, and a dependency upon, those cures by spreading exactly the kinds of diseases that you treat. That is as clever as it is cruel. It would be like Dr. Watson running about London breaking legs and then offering bone-setting at a premium price."

"What I do is incredibly valuable," fired back Oldkirk.

"Is it? Treating asthma with astragalus, cordyceps, slippery elm, and lobelia? New? Hardly. Or this echinacea to calm a troubled digestion. Really, Doctor. You claim your products are better because of secret ingredients, but I purchased some of your blends before leaving London and my rather sensitive nose detected nothing more 'secret' than added oregano and tarragon, perhaps a pinch of nutmeg," Holmes said. "I studied one of your most celebrated products. Even with a brief inspection I was able to identify garlic, ginger, onions, scent leaf, lemon grass, unripe pawpaw, lemon, African pepper, clove, *Gongronema latifolium*, and it comprises your treatment for malaria. I daresay the same ingredients are in your famous treatment for typhus. According to the newspaper interviews, you have visited Africa and worked among the peoples along the Niger River. That is a known cure there, though unknown to the average person in London or New York. Tell me I'm wrong."

Oldkirk merely glared.

"I could go on, Doctor," said Holmes, "but I believe my point is made. But to go deeper into exactly who you are means stepping deeper into the shadows. While in Haiti you became familiar with that island's religion of *vodou*. So misunderstood by most white men who see that island, its people, and the culture there as things to be exploited for profit. You shared that exploitive nature, but unlike the others you studied the herbology and ethnic botany because you did not subscribe to the notion that the *zombis,* the walking dead so popularized in lurid *penny dreadfuls*, were real but not created by magic or religion. You solved the mystery of what they are."

"You have no idea what you're talking about," said Oldkirk, but I could sense that Holmes had actually scored a telling point and that the doctor was shaken. The men holding down Roger merely looked blank.

"The *zombi* is believed to be a dead person resurrected to be, among other things, a kind of slave labor. Controlled not by the whip but by science. There have been speculative articles written on the subject where it is conjectured that they are not at all dead, but living people put into a deep hypnotic state where they are controlled through suggestion. Dr. Fronteau of Paris—who I believe was one of your teachers before he died abruptly of a hitherto undiagnosed heart condition—believed that secretions from the Hyla tree frog, a marine toad, an assortment of plants, and possibly even something from the glands of a puffer fish, were used to create what is called *coupe poudre*. Tell me, Doctor, what kind of laborers did you have working your fields in Haiti? Were they *zombis* of your own creation? Is that why the local *bokor* came out against you and chased you from the island? No answer? I see I have hit the mark. Which makes me wonder even more about the people who work your fields here. Renner told us that there had been a plague in town that you miraculously cured, and that when you bought a farm here from owners who had died in that plague, you were able to get as many workers as you needed. Many, Renner said, had themselves been at death's door before you cured them and hired them. *Zombis* here in England. Who would ever suspect?"

"You are impressive, Holmes, but naïve for all that," said Oldkirk. "You know what they are but not the *why* of it."

"If not pure greed, then, pray, enlighten me."

"You mock, but you are a gentleman of London. You wear fine clothes, eat the best food shipped in from all over the country, and enjoy the luxuries without understanding how they are provided. Every year more labor unions emerge, demanding more pay for less work. Prices escalate constantly, which in turn makes those luxuries harder to obtain. Unless something checks that process, the economy of England will crash, and wither the empire goes, so goes the rest of the world."

"You paint yourself as the savior of the British economy, then?"

"I am a realist," snapped Oldkirk. "Openly I heal the sick, but behind the scenes I am solving an economic crisis that is not merely feared but certain. My workers do not need more than a few hours of sleep per day and are therefore able to work twenty-one hours, seven days a week, year-round."

"That's barbaric," I cried.

He gave me a withering look. "Small talents, small mind, small imagination."

"Whatever you may think of Watson," said Holmes coldly, "he is a man of great integrity and compassion. He is wrong insofar that what you are doing is not barbaric. You are too educated, too enlightened, too clever to ever be accused of barbarity. No, sir, what my friend should have said is that what you are doing is monstrous."

"Bah," growled Oldkirk. "I expected more from someone like you."

"I am entirely delighted to disappoint you," said Holmes. "Now, Doctor, since you seem to excel at rationalization for your actions, explain to me either the medical or financial benefits of turning your victims into ghouls. For that is nothing less than what they are."

Oldkirk glanced down at the hapless Roger.

"What cure is there in the entire world that is without side-effects?" he asked. "Moreover, what cure is equally effective on everyone? Even the most trusted medicines may have adverse or contrary results. What may cure a thousand may bring harm to the thousand and first. It happens. Allergies and intolerances exist in nature, gentlemen. Or does your self-righteous anger disallow you from understanding this?"

"That boy there attacked and killed Mr. Renner," I said. "He attacked and killed the maid and wounded Mrs. Cumber gravely. Just in the few minutes since his attack she began to show signs of infection. Explain that, Dr. Oldkirk."

Oldkirk's eyes met mine only briefly before sliding away. "It is something that I have been studying, and which requires more study. You are incapable of understanding."

"We will be the judges of what we can and cannot understand," said Holmes with a touch of asperity.

Oldkirk looked down at the needle he held.

"Myths and legends often have a basis in fact," he began quietly. "The legends of vampires might simply be ignorant people trying to understand diseases such as rabies and porphyria, not to mention various mental instabilities." He looked at Holmes. "You called them ghouls, and you are not far wrong. Some—a very few—of the people treated with my version of *coupe poudre* have a paradoxical reaction. They become quite ill and present with a number of strange symptoms such as an apparent fever without a rise in temperature. Some even have a greatly reduced temperature. They become listless and their cognitive functions are diminished. Then they lapse into a kind of coma not described

49

in any known medical text. They appear to die, but in truth they have entered a metabolic state so minimalized that their heartbeats are virtually undetectable. The same is true of respiration and even circulation. Left alone, this reduced metabolism will become warped, hoarding only a handful of nerve functions, so that their skin and limbs exhibit signs of necrosis. They rot as a corpse might; though not entirely. Whatever reflexive functions remain take unthinking actions to provide sustenance in order to survive."

"What kind of sustenance?" I asked, though I feared I knew the answer.

"Meat proteins," said Oldkirk. "Specifically living tissue. They…feast upon the living. Humans are the easiest prey, in most circumstances, for them to see and catch; but they will devour anything alive. Animals, insects…"

"God in His heaven," I gasped.

I saw that Holmes was not as shocked, and I had no doubt he had already worked through to this point of horrible understanding.

"Is there no cure for them?" I begged.

Oldkirk shook his head. "The *bokor* of Haiti knew of this, though none that I spoke with ever understood why it happened. They have no cure. There is nothing that works, and I have tried everything. You have no idea the lengths to which I went in hopes of an answer. And so I rely on the two methods I know to work. Not to heal, but to end their unnatural life and quiet those hungers. If you examined Renner's corpse, Holmes, you can probably guess one method."

"Destroy the brain or inflict catastrophic injury to the brain stem," said Holmes matter-of-factly. "Thereby effecting termination of all nerve conduction."

"Yes. A bullet to the right part of the brain will work as well, but you would need to destroy the motor cortex or the brain stem."

"Precisely," said Oldkirk. "And the second…well, that takes more courage, more nerve. It is the oldest of ways according to the sorcerers of Haiti. Fill the mouth with salt and sew the lips shut. Tie the afflicted tightly and place silver coins—only silver, mind you—over the eyes." He showed us the needle threaded with coarse twine, and as he did so he looked suddenly weary. "Yes, I know it sounds like some kind of absurd magic, but it works. I have seen it work every time."

"That is…," I began, but no words I have ever learned were appropriate to my level of horror and revulsion.

"What would you have me do, Doctor?" asked Oldkirk, and now there was an almost plaintive quality to his voice, as if explaining his actions brought home the true scope of his dilemma. "If they are not dispensed with by either method, they will continue to exist in that strange state between life and death. Unlife? Living death? Call it what you will. And worse— far, far worse—those kinds of *zombis* pass along their condition through their bites. I have looked for and have not yet found what pathogen it is that their body creates. It is not a virus, not a bacterium. It is something waiting to be found, but it eludes me, gentlemen. It eludes me. The other *zombis*, the field workers, do not pass along their condition in any way. They are still very much alive, and without my *coupe poudre* will eventually recover completely. As my two servants here have done."

The men holding Roger nodded.

"Their return to normalcy is their reward, for they have worked many months in the fields and I have stored up payment for them. They have all they could want, and they know that they have my trust and my compassion. I see to their wants and, more importantly, I oversee the health and wellbeing of their families."

"Their families?" echoed Holmes. "To what end? To grow the next generation of *zombis*?"

Oldkirk fairly winced, though he looked away to hide it, and I knew Holmes had struck the bull's eye.

Then I noticed that the two former *zombis* were staring at Oldkirk and their expressions were no longer blank. There was surprise and anger in their eyes and the hard lines of their mouths.

"You never said that our kids would be working the fields like we did," said one.

"Be silent," snapped Oldkirk. "This is above your understanding."

"You never told us that you'd give that foul stuff to our wee ones," said the other.

"Nor have I said I would," lied Oldkirk. But it was clearly a lie and all of us knew it. Holmes had done no more than make one of his brilliant deductions, but he had phrased it to speak to the farmhands as much as to Oldkirk.

"You didn't even deny it," said the first man.

"You as much as admitted it," said the other.

"And what about that sickness?" growled the first. "This bloke with the gun said you caused it. Is he right? Did you make us sick just to make us need your cures and all?"

"No, no, of course not," said Oldkirk, but he was scrabbling to save the moment. However, those men, simple farmers as they might be, were not stupid.

The second one pointed at Holmes. "He has the gun. What need does he have to lie?"

"You didn't deny what he said, neither," said the other.

"You don't understand," Oldkirk insisted.

But it was too late.

The men glanced at him, then at Holmes, then down at the struggling Roger. Something passed between them for, as if rehearsed, they both released the lad in the same moment and scuttled backward.

What happened next was blindingly fast and utterly dreadful.

Roger, his hands freed, spat out the salt and before Oldkirk could react, he grabbed the doctor with both hands and jerked him downward toward his snapping teeth.

The screams were the worst I have ever heard.

Holmes had two bullets left in his gun. He fired them both.

The farmhands fled into the fog.

I stared in shock at all that had happened in the space of three seconds.

Holmes and I stood there for a long time. I'm not sure how long. Minutes? Longer? Forever, it seemed.

Then in a voice that betrayed a tremolo filled with pain and sadness, he said, "Do you have extra cartridges for this pistol, Watson."

"Extra...? Yes, of course, but...why?"

He held out his hand, which shook badly. "I fear we will need at least one more."

"One...?" I began and then I heard a scream off in the distance. Back in the direction of Renner's house. It was hoarse and loud and shrill, and it broke my heart.

I fished in my coat pocket and held out a palmful of bullets for the revolver. Holmes took them and I watched him reload as if we were caught in some bizarre sacred ritual. When he closed the cylinder, he also closed his eyes and stood like that for a long moment. I saw his eyes glitter with tears, and that is something I never once saw on my friend's face. His emotions were always under such rigid control. But we were far from

Baker Street, far from crowded London, far from any version of the world that should exist.

He turned toward the sound of those screams.

"We are coming, Mrs. Cumber," he murmured. "Come along, Watson. We have work to do."

Holmes moved off. I lingered a moment longer, looking down at the dead men there among the healing herbs. The distinction between life and death had always been clear to my medical mind. Now that line was partly erased. Many times, Holmes told me that if you eliminate the impossible, whatever remains, however improbable, must be the truth.

This, then, was our truth.

Holmes disappeared into the fog and, once more, I followed his footprints in the direction of madness and horror.

THE PECULIAR CASE OF SWEETLY'S LUCK

Alison Littlewood

It will have become plain by now to the attentive reader that Sherlock Holmes, while accustomed to assisting great men, would never be enticed into taking a case for financial inducement, but rather for the interest it held. He disliked boredom; and yet one particular case astonished me by virtue of its ever persuading him to leave our rooms.

It began in ignominy and from there sank deeper; but I should begin as did our adventure, with the arrival of a note: terse, ill-spelt, blotted, clutched in the hand of a small boy scarcely less grubby than the scrap of paper on which it was written. Waiting only to snatch a coin from my hand, the child fled as rapidly as a mouse into a hole and was gone.

Holmes perused this singular missive in our chambers, shifting his pipe to the side of his mouth and muttering as he read. "Come at once . . . missing . . . taken beneath . . . the Queen!" He threw back his head and let out a laugh along with a puff of strongly scented smoke. "*Tosh* . . . I see." He tossed the note onto the table.

"The – the queen?" was my response. For whatever could our sovereign want with us? It could surely be no personal matter, unless it concerned one of her children – for she had wrapped herself in mourning upon the demise of Prince Albert and had scarcely emerged since. An issue of state, then – I knew that politics held little fascination for my friend, but even so, to declare it *tosh* . . .

Holmes laughed again, this time somewhat mockingly, at me.

"Not Her Majesty Queen Victoria, my dear Watson. Not yet, ha! And certainly not with note-paper such as this. But we are summoned all the same, and by a quite regal fellow, I think you'll find. One with rough hands, a robust constitution, a well-stocked wardrobe and none too keen a sense of smell, I shouldn't wonder."

"You speak in riddles, Holmes." I refused to give him the satisfaction of asking how he had reached such conclusions from so terse a note. I snatched it up, read it myself and frowned. "Why, this is nonsense! I shall throw it on the fire." I made to do so, but Holmes caught my arm.

"You cannot mean to go," I said.

In answer, Holmes went to the window and looked out upon an afternoon that held neither rain nor shine, but was simply gray piled upon gray.

"You know," he said, "I rather think I shall."

*

I have said that we began in ignominy and from there descended, and so it was, for we hailed three hansom cabs before we found one that would take us to the address we had been given. The first driver asked us to kindly step down again, as did the next, but while I rankled, Holmes only seemed to become more amused.

At last, we found means of crossing the river and soon found ourselves standing by our destination: the rather mean and narrow entrance to Metcalf Court. Seeing its sign, half obscured by coal-dust and street-dirt, it rushed in upon me that I had heard the name before. "Why, this is the very place where Dickens had his villain, Bill Sikes, reside, in *Oliver Twist*." I looked about, searching for the squalor that Boz had described. This was once the most notorious rookery in London; now the area around us seemed rather to be given over to warehouses and well-paved streets, though the air still carried the taint of tanneries as well as the burden of too much humanity. There was also the sourness of the river, which could not quite be hidden by another scent: the cloying sweetness that must be drifting from the Peek, Frean and Co. factory, which lent this part of Bermondsey the moniker 'Biscuit Town'.

To judge by Holmes's countenance, my talk of fiction might as well have been in another language. "Come!" he said, and led the way into a warren that must have survived the slum clearances, where children peeked from dirty corners and vanished into mysterious doorways. Holmes was unerring, however, finally rapping on one of them with his cane – the panels were none too clean – upon which a narrow-faced maid admitted us to a small yet rather well-appointed parlor, where our *regal fellow* awaited.

"Mr. Jerry Sweetly, I presume." Holmes did not shake hands and none was proffered by the fellow, who remained seated. Both his hands rested on a cane of his own, as if he was at any moment prepared to rise and leave us. As Holmes had surmised, he did appear robust, even florid, with a generous mop of mid-brown hair, graying a little at the temples. It was difficult to tell his age, and I found myself wondering if he were older than he appeared. His hands were reddened, his shirt immaculately bleached and his waistcoat surprisingly rich; on closer inspection, his cane was tipped with silver. Holmes, I decided, must thus far carry his point.

"Tea," the fellow said. "Pearls." He gestured to the maid, who scurried to obey.

Holmes ignored this puzzling request. "Let us to business, sir," he said, seating himself, without invitation, opposite our host. "You say your daughter has been stolen from you. You say, furthermore, that the perpetrator is not human; that the girl has been taken under the ground; and that the one who took her is a monarch of her realm – one known, furthermore, as Queen Rat."

I had to hold my tongue, or I think I should have laughed.

"I take it from this, sir, that you are one of that breed known as shoremen, or, in some circles, Toshers."

Tosh. Now I understood. They were not shoremen exactly, but rather alike to mudlarks, who search the banks of the river at low tide for such treasures as they can find. Toshers were lower still, however, for they searched not the shoreline but the sewers.

None too keen a sense of smell. Holmes had hit home again, though Sweetly's was a profession surely in constant danger of being stamped out. The Metropolitan Commission had closed up the outflows along the river and prohibited entrance without express permission, for fear such men would be suffocated by poisonous gases; though their efforts must have been much assisted by the improved system of tunnels and embankments devised, greatly to the City's comfort, by Sir Joseph Bazalgette, which was declared finished just over a decade ago.

But the man – Sweetly, of all things to be named – gave a single nod. "Not just *a* Tosher," he said, "but rather *the* Tosher, if you'll believe that. The one who was favored – but p'raps I should go back to the beginning."

It was Holmes's turn to give a deep nod. And this was the strange tale we heard, though for the sake of the reader I shall omit some of Sweetly's more colorful expressions and exclamations, as well as the greater idiosyncrasies of his south London accent. While he spoke, we were only interrupted by the maid's arrival with clattering pots and tea the color of the river, and the solution to one mystery at least: a plate of Pearl biscuits from the nearby factory.

"I was just fifteen when I met her," Sweetly said, his gaze going distant, as if to stare upon those times. "Queen Rat, I mean, though we all knew of her. She'd go after men in the sewers, as they went about their work. She'd follow them, scurrying about in rat-shape, but she could change herself if she chose, and if she liked them – then they'd see her right enough, though they wouldn't see what she *was*. They thought she was just a lovely bit o' jam, see. They'd never have seen her equal for looks. Beautiful.

"And if they went with her, and made her happy, like – you gennlemen know what I mean—" He winked before he went on, "She'd bless them with her luck. They'd find sov'reigns instead of ha'pences in the tunnels, and often too, not just the once. She'd make them rich. And there was the other thing she did – but I'll get to that.

"She didn't find me in the sewers, though. She came to me above ground. I was in the pub."

He spoke with pride and I tried to exchange a glance with Holmes, but he refused to look at me. Perhaps it was just as well; perhaps he too didn't wish to laugh at the fellow.

"My missus was at home. Well, lady friend. Belly getting big by then. So I was on me tod, see, and – well, I didn't know who she was, not at first. In the tunnels, there are signs; the queen's eyes gleam in the dark, like a rat's. Claws on her feet too, if you get a chance to see, but I didn't.

"All I saw was, she were right bonny. Lips; eyes. Got me to take her to a dance, she did. Then an old rag warehouse – empty, it was. And we was just – well – you know – when we gets to the other thing. She bites you on the neck, see. When you're—"

It scarcely needed saying aloud and so Holmes waved him to go on.

"That bite, it's her mark. It means you're hers. And that mark protects you, see – from the other rats, when you're below. There's nothing a Tosher fears so much as a rat bite gone bad. Ulcers come up big and white as a corpse's eyes. Full of nastiness and poison. That's if they don't swarm you in the first place. Rats down there'll bite any bit of skin uncovered and plenty that's not. There's men been picked to bones. Gone below and never seen since.

"Only I didn't suspect who she was, did I? Took me by surprise. Lashed out, I did, and caught her one, and she were gone, just like that. Only when I look up there's this great rat in the rafters, and a shred o' my shirt in its teeth. And she told me – she said, I'd get my luck, right enough. But I hadn't finished paying for it."

He drew a great sigh. "I got my luck, all right. Paid, too. My lass died when the babby came. And after that, when I got married – six chil'ren I had with my wife, we had that long, but Queen Rat must have thought that was enough, because she took her. Fell in the river, my wife did, and gone."

He held up one hand. "You gents'll say it's coincidence. But again, see, there was a sign. My last girl, Edie, was marked too: one blue eye, she's got, but the other's the color of the river, as if to say, *She's mine.* She's the hearing of a rat, too. She can hear a whisper at a hunnerd yards, that one." He paused. "Queen Rat never marked my first daughter, mind, nor the second, but the last. It were like she knew she'd be taking my wife after that."

"And now?" Holmes said. But Sweetly did not all at once answer, for at that juncture the maid returned, and somewhat surprisingly perched herself at the farthest end of the horsehair sofa on which I had seated myself.

Sweetly gestured towards her. "Wife's sister," he said by way of explanation. "Looks after the chil'ren."

At this, the aunt pulled a face, one that Sweetly disdained to notice.

"The boys, they're like me. Do the job we've always done. Our birthright, see, no matter who says we can't or shan't. They've got something o' my luck too, but not the same. It's my girl, see – she's the one, ain't she? The one who's marked. So I've arranged for her to wed. A tosher like me, a good man. Saved him once from the rats, I did, stood in front with that mark on my neck and not a one of them touched us. Respectful lad, he is. Grateful. So I said he can have her, and the luck that goes with her. They'll do well. Their chil'ren will do well."

His hand went to his pocket and, after a moment, he drew something out. It glittered in the lamplight: a golden necklace with a heavy garnet drop, surrounded by crystals.

"I were minded to give this along with her, but now I don't know. I found it in the tunnels, right after I was with *her*. Must've slipped off a fine lady's neck and down through a grate. P'raps Queen Rat made it slip. It was her best gift to me. My greatest treasure."

I frowned. I should rather suppose his greatest treasure to be his children, but what could we expect of such a fellow — one who had left his lady friend, and she with child, to go dancing with someone else? It could not be that he were truly bewitched – this Queen Rat was all in his head; an excuse, one grown to monstrous size in order to allay his equally monstrous guilt. In short, this was a mystery I felt certain I could solve myself, and that, in a trice.

"Which brings us to the present," Holmes prompted. *"Taken beneath."*

"It do." Sweetly roused himself and looked from one of us to the other. "She's gone," he said. "My Edie. Just when I'd decided what to do with her, the Queen took her – she must have. Queen Rat has my Edie and my luck along with her, and enough's enough." He stomped his cane on the floor.

"So when do we go?" Holmes said.

"Now," said Sweetly. "Soon as we get you dressed for it."

It was my turn to look from one of them to the other, the horror slowly dawning on my face.

*

After that, all was activity. Sweetly called for canvas and boots, gesturing to the aunt, who hurried off. Suddenly, Holmes patted his pockets, as if he'd forgotten something. "A word in her ear," he said, stepping after the aunt, just as if this were his home and she his maid.

Sweetly and I looked at each other, though fortunately our *tête-à-tête* did not last long; Holmes returned, and then the scowling aunt, who deposited layers of clothing in a heap on the sofa before she left us once more. I picked out some stout canvas trousers and grimaced. I could only imagine the uses to which they had been put, but for now, at least, they were mercifully clean.

The three of us dressed, all together in the parlor, none commenting on this odd turn of events. After the canvas trousers came voluminous coats with equally capacious pockets; I'd have thought something waxed would be more suitable than their velveteen, but Sweetly said, "It's to cover up the rest," and I understood. To go where we must was not only illegal, but anyone who saw and informed on us stood to earn a healthy reward. We must try to go unnoticed. I glanced at the window to see that it was already growing dark. Good; for it could make no difference where we were going.

Timing her entrance perfectly, the aunt returned, bearing two pairs of tall boots and an old pair of slops, which Sweetly took for himself. Then came a bull's eye lantern, which he secured to his chest with straps. Finally, he took up one last item; a long pole, taller than he was, tipped with an iron hoe.

"Dragged me out o' the mire many a time," he grinned. "And keeps the rats off."

It struck me that he'd claimed to be safe from such creatures – but of course, that was nonsense. Suddenly, I pictured them: numerous eyes gleaming in the dark, their bodies almost invisible, their fur dark and foully slimed. Thin. Hungry. Fast. Hissing at us, baring sharp yellow teeth. I suppressed a shudder. It could be of no matter; Holmes would reach the entrance and declare some revelation, and we need not go in.

For now, "Do you have the bauble, Sweetly?" was all he said, his tone as bright as if he were going on a day-trip to the seaside. Then he turned to me. "Come, Watson, don't be glum. We are about to witness one of the wonders of our age."

*

And so, we walked through the darkening streets towards the Thames, Sweetly going on ahead, Holmes and I a little behind him. I tried to arrange my expression as if I were out for an evening stroll, though I rather doubt I succeeded. I avoided the eyes of my fellow men, whether they be costermongers, crossing sweepers or stevedores going to and from the docks at St. Saviour's, though none showed any interest as we slipped by.

"Strange, is it not, Watson?" Holmes spoke softly, without turning his head. "All this talk of Queen Rat. Once, every river, lake, pool or well had its guardian spirit – or its goddess. Men have paid obeisance to them for centuries, since to them water meant life itself."

"True," I said. "I suppose we should not be surprised if the same story is told of the sewers."

"Ah," he replied, "but the sewer system swallowed the rivers too, did it not? The Fleet, the Tyburn . . . and if I am not much mistaken, beneath our very feet, the notorious old Neckinger. The river was named for the Devil's neckinger –

64

the Devil's neckcloth – in honor of the noose used to hang pirates at the very place where it empties into the Thames."

"A sorry kind of river, then," I muttered.

"Not so, Watson, not then; it was once navigable all the way to the old Bermondsey Abbey. Now there's not a trace of it, you see? It too has been *taken beneath*. It sees nothing but bricks and tunnels. Yet the pagan survives in many of us, particularly those bound to uncertain and dangerous occupations. We are atavistic creatures, and such things live on, in the back of the memory if nowhere else." He paused. "If we were ever to believe a word of it, of course."

I considered his words as we went, though they cast my spirits even lower. Was Queen Rat, then, the remnant of some ancient spirit of the river? A sorry goddess she must be, to have been forced to such depths – choked by every miasma, wading in filth, and never to see the sun or the sky or a bird again. Keeping the company of nothing but rats, until she became little more than a rat herself. What poisonous thoughts would have come to her in the dark? And what kind of offering could possibly appease such a creature?

But I could dwell on such fancies no longer, for our destination was before us. We made our way down some narrow steps, slippery and green with slime, onto a ledge that ran alongside the river. Before us the Thames slid by, brown as tea and thick as soup, and at its side: a metal grate, just a little awry on its hinges. A trickle of something foul seeped from the opening, like infection from a wound.

Sweetly, ahead of us, paused. As we drew in close, he murmured. "My luck'll change, now. That's what happens, if a man speaks of Queen Rat. Like as not, he'll drown. Come to a bad end, anyway. But what price a man's luck, Mr. Holmes?

I made a promise. A promise I mean to keep." He reached out and with a single motion, drew the grating back. Its hinges did not groan or shriek; they must be kept well-oiled.

Sweetly raised the cover of his lantern. A beam of light – not bright nor wide enough for my liking – shone ahead of him into the tunnel.

Before he stepped inside, he scrabbled with one hand, reaching for the back of his neck where, for a brief moment, he pressed his fingertips to an old white scar. Then he walked into the dark before turning to close the grate behind us.

*

The stench was like a solid thing we pushed against. It forced its way into my nostrils and between my lips and down my throat. Words passed through my mind, words tinged with horror: *Loathsome. Pestilential. Mephitic. Foetid.* I could not stop their flow. It overwhelmed my senses. From time to time, as we went, I would begin to think the smell almost bearable; then it somehow gathered itself again, rolling over us, thickening on my tongue. And at our feet – we waded through every sort of filth known to man. There was not just the expected ordure, which was plentiful, but also rotting vegetables, slimy orange peels, discarded oyster shells, broken clay pipes, fish heads with and without their black little eyes, offal and other waste from the slaughterhouses, putrid fare and decaying flesh. Here and there, surprising flashes of color betrayed chemical run-off from the tanneries or some other hellish manufactory. Once, there was a glimpse of what was barely recognizable as a dead cat, its grimace revealing little white teeth.

The sounds were scarcely better. Constant dripping and rippling and trickling, and worse: the wishful, almost fantastical airs of water babbling and air whispering, that tricked my ears until I could almost believe the atmosphere of some mythical glade or garden had reached us in these depths. Then we would pass by this tunnel or that opening, and it would be gone, no breath of sweet air or sip of clean water to leaven the misery of it.

I did not know how the Toshers could bear it. I did not know how Holmes could; he was somewhat untidy, but fastidiously clean, and his olfactory powers were legendary.

All of this was lit by that single narrow beam of light. And even that, since I followed behind, was by turns blocked by shoulders or limbs, sending mad shadows flying about the walls, making it seem as if the ceiling was lowering, the tunnel closing in. At times I could hardly see where I put my feet, though I heard the sounds made by my steps and tried to close my ears against them.

I was, in short, glad of the boots on my feet. Doubly glad they were not my own.

Then the thought came of the dangers that existed besides the dirt.

Rushing gallons of filth released by raised sluices further along the system. Rising tidewater pouring in along the shoreline to fill the tunnels to the roof. Older tunnels crumbling at the brush of an elbow. Air pockets so noxious they could kill a man in an instant. Involuntarily, my breath quickened, bringing yet more fetor to my throat.

Thankfully, at that moment Sweetly paused, providing some little distraction.

"You see," he proclaimed, "we're not shoremen, not really. Riverbanks – they're for mudlarks. Those fellows, they're glad to grub up a bit o' coal or wood or rope. Something for the ragman. Not us, though. Toshers are after *tosh* – metal."

He stooped, burying his hand to the elbow in muck. When he withdrew it, he held aloft a small round shape, unrecognizable in its filth. "Half-sov," he said, so much pride in his voice I almost expected him to bite down on the gold there and then. "You have to know where the cracks are, see. Coins get washed down and wedge into them, just waiting for me to pick them up."

He grinned around at us, his features made grotesque by the lamplight beneath his chin, but all I could think was, *Cracks?* In these tunnels? I glanced at the ceiling, half expecting to see fissures opening all around us.

Holmes nudged my arm. "Don't forget Bazalgette, my dear Watson," he said. "He insisted on good Portland cement – as strong as it is water-resistant. These tunnels will last a century yet. Now, Sweetly, are we almost at the Neckinger?"

Sweetly looked surprised. "I thought we'd head that way, aye."

"Then we are of one mind," said Holmes. "Lead on, good fellow."

And Sweetly did, choosing this tunnel or that, until *Getting hopelessly lost* was added to the list of dangers already present to my mind. Then, of a sudden, I realized the tunnel was widening. With another step, I could not have touched the walls if I stretched out my arms; a rushing sound became apparent to my ears, and I knew we had arrived.

Sweetly stopped, as did Holmes, and I stepped aside to see better. I had to stop short; a rush of dark water ran at my feet, which, if I had taken another step, would have swept me away. It was set into a deeper channel that emerged from what appeared to be an ancient bridge, forming part of the tunnel to our left. Its arch, embedded in the tunnel wall, remained discernible even in the dim light: its span was around ten feet across, and I made out six distinct ribs amid the enclosing brickwork. This tainted water must be what remained of the Neckinger; this bridge, once open to the elements. It was a landmark only for the sewer folk now.

"Here," said Holmes, "is where you make your offering, Sweetly."

The man frowned. "My what?" he said.

"You already know what you must do," replied Holmes. "That is why you brought the necklace – your most treasured possession – the thing she gave to you first; it will take no less, I think."

The man pulled the necklace from his pocket, then went on staring into the black water.

"Come, man. This is why you led us here – you persuaded yourself you needed my services in the hope I would dissuade you from it, but how can I? Indeed, I shall explain it if I must. You have displeased Queen Rat. She is unhappy with you and the choice you made for her daughter – the child she claimed as her own. Who is this fellow she must marry, after all? Someone upon whom the Queen once set her rats. You saved him, but does that make him fit to be her son-in-law – or yours?"

Sweetly glowered. He did not meet Holmes's eye, or mine.

"Give her what you brought," said Holmes. "And then give her what is truly important – the thing any parent ought to desire. The happiness of their child."

For a long moment, the only sound was the inexorable flow of filthy water. Then Sweetly walked to the very edge of the channel, by the bridge. He reached out and hung the necklace from a loose nail jutting from the brickwork, as if it had been set there for the very purpose.

In a moment, the sound changed. The rushing grew louder – I found myself peering beneath the arch, ready to run if a flood was upon us, but the water level did not change. Instead, the noise resolved into rustling – a shifting that seemed to echo all around us.

Something caught my eye, against the wall by the mildewed bridge. Had something moved in the liquid dark, emerging from the tunnel? I almost felt I'd glimpsed it, from the corner of my eye – and then the shadow moved again, growing larger; taller.

Sweetly whirled about, sending a madness of light around the walls and barreled ceiling. And I saw them: two brighter points gleaming from out of the dark, like a cat's eyes caught in the light of a lamp.

Queen Rat?

The words were on my lips, but I was not to say them. "Quick!" Holmes called out. "Both of you, back along the tunnel."

We needed little bidding. We started away, raising splashes and ripples around us, subsuming all other noise, any other movement.

I only glanced back once. I do not know if the shadow remained; but I was certain that the nail where the necklace had hung was empty.

*

I do not know how swiftly Sweetly thought his offering might have its answer, but I was as astonished as he when we reached his parlor once more and found the aunt waiting there with a young lady standing at her side. At first, no one spoke; it seemed that any word might rend the air and dissolve the vision. But she remained standing there, a rather curious girl, so calm and self-composed she might have been called dignified; even, perhaps, regal.

"Sent you back to me, did she?" Was her father's eventual greeting.

His daughter, unsurprisingly, kept tight-lipped.

"Well, girl, wherever she's been keeping you, you should know that I've changed my mind," her father said. "You're not to marry Lanky Harry, after all. And that's that."

She brightened, then tried to hide her sudden delight.

"Well, you should know your necklace is gone." Sweetly seemed to have forgotten that he'd ever prevaricated about giving it to her. "Queen Rat wanted it back, see. Seems a lady likes a bit o' glitter, even in the sewer." His laugh came out in a bitter choke.

Holmes interrupted this sentimental exchange with a polite cough. "Perhaps it is time to enquire," he said, "after the alternative. Maybe Queen Rat has put your daughter in mind of something else."

Sweetly scowled, but he had no time to ask the question before the girl announced, "I'm to wed Tom Huckell."

71

"Huckell!" Sweetly's face dropped. "He's no Tosher, girl. He's a lighterman, Tom Huckell is. He lives *on* the river, not under it."

"I know," she said, and smiled.

In that moment, it struck me that there really was something almost uncanny about her – or at least, about the brilliance in her eyes: one the color of river mud, the other as clear as light shining on water on a sunny day.

*

After that, Holmes and I were left alone for a while, and water was brought so that we could wash and change. He kept silent, and so I said, "You will make me ask, then?"

He answered with a smile.

"So tell me, Holmes. How did you do it?"

He gave a brief laugh before replying in a low voice. "Well, Watson, you must have noticed me slip away before we donned this very attire. I did so in order to tell the aunt – whose name is Nell, by the way – that I knew perfectly well she was aware of where her ward was hiding, and indeed why, and that she would do well to have her waiting for us upon our return, when the young lady would hear something to her advantage."

I was all astonishment and could only repeat my question. "But *how*, Holmes?"

"It may surprise you, Watson, that I do not always take clues from the cut of a gown, or the stains on an apron, or the state of someone's fingernails or their shoes. Sometimes, all it requires is the expression in an eye when a particular person is spoken of; in this instance, Nell's niece. What I saw on her face was love, mingled with disdain for the father, and not a little smugness beneath it all." He paused. "The female sex may hold little attraction for me, Watson, as you know, but that does not mean I cannot read them."

"And from that you surmised—"

"That the young lady had, with her avowedly exceptional hearing, eavesdropped as her father planned her wedding. And that to a Tosher, no less, most likely one cut from the same cloth as Sweetly himself. I also deduced that her father's success may have given her hopes for better. Marrying whom one chooses, after all, is a privilege often enjoyed by the lower classes rather more than royalty.

"In short, it was obvious that she had run away – most likely to the family of this Huckell fellow. Her aunt, of course, was her willing confidant."

"So Sweetly's offering – why, Holmes, you have duped the fellow. And furthermore, you have made a believer of him."

"He was already a believer, Watson. Many such small and closed-in communities insist on their tall tales, do they not? I rather think I turned it to the best, though, don't you? Now, there is just one more thing to be done."

At that very moment, the door opened. It was the aunt standing there – Nell, a person I had observed heretofore only to mark the way she had clattered the cups at tea. Now she was beaming, her eyes shining almost as brightly as her niece's had earlier.

Holmes handed her his bundle of odiferous clothing. "Thank you," he said. "There is among these – I think you know – something you may wish to boil in vinegar before it is made use of again."

It was odd to hear Holmes suddenly leaving off his tale in order to give advice on laundry. But then I glimpsed something nestled amid the soiled cloth – something that glinted in hints of gold and deepest red, indeed, that fairly glittered, before the aunt gave her curtsey, smiled fit to burst, and carried it away.

And there rests the body of my tale; but there was one more peculiar thing to report as we turned our back on Sweetly's residence and indeed on Bermondsey and the whole district of Southwark. It was quite dark by then, the gas-lamps giving off a soft glow through a mist that had crept up from the river, and I do not entirely know what possessed me to turn back.

There, standing close by the wall of the court from which we had emerged, was the figure of a young woman. The light caught and snagged at something hanging about her neck – a deep red jewel that, pretty as it was, gleamed never so brightly as her eyes. For just a moment, the way they reflected back the gas-light put me in mind of a cat's eyes; or those of some other, more subterranean creature, one well accustomed to finding its way through the dark. I found myself wondering if she also had claws on her feet, but even if I had indulged such a thought far enough to look, from that distance I never could have made them out.

*

Once more ensconced in the warm comfort of our rooms on Baker Street, as late as it was, we did not at once betake ourselves to bed. Instead, we sat a while in the parlor, Holmes filling the air with the most pungent pipe-smoke he possessed, and for once I did not mind it. After a time, his question drifted through the air with the scent.

"Will you write about our villain, Watson?"

I gave a wry smile. "A debased goddess, the monarch of the rats? You will no doubt accuse me of romanticizing when I do, Holmes, but of course I shall."

"Queen Rat? Ah, but I wasn't thinking of her. Do you think her the villain here, then? She must have seen how we treat her river – despoiling it, filling it with our filth, then burying it away from sight. Just as men so often do with all that is clean and free and noble."

"Now I half believe that *you* are romanticizing, Holmes."

"Ah – perhaps. In that case, may I propose another villain: Jerry Sweetly himself. Controlling as a lord, and planning his children's marriages with quite as much care; building a dynasty as grand as any princeling. It seems that any man can be a despot, if the circumstances are right. Of course, one might say he has good reason to stand on his pride. Toshers have money, after all – they pick it from the filth – but they rarely have respect. Certainly few would look up to them, deep as they are in the mire."

With a nod, I conceded his point. Though it had already struck me that Holmes, so little concerned with matters of the heart, might never have interested himself so closely in the fate of the daughter if it were not for a certain aversion to the father.

We sat a little longer, so that I almost thought Holmes had fallen asleep in his chair, when his voice drifted up again. "Wasn't she magnificent, Watson?"

With a start, it was before me again: a shape emerging from a tunnel; a shadow straightening against a wall; the gleam of two eyes shining out of the darkness. Sitting as we were in the half-dark, it seemed more real than ever, and before I'd known I was going to speak, I said: "You saw her too, then?"

He let out a low sputter. "I did, my dear Watson. A hallucination, as must have been experienced by many before us, arising from the foulness of the air. Her eyes, a reflection of the light from some grate or from the lamp. Her hair, the slime clinging to the walls. Her step, the natural stirring of the water."

I forced myself to laugh. "Well, perhaps you might have spoken with her, Holmes. You too might have been granted good fortune."

"Ah, but that would not do. Have I not made it plain before, Watson? Logic has no need of luck."

I nodded, but I could not help thinking of Jerry Sweetly, who would no doubt soon venture again into his black underworld. Would his luck indeed have changed, as he feared? Queen Rat had received no offering, after all. She had no child; no necklace. But perhaps she was, in her way, like him. Perhaps all she really desired was a modicum of respect. Still, I could not help dwelling on his words: *Like as not, he'll drown.* What kind of terrible fate might await him, in those awful tunnels?

Or perhaps, trapped in the dark as she was, the queen's powers were failing. Perhaps mine were also, for Holmes's next words caught me by surprise. Indeed, they made me feel I had seen everything, yet observed nothing.

"Did you recognize the necklace, Watson?"

I conceded that I had not.

"Did you think it garnet and paste, my dear fellow? You should look more keenly. That was most certainly a ruby, surrounded by diamonds, if I'm not mistaken. Indeed, I have seen it once before – hanging about the neck of the Princess Helena, as she went about some public duty or other. An unfortunate thing for her to lose, was it not? A fine wedding gift, though, for someone. Indeed, a necklace fit for any princess."

I think my mouth fell open at the thought of the riches Holmes must have plucked from that nail by the bridge when Sweetly and I were distracted by shadows – the same one he had handed to the aunt in a bundle of soiled clothing. I started to chuckle; and then I realized that I *had* been right about something, all along. This case, as ignominious as any we had encountered, had indeed involved one of Queen Victoria's children – if only she had known it. On that, at least, I had speculated aright, and I opened my mouth to say as much to Holmes, but as ever, he forestalled me; knocking the ashes from his pipe, it was he who spoke first.

"Good night, Watson," he said.

THE CASE OF THE STRANDED HARLEQUIN

Mark A. Latham

"Watson, this so-called 'holiday' is really quite interminable! If this is the kind of thing you prescribe to your patients, I'm sure your practice must be on its last legs."

My friend Sherlock Holmes sneezed for the umpteenth time, and shot me another barbed look down his aquiline nose.

"Come now, Holmes," said I, conjuring as much cheer as I could, "other than catching a chill, it's hardly as bad as all that. These rooms are rather pleasant. And that view!" I gesticulated grandly towards the window, where the Downs sprawled majestically away towards the admittedly gray and misty horizon. The weather had proved untypically inclement for the time of year—another thing Holmes, despite his famous reliance on logic, seemed to blame me for.

Holmes's pale ankles jutted from a bowl of steaming water like the limbs of the grey heron, and Holmes, avian as he often appeared, looked at me unblinking, much like that majestic river-bird might eye up a fish.

"I confess, the landlord keeps a good cellar and comfortable rooms," Holmes said. "And this stop might have been tolerable... had you not foolishly blurted out my name to all and sundry."

"Hardly 'blurted', Holmes..." I reddened all the same. Whilst in the bar of the White Hart, on the first night of our stay, I had been discussing with Holmes my notes on our recent case—the Adventure of the Popish Relic—and perhaps, somewhat the worse for tokay after a long day of travelling, I might have referred to my friend as "the great Sherlock Holmes" a little too loudly.

"Blurted." Holmes asserted. "And now I cannot move in this village without someone or other bothering me. Yesterday, the landlord himself hoped I might deduce why his takings were short by three-and-six last Sunday week. This morning, while you were out in search of a game of golf—*golf!*—the postmistress came calling to see if I might find her missing cat. No, this won't do."

Having bumped into the rather flustered postmistress as she'd left the White Hart, I could only imagine how that interview had gone.

"*Aah-choo!*" Holmes's sharp sneeze caused the water in his bowl to splash onto the patterned rug.

"Two more days," said I. "It will give you a chance to get over your chill, and then we shall press on to Hungerford. I'm sure that will be more to your liking."

Holmes *harrumphed.*

79

My hopes of going onwards to Oxford, then perhaps to the Essex coast, were now as dampened as the rain-soaked hills. I had thought a little tour by rail might provide a welcome change of scene, for my friend had been much troubled of late. In truth, I suspected his active mind found conflict, even if he must create it himself.

I was about to make some remark to this effect when there came a knock at the door.

Holmes rolled his eyes theatrically. "If that's the local farmer asking me to investigate a missing heifer, I shall throw myself from the window."

The person on the other side of the door was no farmer. Indeed, it was a woman who stood before me—handsome, in her late thirties perhaps, and well-attired. She clutched a large, rolled paper tightly: her hands shook with agitation. Dark rings about her eyes attested to sleepless nights. Breathlessly, she inquired after Holmes. Before I'd a chance to reply I heard a splash of water behind me, and a brief flurry of activity, before my friend's voice called out, "Where are your manners, Watson? Show the lady in."

The woman introduced herself as Mrs. Eleanor Basford. Once she had been made comfortable on the small sofa of Holmes's room, I set about making some tea.

"I am here about my husband, Harold," Mrs. Basford said.

"Missing," said Holmes. The woman's eyes widened, and Holmes explained simply, "A married woman would not be here alone, in such a state of distress, if her husband were available. That paper you hold bears the letters 'M&SWJR' – I expect Mr. Basford has something to do with the Midland and South Western Junction Railway?"

"Remarkable, Mr. Holmes," the woman said.

"Elementary."

"Perhaps you are just the man to help me…"

She unrolled her paper and spread it out across the coffee table unbidden. It was an ordnance map of the local area, dominated by the railway and canal to the north of the White Hart.

"You have heard of the tunnel collapse?" she asked.

"I have not," replied Holmes. "In fact, I have barely left this establishment since we arrived yesterday, on account of this chill—caused, I might add, by somewhat poor advice on the part of my doctor."

I sighed as I set down the tea-tray, and helped Mrs. Basford anchor the corners of her map with saucers and sugar-bowl.

The woman tapped her finger upon the map. "The Bruce Tunnel," she said. "There was a partial collapse the day before last. It buried a narrowboat, although there was no sign of any crew. Harold is a shareholder in the canal, and the adjoining railway. He runs a local stone quarry, and it is in his interests to maintain the freight routes. Harold could find no one to help investigate the collapse, and so he went alone yesterday. He… he's not been heard of since."

"You have spoken to the police?" Holmes asked.

"Of course. They sent a local man to make sure Harold hadn't been injured in the tunnel or anything of the sort, but found nothing. That's all they would do: they say he has not been gone long enough to start a search."

"Did you hear that, Watson? The country constabulary are slower even than the London breed." Holmes steepled his fingers, then to Mrs. Basford said, "You say he could find no one to investigate. Why not? He must have strong men at his disposal."

"He does. But… Well, people around here are superstitious. There have been stories lately… of strange noises in the tunnel. The locals put it down to an old wives' tale. But it has hurt business these past months. We can barely find any men to operate the cables now, and the collapse has been blamed on vengeful spirits."

"I've heard of this, Holmes," said I. "Just this very day on my walk, I encountered a fellow going on about 'Grindylows' or some such. 'River fairies', I think he said."

"That's a common story around here, Doctor," Mrs. Basford said.

"Ridiculous," Holmes muttered. "It beggars belief how the brain of the most stalwart Englishman can be so softened by fairy stories. But your husband surely went to the police?"

"He did. And his requests fell on deaf ears, as expected. You see… we do not believe the collapse was an accident."

"Industrial espionage?"

"Yes. There are three Bath-stone quarries in this borough. Two of them—ours included—are serviced by the canal, and the new rail junction." She again pointed to the map, this time to a sprawling quarry bordering the vast Savernake Forest. "The third is the Savernake Works, owned by Roderick Harrington. It is the largest and most profitable. Harrington doesn't use the canal, and has opposed every improvement plan over the last five years. Every day that tunnel is closed to freight, Harrington increases his monopoly. He owns almost everything around here: the land, the labor… the police."

"Quite an accusation," Holmes said.

"It's the truth, I swear. Roderick Harrington has been expanding his mines exponentially, using the most dangerous practices."

"Mines?" said I. "I thought you said he owned a stone quarry."

Holmes waved a hand at me. "Bath-stone quarries *are* mines, Watson. Honestly, you should try reading that Bradshaw's you insist on carrying around. Dear lady, do proceed."

"A number of sinkholes have been found all around the county of late, though nobody has been able to inspect them closely before Mr. Harrington cordons them off or fills them in. My husband has long suspected Harrington of undermining beyond the boundaries of his own land. You see, Mr. Harrington has a penchant for blasting deep-level mines, and the safety of his workers is secondary to profit. He has had three serious accidents in as many years—the last resulted in four deaths when a whole shaft collapsed. It is only because he is firm friends with the local magistrate that no charges were brought against him."

"Hence your belief about the loyalties of the constabulary," Holmes said.

"Indeed. They will do nothing about my husband if there's even the merest suggestion Harrington is involved."

"Tell me, Mrs. Basford—these strange stories and superstitions… They must have been told for many a year. Why only recently have grown men been afraid to explore that stretch of the canal?"

"It is beyond me, Mr. Holmes. The locals tell of whispering spirits, and even strange figures rising from the waters at night. It has become worse of late."

"When did these rumors start to gain a hold on the locals?"

"Last winter, directly after the accident I mentioned. It was my husband's belief that Harrington invented the stories, playing on old superstitions, as a way to hamper our business while he got himself back on his feet."

"Plausible," Holmes agreed.

"The fact remains that Harold has been missing a full day. It is most unlike him. None of his friends have seen him…" She suppressed a small sob. "Mr. Holmes, can you help find him?"

Holmes stood, a thin smile rippling across his lips. "Mrs. Basford, it would be my pleasure to assist you. This little holiday was already becoming tiresome, and nothing invigorates me more than a case. I will do what I can."

Mrs. Basford was grateful to the extreme—the sheer relief of being listened to, and believed, was evident. And Holmes did not stop there. He insisted on starting at once, before I could have any say on the matter at all. He bade our client wait whilst he went to the adjoining room and dressed for an excursion. Then, we accompanied the lady downstairs.

We passed through the bar, under the curious stares of the afternoon drinkers. Before saying her goodbyes, Mrs. Basford nodded towards a tall, fair-haired fellow, identifying him as one Dennis Wigram, who had apparently refused to assist her husband. Indeed, she said, he had resigned from Harold Basford's employ that same day, and was now already known to be working at the Savernake quarry.

Holmes bade the lady farewell. As soon as she'd gone, his smile evaporated. Holmes made straight for the fair-haired man, who rose clumsily to his feet, ale slopping onto his shirt.

"Mr. Wigram, is it?" Holmes said. "I'm informed that the other day you were asked by your employer, one Harold Basford, to inspect a tunnel collapse in the nearby canal. Is that correct?"

"He ain't my employer," the man said. His drinking companions eyed Holmes warily.

"He was at the time."

"Well, he was a bleddy tyrant, trying to get us to go in that tunnel, on our day off! So I quit. Had a better offer."

"From Roderick Harrington?"

"I... Eh, what's it to you?"

"Mr. Basford is missing. His wife has tasked me with finding him."

"Run off, has he?"

"I was hoping you could tell me."

Wigram pulled his confidence about him like a cloak, drawing up now to his full height, which rivalled Holmes's. "Maybe you should keep your beak out of local business, Mr. Sherlock Holmes. Oh aye, we know who you are. If you ask me, Basford got sick of sinking all his money into a failing business, so he did a moonlight flit. Shame about his good lady, left all alone like that, but that's how it goes."

This drew a few cruel sniggers from Wigram's fellows.

"And no one has seen fit to inspect the tunnel and clear the blockage?" Holmes persevered.

"Give over. Railway company'll get round to it when they get round to it. Nothing happens quick 'round here."

"There's a boat trapped in there. I don't suppose you know who it belongs to?"

"Maybe it belongs to the fairy folk. *Grindylows*. Maybe it was them what stole Basford away. Good luck finding him in fairyland."

Now the whole gathering exploded into raucous guffaws. I felt my color rise, though Holmes remained stony faced.

There was little more to be had from Wigram. Holmes went instead to the landlord, whose disposition was far more favorable on account of us renting his best rooms. Holmes secured the name of a dependable local boatman, a certain Eli Collins, and took the loan of lanterns, rope, and a pair of waders. If no one could be found to inspect the collapse, Holmes declared, then we must go ourselves.

*

Collins was an earthy sort, with a bulbous nose and great white whiskers. He led the way through the tunnel, explaining that the path was far too narrow for horses, and so canal-boats were pulled through this stretch by men on foot, or by oared launches.

"Watch yer footing," he said.

The light of our lanterns danced off the silty, dark water.

"What of the strange noises heard by the locals recently?" I inquired.

"Noises, sir?" replied Collins.

"Yes, voices and whatnot. Have you seen or heard anything out of the ordinary?"

"I've heard the stories. You get all kinds of strange noises in tunnels like this. Learn to live with 'em. But as fer seeing things... well..." He trailed off.

"So you *have* seen something strange?" I pressed.

There was a long pause, then, "Here we are, sirs. There's your blockage right there. *Tsk.* Terrible mess—I 'spect the railway company will have to send a whole crew for this. And an engineer to repair the damage. Yes, terrible mess…"

That Collins had changed the subject seemed of less import now, for before us the collapsed tunnel presented a severe obstacle indeed. An entire section on the far side had given way, leaving a pile of bricks and rubble blocking more than half the navigable waterway. The debris terminated near the tunnel ceiling, where a small, dark hole penetrated the hillside beyond, tree roots and mud spilling from the fractured earth. In the water, the bow of a narrowboat jutted from the mound of fallen stone at an awkward angle, its stern clearly pinned to the canal-bed by the weight of the debris.

We stood in silence for a moment. There came no sound but the occasional, soft drip of water from the slimy ceiling.

"How deep is the water here?" Holmes asked.

"No more than four feet," Collins replied.

"Excellent. In you go, Watson."

I looked at Holmes agog. "Into the water?"

"How else are we to ascertain the facts?" my friend replied.

"What facts?" I protested. "We can see very well from here."

"The name of the vessel, for one," Holmes said. "Its cargo, for another. We must determine whether the vessel had anything to do with the collapse, or if its presence here—suspiciously crewless—is pure coincidence."

"Well… Why can't you go?"

"My dear Watson, have you not been telling me to keep warm this past day, to stave off my chill? What kind of doctor are you? *Aah-choo!*" The sneeze, it seemed to me, was pure theatrics. He held up the waders. "You'll need these, of course."

It was with great annoyance that I found myself in the cold murk of the canal. The black water lapped dangerously close to the brim of the waders, such that I had little doubt I'd be soaked through before my work was done. I forged over to the trapped boat, the canal-bed beneath my feet uneven and treacherous with detritus.

"Just there," Holmes called. "Clear away some of that rubble from the bows. See if you can't see the name of the boat, then perhaps we can find her owner."

I was too cross to reply, so I simply set about my task half-heartedly. Every time I moved a large lump of stone, or splintered plank, the whole precarious pile seemed to shift, and the boat creaked ominously. I muttered curses under my breath as my excavations created a small landslide. I stepped back from the avalanche a little too quickly, and felt the first trickle of cold water leak over the waders.

The light of Holmes's lantern swept across the exposed bow of the narrowboat.

"The *Harlequin*," he said. "Well done, Watson, we have our name. Now look—you've exposed something there on the deck. Looks like cargo."

I found a little purchase on the rubble now piled on the canal-bed, and heaved myself up onto the boat. Now the whole vessel groaned, and detritus skittered down the great pile. Remarkably, it did not give way entirely, and with yet another curse I pried at the top of the nearest crate. It wouldn't shift fully due to the weight upon it, but it moved sufficiently for a chink of lantern-light to fall on the contents.

I gasped, and stood bolt-upright.

"What is it?" Holmes called. Was that concern in his voice?

"Explosives!" I said. "Dynamite, and lots of it."

"Good heavens, Watson. What are you dilly-dallying for? Best get out of there this instant!"

I scowled, and clambered back into the water. A little more spilled over the waders, and I resigned myself to squelching all the way back to the White Hart.

I'd barely taken two strides back towards my companions when I felt something move against my leg. At first, I assumed something had been dislodged from the *Harlequin* and was now drifting towards me. But then my ankle was—unmistakably—*squeezed*. Instinctively, I took a great stride away, but my foot did not find solid ground. Instead, my standing foot was yanked violently, and to my utmost horror I was submerged abruptly in the water. My head was fully under. My knee touched the canal-bed. I was blind in the darkness, but again, for a moment, I felt some indescribable dark mass brush past me. I flapped and floundered, swallowing a little of the disgusting water in my panic, until at last I regained my senses and pushed myself upwards.

Now I stood in the light of two lanterns, coughing and spluttering, hair plastered to my forehead. Holmes and Collins pulled me from the water. Soaked through and flustered, I must have sounded like a lunatic, raving about deep holes and unseen things grabbing my leg. Then, at once, we were all silenced by noise behind us—a splash, followed by a bubbling, as of something submerging.

Collins had already been looking towards the water, lantern in hand. Now, uttering some indecipherable local curses, he raced off down the tunnel whence we'd come, holding onto his hat as he went. No amount of calling would stop him, and he offered no reply, and no explanation for his sudden exit.

Holmes scanned the water. "Whatever did he see that alarmed him so?"

The cold hit me now; my teeth chattered. "For all we know," said I, "a box of dynamite might have fallen into the water. We should leave too, unless we wish to be blown to Kingdom Come."

"Hmm?" Holmes mused absent-mindedly. Then he snapped to attention. "Yes, of course. Let's depart—I've seen all I need for now."

He strode away in the opposite direction to the way we'd come.

"Holmes!" I called, exasperated. "You're going the wrong way."

"No, Watson. We must take a detour."

"I shall catch my death!"

Holmes didn't stop. "I thought you were made of sterner stuff, Watson," he called back. "Come along!"

The dark tunnel ran for another half-mile. Every so often I afforded a glance over my shoulder, but without a lantern I could see barely anything.

"You say you stepped into a hole?" Holmes asked.

"That's hardly the point," said I. "Something snagged my leg."

"Grabbed," Holmes said. "Before, you said 'grabbed'. Which is it?"

"I… *ahem*… Cannot say for sure." The further from the scene of the incident we walked, the more ridiculous it felt—as though I'd imagined the whole affair.

"There was a swirling current in the water near the boat," Holmes said. "I saw it just a second or two before you fell. It would support the hypothesis that there's a sinkhole in the canal-bed."

"You think I stepped into a sinkhole? And perhaps… it was simply debris from the wreckage I felt under the water…"

"I'm sure of it, Watson," Holmes said.

Soon we reached the other end of the tunnel, squinting against the influx of daylight, as abrupt as it was welcome. We were out on a graveled towpath before our eyesight had adjusted fully to the light, and it was at that moment we were caught unawares.

Rough hands landed on our shoulders. Rougher voices gave warning.

"Snooping about, are you?" one said.

"Outsiders, sticking your noses into other peoples' business!" said another.

There were four men, thickset and hard-faced. They all wore heavy jackets, and had caps pulled low over their brows. Two of them had hold of me; one held Holmes likewise, while the fourth stood before us—evidently the leader, due to his bearing, the smirk on his square face, and his lack of willingness to sully his hands.

"And who are you to accost us so?" Holmes said, with remarkable calm. "Is this not a public right of way?"

"Not for you," the leader said. "You're here chasin' ghosts for Basford's wife. Making acc'sations."

"Ghosts?" Holmes said. "That's only true if Mr. Basford is deceased. And there's only one way you could know that."

"See?" said the man. "Acc'sations. Seems like somebody needs teaching a lesson."

He nodded to his men, who tensed, ready for violence at their leader's command. But the signal, intended for the thugs, was read instantly by Holmes and by myself, for this was not, as they say in the Americas, our first 'rodeo'.

I heard a loud splash, and knew without looking that my friend's assailant had gone into the canal. Despite being slight of stature, Holmes was well-versed in the gentlemanly art of Japanese wrestling, *baritsu,* which meant I rarely had to worry about him holding his own against less skilled opponents.

For my part, I threw myself backwards, crushing one of my assailants against the stone wall of the tunnel, while the second threw a clumsy punch that struck nothing but thin air. An elbow into the ribs of the first man finally forced him to release me. Another elbow to his nose dropped him in short order.

Now it was two-against-two, and the common thugs backed off warily. One took out a knife, another pulled out a cudgel, wrapping its leather strap tightly about his ham-sized fist.

"That's quite enough of that!" a new voice called out.

The two thugs, startled, looked up the canal-bank at a short, well-dressed man, hands in his pockets, face shaded by the brim of a homburg. Immediately, the men stepped away, looking sullen and disappointed. The man behind me staggered to his feet and edged around me timidly, before hurrying to his comrades.

"Mr. Holmes, is it?" the newcomer called down. "And you must be Dr Watson. Forgive my men—they can be a bit... overzealous."

"Roderick Harrington, I presume?" Holmes called up.

"The same. Come up here if you will, and let me make amends. Doctor... you're soaked through. I hope my men didn't do that? I've a carriage up here, please come with me up to the house and dry off." He looked to the leader of his men and said, "Hapgood, I'll deal with you later. And help Smith out of the bloody canal, will you?"

*

We sat in comfortable chairs in Harrington's lounge, me in borrowed clothes, and Holmes as inscrutable as ever but for the occasional sniffle. A black Labrador lay curled up snoring beside a crackling fire. For a large house, it was surprisingly homely. To reach it we had driven through a somewhat dreary and desolate industrial wasteland. Roderick Harrington lived on the edge of his own business enterprise so he could, as he'd put it, "look upon his empire from his own doorstep."

"You have not spoken with Mr. Basford these past few days?" Holmes asked. In typical style, he had not been intimidated by Harrington's show of wealth and power, and his line of questioning had been as direct and as pointed as I had ever witnessed. The scuffle with Harrington's men—for which our host had apologized profusely—had not set Holmes in a particularly courteous disposition.

Harrington took a sip of tea, then set down his cup. His deeply wrinkled brow furrowed further, rolling into his bald pate like some kind of geological formation.

"I've not spoken with him this past month," Harrington said. "Basford is an odd fish. Builds a canal tunnel with backing from the railway company to monopolize business, then accuses *me* of funny business."

"Funny business?" Holmes asked. "You mean the safety concerns over your mining operations?"

"Among other things, yes. And those complaints have been investigated. We had a few unfortunate accidents in the quarry—I'll not deny it—but there was no suggestion of negligence. I have a signed statement by a magistrate to attest to it. So, I ask you, if there was no blame at this end, who is really under suspicion of 'industrial espionage', hmm?"

"You're referring to the tunnel collapse. But if you haven't spoken with Basford for a month, how has he accused you of anything?"

"His bloody wife!" Harrington snapped, his mask of patience slipping. "She's been saying it to anyone who'll listen. You included."

"I see. About the tunnel—you call it a monopoly, but is there not another quarry who uses the canal quite happily?"

"I imagine they pay through the nose for it."

"Ah. And is it money preventing you from exploiting the waterways for your own business?"

"Not at all. We're not favorably located to use the new branch of the canal, and so we rely on road freight through the Savernake. Always have."

"Mrs. Basford says you own most of the land around here. I imagine that gives *you* a monopoly when it comes to road freight."

"That's where you're misinformed again, Mr. Holmes!" Harrington clearly relished saying this, as much as Holmes was irked by it. "I do not own any part of Savernake Forest. My land is simply contiguous to it. I have a long-standing gentlemen's agreement with George, and his father before him."

"George?"

"The Earl of Cardigan. Influential man. *Very* influential."

"And he doesn't mind you mining under his land?"

"Because we don't. Indeed, that's part of the agreement. Our wagons cross his land, that's all."

Holmes pursed his lips. "You do, however, keep canal boats?"

"Why?"

"I hear you've been hiring boatmen. Boatmen previously in Basford's employ."

A scowl momentarily crossed Harrington's face. "I keep a few boats, out of necessity."

"Is the *Harlequin* one of them?"

"Couldn't tell you. What the men call their own boats is up to them."

"Mr. Harrington, we have reason to believe that the tunnel collapse was in part due to the formation of sinkholes— sinkholes probably caused by nearby undermining. If we could take a tour of your operation, I'm sure we could quickly put this matter—"

"Quite impossible, Mr. Holmes," Harrington said abruptly. "Beyond the safety issues with having civilians near the quarry, you are currently engaged by one of my main business rivals. I take my trade secrets very seriously."

"Your rival is missing, Mr. Harrington. I am engaged by his wife, who's sick with worry."

"You work for the Basfords; that means you're taking railway money. I'm sorry Mr. Holmes, but that's the way it is. I'm glad of the chance to clear things up with you, but as far as I'm concerned this is the end of it."

"There is no end to this matter until Harold Basford is found."

Harrington and Holmes locked eyes. At last, Harrington rose from his chair and said, "I'll have my man take you back to the White Hart."

"I'm sure we can make our own way," Holmes said with a thin smile. I expect he hoped to take a jaunt across Harrington's land at any opportunity.

"I *insist,*" Harrington said. And the glower suggested he, too, suspected Holmes of duplicity.

There was little more to be said. With a promise that I'd have the spare clothes cleaned and returned post-haste, and a few icy cordialities, we took our leave, making the journey in silence to spare us from prying ears.

*

"Enemies? Harrington?" The landlord scratched at his bushy sideburns thoughtfully. "Now, why would you ask such a thing, sir?"

"On account of the mining accidents," Holmes said. "A small place like this… there can't have been too many families unaffected by Roderick Harrington's operation."

"That's true enough, but most of the men round here are boatmen. The quarry workers come in from all over. Crofton men mostly and a few from Bedwyn. No… Apart from Mr. Basford, there's nobody I can recall having a harsh word to say about Mr. Roderick. 'Cept of course fer…" The landlord trailed off, looking abashed.

"Except for whom?" Holmes pressed.

"I was going to say Lord Savernake himself, but that seems a mite remiss."

"The Earl of Cardigan?"

"The same."

"I'd heard the arrangement between Harrington and the Earl was an amicable one."

"Most of the time, aye. But… Well, it's the sinkholes, y'see. They open up in the forest now and then. His lordship accused Mr. Harrington of tunnelling under his land more than once, but when the inspectors came to check they didn't find nothing."

I looked at Holmes, and ventured, "Inspectors sent by the local magistrate, I presume."

"I s'pose so, yes," the landlord replied.

Mrs. Basford had told us the magistrate was in Harrington's pocket. Holmes pursed his lips in that familiar expression of deep thought, then his eyes darted left and right. He'd noticed several men in the bar eavesdropping.

"This is all very interesting," Holmes said, loudly. "We did, in fact, find blasting equipment aboard the stuck boat in the Bruce Tunnel. A boat called the *Harlequin*. Do you know it?"

The landlord looked guarded. "N—no," he mumbled.

"No matter. A thorough search must be made of the boat. I've already arranged to meet with the Marlborough constabulary at first light. We'll soon have the thing dug out, and then we'll get to the bottom of things."

With that, Holmes ushered me away, and we returned to the room.

"What was all that about, Holmes?" said I. "Marlborough constabulary, indeed!"

"Now that my little deception has been overheard by those men in the bar, I expect someone will go to dig out the boat themselves. Or perhaps even detonate that dynamite so no evidence can be found. Tonight, Watson, you and I shall return to the tunnel, and see what we can see."

"Good heavens, Holmes! So it is industrial espionage, then?"

"More than likely. I think you should get some rest—we have a long night ahead. Did you pack your service revolver?"

"As always."

"Excellent fellow. I think you may well need it…"

*

Holmes and I lay on our bellies atop the canal bank, hidden within a tousle of thick shrubbery. The cold and damp seemed to seep into my very bones. A fine, mist-like rain floated in from the Downs, settling miserably over us. I fidgeted uncomfortably, whilst Holmes was, as ever, unflappable.

We waited in this manner for well over an hour, until I could no longer feel my fingers and toes, and the clouds blew in so thick they masked even the scant moonlight. But then, in the moment I'd almost decided to give up on the whole affair, several dark figures emerged just ahead of us, scarecrow shadows against a dark and misty horizon. One of them lit a lantern, revealing their faces briefly. At least one I recognized from the hotel bar. Another was Hapgood—Harrington's square-faced thug. As the men descended the bank toward the tunnel-mouth, Holmes signaled that the time had arrived. I forced my leaden limbs to move. Now we'd catch these rogues in the act, and hopefully get some answers.

Once the men had vanished into the tunnel, we waited a few minutes longer before commencing our pursuit. We entered the tunnel and followed the yellow lantern-light that swung to-and-fro ahead. We continued cautiously, quietly as possible, until the voices of our quarry became louder, and their lamplight brighter. Then at once, the voices stopped. The light fell, as if laid on the ground. Holmes checked his stride.

I started as something moved in the water beside us. In the low light I gleaned the impression of a sleek, black shape breaking the surface, before gliding on around the tunnel bend.

"Holmes..." I hissed.

There came a scream, of abject terror, echoing through the dark. Then another. There was a loud splash, followed by footsteps pounding the tow-path, drawing swiftly closer.

I drew my pistol instinctively, and would have fired upon the dark shape that now fled the tunnel had Holmes not stayed my hand. Holmes lifted the hood of his lantern as the man almost crashed into us.

Hapgood's face was a pale contortion of horror, covered in bloody scratches that looked all the world like the rake-marks of large claws.

"They're real..." he babbled. "They're bleedin' real!"

Holmes seized the man's shoulder. "Pull yourself together, man! What's real? What do you mean?"

Hapgood pulled away, his anger at Holmes momentarily overcoming his fear at whatever he'd left behind. His eyes widened, and he growled, "The *grindylows!*"

Holmes began to remonstrate further, when we both noticed an object clutched in Hapgood's hand.

Dynamite.

"They killed my mates," Hapgood said. Then, louder, hysterically, "Now I'll bleedin' kill them!"

He turned back the way he came, and began to run away from us. We saw the flare of a match.

Without hesitation, Holmes took off after the man. "Come back!" he cried. "Don't light that dynamite; it's suicide!"

I gave chase, but what came next seemed to unfold painfully slowly, making of me a spectator to disaster.

We rounded the bend just as Hapgood hurled the stick of dynamite towards the wreck of the *Harlequin*. It arced towards the pile of debris, leaving a trail of smoke in the air. For a briefest moment, I saw beneath its trajectory the fallen lantern, casting its light upon a bloodied and broken body. And over that body, though my brain tried to deny the truth of my eyes, a dark, slimy figure, hunched.

I called out to Holmes, but there came a deafening blast, muffling all else but the ringing in my ears. A warm wind ripped towards us, carrying a plume of thick dust and sharp projectiles of chipped stone.

And then the tunnel collapsed all around us.

*

I don't know how long I lay in the darkness, nor how long before that I'd been unconscious. All I knew now was that Holmes was speaking to me, his hand pushing through rubble to grasp mine, and Holmes's lamplight illuminated our predicament.

"Watson!" Holmes's face appeared at the hole he'd dug. "I've found a way out, but we must be careful or we'll be crushed to death."

It was only then that I really saw how precarious the situation was. Were it not for several large capstones that had collapsed near to me, I'd certainly have been crushed already. As it was, I was cocooned within a tight pocket of debris, my upper half covered in thick dust that cloyed at my lungs, but my legs soaked in water so cold I'd been entirely numb to the situation until now.

Together, we dug away at the rubble until I was able to wriggle free and move through the gap towards my friend. Holmes occupied a slightly larger cavity, and dryer too.

"Hapgood?" I croaked, through dusty throat.

Holmes swung his lantern to the right, shining the light on a lower leg, jutting from the detritus, the foot twisted awkwardly at the ankle, Hapgood's boot dripping with blood.

"So, what now?" I asked. "Someone must have heard the explosion. I expect they'll come to dig us out soon."

"Not soon enough," Holmes replied. "Listen."

We both went very still and sat huddled in silence. Then I heard the noises to which Holmes had alluded. At first a tapping and scraping, as of something digging outside the rubble. Then the faint echo of some guttural, bestial sounds— a snapping and clacking in wet throats, dreadful and unhuman.

"Whatever's out there," Holmes said gravely, "cares not about us. Their digging will bring this whole mess down on our heads, unless we first escape."

"But how?" said I.

Holmes now shone his light at our feet, where the debris entered the silty water, which swirled and gurgled.

"A sinkhole," Holmes said. "That disturbance in the water means it's being drawn away somewhere. I mean to find out where."

"Are you mad?" I hissed. "It'll be pitch dark, and there's no saying it comes out anywhere but a submerged cavern. You'll drown."

"I think not. In fact, after studying the map, I think we're closer to salvation than you might think. What's it to be, old friend? A swim into the breach, or a gruesome death in here?"

"Well, when you put it like that…" I grumbled.

A moment later, without further discussion, Holmes was gone; vanished beneath the ink-black water. Even then I reconsidered, unmanned by the idea of drowning beneath a pile of rubble. But again came the scraping, this time causing dust to fall on my head. And it was followed by a growl so unknowingly *alien,* that I could not bear the thought of waiting to see what was coming for me.

And so, I lowered myself into the freezing water, took a deep breath, and followed Holmes.

*

For what seemed the longest time I lay in cold mud, coughing and spluttering the disgusting, silty water from my lungs. Holmes had been right about the sinkhole, and had fished me from a narrow, water-filled tunnel just as I thought I would run out of breath. But I couldn't see him—nor anything else— for wherever we were was entirely pitch dark.

There came a spark, followed by the yellow glow of the lamp. A large cavern flickered into view.

"How does the lamp still work?" I asked, in spite of my relief.

"Rudimentary science, Watson. I loosened the glass chimney-stock before entering the water, and submerged it quickly to trap the air within. The wick may still have become a little wet, but as oil repels water that's hardly a problem. We're just lucky the sudden temperature change didn't crack the glass. Lucky also that I remembered to pack my flint rather than matches, or we'd be truly stumped. Fortune favors us, it seems."

I looked ruefully about the cavern, with its moss-slick rocks, jaw-like stalactites, and darkened corners hiding who-knew-what. "Oh yes," I said. "We're fortunate indeed."

"I'll forgive your sarcasm this once," Holmes said. He held up his hand, cocked his head for a moment, then pointed the way, "There's fresh air coming from that direction. Let's go—this oil won't last all night."

We followed a trickling, underground stream for what seemed like hours, taking many twists and turns through the gloom. In some places, the tunnels tightened so much Holmes, being the more slender of us, had to crawl through and physically pull me through after him. In others, the caverns opened up into yawning maws, toothy stalactites hanging ominously overhead, dripping water onto moss-slick rocks beneath our feet. When one such cavern opened out to reveal an underground lake, I gasped in amazement. The lantern barely illuminated the opposite shore, but through what dim light we had, we discerned a large tunnel leading away from us, surrounded by unmistakably man-made debris—scaffolds of wood and iron, and large square lintels—the workings of a quarry, now collapsed, forming a slope into what we hoped was salvation.

But the light shone upon something else, too. Something dreadful.

The banks of the lake were littered with bones. Even as we noticed this for the first time, I stumbled clumsily, my foot cracking through the ancient skull of some mammal—a deer, or sheep, I could not tell. And as I looked down in disgust at the bone-beach, I saw also scraps of cloth, and human skulls poking out from the mounds.

This gruesome discovery only served to make Holmes more animated. He picked his way deftly through the charnel remains, casting his light about the ground. And then he stopped.

When I caught up, I saw that the remains grew fresher the closer we got to the mine workings. Instead of bones, there were now carcasses of deer, badgers, and an abundance of waterfowl. Some were partially devoured, some almost untouched. And amidst them was the body of a man.

I shudder to describe the condition of the corpse, even in medical terms, save that it was unidentifiable.

Holmes held the light while I searched through the bloodied and torn clothes for some means of identification. The man's wedding ring was uninscribed. He had no wallet, and his pockets contained only a few coins.

"The watch-chain," Holmes said.

Of course, it was Holmes's keen eyes that saw the broken chain at the man's button-hole, and I dug around in the mulch and nauseating animal remains for the watch that must have once hung from it. At last I found it, and after wiping it clean, the discovery confirmed our worst suspicions. It was inscribed, *For the man who is so often late. All my love, Eleanor.*

"I'll bring the watch and ring back to his wife," I said, sorrowfully.

"Indeed," Holmes said. "But we should tarry no longer down here."

Almost in answer, there came an echoing splash, as of something entering the lake in the darkness. And following that sound, a dreadful skittering of claws on rock, and a throng of low, throaty growls.

"Run!" Holmes hissed.

It was pure instinct that spurred me to movement. I had never before seen Holmes given to panic, and now I followed him as closely as I could, though it was a struggle to keep pace with my sure-footed friend. Several times I stumbled, falling beyond the comforting radius of lamplight. Each time I dared look back, many pairs of eyes gleamed in the cold dark, drawing ever nearer.

As we at last reached the slope of the mine-tunnel, I sensed movement to my left. Something dark and slimy broke the surface of the underground lake. An indistinct shape leapt from the water, and scurried towards us on all fours.

"Watson!"

Holmes's call shook me from my momentary stupor, and I climbed desperately. When at last I thought I might reach the imagined sanctuary of the tunnel-mouth, a cold, wet hand gripped my ankle, squeezing with uncommon strength. I felt the tips of needle-sharp claws pierce my skin, and yelped as much from fright as pain. The strength of my pursuer was uncanny. I slipped back down the slope, even though I was clinging on for dear life.

Holmes's hand grasped mine, his grip like iron. I was pulled then in two directions, and with all my strength I kicked out, my foot connecting with something solid.

The clawed hand at my ankle slipped away and Holmes hoisted me up into the tunnel.

The skittering of debris grew louder. I gained a sense of not one, but many creatures climbing the slope inexorably towards us.

Holmes ushered me from the tunnel-mouth. I limped away, turning back as those terrible, gleaming eyes appeared at the opening. Sherlock Holmes stepped in front of me, and threw the lantern.

The glass cracked, the oil spread and ignited at once. With hisses and baleful screeches, our pursuers fell back from the flames. But there was not much oil remaining, and the fire began to die almost as quickly as it had spread.

Again, we ran. At first, I felt sure we would be lost in the darkness without the lamp. But then, ahead, I saw faint, crepuscular rays forcing their way irregularly through the tunnel roof. And soon we found an upward slope, then wooden ramps and tread-boards. I know not how long we wandered, but I remember clearly the relief when we emerged from a sinkhole in the Savernake woods. I lay on my back in soft loam, gulping the cold, clean air, as the first rays of morning light bathed my face. And I knew in my heart, like a man of true faith, that those hideous things in the dark tunnels would not brave the daylight. We had escaped.

*

"You say he *fell*?" Lord Savernake looked dubious. He hazarded another glance down into the sinkhole, from where three bodies had now been retrieved.

"There are sinkholes all the way from here to the tunnel," Holmes said. "Mr. Basford must have been searching for evidence of undermining after seeing the tunnel collapse. He found more than he bargained for."

A policeman covered Harold Basford's remains, and then he and two others solemnly carried the body away on a stretcher.

"And you say animals did that to him? And the others? Mr. Holmes, this is *England*."

"What else could it have been, Lord Savernake?"

Holmes held his lordship's gaze for a little too long, and I saw in the Earl's eyes that he suspected more than he would ever say, and knew more than he cared to.

"Well," the Earl said after a while, "it goes without saying my agreement with Harrington is over. Irrespective of the damage caused, these workings encroach well beneath the forest—ancient land, that my family has long sworn to protect."

"It seems nature found a way to protect itself, my lord," said Holmes.

The Earl paled. "Quite. I'll see justice done; don't you worry."

"It's said that Harrington has the local magistrate in his pocket," I interjected. I couldn't help but be angry. Mrs. Basford's loss was egregious, and her despair when I had returned her husband's things had been heart-breaking. Whatever evil had been awakened beneath those damned woods had been so roused due to Harrington's greed.

"Wealthy men have always exploited the system of law, Dr Watson," the Earl said. "But you will find my influence extends considerably further than a local magistrate. For undermining my land, and inculcating dangerous working conditions, he'll lose his license. If he really was behind the sabotage of the canal tunnel, as Mr. Holmes suggests, he'll face criminal charges, you can be sure of that. However, of more immediate concern is the matter of these sinkholes. What am I to do with them?"

Holmes looked the Earl square in the eyes, and said, "My lord, if I were you, I would seal every ingress to that underground lake as a matter of urgency. For the good of all."

So solemn was Holmes with his final words, that the Earl could summon no direct reply. Instead, he asked only what Holmes and I planned to do next.

"This holiday has been quite eventful enough," Holmes said. "We shall return to London post-haste."

And though it was the first I'd heard of our change of plans, I did not argue.

Instead, I at last succumbed to the chill that had been growing in my very bones since my impromptu dip in the canal-waters, and I had but one reply.

"Aah-choo!"

THE ADVENTURE OF THE STONE MEN

Charles R. Rutledge

"Every word of this story is as true as despair-" Edith Nesbit

During my long acquaintance with Mr. Sherlock Holmes I have attempted to set down some of his more remarkable cases, and, I think, in general my accounts have served him well. There have, however, been a few such investigations which Holmes insisted I not commit to paper, even without an eye for publication. Most of the time this was to protect a client or witness, but sometimes it was because Holmes simply thought the circumstances to be too outré to lay before the public.

There is one case that has haunted me for many years, and I had asked Holmes, on several occasions, to allow me to write it down, if only to exorcise it from my memory. A week ago,

I sent him a telegram in Sussex to inquire once more. His laconic and surprising answer was, "Very well. No one will believe it anyway."

Thus, I am finally free to chronicle one of the most bizarre occurrences with which Holmes and I were ever involved. When I have finished, I shall place the manuscript in my old dispatch box. It may be that someday the story will be read and either believed or dismissed. Time shall be the judge.

*

On a cold, rainy morning in early November, I was seated before the fire in our sitting room in Baker Street. Holmes was lingering over his breakfast, or rather I should say he was pushing the remains of it around on his plate, obviously lost in thought. He had been without a case for almost two weeks, and he was chafing at the inactivity.

Neither of us could have known how quickly things were about to change when we heard a swift, heavy tread on the stairs. The sitting room door burst open with such force that both Holmes and I rose to our feet. A burly man, with a great shock of red hair, stood in the doorway. His ruddy face glistened with rain and water dripped from his coat.

"I'm sorry to barge in at this hour, Mr. Holmes," the man said. "I knocked downstairs, but no one answered."

The man, having a thick accent, was obviously Irish. I shall not attempt to reproduce his brogue here, for it might cause my readers some confusion and add an air of unintentional humor to my tale that it does not warrant.

"Our landlady is away doing her shopping, Doctor," Holmes said. "If you would be so kind as to hang your coat in the hall, you may dry yourself at our fire."

Shrugging out of his coat, I showed him where he might hang it. As he turned back, he paused and looked to Holmes. "How did you know I was a doctor?"

"Simplicity itself. Part of your stethoscope is hanging from your coat pocket. Now, what has brought you here from the country at this early hour? No mystery there either, Doctor. The country sun has affected even a normally fair complexion like yours."

"You are right, sir. I am a doctor. Kelley is my name. My practice is in the village of Brenzett, near the southern marshes in Kent. We had a tragedy there the night before last."

"And the nature of this tragedy?" asked Holmes.

Kelley stretched his hands out toward the fire. "A young woman, the wife of a friend and neighbor, died in very mysterious circumstances."

"What was the cause of death?" I said.

"Truthfully, I'm not sure."

"You haven't had a chance to examine her?"

"Oh yes, I've done that. At the request of the local magistrate. I've given heart failure as the official cause."

"Then why come to me? I can hardly investigate a failed heart," said Holmes.

Kelley looked at the floor. "There's more to it than that, Mr. Holmes. I said I'd given heart failure as the *official* cause of death. But it is what might have caused such a reaction that vexes me. I could not include my own suppositions in my report, but I will tell the both of you. I believe the young woman died of sheer terror."

"Terror of what, Doctor?" said Holmes.

"Here I must ask you gentlemen to indulge me, for the rest of my story will make me sound like a madman."

111

Holmes raised an eyebrow, but he took his customary chair near the fire and motioned Kelley toward the settee. The Irishman gave a grateful nod and settled his bulk on the cushions. I resumed my own seat.

"As I told you," he began, "I live in the village of Brenzett. I am currently the only doctor there, so I am kept quite busy and do a great deal of walking about the countryside. Two nights ago, I was on my way to see the young daughter of a man named Palmer. The child was only slightly ill, and Palmer had asked me to stop by if my schedule permitted it. I was going across the fields to save time, and I must admit I was concentrating more on the uneven ground than looking ahead, so I was very surprised when I almost collided with David Marsh, a young artist who had recently moved to the village with his wife.

"Marsh attempted to push past me. I knew him to be a nervous man, but he seemed in a dangerously high state of agitation. I grasped him by the arms and held him in place. He struggled, shouting that the marble figures had gone from the church."

"Figures?" Holmes said.

"Yes, Mr. Holmes, and there we come to the heart of my story and my consternation. There is a very old church in Brenzett, which stands well away from the village itself, near a patch of woods. It is a large and lonely place, surrounded by great yews and elms."

"You have a flare for the poetic, Doctor Kelley," Holmes said.

"The place inspires that sort of thinking. Inside, the building is quite ornate, with a high ceiling and reticulated windows. Within the chancel, on each side of the altar, lies a gray marble figure of a medieval knight in full plate armor."

"And it was these figures your young friend thought had somehow been taken from the church?"

"He didn't think they had been taken," Kelley said. "He thought they had gotten up and left the church under their own power. Oh, I see the look of disbelief crossing your features, Mr. Holmes, but please hear me out to the end of my story."

Holmes spread his hands. "Pray continue then."

"You see, there is a local legend about those two figures. Apparently in life the two men had been devils incarnate, guilty of every wicked act imaginable."

"The names of these demons?" Holmes said.

Kelley shook his head. "Lost to time. I think the villagers had tried to forget them."

"Then how did they come to be so honored in the church?" I interjected.

Kelley gave me a wry smile. "How do such men ever achieve honor after death, Doctor? The gold of their heirs bought them their places in the chancel. In any case, according to the rest of the legend, the men's evil acts eventually caught up to them, and a bolt of lightning struck their house. It burned to the ground with them and all their servants inside."

"Dear me, Watson. This story has everything, including divine retribution. I suppose the cottage where the young couple resided stands on the ground formerly occupied by the home of the knights." Holmes said.

"You anticipate me, Mr. Holmes. Yes, that is correct. I believe the cottage was actually built from stones remaining from the big house. And the legend says that on All Saints' Eve, when the church bells toll eleven, the two marble knights rise from their slabs and return to their home, and woe betide any who cross their path. And, of course, the night before last was All Saints' Eve.

"I managed to get young Marsh calmed down enough to return with me to the church so I could show him the folly of his actions. We walked up to the church and the air was filled with a damp, earthy smell. A storm was approaching. I was still holding Marsh's arm and I could feel him tremble as we entered the dark building.

"I confess to a certain thrill of uncertainty as I fumbled for a box of matches in my pocket, but when I lit the match both figures were lying on their slabs, as they had done for many years. Marsh shook my hand and thanked me for saving him from his own strained nerves, but as he was talking, I leaned down for a closer look at the nearest statue and saw the hand was broken, with one of the fingers missing.

"I'm not sure what it was about that missing digit that caused a feeling of dread to wash over me, but it was as if a cold shadow passed over my heart. Marsh invited me to return with him to his cottage and see his wife. I readily agreed, as it was growing too late to call at Palmer's and I could go there in the morning.

"My uneasy feelings were only intensified as we approached the cottage, for I could see the front door hung open and light streamed out onto the garden path. Marsh and I hurried inside and found the parlor door open as well. The room was ablaze with candles, as if Laura Marsh had been trying to hold back the night.

"At first, we did not see the girl, but then Marsh cried out and rushed across the room to a window recess. His wife lay there unmoving, slumped across a small table and half on the window seat. Her lips were drawn back and her eyes wide open. I tell you, gentlemen, I have never seen such a look of sheer horror as the one etched across that young face."

I said, "What did you do then?"

Kelley heaved a great sigh. "Young Marsh drew the girl to him, talking to her as if she were merely sleeping, but I knew, even before I examined her, that she was dead. When I was able to calm Marsh enough to let me close to the girl my fears were confirmed. It was during my examination I realized her fist was clenched tight around some object.

"When I was able to pry her hand open, I saw she was holding a stone finger."

"A trick," I said. "Some sort of cruel prank."

"I thought the same, Doctor Watson, and I still can't say that isn't the case, but as I heard the first patter of the coming rain, I hurried out to the garden to look for any signs of visitors before the storm fell and wiped them out."

"And you found...?" Holmes said.

"Footprints, Mr. Holmes. Wide and very deep, as if made by an extremely heavy man, or... something else. All such signs were destroyed by the storm, of course."

"Of course," Holmes said. "I am inclined to agree with my friend Watson. Someone was playing an elaborate joke or hoax on the unfortunate young woman and it ended in tragedy."

"I should like nothing better than to believe just that, but if that is the case, then the perpetrator of such a cruel hoax is responsible for Laura Marsh's death. I have come here to ask you to find the truth, Mr. Holmes. Whatever it may be," Kelley said.

115

"Do you suspect anyone yourself, Doctor Kelley? Is the husband capable of such a prank?"

"David worshipped his wife. I do not think he would have done such a thing, though I had considered it."

"Where is he now?" I asked.

"I thought it best not to leave him alone, so after I saw to the proper care of the girl's body, I bundled Marsh off to my home. My sister keeps house for me and she is watching over him."

Holmes asked, "Can you think of anyone who would have anything against David Marsh or his wife?"

"The only thing that comes to mind is I heard that their housekeeper, Mrs. Dorman, left them with scant notice."

"Worth noting," said Holmes. "Though something that complex hardly seems within the purview of a housekeeper. Very well, Doctor Kelley. You have intrigued me."

"Then you will look into the matter? You will return with me to Brenzett?"

"I will join you in the village but a bit later, I think. Can you tell me who owns the cottage the couple was renting?"

"Yes, well known in Brenzett. The cottage and land are owned by a woman named Constance Brewer. She inherited from her husband and spends as little time in the village as possible. She is always away to London well before All Saints' Eve."

Holmes rose from his chair. "I shall begin my investigation with Mrs. Brewer then. You will hear from me soon, Doctor."

Kelley stood and shook hands with each of us, and with a final word of thanks, rushed out the door as abruptly as he had entered.

"What an amazing story, Holmes," I said. "Why would anyone perpetrate such a terrible hoax?"

Holmes lifted a pipe from the rack near the mantle. "That is what we must determine. Now, let us see if I can obtain an interview with Mrs. Constance Brewer."

"May I join you?" I said.

"I would not think of making a move without you, old fellow."

*

Mrs. Constance Brewer lived in an elegant, white brick house on Arlington Street in St. James's, which commanded a fine view of Green Park. Holmes and I arrived there around 2:00, hoping she would receive unexpected visitors.

Holmes presented his card to a footman, along with a few words of brief explanation, and a few minutes later we were ushered into a large and well-appointed parlor. A cheery fire crackled in an enormous fireplace and a tall, slender woman stood before it. She was clad in a deep purple dress of a rather severe, though elegant, cut. I judged her to be about fifty years of age, and she had made no attempt to hide the iron gray strands in her hair.

Without preamble, Mrs. Brewer said, "I had thought the police might consult me at some point, but I hardly expected a visit from the famous Mr. Sherlock Holmes."

"You flatter me, madam. May I ask why you thought Scotland Yard might call?"

"That terrible business in Brenzett, of course. I own the property where the young woman died, so thought it likely I would be involved sooner or later, though I hadn't thought it would occur this quickly. Please be seated gentlemen. Shall I ring for tea?"

"Please do not trouble yourself on our account. We shall endeavor to keep this interview brief. Since you are already aware of the situation in Brenzett it will make things easier. May I ask, had you met David Marsh and his wife?"

Mrs. Brewer shook her head. "Since my husband's death, I have tended not to frequent Brenzett. He was born there, and his people were from the area, but without him I have no connection there myself. A housing agent handles all my business in the village."

"One of the locals indicated you make occasional use of the cottage, but were careful to absent yourself well before All Saints' Eve."

"Is that what they say about me, Mr. Holmes? That I hurry away before the local legends can come after me?"

"That does seem to be the general opinion. You are familiar with the legend of the stone knights?"

"Of course. No one could live in the village for long and not have heard that tale. But I can assure you, Mr. Holmes, my desire to be away from Brenzett by November has more to do with wishing to spend the cold, damp months of winter ensconced here in more comfortable surroundings."

"I suppose your agent will have to seek other tenants now," I said. "I cannot imagine Mr. Marsh will remain."

"As it happens, it may not be a concern for me much longer. I have had a generous offer on the house and property and have almost made up my mind to accept it."

"May we know the name of the interested party?" Holmes said.

"I can see no reason to withhold it. His name is Karl Charnock."

Holmes raised an eyebrow. "Indeed?"

"Are you acquainted with him, Mr. Holmes?" Mrs. Brewer said.

"Only by reputation. Tell me, madam, when did Mr. Charnock first approach you about purchasing the cottage?"

"Several weeks ago. Near the end of September."

"And you were not inclined to sell to him at that time?"

"Truthfully, I wasn't interested in selling the land at all. But this recent business is really too much. I don't think I would ever feel comfortable in the cottage again, knowing that young woman had died there."

Holmes stood up from his chair. "I completely understand. We have taken quite enough of your time, Mrs. Brewer. Thank you very much for seeing us. No, no. Don't ring for the footman. We can see ourselves out."

Holmes inclined his head and then hurried from the room. I thanked Mrs. Brewer for her help and then followed after him.

"I say, Holmes. You ended that interview rather abruptly."

"With good reason, my dear fellow. This case has suddenly become much more interesting."

"Has it?"

"I can tell from your lack of reaction, Watson, that you don't recognize the name Karl Charnock."

"It is not familiar to me, no."

"I am not surprised. Charnock's name is known primarily to the occult community."

"He is an occultist?"

119

"And one of the most notorious. The fact that he is connected to a death that is linked to the supernatural is unlikely to be a coincidence. I will tell you more about him presently, but for now, let us return to Baker Street and pack two suitcases."

"We are leaving for Brenzett, I take it."

"We shall take the afternoon train from Waterloo and I doubt we'll be returning to London before morning."

We followed Holmes's plan and prepared for our trip to Kent. As a former military man, I had no trouble with a sudden departure and my needs were simple. The weather continued cold and damp through the day and a desultory rain was falling when we reached Waterloo.

The train, unexpectedly crowded, forced us to share a compartment with another traveler. Holmes and I were obliged to sit side by side as our fellow passenger was so broad through the shoulders it would have been difficult for anyone larger than a child to sit beside him. He was, without a doubt, the largest man I had ever seen. I wished him good afternoon, but he merely nodded.

As the train left the station, the man stared out at the rain and seemed completely uninterested in us. Holmes studied him for a moment, but whatever inferences he drew from the man's appearance, he kept to himself.

When we were well on our way, I prompted, "You were going to tell me about this fellow Charnock."

"Indeed. As I mentioned, he is an occultist of some note. Reportedly an author, a poet, and a philosopher. A man of incredible erudition and personal magnetism. He collects followers, usually neophytes in the study of the supernatural, and they make him gifts of money and valuables. From what

120

I have learned, he holds no actual occupation, yet lives like a gentleman."

"And can afford to buy property in Kent. Perhaps his family had money?"

Holmes shook his head. "I have found precious little information about his history, but there does not seem to be any family fortune. There are, however, more sinister intimations about the nature of his influence over his followers.

"In more than one case he has convinced those who sought out his knowledge and good will to name him as beneficiary in case of their deaths."

"Good God, Holmes. And you mean those people died?"

"That is precisely what I mean. However, let me add that in none of the cases was there even a hint of Charnock's involvement in his follower's deaths."

"But they died just the same. Then you suspect he had something to do with the death of Mrs. Marsh? Surely, he wouldn't perpetrate such a hoax merely to gain ownership of the cottage and property?"

"Who can say what a man will do, Watson? I shall restrict myself, for now, to the available facts. However, Charnock's history is suggestive."

"You're investigating the death in Brenzett," a deep, rumbling voice interjected.

I looked up to find the man in the opposite seat regarding us. Seen up close he was a striking individual, with a deeply tanned face and cold blue eyes. An old, white scar ran from the corner of one eye down to his mouth.

"We are," Holmes said. "Is that where you are traveling as well, Mr…"

"Kharrn," the man said. "Yes, that is my destination and for the same reason."

"My name is Dr. Watson, and this is Mr. Sherlock Holmes."

The man's eyes narrowed for a moment. "Sherlock Holmes? You shouldn't..."

"Shouldn't what?" said Holmes.

"Never mind. You're the consulting detective."

"That is my occupation. You said you were going to the village to investigate as well. Is your inquiry an official one?"

"As official as I need it to be," said Kharrn.

"I meant no offense," Holmes said.

"I took none," Kharrn said. "I merely stated my position."

"I see. Mr. Kharrn, I pride myself on my knowledge of languages and dialects, but must confess that, other than the fact you've spent considerable time in America, you possess a slight accent I cannot identify. Would you mind telling me where you are from?"

"Nowhere you'd have heard of," said Kharrn, in a tone that did not invite any further questions along that line.

"My, my, you are not very forthcoming," said Holmes. "I nearly fell into the error of thinking you a policeman. Now I see you are a mercenary soldier."

The big man smiled. "You deserve your reputation. I don't know how you would know that, but you're correct."

"That scar on your face, and those on your hands, show you have seen considerable conflict. You acquired your deep tan in climes far warmer than England's. You have a military air, but there is a strong sense of the intractable about you. I do not see you serving in the regular army."

"Right on every count," said Kharrn.

"Now, why your interest in this murder investigation? Did you know the young lady?"

Kharrn shook his head. "Let's just say I'm something of an expert on the occult, but not like Karl Charnock. In fact, I was already investigating him before the incident in Brenzett. Charnock has been acquiring some dangerous books of late."

"Dangerous books?" I questioned.

"Grimoires," said Kharrn. "Books of ancient knowledge that are best kept from the general public and especially from men like Charnock."

"You think him capable of actual sorcery, then?" said Holmes.

"I admit the possibility."

Holmes nodded. "Are you familiar with the local legend of the stone knights and their part in all of this?"

"I am. It's why I'm going to Brenzett. As you noted, the strange circumstances there and the involvement of Charnock are too much to be coincidence."

"And have you formed any opinion on that part of the occurrence?"

"You mean do I believe the stone knights walked? I'll wait until I get to Brenzett."

"Capital," Holmes said. "You do not care to speculate before the facts."

The conversation fell away after that, and Kharrn resumed gazing out the window. We reached the station at Ashford about a quarter hour later. As we left the train, I noticed Kharrn had only a worn carpet bag and a wide, flat leather case for luggage.

"We have arranged for a carriage to take us to Brenzett," I said. "You are welcome to accompany us."

"Thank you, but I have a horse waiting at the livery stable," Kharrn said. "There is only one hotel close to the village. I expect I shall see you there."

As he strode off, I said, "What an extraordinary fellow."

"He was indeed, Watson. He sidestepped most of my questions quite handily."

We found our carriage and stowed our luggage. It was an open carriage, and we were fortunate that the rain had abated, at least for the moment. The road from Ashford was muddy, but our driver seemed to know how to avoid the deepest ruts, and in less than an hour we reached Brenzett.

The village was indeed a small one, with scattered cottages and a few larger buildings including a sizeable hall. The carriage driver deposited us in front of Doctor Kelley's surgery, which was attached to his residence, an old, red brick house, which stood about two miles from the village proper.

We had been told there was no actual hotel in the village, so would have to stay in the nearby town of New Romney, which sits just on the edge of the famous Romney Marsh. For the moment, we carried our suitcases into Kelley's receiving room.

We had barely stepped inside when Kelley came through a door at the back of the room. He said, "Mr. Holmes. Dr. Watson. Thank you so much for coming. Just set your bags down. I'll see that you get to New Romney later. I've reserved rooms there for you, already."

"Thank you, Doctor," Holmes said. "It is always pleasant to know one will sleep with a roof over one's head."

"David Marsh is waiting for you. I'll take you through, but I beg you, do not tax the poor man too much."

Kelley led us back the way he had come, down a short hall that led past his consulting room and through a doorway into his personal quarters, arriving in a comfortable sitting room. A young man with a tangle of wild, dark hair and haunted eyes regarded us as we entered.

"My friends, Mr. Sherlock Holmes and Doctor Watson," Kelley said. "Gentlemen, this is David Marsh."

I said, "My deepest condolences on your loss, Mr. Marsh."

Marsh nodded at me, but it was to Sherlock Holmes he directed his first words. "Have you come to help me, Mr. Holmes?"

Holmes removed his hat and coat and moved quickly to take a chair close to the sofa where Marsh sat. "I shall endeavor to render you every assistance. Please tell me of your experience in the church."

Holmes, who could often be trying in his arrogance, could also be remarkably solicitous. I think that the young man's appearance and attitude had affected him as it had me.

"I shall tell you what I saw, though you will think me mad. God knows I wonder now myself. I am sure Dr. Kelley has given you the outlines of what happened. Two nights ago, at about half past ten, I stepped out for my evening pipe. I left my…I left Laura sitting in the cottage.

"I'm not sure exactly why I decided to walk to the church. Laura and I often went there on our walks. I went along the edge of the woods, admiring the look of the place under the moon and clouds. Everything seemed very still, and then I heard something, a sound, like something moving in amongst the trees.

"But you saw nothing," said Holmes.

"Nothing at all. I kept walking and then heard the sound again. It seemed as if someone might be keeping pace with me, though staying just out of sight. I then picked up my pace along the path that led to the church. In the gray light, I saw the front door stood open, so went inside to make sure nothing else was amiss. I was halfway up the aisle when I suddenly remembered the macabre legend of the place and that I was there not only on the day, but near the very hour, when the stone knights were said to stir.

"I will tell you, Mr. Holmes, that a wave of panic surged over me. I was immediately ashamed of my reaction. So, I stalked up the aisle to the chancel to prove to myself that I wasn't a coward. The moonlight was streaming through the windows and in that cold radiance I saw that the slabs on either side of the altar were empty.

"I crouched down and ran my hand across one of the slabs and through the empty space where the statue should have been, just to be sure. At that moment I was seized by unreasoning and indescribable horror, and an almost overwhelming sense of approaching calamity. I ran from the church like a man possessed, and perhaps I was. I felt I had to get home to Laura as soon as possible."

"And then you came across Dr. Kelley," said Holmes.

"And I made you go back to the church," said Kelley.

Marsh held up his hands. "It doesn't matter, Kelley. What was done was already done at that point. It wouldn't have helped Laura had I gone straight home."

Holmes said, "Forgive me for asking, Mr. Marsh, but can you think of anyone with a grudge against either you or your late wife? I understand your housekeeper left without notice."

"Mrs. Dorman? She left out of fear of the statues. And she was right to do so."

"Then you lean toward a supernatural explanation?" I said.

"I truly don't know," Marsh said. "But to answer your question, Mr. Holmes, I can think of no one who wished to harm either of us."

"Have you, Mr. Marsh, had any dealings with a fellow by the name of Karl Charnock?"

"The name is meaningless to me."

Holmes stood. "We shall trouble you no more."

"But you will let me know if you learn anything?"

"I can assure you of that," said Holmes.

Kelley led us from the room. I glanced back at David Marsh, who sat slumped on the sofa, staring at the floor. Having lost a wife, myself, I knew that he would have many long days and nights ahead.

When we were back in the receiving room, Holmes said, "Now I would like to see the cottage, if I might?"

"Of course. I have the keys and it is not far. I will take you there myself."

"I think it might be best if you remained here," Holmes said, "should young Marsh have need of you, Doctor. Simply point us in the right direction and I'm sure Watson and I can manage."

Kelley did as Holmes requested and gave us the keys and directions. The sky had begun to clear, and it looked as if the rain was done with us for now. We walked down a narrow country lane. Kelley was Marsh's only near neighbor, so we passed no other dwellings along the way.

"I can make nothing of this, Holmes. You can tell that Marsh still believes he saw the statues gone from the church, and I think even Dr. Kelley has begun to wonder. I know that you give no credence to the supernatural, but it seems this entire village does."

Holmes shook his head. "It won't do, Watson. Consider the facts. Even if we allow ourselves to believe stone statues capable of motion, why has no one ever seen them walking about? In all the years since they were placed in the church, surely some brave soul would have waited on All Saints' Eve to see them, or some unfortunate traveler would have crossed their path. And if these stone specters are so fearsome, why has there never been another death attributed to them?"

"Well," I said, "when you put it like that, it does seem rather improbable. Over the years the cottage must have had many tenants. It is unlikely all of them vacated the place on the night in question."

On reaching the cottage, I could scarcely believe such a picturesque place had been the scene of such a dreadful tragedy. It was a long, low building, of large stone blocks, presumably part of the old house that had belonged to the unknown knights. It was moss-grown, and covered in ivy and rose vines, which in the bloom of spring would make the house quite lovely. Even on this gray autumn afternoon, it had a certain rustic charm.

In the distance, across two fields, I could see the old church where the stone men lay.

I used the keys to open the door and we stepped inside. The place had that somber stillness that seems to breed in empty houses. The house had only two rooms. Under other circumstances the foremost room would have been quite cheery, but now held an oppressive aura of gloom.

Holmes stood just inside the doorway for a moment, taking in the room. Then he walked slowly across the chamber to the window recess where Laura Marsh's body had been found. As was his habit, he got down on all fours and made a careful examination of the carpet. I heard him grunt, then he removed his magnifying lens from a coat pocket and gave the rug an even closer inspection. He produced a small envelope from another pocket and swept something from the carpet into it.

"Have you found something, Holmes?"

"Several particles of rock."

"Marble, do you think?"

"Perhaps. And what's this? Some dried mud here near the window seat. Unless I am mistaken, this comes from the same path we just walked, as one would expect. Anyone could have tracked it in."

As Holmes continued to look around the room, I was seized by a sudden feeling of being watched. I turned to find a man standing in the open doorway. He was of medium height, quite gaunt, with a thick mass of bone-white hair swept back from a high forehead.

"Good afternoon," the man said. "You would be Dr. Watson. I am…"

"Mr. Karl Charnock," Holmes said.

Charnock turned to Holmes. "What gave me away?"

"No deduction was necessary in your case. You were pointed out to me by the wife of a man who, after becoming involved with you, took his own life."

"That is close to slander, Mr. Holmes," Charnock said.

"Slander would need to be untrue and would require witnesses. I hardly think my good Watson could be persuaded to testify on your behalf."

Charnock glared at the two of us. I will admit there was something in his stare that gave me a definite chill. Holmes seemed unperturbed.

"No matter," Charnock said. "Your theories mean nothing without proof. How do you like my new cottage, by the way?"

"I do not believe you have taken possession just yet," said Holmes.

"But I will. You spoke with Mrs. Brewer. You know she intends to sell me the property."

If Charnock hoped Holmes would ask him how he knew we had met with Constance Brewer, my friend didn't give him that satisfaction. Holmes said, "I do wonder what interest you could have in such a remote property. From all I've heard, you much prefer the city to the country."

Charnock smiled. "That is true. Tell me, Mr. Holmes. Do you know what the word 'liminal' means?"

"By strictest definition, a boundary or threshold, but I take it you mean something to do with your particular field of interest."

"Your definition is essentially correct, but yes, in occult terms it means an area where the walls between worlds are thin. Where things can be accomplished which would be impossible in any other place."

"He means a place of power," a familiar deep voice said.

Charnock turned and I followed his gaze. Kharrn had entered the cottage far more silently than I would have expected from such a large man. His head almost brushed the ceiling.

"You!" Charnock said. "Can I find no escape from your persecution?"

"I see that you and Mr. Kharrn are already acquainted," Holmes said.

"He convinced the owner of Thackeray's Book Shop in Charing Cross not to sell me certain volumes, and he has harassed me about my library, at my own home. Were I already the owner of this house, I would eject him for trespassing. In fact, I may speak to the village constable all the same."

"I would remind you that Watson and I have permission to be here and Kharrn is assisting us in our investigation. I shall also note, Mr. Charnock, that you are not yet the owner, and if I can work my way, nor will you be."

Charnock's brow furrowed. "I don't see how you can stop me."

"Were I to convince Mrs. Constance Brewer that you played some part in what happened here," said Holmes, "I think it likely she might decide you weren't a tenant she would welcome."

"I warn you, Holmes, if you interfere with me…"

"Yes, yes," Holmes cut him off. "Many have said such things, yet here I remain. Good day, Mr. Charnock. You don't have permission to be on these premises, so I would appreciate it if you would go."

"You can't force me to leave," Charnock said.

"I can," said Kharrn.

Charnock leveled his gaze at the giant man and something in his expression changed. "You…you don't belong here. You're…"

"A few moments from tossing you through the door," Kharrn said. "Go while you can."

Charnock continued to stare at Kharrn but he hurried to the door. He stopped on the threshold and looked back at us. "There will be a reckoning. For all of you."

"What an erratic fellow," said Holmes. "He seemed, all of a sudden, absolutely terrified of you, Kharrn."

The big man nodded. "Perhaps in his place of power he saw me more clearly."

I said, "Or perhaps he believed you would really hurl him through the door."

"There was no question about that, Doctor."

"I think we have seen all we need to here. Do you wish to look over the house, Kharrn?" asked Holmes.

"I haven't your gift for deduction, Mr. Holmes. I simply wanted to see the place and now I think I'll walk over to the church."

"If I might suggest," said Holmes, "I plan to inspect the church after dark to more closely approximate what the unfortunate Mr. Marsh saw. If you don't mind waiting, you are welcome to dine with us, and then we'll carry on to the church together."

"That will suit me. A few hours difference won't matter, and I think that's a good idea of yours to see the place at night."

Kharrn's horse was tethered to a tree not far from the cottage. He told us he would meet us at the hotel and swung into the saddle like a born horseman. Holmes watched him ride away.

"You know, Watson, that man is a fascinating subject for my art. One moment he speaks like a gentleman and the next he is almost brutish. He appears to be perhaps thirty, yet there is something about him that makes him seem older."

"Have you been able to identify his accent yet?" I asked.

"No, perhaps after talking with him at length tonight over dinner."

We returned to Kelley's surgery and informed him of our plans and he decided to join us for dinner at the hotel. Marsh had been resting and we didn't see him before leaving. Kelley had arranged for a cart and driver to transport us to New Romney.

Accommodation had been arranged for us at the Ship Hotel, which our driver informed us was a sixteenth century coaching inn. He also told us it had originally been built from ship timbers brought from New Romney's port, hence the name.

Looking at the hotel, I could well believe in its antiquity. The plaster façade and the tile roof had obviously witnessed much of the passage of time. The driver agreed to wait and take us back to Brenzett after dinner. The bar was open, so he was easily persuaded.

Dinner passed pleasantly, but Holmes's hopes of learning more about the mysterious Kharrn were left mostly unfulfilled. The man was a fascinating conversationalist, but he stuck primarily to accounts of his various military experiences. It did turn out we had briefly been in Afghanistan at the same time, but we weren't stationed close to one another.

It was full dark by the time we asked our driver to return us to Kelley's residence. We had decided we would go to the cottage and walk from there to further replicate David Marsh's experience. We were somewhat taken aback when Marsh suggested he accompany us.

"Do you think that's a good idea?" Kelley asked him. "I'm afraid it may have a negative effect on your recovery."

Marsh said, "I might be able to offer some useful information for Mr. Holmes. Since he was good enough to come here, I think I should make myself available."

"That is very brave of you, my friend, and I will accept your offer, but only with the provision that if at any time you think the proceedings too much for you, you will tell us, and we will send you home."

Marsh agreed to this and the five of us set out on foot. I noticed that Kharrn had brought the long, flat leather case I had seen back at the train station. Kelley led the way, and Holmes and I were right behind him. Kharrn walked side by side with Marsh, and I wondered if the younger man took some strength from having the giant at his side.

The clouds had completely vanished, and the gibbous moon seemed to have a halo all about it. The moonlight spread across the fields, throwing stark shadows from every object its light enveloped. It seemed to me that our procession had an ineffable strangeness there under the deep blue arch of the sky.

We made our way up the bier-balk, then passed through the corpse-gate and between the graves to the low front porch. We paused there. Unlike the night in question, the heavy oak door was firmly closed.

"You don't have to go in with us," Kelley told Marsh. "If Mr. Holmes has any questions we can come and find you."

"I'll go in. I've come this far."

Kharrn stepped up and under the Norman doorway and pushed the door open. He entered the building and none of us, not even Holmes, seemed to doubt the giant should be the first one inside. But Holmes and I were close behind him. Inside the arches rose into darkness and the ceiling was lost in the gloom.

We had no trouble seeing. Silver moonlight streamed through the reticulated windows, throwing rectangles of radiance on the floor. The light made the old, black oak pews seem darker by contrast. No one spoke as we moved up the aisle to the chancel.

I think I half expected the stone knights to be gone, but there they lay, fully life sized and rendered in intricately detailed marble. My gaze fell to the clasped hands of the figure on the right, and I saw that a finger was indeed missing. It occurred to me that neither Holmes nor I had thought to ask what became of the finger.

Holmes stepped up to the closest of the statues and examined its feet. I realized he was looking for traces of mud on the soles. Holmes might not have believed in the supernatural, but he was always thorough in his attention to small details. He had lectured me more than once on the importance of trifles.

"Nothing to show that this stone fellow has walked anywhere recently," Holmes said. His voice sounded loud in the unnatural silence of the church.

"Did you expect to find anything?" Kelley asked.

"Not particularly."

"So, you think me mad too, Mr. Holmes," said David Marsh.

"Not at all. While I can offer no explanation for what you saw, it doesn't mean there isn't one. We've far to go yet. There are more people in the village with whom I should like a word. I don't think…"

Holmes next words were cut-off by a sudden loud booming. I looked down the length of the church and saw that the great, iron-studded door had closed.

"The wind must have blown it shut," Kelley said.

"There is no wind," said Holmes.

Kharrn strode down the aisle and grasping the door's iron handle, pulled. The door didn't move. He grunted with effort and tried again, but his exertions had no effect.

"That door doesn't have a lock," Kelley said. "It can be bolted from within, but it obviously isn't."

"Somehow it has been sealed shut," Kharrn said.

At that moment David Marsh screamed. I turned and saw that he was pointing with a shaking hand. I looked back into the chancel. One of the stone knights was sitting up on the slab.

"Holmes!" I said.

Sherlock Holmes stared at the knight, who in turn was staring at all of us with cold, lifeless eyes. Holmes said, "It has to be a trick. A man in a costume or some such."

But even as Holmes tried to come to some sort of rational understanding, I knew that he was wrong. The statue was alive. My heart was thudding hard in my chest as I watched the eerie thing.

Holmes started toward the knight. As he did so the second statue sat up. Together they swung their legs from the slabs and stepped onto the stone floor.

"Stay away from them, Holmes!" I heard Kharrn shout.

The giant man hurried up the aisle, unsnapping the latches on his case as he came. But Holmes had already reached the knights. He sought to grasp one of them by the arm, but the stone effigy swung out its hand and knocked Holmes off his feet. Senseless, my friend rolled across the floor and struck one of the pews. I started toward him, but Kharrn warned me back.

David Marsh stood rooted to the spot as the other knight closed on him. I saw one gleaming marble fist rise, and then Marsh's head was crushed by a downward blow. A moment later I saw a glint of metal and then the blade of a great axe struck the knight's head, cleaving off a chunk of stone.

Now I saw what Kharrn had kept hidden in the leather case. It was a huge, double-bladed axe, like the Vikings of yore had once carried. He swung the axe again, this time at the torso of the stone monster. Sparks flew and bits of marble rattled to the floor, but the statue kept moving forward.

The big man continued striking with the axe, damaging the stone man but not enough to stop it. Given time and room to maneuver, I think he could have smashed the creature to rubble, but he had the luxury of neither.

The second knight had reached Kharrn by that time and it struck him on the shoulder. I heard bone snap and the arm hung useless. Kharrn grunted in pain but continued to wield the axe with one hand. The twin horrors closed on him, backing the big man toward a wall.

I looked around for a weapon, and seeing a large, brass candle holder, I ran forward. The object was so heavy I could scarcely lift it, but I managed to get it over one shoulder, and lumbering up to the closest knight, I swung the holder at its head. I was rewarded with a loud cracking sound, as part of a marble helmet broke free.

137

The stone knight turned and struck the holder from my grasp, then made a grab for me. I ducked away, just evading its lunge. I had succeeded in distracting it from Kharrn and it lurched after me.

Out of the corner of my eye I saw that Holmes had recovered and managed to regain his feet. He stood for a moment, looking all around the sanctuary, then started toward a curtained alcove on one side of the chamber.

I ran between two of the pews, slowing the statue's pursuit. I heard a loud cracking sound and risked a glance back toward Kharrn. The big man had succeeded in smashing one of his opponent's legs at the knee. The statue was on the floor, but still trying to crawl after him.

I dodged away from my own pursuer again and hurried toward Holmes just in time to see him pull the curtain away from the alcove. Karl Charnock cried out in rage and lunged from the recess brandishing a dagger. Holmes twisted to one side, and grasping Charnock's arm, redirected his attack and hurled the man to the ground. Once again, Holmes's knowledge of the Japanese science of wrestling had served him well.

Charnock struck the stone floor with considerable force and didn't move. The two marble figures stopped moving, and the one still on its feet toppled to the ground.

A dark bruise was already forming on Holmes's face, and I said, "Are you all right, Holmes?"

"As well as can be expected," Holmes said.

I said, "How did you know Charnock was here?"

"I reasoned that if the statues were truly moving on a day other than All Saints' Eve, then the curse wasn't the explanation for their animation. It seemed likely whomever was controlling them had to be close enough to see them and direct their homicidal ambulation.

"I looked about for a place of concealment, and the alcove seemed the most probable, since it commanded an excellent view of the entire chamber. In the semi-darkness we didn't see Charnock peering from behind the curtain."

"Mr. Holmes," Kelley said.

We turned toward the burly Irishman. He was kneeling on the floor next to the still form of David Marsh. Even as we approached, I could see there was no hope for the younger man. His skull had been caved-in by the stone man's fist.

"I never should have let him come with us," Kelley said.

"You tried to dissuade him, Doctor, and more than once," replied Holmes.

"And now Charnock is responsible for the deaths of man and wife," said I. "But how will we ever convince a British jury of his culpability?"

Kharrn said, "You won't have to, Doctor Watson. Charnock fell on his knife."

Holmes turned to the giant man, who was standing beside Charnock's body. "Did he? I was certain I had held the blade away from his body as I threw him."

Kharrn rolled Charnock over and said, "See for yourself."

The dagger was buried in Charnock's chest, directly in his heart. I looked at Holmes and he raised an eyebrow. I think neither of us doubted at that moment the knife had some assistance in finding its target.

I walked over to Kharrn. "Let me have a look at that arm."

To my astonishment Kharrn raised the arm and flexed it. He said, "It hurts, but I've had worse."

I said, "I was certain it had been broken."

"I heal faster than most men," Kharrn said.

"Merely one of your astonishing talents, Mr. Kharrn," said Holmes. "Will you tell us now, who you are?"

"I think you mean what I am, not who. We have fought side by side so I will tell you. If I said I have lived for thousands of years, would you believe me?"

I said, "Right now, after what I just saw, I would believe almost anything."

"Wait for the cold reason of morning, Doctor, and you might not, but that is the truth. I have lived for more years than I care to think. I serve a goddess from a time-lost age and she sent me here to see justice done."

"Was that what Charnock meant when he said you didn't belong here?"

"That was part of it, but the rest would be too much even for your current state of open-mindedness. Let us just say that he was right, and I don't belong in this world. As I hinted before, I think being in a place he found receptive to his powers allowed him to see more of my true nature than he had at our other meetings."

Holmes said, "If I accept your claim that you are from some other realm, would that explain why you seemed surprised to meet the good Doctor and myself?"

"Yes, Mr. Holmes. Where I come from you don't actually exist. I didn't expect to run into you."

I said, "But you knew of us?"

"I did, but it's probably best I don't explain too much. I should be away in any case."

"As should we," said Holmes. "We'll need to see to Marsh's body and formulate some sort of explanation for the authorities."

140

"I don't envy you that," said Kharrn.

With that, the giant man turned and walked back up the center aisle. He paused only to retrieve the case for his axe, then, opening the front door, vanished into the night without another word.

I looked around the room at the shambles of the statues and the two dead bodies. "What are we to make of all this, Holmes?"

"There are times when even the most logical of minds can find no reasonable explanation, Watson. I fear we have all the knowledge of these events we are ever likely to get."

In the end, Sherlock Holmes was able to convince the local coroner's court that Karl Charnock had been responsible for the deaths of David and Laura Marsh while attempting some strange occult ceremony. He had somehow got the two statues off their slabs to simulate them moving of their own volition for his mad scheme. I'm not sure the coroner, or anyone else really, believed the explanation, but they were content to put the matter behind them.

Dr. Kelley moved from Brenzett not long after the events recounted here. The last I heard of him, he had established a successful practice in Hampshire. Holmes and I rarely spoke of the affair of the Stone Men, and as the years passed, I think we convinced ourselves we had imagined most of it. I will admit though, I can never pass a life-sized statue of a human form without a feeling it is watching me.

THE ADVENTURE OF THE SEVEN UNNATURAL WOMEN

Stephen Gallagher

The Barts reunion was an odd affair. Of the twelve who attended there were only two that I'd run across since our student days, most having scattered to hospitals and practices across the nation. Our number included two senior surgeons, one man who'd left medicine to join his father's bank, the founder of a private orphanage, and a Scot who had thrown his education to the winds and now performed bawdy songs on the Music Hall stage. We gathered in one of the smaller function rooms at De Keyser's on the Embankment, a hotel largely patronized by Germans, Frenchmen, and other foreigners. Our conversation was stilted at first, energetic as the memories resurfaced, and maudlin by midnight.

I arrived home in the small hours looking forward to my bed. I had the rooms to myself for several days and had made plans for a late rise and a leisurely breakfast.

Inevitably I found a waiting telegram with an urgent summons to join Sherlock Holmes in the Romney marshes at my earliest opportunity.

Can one's heart surge and sink at the same time? My 'earliest opportunity' was a 6.20 train from London Bridge with a change for the New Romney branch. Holmes had been several days on the south coast, with an assignment to locate a set of holy relics missing from a remote abbey. "Go," he'd said, "Go attend your medical men's beano, this is a case I can handle with ease. I already fancy the dean for it, though I'll keep an open mind."

This was the mystery whose solution, you may have read elsewhere, called for a trained monkey and some chicken parts masquerading as finger bones.

I reached my destination late in the morning to find Holmes himself awaiting me on the platform of a little-used rural halt. Open country extended in every direction, empty, flat and reedy under a wide oppressive sky. He was seated on a bench under the railway company's painted wooden shelter. He did not rise to greet me. His portmanteau bag was turned on end and one leg was extended to rest on it, while the opposite hand gripped a stout walking cane meant for support rather than show.

"Good lord, Holmes," I said. "What have you done to yourself?"

"A poor choice of words, Watson, but I can appreciate the note of concern. Did you buy a return ticket?"

"As per your telegram."

"We've an hour until the next train back. I'm sorry to inconvenience you. Be assured that I hadn't planned for a loss of independence."

An apology, no less? This show of consideration so alien to his character caused me some concern. I bent and looked closely into his eyes and then I said, "Morphine, Holmes?"

"The local doctor is generous with his pharmacy," he said, avoiding my gaze. "Given his touch with a displaced patella, he needs to be."

"You must tell me how this happened."

"It's a long story."

"We have the whole hour," I said, and settled onto the bench beside him.

He considered for a moment, and then conceded. He shifted his weight to ease the discomfort of his injured leg; the reduction of a misaligned kneecap can be as painful as the original injury, and they go back into place with quite a crack.

This is the story. I set it down much as Holmes told it to me.

*

The case of the missing reliquary brought me no satisfaction, *he began.* Quite the opposite. On learning of my arrival, the Dean confessed with such haste that there was little left for me to achieve. I briefly considered waiving my charges until I saw the rich appointments of the Abbot's personal apartments, and then I briefly considered doubling them.

The abbey stands beyond the reach of the branch line so I set out on the return journey in the Abbot's Victoria, only for the horse to throw a shoe some three miles short of my destination. The weather was fair and the way was well-marked, so rather than waiting for help I chose to complete the remainder of the course on foot.

I should, in retrospect, have left my bag with the coachman to be sent on. It seemed to weigh so little in the beginning, but was a burden by the end of the first mile. The countryside there was much like it is here—marshland, cut for drainage, the earth banked up where the causeways run. I stopped at a crossing where I saw a distant group of figures moving in my direction, far off and to my right.

I set my luggage on the embankment and sat on it to watch their approach. As they drew closer the group resolved itself

144

into three individuals, two of them leaning into the handles of a wheeled handcart while a third followed close behind. Local men, rough-hewn, their clothing coarse and rustic. Theirs was a struggle, fighting to keep the handcart's spoked wheels from sinking into rutted ground. A few yards closer and I could see that the third man wore the uniform and headgear of a Kentish police constable.

Closer still, and the shape on the cart itself became unmistakable. Though covered with a canvas, it had the clear outline of an adult human form. I rose to my feet and moved onto the track.

When the party and their melancholy load were almost upon me, I called out, "Good day to you, Constable. Do I take it there's been a tragedy?"

"You assume correctly, sir," the policeman said. He was a young man with a thick moustache, no doubt grown to add to his authority. "And now I'll thank you to make way."

"Accident or criminal act?"

"Not for me to say."

"The name's Holmes. I've some knowledge in such matters. May I see?"

"No, sir, you may not. Now if you please. . .?"

"Perhaps I can accompany you."

"No, sir."

I'd been eyeing a corner of the cart for my hand luggage, but it was not to be. He was so adamant in his refusal that I could only step aside. As a result of your literary efforts, Watson, if I can call them such, I can count on the occasional gesture of deference from the London constabulary. But here I went unrecognized.

I returned to my perch and continued to observe their progress. They were now making toward the only building on the far horizon, an inn that I'd passed on my arrival. I recalled a village beyond it, and beyond that the line of the Royal Military Canal. But for now it was as if those diminishing figures were toiling toward the loneliest spot on earth.

I could tell you that my interest was a matter of common humanity, but you know me better than that. You understand why I do what I do, Watson. It brings me the only true peace I know. My brief time at the abbey had given me no satisfaction. Now the draw of an unresolved mystery was enough to make me brave even the horrors of a country inn.

This one was half stone, half brick, a wide low building with a roof of red tile. The garden was a vegetable patch and I had to step over an old dog in the doorway, above which the licensee's notice bore two spelling errors. Inside I faced an empty bar with no light, thick wooden beams, and walls stacked with bad taxidermy. When the landlord appeared, a stocky man of forty-something years, I could see that he was distressed and distracted; but he agreed to my request for a room, and produced the guest book for me to sign.

As I was writing I said, "You seem disturbed. Are you worried at what a visitor might think of a deceased person laid out under their feet?"

His eyes widened. "I swear I don't know what you mean, sir," he said.

"Have no fears on my account, Mr. . . Murphy?" I glanced up at him for confirmation.

"Hawkes, sir," he said. "Edgar Hawkes."

"I saw the remains being wheeled in from the marsh," I said, and I pushed the book and pencil back to him. "A beer cellar's a cool and private place to store them while proper arrangements are being made. Certainly more secure than a lying-out on a handcart in the yard."

I'd at least relieved him of the need to deceive. "We're a small community here and Tom Tweedy is our law," he said. "I could hardly refuse."

He called a skivvy to take my bag upstairs, and we were joined in the bar by the two men who had been pushing the handcart.

The first said, "Any chance of a glass for two thirsty workers?"

146

And the second added, "What has done their civic duty despite their harrowing experience?"

I said, "Allow me, gentlemen," and invited them to join me in the snug while I stood their drinks.

What the constable would not disclose, they freely gave. They made their living as eel fishermen, trapping their prey in home-made willow baskets baited with bad meat. One stretch of water had been particularly productive, and that morning they'd found a possible reason. From the depths had risen the unclothed body of a woman, mutilated beyond recognition but otherwise almost whole. One man had gone to fetch the constable, while the other sat vigil with the body and smoked a pipe.

They seemed unruffled by their experience though Constable Tweedy had parted with his breakfast at the first sight of those remains. Poking around in the water with a gaff, they'd recovered traces of a canvas sack and the stones that had been used to weigh it down.

It was at this point that Tweedy made himself known from the adjoining bar with an expression of outrage.

"Hey," he said, appearing in the doorway. "What's this talk? What did I say?"

"Just conversing, Tom," one of the eel trappers assured him.

"It's Constable Tweedy when I'm wearing this," he said, pointing to his duty armband, "and we'll stop the conversing right here." Then he turned to me. "You, sir."

I rose to my feet. "Sherlock Holmes. Consulting detective. When I said I have experience of criminal matters, I did not lie. You may have heard something of my work."

From his unchanging expression, he clearly had not.

I said, "I am willing to offer my services, if you would let me view the remains."

"That's twice you've asked," he said. "I find an interest in the sight of dead women more than a little unhealthy." He turned to the landlord, who stood on the other side of the bar. "Is he staying here?"

Hawkes gave a nod.

"No one goes in the cellar," Tweedy went on. "Lock it up and keep the key about you." Again he turned to me, and drew out a notebook. "Holmes, you say?"

He questioned me then, closely and in detail, and I answered openly. I saw him grow a little uneasy as he grew to appreciate my background and connections, but to his credit the questioning remained thorough and he showed me no deference.

The interview ended with an implied dismissal, so I went up to inspect my room and lay out my kit. If we were not to cooperate, I must gather my own information by whatever means I could. Through the boards underfoot I could hear the voices of Tweedy and Edgar Hawkes in conversation with the name 'Charlie' coming through several times. I stood still and did my best to follow but the thick oak muffled any further sense.

*

The early evening found me alone in the dining room, served by the skivvy with a simple meal of ham and potatoes. Hawkes was elsewhere and so I took the opportunity to draw on her knowledge of the area. She was more than forthcoming.

The Charlie in question was Charlie McGrath, a local man and tenant smallholder who made a bare living from his vegetable crop and whatever marsh life he could trap or shoot. Each year he'd raise a pig for slaughter and turn the carcass over to Hawkes, who'd cure and hang it and sell the meat on. No one had seen Charlie's woman in months. Everyone had good reason to assume that she had left him but Charlie sat in the snug every night, drinking his credit and complaining about his loss, as self-pitying and sentimental as only a deserted wife-beater can be. His loudest complaint was that the love of his life had been taken from him by 'that coven of

148

unnatural women' after a stranger had remonstrated with him on the common. He'd been driving his animal home with a switch and this loss, he reasoned, was his punishment for answering her back.

I tipped the skivvy and asked her to let me know if McGrath should make an appearance in the bar that night. Later in the evening there was a soft knock on the door of my room. When I opened it no one was there, but when I descended to the saloon bar, I saw a group of road menders ending their working day over ale while in the adjacent room sat a lone figure, hunched over a bench in a dark cloud of his own misery.

I went through and stood before him and said, "Charlie, is it? May I sit with you for a while?"

He looked up, slowly. The drink had him already. "And you might be?"

I introduced myself, to no effect.

He said, "They found her, didn't they? He won't let me see."

"Tell me her name."

"Polly," he said. "My Polly. I curse the day she left and I curse those unnatural women."

"Did you see her leave?"

"I did not. But others did. And they saw which way she went."

"These unnatural women you speak of. . ."

"Who are they? A coven of witches is what they are. My woman's gone and they're behind it. She was seen on the path to their manor, and never seen again."

"What do you imagine happened to her?"

"Spirited away or worse. Go look at that moated castle of theirs. They've a stone altar carved by no Christian hand, the haunt of Beelzebub himself. There's talk of human sacrifice, babies and more. People round here laugh at me when I say it. But my woman went up there and she never came back."

"Women have been known to leave their men with no supernatural agency involved."

"Not mine. She was a good woman. I hardly ever had to raise my hand to her, except in love."

One of the road menders was banging on the bar and calling for service, which brought Hawkes hurrying in from the nethers of the hotel. He didn't take kindly to his customer's attitude, and an argument began. It became impossible for me to question Charlie any further. Charlie sank back into his depression, and I withdrew for the night.

I'd taken along a copy of Vidocq's *Memoirs* for the journey, and for a while I read. I laid the book aside after concluding that these were not the words of the man himself but those of a paid hack, and that I would learn nothing from a mimic. I went to my window and looked out across the marsh. The full moon and the new moon were the best nights for catching eels, I'd been told today. I did not dismiss it, but I thought it unlikely. Folk tales are no substitute for evidence.

The full moon is also said to mark the time when the powers of witches and other occultists are at their height.

This, I *did* dismiss.

I slept more deeply that night than on any other I can remember.

*

The morning found me back in the dining room. I was breakfasting on sausages from Charlie McGrath's rather excellent pig when I heard Constable Tweedy's voice in the building. He was moving my way. I imagine he was speaking to Hawkes, for he was saying, "Maybe he's right and maybe it's Polly. But I'll leap to no conclusions."

When he came into the room, I sensed a difference in his attitude toward me. He'd removed his headgear—the ceilings were low, the wooden beams a hazard—and held it tucked under his arm.

"Mr. Holmes," he said. "My Abi tells me you have a reputation to be respected."

I pushed my empty plate away and suggested to him that Mrs. Tweedy might be one of your inexplicably devoted readers, Watson, and he confirmed the notion.

"She runs our little school," he added. "To be honest, I don't know what she sees in a man like me. I tend to speak before I think, sometimes."

It was an apology of sorts, though it came where none was needed. I said, "All forgotten. I have seen more than once how a death in a small community is a shock to all."

"The poor woman was stripped naked and weighted with stones and sunk in a marsh pond. You can hope it's not someone you know. But Polly Cook's been gone these past twelve weeks and it's fair to assume the worst."

"Charlie McGrath seems to think that some form of human sacrifice must account for it."

Tweedy's response was not as I expected. He looked down. He was silent and serious for a long moment as if measuring his next words, and then he looked up and said, "What do you know of witchcraft, Mister Holmes?"

"All very well in its place, which is in a Grimm's fairy tale. In this world not so much."

"I once thought the same," he said. "But try living out here amongst these people, and see how your certainties last. I don't say I'm a believer. But what folk do, I have to deal with."

"He claims there's a coven."

"Women who believe they can live without need of men, for a start. Can you imagine such a thing?"

"It's a school of thought in the city."

"Well, now it has a college in the country. Edith Appleby is the one they call Lady of the Manor."

He explained further. With all the advantages of an old name and a good family, Edith Appleby took up her inheritance and moved into the run-down grange with her companion. Both were stalwart, sturdy matrons who dressed

151

like a couple of gamekeepers and were joined by others of varying ages over the following months, to form what Tweedy described as a colony of New Women.

I said, "And a colony is how many?"

"They come and go, but it's mostly the same seven or eight. Growing food and keeping chickens to sustain themselves. They wear garlands of flowers and dance on the lawn at sunrise. Barefoot! As if that's decent."

"Not decent, but hardly sinister."

"I see them out on the marsh picking strange herbs and poisons for their rituals. And I know for certain they once burned a goat for a sacrifice. Those stones that held down the body—they had magical symbols and words in some strange tongue, carved by some ancient hand. And around the time Polly Cook went missing, a hooded woman was seen heading over the marsh to the house. She was flying as if some great force carried her."

"Did you secure these stones for evidence?"

He was a little embarrassed. "I did not. They were very heavy."

"So where are they now?"

"By the leat where we left them, I expect."

"Then let us proceed to the leat."

As we crossed the marsh together, I learned that on the night of Polly Cook's disappearance Charlie McGrath had been sobering up in the one-roomed lockup on the side of Tweedy's house that served as the district's gaol. Tweedy had arrested him that evening at the inn, where he'd taken a knife and was threatening some man in the bar who he claimed had passed by his home and 'looked at' Polly.

"And this man. . ." I prompted.

"Just a bargee passing through," Tweedy said. "A recently-married boatman of decent character and the keeper at the Iden Lock confirmed it. I may regret it now, Mister Holmes, but with no suspicion of foul play I left it at that."

"As if no married man of decent character ever found his way to the gallows."

"Everyone assumed she'd simply taken the opportunity to move out. Charlie can be a bit of a brute and no one would have blamed her."

Did one night of detention exonerate McGrath? Of course not. And his loud and lengthy lament could be a performance to equal Dido, calculated to deflect suspicion.

The tracks of the handcart led us to a place where marsh and river met, of deep channels and flat mud where at some time in the distant past a wooden barge had been scuppered and sunk. Reeds grew up through its carcass. Whoever submerged the body in this desolate spot had not expected it to reappear, but had underestimated the sharp teeth and determination of the Kentish freshwater eel. Some of the heavy canvas dragged up by the gaff lay shredded on the banking, spilling out the stone weights and their 'occult symbols'. With both hands I turned over one of the stones and studied the carvings thereon.

I said, "Where was the Roman camp located?"

Tweedy began, "I know of no such. . ." but to spare his embarrassment I spoke across him.

"Your magical symbols in a strange tongue are Classical Latin. A military officer's memorial, from the fragment I can read. There was surely a Roman fort somewhere close, and there is no source of natural stone on the marsh. I expect Roman materials have found their way into every wall and building for miles around."

"Our vicar is a student of the history hereabouts. He might know."

I had Tweedy carry one of the stones to the vicarage. From there we were directed the short distance to the village church. The resident cleric was a Cambridge man of advanced age and he seized upon the opportunity to converse with a city-dweller he imagined might share his education and his interests. As he spoke, I took the opportunity to leaf through the Parish

Register and observe that, as I had expected, there was no marriage entry for Charlie McGrath and Polly Cook. The turn of the pages inspired a commentary on those my new friend had christened, wed, or buried; here was Peg-handed Meg and her sister fetching pots for their father at the inn; there, William Barker who moved north to live as a paid hermit in the folly caves on a rich man's estate; on this page Jarvis Appleby, grandfather of Edith, who died of a fit while laughing at the sight of a busker's dancing dog.

When I asked him if the Appleby family kept a pew in the church, he grew grave.

"They have their own chapel up there," he said. "And their own ceremonies."

*

We were away within the hour, with the knowledge that the Romans had occupied a site within the boundaries of the controversial manor. It gave me fair cause for an approach to Edith Appleby and her so-called coven or colony of women. Tweedy asked me if the ancient stone could be left in the churchyard, but I urged him to bring it along.

The manor house was reached by an approach that had once been a fine driveway, reduced by neglect to an overgrown country lane. The house itself was mostly Elizabethan with some Georgian remodeling that fell short of bringing symmetry. Around it was a moat that had been cleared of weed, crossed by a bridge in good repair. The overall effect was of a dwelling revived and restored to use on an otherwise run-down estate. Though I did not take him for a nervous man, I sensed the constable's discomfort as we drew closer.

Half of the courtyard between two wings of the building had been turned over to create a kitchen garden, where hens roamed and three young women were working. The nearest set down her basket and came over to meet us. She was around twenty-five years of age, and wore a gray calico dress and apron. On hearing the reason for our visit she asked us to wait and went inside to fetch Miss Appleby.

Edith Appleby was much as Tweedy had described her and had a grip like a bricklayer's, exercised in a handshake for which I was unprepared. I asked about the Roman works and she said, "You're standing on it, Mister Holmes. The manor was built on the site of the Roman commander's house. The gardens were the barracks and the ditch became the moat. But I don't think that's really what you want to ask me."

I said, "You have heard that a body's been found?"

"I did so hear," she said. "None of my women is unaccounted for."

"In the past year?"

"Longer. And those who leave us stay in touch. You don't have to take my word for it." She gestured toward the house behind her, as if we were free to enquire further. "We're a community, Mister Holmes, not a secret society."

"With that in mind, did you ever have any dealings with a woman from the village named Polly Cook?"

She looked from one to the other of us. "Is she your victim?"

Tweedy said, "That's what I'm trying to establish."

I explained about the stones used to weigh down the body, our example of which was now set down at Tweedy's feet. Miss Appleby said, "The fortifications may be long gone but the soldiers built a temple to Mithras outside its walls. Some trace of that remains. Would you care to see it?"

"I would," I said, and Edith Appleby turned and called to another of the three young women.

"Lily!" she called. "A respite from the cabbages."

This time it was the farthest of the three who broke off from her work and came over. Pulling off her gloves as she reached us she said brightly, "Constable Tweedy. How is Abi?"

"She is well, thank you for asking," Tweedy said.

Introductions were made. This young woman's name was Lily Cleminson and she had joined Edith's community from

London some eighteen months before under some personal circumstance that was not disclosed to us. She was dark-eyed and sharp, with manifest confidence. As we moved to leave, Tweedy picked up his rock with both hands and followed with the resignation of a Sisyphus.

Lily glanced back.

"That looks ever so heavy," she said.

"No, not at all," Tweedy insisted.

This time his burden was short-lived. The soldiers' temple was located just outside the walls of the fort, barely a few strides from where the nearest gate had stood. It was represented now by a shallow depression in boggy ground, in which were sited two rows of broken columns and a stone altar. Of the surrounding walls only traces of the foundation remained, suggesting the outline of a long-lost building hardly bigger than a cabman's shelter.

Like the pillars, the altar was badly weathered. There was a depression worn into its surface where recent visitors had left coins, much as one might throw pennies into a well for good fortune. These coins, I was later told, were an offering from locals to keep bad spirits from roaming.

Such was the nature of this damp hollow that flies rose in a noxious cloud as we descended. I said, "I see a possible place for our stone. Tweedy, see how it fits."

I pointed to a bowl-shaped hole in the dirt against the altar. Tweedy crouched and tried the rock this way and that, and it slotted perfectly into the space where it had previously lain for some hundreds of years. He stepped back, swatting away flies from the sheen on his brow.

"A truly Godless spot," he said.

"Depending on your choice of gods," Lily Cleminson said. "There's nothing Satanic or Divine about those flies. The altar's hollow. Things crawl in there and die." She gave Tweedy a look of barely-disguised amusement. "Unless you think they spring from one of our ritual sacrifices to Beelzebub."

Tweedy blushed. Lily moved around behind the altar and said, "We've heard all the stories. Come. Let's set your mind at rest." Then she took hold of the altar's slab top and looked at both of us, from one to the other.

"I can't do this alone," she said.

We hastened to the slab, and together all three of us managed to make it slide. The masonry of the four upright sides had suffered over time, and there were gaps where the sections had been undermined. We looked inside. Newly exposed to daylight were animal bones, lying in a mess of skin and fur.

"A fox, perhaps," I opined.

Lily Cleminson covered the lower half of her face with a hand and leaned in for a closer look.

"The leg bones are too short and the cheek teeth are flattened," she said from behind her hand. "*Meles Meles*, the European badger. I doubt there's ever been one with so grand a tomb. Nothing to be gained by removing what's there. We'll let nature take its course."

With a motion of her head she indicated for us to help her return the lid, and we pushed it back into its original place. Then we wasted no time in withdrawing from that unclean spot.

"Other than the women of the manor," I said, as we reached level ground, "who might come here?"

"Anyone," the young woman said. "The temple is on the land but it's outside the property. And you'd never be seen from the house."

As we turned to leave, we were met by a boy from the village, sent with a message for Constable Tweedy. An undertaker was at the inn with a parish order to release the body from the beer cellar to more appropriate accommodation. Tweedy begged Miss Cleminson's leave and set off with the boy, while I offered to escort our hostess back to the house.

"That is hardly necessary, Mister Holmes," she said.

"But it will be my pleasure," I said, seeing an opportunity to probe a little deeper.

As we walked, I said, "I note you have a scientific education, Miss Cleminson."

"Your observation is correct," she said.

"Comparative anatomy at the Central Imperial College. Undertaken without your father's approval, I would say."

"How would you know that?"

"Pure deduction," I assured her.

"Please explain."

"The level of detail in your knowledge points the way. It's a course popular with young women educated to a certain standard and I know Russell's methods. When his students speak it's with their teacher's confidence. Your clothes are of quality but—forgive me—shabby and sufficiently out of style to suggest the withdrawal of financial support around the time that your studies began. Which leads me to conclude that your father wished to discourage you from your chosen path."

She said, "You do my teacher justice and my father none. These are my old gardening clothes, Mister Holmes. The rest of my wardrobe is both serviceable and presentable."

This seemed like a good moment to move on.

"You are acquainted with Constable Tweedy's wife," I said.

"We do engage with the village. Many of them are our tenants."

"But it's mostly the women."

"The women trust us more. It's the men who spread the Old Wives' Tales. Have you heard the animal sacrifice story? We kept a goat. It died of a disease and we had to cremate it. By the time the story came back to us, we were all dancing naked around the bonfire. So ridiculous. Our Jane Graham is a qualified herbalist. Hannah Whitbread was a nurse. Of course the women come to us for advice."

"Was Polly Cook one of them?" I asked.

"I can't say that she was," Lily Cleminson said.

*

We parted at the bridge and I made my way back along the lanes and causeways. There I passed my eel fishermen from the day before, their handcart now piled high with griggs and baskets. They knew I'd been to the manor and the elder told me of the Pococks' boy Seth, who'd thrown stones at Edith Appleby's carriage and was drowned within the year, and if that wasn't proof of something then he didn't know what was.

I reached the inn just in time to see Charlie McGrath being thrown out of it, observed with interest by the dog Patch, who seemed to spend all his days lying out and watching the world go by.

Charlie was not going quietly. "That's my Polly dead and cold and those women took her from me," was his strident complaint. "Nobody believes me and Tom Tweedy does nothing. He won't even let me say my goodbyes."

Edgar Hawkes would have none of it. "You can't say any goodbyes to anyone," he said. "The cellar's empty now. She's gone from here." He was blocking the doorway against Charlie's return.

"Then at least spare a tot of rum for my grief."

"You've drunk up your credit twice over this year. Away with you."

Charlie turned to appeal to me. "Mister Holmes?" he said, but I shook my head.

"Not today, Charlie," I said.

With Charlie gone I followed Edgar Hawkes into the inn. Glancing back over his shoulder he said, "Do you want to know what I think? If the stories about Charlie and Polly are true then there's one sure way to put a name to that body."

"What stories are those?"

He indicated for me to keep following. We went on through the bar, past the stairs, and into the kitchen. There he opened the heavy door of the cold safe where the meats were kept. From it he brought out a plate bearing an enormous cured ham, and placed it on the preparation table.

159

Hawkes said, "He plays the grieving lover now, but Charlie has a temper. Some say he pinned her down and put his mark on her like one of his pigs. This is how he marks his pigs." He turned the plate around to show me a crude symbol that had been burned into the skin during life, and which had survived the scalding and brining involved in preservation.

"You're saying he branded her?"

Hawkes nodded, his face set. "Some say."

Such marks are not unusual, I know. Any pig released onto common land for pannage would need some way for the owner to reclaim it. But to brutalize a helpless woman so. . . it would be deeply shocking, if true, and any man guilty of such cruelty must surely be capable of worse.

Hawkes said, "If that poor girl bears such a mark, then it's Polly for sure."

"Thank you, Mister Hawkes," I said. "That is more helpful than you can know."

My next step was clear. From Hawkes I learned the location of the undertaker in question, a third-generation carpenter and cabinet maker with a secondary avocation and a family willing to dress in mourning and weep to order when funeral attendance was low. When I reached his workshop, he was in apron and shirtsleeves and expressing his displeasure to Constable Tweedy. The reasons for his displeasure; he was dismayed at the condition of the body he was expected to handle, and doubly dismayed at the prospect of having to store it while Tweedy's investigation continued.

Neither man was aware of Edgar Hawkes's rumor of a drunken Charlie McGrath putting a mark of ownership on his woman. The act of a monster, Tweedy called it, and almost beyond belief, but he conceded that it could not be ignored. He withdrew his objection to my viewing the body.

We are neither of us a stranger to the dissecting-room, Watson, and I am sure you can imagine what lay on the table before us after so many weeks in the water. I am rarely given to strong emotion though what I felt here was not revulsion, but a powerful sense of pity. The face was gone, and most of the extremities, and a good part of the right arm, but the torso was largely intact.

When we turned her over, there was the mark.

The carpenter spoke then.

"The devil's mark?" he said.

All were silent for a while and then Tweedy said, "Where does this take us, Mister Holmes?"

"One more day will make no difference to this poor woman," I said. "But it may help to complete my understanding. I believe I am within reach of an answer to your witchcraft mystery, Constable Tweedy. Will you bear with me one day longer?"

"I suppose I must."

"I'll need a cart and driver at my disposal tomorrow. Have him pick me up at the church."

When I went to my bed that night it was with the inconvenience of one of my slippers gone missing, the significance of which would not become clear until much later. I did not trouble to pursue it, as it played no part in my theory of the case and my plans for the morning required my undivided attention.

*

While the skivvy cleared breakfast, I gave her a mission and a message to carry. Then I made my way over to the church, where the waiting carriage proved to be a one-horse dog cart driven by yesterday's messenger boy. It made a serviceable ride and I was pleased that he attempted no conversation, though I would have appreciated a more comfortable seat for the hours we spent crossing the county. It was, in the end, a fruitful day, and it was late in the afternoon when I returned to the inn. Through the window I could see that the skivvy had carried out her task and Charlie McGrath was in the bar. I sent the boy to fetch Constable Tweedy and then I went inside.

161

Hawkes stepped out into the hallway, glanced back toward the snug, and said, "Charlie says you sent him a message. Promised to stand him a drink."

"Just the one," I said. "He's going to need it."

Tweedy arrived a few minutes later and we went through to sit, one to either side of Charlie. Our landlord placed the glass before him, a generous measure at my expense, and retired to listen from behind the bar counter.

"Now, Charlie," I said. "I must tell you what happened to Polly."

"She is—"

"She is alive. She is well. She is gone."

My first call that morning had been on the keeper at Iden Lock. With a little prompting he'd remembered Tweedy's enquiry and was able to direct me to the mooring of the bargee in question. I'd found him in good time; another hour, and he'd be departing with his load. He seemed a decent man but he treated me with suspicion. Only when I'd explained did he call his female companion out from the cabin. When challenged, she conceded that her name had once been Polly Cook.

"I will find her," Charlie McGrath said, rising to his feet, and both Tweedy and I put a hand on a shoulder and drew him back down.

"She is a wife now," I said, "but not yours. I urge you to accept her wishes and move on."

She was happy with her boatman. Theirs was no broomstick wedding; they had been legally wed in another parish two months before, after three Sundays for the calling of the banns. I took care to tell McGrath only the bare facts, giving him nothing that would help him to pursue the pair. My glance through the local register had confirmed that McGrath and Polly had been husband and wife in common law only, and he had no power to compel her return. Her boatman had courted her in the way Charlie never did, and had begged her to leave with him. A perverse sense of loyalty held her back.

When she found that she was with child she had gone to the women of the manor to seek a remedy. On learning the details of her unhappy life, Edith Appleby had helped to arrange her escape to a new and better one.

Tweedy said, "So if Polly is alive, we're worse off than where we started. A dead woman with no face and no name."

"And yet," I said, "the body has Charlie's mark on it. How do we explain that?"

And a voice from the doorway said, "I believe I can."

Our landlord raised himself from his elbows on the bar. "Out with you, miss," he barked. "No women in the snug."

"Break a rule, Hawkes," I said. "We have greater matters to concern us. Miss Cleminson."

Tweedy and I rose to our feet while Charlie stayed seated, staring darkly into the glass in his fist. Lily Cleminson moved in to join us, tugging at the fingers of a rather more elegant pair of gloves than those she used for the garden. Tweedy drew out a chair for her to sit.

She thanked him and then turned to me and said, "I paid a visit to the local undertaker, as you requested."

"Was he helpful or obstructive?"

"He's one of our tenants. I had to remind him of that, and then he was helpful. I made a close examination of the body and I can confirm your suspicions. The bone of the arm bears the marks of a saw. The brand on the buttock was made post-mortem."

Tweedy said, "I don't understand."

"One was done to disguise," I said, "the other to misdirect. Who is Peg-Handed Meg?"

Charlie stirred himself, recognizing the name. "Margaret Murphy," he said. "Peg-handed Meg is what we called her, growing up."

I looked toward our landlord and I said, "The same Margaret Murphy whose name is above the door here, as licensee. Check your spellings, by the way."

"She's gone to be with her sister," Hawkes said. "Sally's been widowed and needs her care."

"And if we send for Margaret, will she come?"

Hawkes struggled for a response. Charlie was staring at him.

Tweedy said, "Edgar?"

In the continuing silence Charlie said, "Old man Murphy had the inn for thirty years. It passed to Meg when he died. We called her peg-handed because she wrote with her left. Her right arm got broke and never healed."

"The right arm of the body is missing," Tweedy said, beginning to understand.

"You took care to remove the bent arm, did you not," I said to Hawkes, "in case the bones were ever found." I got to my feet and moved to the end of the bar counter, in case he should attempt to bolt. "But the dead rose too soon, so you sought to shift attention by putting Charlie's mark on the body while it lay in your cellar. He was out of credit but you allowed him one more night of drinking, just so you could slip out to his cottage and steal the brand for the purpose. You didn't care who might be blamed for the murder. Only that the body be taken for anyone other than Margaret Murphy, Peg-handed Meg, your common-law wife and the owner of these premises."

Hawkes spread his hands in bewilderment and outrage. "Why would I ever do such a thing?"

It was Lily Cleminson who spoke up. "Because with her dead, you have no right to keep the inn. A common-law marriage is not a legal union, so the sister now inherits."

"How long did you expect to maintain the pretense?" I asked him. "What was your plan for explaining Margaret's absence?"

Hawkes lowered his hands, and his face set in a stubborn mask.

"None of this is true," he said. "And no one here can prove otherwise."

"No?" Lily said, and she indicated the window. "Have you seen what the dog's doing?"

Here's the thing about dogs, Watson. Old dogs have their habits. On her way in Miss Cleminson had seen Patch at work in the garden. While burying my missing slipper he was also in the process of unearthing one of his previous treasures.

We went out, leaving Charlie behind, and amongst the stolen socks and pork bones Miss Cleminson identified the radius of a human arm. It had been broken and badly reset at some time in the past.

"Saw marks," she said, thrusting the dirt-encrusted bone under the nose of a disconcerted Tweedy. "Marks that I can testify will align with those on the body."

"Well, Hawkes," I said. "Do you still deny it?"

"There was no murder," Hawkes blurted. All eyes were on him now. "I swear it," he said. "In all our time together, I never struck her once. One evening she complained of a terrible aching head and went to bed early. When I woke in the morning, she was lying dead beside me. She'd taken her last breath and I never even heard her go. What was I to do? Everything is hers. I have nothing to my name. I meant no real harm."

"But you abused the dead," I said. "You disrespected a decent woman's memory, and worst of all, you would have stood silently by while some innocent was hanged for it."

"She was never supposed to be found."

"And that's your best defense," I said.

*

Holmes now leaned forward to peer down the track. His hearing is so much sharper than mine.

"I believe our train is on time," he said. "I can have the conductor see to the bag but I'll need your arm to board. A nuisance, I know, but there it is."

"But Holmes," I said. "Your injury. The entire reason for me making this journey. How does anything in your account explain it?"

He seemed not to hear me. "This d—— stick," he complained, struggling to his feet. "I'll be glad to be rid of it."

"I said. . ."

"I heard what you said, Watson." He paused, and would not meet my eyes.

"I packed my bag and I paid my bill," he said. "Then when I went to leave. . ."

Again, he paused.

"Well?" I said.

"I fell over the dog," he said.

THE KINGDOM OF THE SEA AWAITS YOU

Wendy N. Wagner

He awoke to the sounds of the sea: waves, and gulls, and the throbbing moan of a foghorn, very nearby. Awoke, too, to the hollowed sense of a body climbing from a pit of fever and great quantities of laudanum holding back a cough that had been so fierce his throat and ribs still ached. His very sense of himself hung about his consciousness in filmy rags, and he had to force himself back together as he sat up on the edge of the small bed. There was no sign of Holmes in the one-room cottage, and that brought him back to himself more powerfully than any amount of introspection might have done.

"Holmes?" Watson called, but only the seagulls replied. He dressed himself in clothes he found on a chair and made his way outdoors.

The wind battered the vegetables inside the tiny cottage garden, where a waist-high wattle fence formed a flimsy barrier against a dizzying drop to the sea. Watson leaned against the cottage wall, breathing as deeply as his aching lungs would let him. Sea air. It was just what he would have prescribed himself for a bad bout of bronchitis or pneumonia, whatever had befallen him.

"Holmes?" he called out again, his voice cracking. How lonely he felt, how exposed. He could drop into the sea and no one would know.

"Mr. Holmes has gone up to the lighthouse."

The cracked voice came from the gate at the end of the garden, its accent thick, reminiscent of some ancient Breton. The old woman standing there drew the top layer of her shawls more tightly around herself and took a step forward. Her fingers looked as gnarled and knotted as an oak's branches, her skin wind-stung and so heavily creased her features nearly vanished into the folds.

"Can you point me the way?"

She shook her head. "You ought to stay here and rest. I brought you your breakfast." She patted a basket dangling from the crook of her elbow, and he noticed the jaunty checked fabric, the rustic loaf of bread, a wax-sealed jar. "Come inside, and I'll make you tea."

Tea had never sounded so fine, but he burned to find Holmes and learn why they were here and how long he had been sick. "I must find my friend."

Again she shook her head. "The lighthouse is not for you. Come. Eat. Drink."

He followed her inside, because what else could he do? She was already stoking the fire in the iron stove. He dropped onto the small wooden chair where he had found his clothes and watched her work, while rubbing his chest. Congestion squeezed like a fist inside his lungs, stopping the air from filling them completely. His head floated strangely.

"Where is this place?"

She grunted. "No name you've ever heard of."

"But where? You said Holmes was at a lighthouse? Surely it has a name."

"Rinnick Head Light," she said, finally, dumping a handful of leaves into a pot. "Not so far from St. Ives," she added, as if she resented the need to put her world into some larger context.

Rinnick Head Light. He'd read about the place a few months earlier—the most state-of-the-art lighthouse in the Empire, recently installed on the Cornwall coast. The light could be seen up to one hundred fifty miles on a clear day, and the gears that turned the Fresnel lens, giving the beacon its own signature flash of white and red lights, were the largest ever installed in a British lighthouse. He could understand why Holmes would wish to see such a tremendous technological achievement.

The old woman drew out the loaf, a crock of butter, and the jar, which proved to be some kind of red preserve. She didn't ask if Watson wanted any; merely cut a thick slice, smeared it with butter the color of daffodils, and loaded it with preserves. The strong blend of sugar and salt and sour soothed his throat as he swallowed.

"You ask too many questions," she said, handing him a mug of tea so dark it might well have been coffee.

"If you think I ask too many questions, you should meet Sherlock Holmes."

"I have." She studied his face for a moment and then reached into the basket again. She held out a loop of red yarn, a smooth rock strung on its length. "Promise me you will wear this while you are here."

Watson hesitated, so she came around the table to pull the thing down over his head.

"Promise me!" She set her hands on his shoulders, and their strength startled him. Her eyes flared like the dark embers of a banked fire.

"I promise." The words surprised him as they escaped his lips, but they stirred his sense of honor. This talisman, as simple and superstitious as it might be, clearly meant something to her, and she just as clearly cared for his well-being.

She smiled and cut him another slice of bread. "Good. I told Mr. Holmes I would keep you safe."

A coughing fit overtook him then, and she pounded his back and urged tea upon him before tidying the cottage and leaving. He opened the shutters and pulled the chair to the window to watch the clouds scuttle across the sky for a few peaceful moments, before he realized he had not asked her name, or thought to ask her why Holmes worried about his safety. Such things rarely concerned Holmes, and it seemed even odder in this quiet place.

A seagull settled on the woven garden fence, its head cocked so it could fix its yellow eye upon him. As a rule, Watson didn't mind gulls, but this one's size and posture unsettled him. It stood boldly, its glare so fierce, it reminded him more of a raven than the usual stupid seabird. He rapped on the window, and its head swiveled, revealing its other eye: a deep and baleful red. It fixed the glowing eye upon him and held his gaze. The skin on the back of his neck began to prickle.

"Go away, bird." His voice came out soft, so he cleared his throat and again shouted: "Go away!"

It fluttered onto one of the stakes supporting the peas, now only a few feet from the window. The red eye did not blink.

Watson jumped to his feet and slammed the shutters. On second thought, he slipped into the jacket hanging on the back of the door and went outside, but the bird was gone. He found himself panting as he stood in the garden alone, which stirred his anger further. He wanted answers, not more molly-coddling.

He pushed open the gate. Within a few steps, he could see the path led downhill, away from the sea, but a parallel track led farther along the cliffs, climbing to the lighthouse in the distance. Its gray tower thrust itself against the sky, its great lens flashing across a few white clouds.

A flock of sheep blocked his path to the lighthouse. A shepherd strode in their midst, border collie at his heels. He held his crook like Poseidon gripping his trident.

"You Dr. Watson?"

Watson nodded to save air.

"You're wanted down at the Sea's Arms. With your doctor's bag, too."

Watson tried to remember if he'd seen his bag inside the cottage. The man squeezed past him with an exasperated sigh.

"I'll get it, your nibs."

Watson opened his mouth to argue, but the man had already hustled inside the cottage and, in a moment, reappeared with the trusty Gladstone. Watson stuck out his hand for it, but the man marched past him. "You'd best follow me."

The shepherd's pace left Watson wheezing as they hurried downhill. The stink of fish and smoke announced the village's presence before he caught a glimpse of it: a few commercial buildings hunkering along the lone cobblestone street; a boat or two at moor in the sheltered harbor. Watson guessed there were slips for at least five or six more vessels. Not much of a town.

Beside the harbor sat a square building with a gray slate roof, its character more formal than the thatched buildings along the road. A glinting brass sign over the doorway announced it as the harbor master's office. But beside its front steps, a strange structure a little larger than a post box perched, its sides bedecked in garlands of ivy and late spring flowers. A bouquet of lilies lay on top, a handful of new potatoes, and what looked to be a few guineas glinted in the sunshine. An altar of some kind. Watson found himself staring at the thing. His hand went to the stone at his throat, fever hot to the touch.

The shepherd clicked his tongue impatiently, and Watson realized the man had pushed open the door to the largest of the town's other buildings. A sign suspended from the thatched roof marked it as "The Sea's Arms." Beneath the words a stylized octopus gripped a woman in its tentacles. Though crude, the artwork held an unsettling fury. Watson wrenched his eyes from it and followed the shepherd inside.

A group of men still wearing their fisherman's oilskins crowded around a table. The patter of dripping water made the only sound besides a soft and terrible gurgling. The knot of fishermen broke apart when the shepherd announced Watson, and one pulled him by the hand to join them beside the table.

"Can you help him, doctor?" the man asked, his voice thick with emotion. His hair looked wet.

Someone pulled back the blankets piled on the table, and Watson took stock of his patient. All the color had left the man's skin, and it was clear from the water trickling from his hair and clothing that he'd spent some time fully immersed. When Watson laid his hand across the man's forehead, the skin felt like ice.

"The captain jumped in after him," someone said.

"He wasn't breathing when I found him, but Johnny knocked the water out of his lungs," the wet man—the captain, presumably—explained.

"What happened to him?"

"It came out of the sea!" a man shouted. Another shushed him, but he pushed on. "T'was the morvoren, for sure. We didn't consult the harbor master—"

The shepherd hauled the speaker outside by the arm. Watson wanted to ask more, but now he saw the red holes punched in the victim's skin, each wound a circle of flesh the diameter of a cordial glass, the skin and fat scooped out like the hollow in a roasted apple.

"What the devil did this?" he gasped, and then the sign over the pub's door leaped into his mind. "An octopus? He was attacked by an octopus?"

The captain hesitated. "Yes. An—an octopus."

Watson wrenched open his bag, his hands moving over the familiar instruments without need for thought. The flat-tipped scissors sliced open the man's homespun shirt, revealing a pattern of mottled bruises wrapping around the entire torso. It took no act of imagination to envision the enormous tentacle twining around his body, the beast's muscles contracting over

173

his flesh, squeezing the bones, crushing the inner organs. Watson's fingers found the distended soft tissue of the man's abdomen and knew the worst.

"This man's been squeezed to a pulp." He flung down the scissors and caught the captain's eyes. "The best we can do is make him comfortable."

The dying man's breath gurgled in his chest, punctuating the truth in Watson's words. But the shepherd's face twisted. He raised his fist. "Goddamn you, Doctor. Do *something!*"

One of the fishermen caught the shepherd's hand. "Liam! Stop. Your brother was doomed the minute Captain Michaels raised the sails. The morvoren—"

The shepherd struck him hard enough that Watson heard the fisherman's nose crunch. A scuffle while the others grabbed the pair, dragging them outside. The man on the table gurgled louder than before.

"Please, Doctor," the captain whispered. "This is my fault. Help my man."

Watson took the bottle of morphine and a syringe from his bag. The dose he drew would have stopped a cow's heart. "This is all I can do for him."

The job done, he broke into his own coughing fit and had to sit. The publican brought him a hot toddy, and Watson clutched it while holding the dying man's wrist. Beat by beat, the man's pulse slowed. Watson sipped his toddy and watched the captain. They were alone now, facing each other across a broken, dying body. Watson thought he had never seen such anguish as the captain's face emanated, and he wished Holmes was here to observe the moment. Watson's own faculties were such simple, blunt things; Holmes would have understood everything about the situation. He would have known what to say to soften this terrible blow.

The dying man's eyes flew open. Watson flung himself backward in his seat. No man's eyes should glow like that, that baleful red, same as the seagull's. A pink foam boiled up on the man's lips.

Watson shook off his terror. Just burst blood vessels, caused by the pressure of the creature's squeezing. He reached for the man's hand. "It's all right," he said.

"She's coming," the man gasped.

The captain's bench toppled as he sprang to his feet.

"What?" Watson asked. "Who?"

"She's coming!" the man repeated, froth spraying from his mouth. The air caught in his throat. Blood dripped from the corner of his eye. "Michaels," he whispered, and then convulsed.

"I'm so sorry, Connor," the captain murmured, but the man was gone.

"What's the morvoren?" a voice said from the tavern doorway. Watson turned in his seat, relieved to see the comforting figure of Sherlock Holmes.

The captain righted the bench and sank onto it. "It's my fault he's dead," he said. "We've always consulted the harbor master for the proper observances to keep her happy, but this morning, he had gone to visit the lighthouse keeper, and I would not wait for him to return. All these years, I figured it was all superstition. The kind of nonsense parents tell their children to make them behave, you know?" He raised tear-stained eyes to meet Watson's. "But they were right. All of them."

Holmes strode to the captain's side and hauled him to his feet. "We don't have time for guilt. Take me to the harbor master this minute."

"Holmes—" Watson began, but his friend cut him off. "You get back to the cottage where I put you, Watson. I won't have you caught up in this mess, not as sick as you've been."

Ignoring the command, Watson followed the two men out of the tavern. The weather had changed in the wild way of the seaside: black clouds raced in from the west, and a screaming wind buffeted the tiny town. The boats in the harbor leaped and yanked on their moorings.

A large group had formed in front of the harbor master's office, some of them the fishermen Watson had seen in the tavern, as well as some new faces. The woman who had tended to him was not in their midst. Her absence drew Watson's hand to the stone tied at his throat. It felt strangely warm against his flesh.

The shepherd stood beside the altar. Wind whipped at his hair and ripped at the white petals of the lilies. "Michaels!" the shepherd bellowed. "This is your fault!"

"Where is the harbor master?" Holmes's voice rose over both crowd and wind. "I believe he is the man to blame for today's calamities."

"It wasn't Captain Overton who drew the wrath of the morvoren." The shepherd rushed forward, jabbing his finger in Michaels's face. "You're the one who got my brother killed!"

"You fools!" Holmes roared. "Don't you know what Overton has been up to?"

At that moment, a finger of lightning drove down from the black clouds, striking the roof of the harbor master's office.

The top line of slates burst into pieces, the roof beam beneath it catching fire. The shepherd dropped to his knees, his back prickling with tiny shards of slate. Blood ran from his wounds as he howled at the sky.

The ground shook beneath their feet, and a woman screamed, pointing out to sea. Something gray and slick, much larger than a boat or a porpoise, rose up from between the clashing waves. White foam sluiced down its rocky flanks, the water hissing loud enough to be heard over the roar of the waves and the sizzle of the flames. Holmes stared for a second, pivoted, and then raced up the path leading into the cliffs.

"The coward," Michaels spat.

Watson grabbed his shoulder. "We must follow him. If there's one thing I know about Holmes, it's that he's no coward. If he knows a solution, he deserves our help."

Michaels glanced back out to the sea, where the rocky shape still climbed from the water. A new island? A whale vaster than anything recorded by man? The clouds and storm clung too closely to its shape to be sure, and the mist grew thicker around it by the second. The village had been plunged in gloom as deep as twilight.

"All right," he said. "If nothing else, perhaps we'll find the harbor master."

"Tell me more about Overton," Watson demanded, clinging to the man's arm as they hurried up the path.

Another temblor rocked them so hard they nearly fell from the path. Rocks crumbled down the edge of the cliff. The pair turned to face the harbor. The rock—the island—the *enormity* cracked open on one side, steam belching from the interior. Things moved inside the gap, springing free and plunging into the harbor. Some arced like leaping fishes, some dropped like spiders from their webs, but they were all large, the size of a man or more. Creatures of nightmare.

"The morvoren," Michaels breathed. "That must be where it comes from."

Watson spun him around. "We must get to the lighthouse, and soon!" He risked running, even though his lungs felt abraded by the simple act of breathing. Lightning flashed on the horizon, illuminating the pale form of the lighthouse.

Something burned at the top of it, not the bright glow of a kerosene lamp behind a Fresnel lens, but a ruddy glow all too akin to the light Watson had seen in two sets of eyes this day. He shuddered and would have fallen if not for Michaels catching him.

"What is happening, Doctor?" Michaels moaned. "The lighthouse, the harbor—is it the end of the world?"

Watson set his teeth against a burning need to cough. "Holmes will know," he managed, and they trudged onward, up the bucking flanks of the cliff. The earth felt as if it might shatter or dissolve beneath their feet. Every living thing seemed to scream in pain and terror.

As they came up the final rise beside the lighthouse keeper's cottage and the two oil houses, Watson could see the door to the lighthouse stood open ahead of them. Even at this distance, Watson could see the way the lighthouse's walls vibrated. The windows in the keeper's cottage rattled in their frames. Far above, gears squeaked and ground against each other.

Michaels trembled beside him. "I can't go in there. You feel it, don't you? There's something horribly wrong inside."

Watson doubled over, unable to control the coughing any longer. He fell to his knees. At this level, he couldn't help but see the plaque beside the lighthouse stairs. He forced down the coughing and yanked Michaels down to his level. "It says Captain Overton organized the funds for this lighthouse. Explain."

Michaels shook his head, confused. "Captain Overton is in charge of everything in this town. He takes the readings for the tide charts. He makes the offerings to the morvoren. He gives us permission to fish or not to fish."

"But why?" Watson had to shout to hear himself over the noise of the sea, the wind, the rattling lighthouse. "Why Overton?"

"There's always been an Overton at Rinnick Head!" Michaels bellowed. "They were the first family to settle here!"

"And we'll be the last, too," a voice announced from the stairs of the lighthouse.

Watson stared up at the man standing there, his red hair waving in the wind, his black peacoat streaked with something wet and glossy. A pattern of three cordial glass-sized circular scars ran down the right side of his face, drawing up the corner of his eye and mouth into what should have been a merry twinkle.

There was nothing merry about the bloody gaff hook in his hand.

Watson scrambled to his feet. "What did you do to Holmes?"

"I? I did nothing. Show him, my queen." And Overton stepped aside to reveal the woman standing behind him.

No, not a woman. A woman's face, a woman's slender arms and shapely bosom, but all of it wed to a fleshy white monstrosity his brain couldn't assemble into meaning. Watson stumbled backward as she rolled, no, slid, no, *oozed* down the stairs, her tentacles furling and unfurling as she came toward him. The pale flesh of her rubbery torso shifted color and pattern as she went, turning green as she pulled herself onto the grass.

She smiled, and each of her teeth were the needle points of some deep-sea fish. This close, he could see the strange shape of her face, too thin in places, too wide in others. Her eyes were pure black pools, like looking into the bottom of the sea. The stench of rotting fish came off her in waves. Around her neck, swinging over her blood-spattered breasts, hung a necklace strung with what could only have been bones.

"God help us," Watson said, but it came out in only the harshest of whispers. The fist in his chest squeezed so tight he could barely sip at the air.

Michaels threw himself prostrate and cried out: "Oh, Great Morvoren! Please spare us!"

The morvoren's lips moved, but the sounds coming from her mouth sounded like rocks grinding against each other. Overton responded in kind as he dropped to kneel at her feet. She extended a tentacle to cup his face, staring down at the two men.

Then, another of her tentacles shot out, hoisting Michaels into the air. He screamed as it tightened around his waist.

"You thought you could fish without Her permission?" Overton shouted.

Michaels's mouth fell open. Vomit spurted from his throat as the tentacle tightened, lifting him high. Blood dripped from the bottom of his trouser legs, soaking into the morvoren's flesh. She threw back her head and laughed horribly. The ground shook and lurched.

Something brick red and blood-streaked bulged from Michaels's gaping jaws, and Watson turned away, unable to watch the man's organs be squeezed from his body. But behind him, the tower of green stone had risen to heights known not even to the Cairngorms. A tremendous mountain towered over the Cornish coastline, the town itself vanished in the hot steam boiling off its sides. The air stank of cooked seaweed.

A hand closed on the back of Watson's jacket, or perhaps something worse than a hand. He flew through the air and felt his head slam into something hard. For a moment, the lighthouse spun above him, a flash of ruddy light against the blackest sky he had ever known.

Then there was only darkness.

*

He awoke to the slow *ting-ting-ting* of footsteps on metal and the sensation of his heels bouncing against what could only be steps. Someone was dragging him to the top of the lighthouse. He struggled, but to no avail. Above him, he saw the brilliant glow of the lighthouse, the pure bright light at the base of its lens. It made no sense, this white light, not when the last time he had seen the beacon, it had glowed red. He squeezed his eyes against the light and wished for Holmes's reason.

Then he rose above the base of the mechanism and understood. The lighthouse keeper's head sat on the far side of the Fresnel lens, his arms and legs making the points of some grisly star, and his body—his body smoldered on the crown of the light, the heat so fierce it sent tendrils of wool-

181

stinking smoke to the very ceiling. His blood dried almost as quickly as it dripped.

"What have you done?" Watson gasped.

"I love my queen," Overton said. "And it's her time to walk this earth."

Overton dropped Watson so his back hit a glass wall. The gears crashed and growled as the light room spun at speeds its builders could have never intended. There was very little space in the room, and the heat infernal. Now Watson saw the tiny lines of script connecting the torn limbs of the lighthouse keeper, letters shaped like nothing Watson had ever seen before.

Watson's head ached and his chest burned, and the smoky air made his lungs falter even more. But there was no sign of Holmes and, curiously, that gave him hope.

A clanging from the stairwell then reminded Watson of the horrible creature, the morvoren. He struggled to sit up more. Shadows played on the railing below.

Overton hunkered down so his eyes could meet Watson's. "Did you know this was all ocean once? And we were once all sea creatures. Even the geologists are starting to say such things."

"Heresy," Watson gasped.

Overton shrugged. "Think what you like, Doctor. You're only here to provide more blood for the gate. By the time the moon rises, the kingdom of the sea will be upon the Earth forever, and your death will have been as big a part of it as this lighthouse I designed." He drew himself up to his full height and drew out his gaff hook. "By the will of my gods, it will be done!"

He pressed his lips to the filthy weapon. An enormous boom shattered the air. Watson threw up his arm to protect his face from flying shards of glass. Overton went stiff, then toppled backward. His head should have struck the glass wall of the light room, but the glass was gone, exploded in a million pieces, some of them driven into Watson's exposed arm and cheek. With one last howl, Overton fell through onto the exterior catwalk.

"Watson!" Holmes shouted. "Behind you!"

Watson threw himself sideways, onto Overton's still twitching legs, just as the tentacle lashed out. The morvoren hissed and snarled as she scuttled up the last of the stairs, her body sliding up onto the walls of the light room as if gravity had no meaning for her disgusting kind. Part woman, part octopus, part something so ancient and terrifying it stole the last of Watson's breath from his chest.

"Holmes," his mouth moved, soundlessly, but she was rushing out the open window onto the catwalk where his friend perched. The world went gray spangled. Watson pounded at his chest and felt his hand touch the hot stone at the base of his throat.

His doctor's hands knew an instrument of life when they felt one. He ripped the stone from his throat and spun it on the rope of yarn. It flew from his hand and connected with the back of the morvoren's head just as her tentacle shot out toward Sherlock Holmes.

Over the sounds of the lighthouse's grinding gears and the rush of the wind through the broken glass, he couldn't have heard the sound of the rock striking her skull, but years later, Watson would still wake in the night, certain he heard the sound of a melon splitting open beside his screaming face.

Blood as black as ink sprayed out, and the morvoren's momentum plunged her over the side of the lighthouse. For a second, her tentacle caught on Holmes's arm, and he grabbed the railing of the catwalk just before he himself went over. With a squelch, the boneless organ ripped free and hung trembling from his coat. Holmes flung it away with a face of revulsion.

"Watson!" he roared, and rushed to Watson's side. "Damn it, you were supposed to stay inside the cottage while I dealt with all this!"

"That's what the old woman said," Watson laughed, coughing between words. "But it's a good thing I didn't listen to her."

Holmes's brow furrowed. "Old woman?"

Watson pulled himself to his feet. "You know, the one you asked to make me breakfast. Nice old thing."

Holmes just shook his head. Watson's fingers went to his throat, where the skin was still strangely warm.

The lighthouse gave a tremendous shudder, the remnants of glass panels in the light room cracking free of their lead frames and tumbling into the darkness outside. Watson stumbled and caught himself on the stair rail. "We have to get out of here!"

Holmes went ahead, the pair moving as quickly as they could. Slabs of masonry slid from the interior wall of the lighthouse as they went, the metal staircase shrieking as its supports yanked free of their bolts. Bricks tumbled down from above, nearly braining them as they leaped out the door.

The sunset beamed back at them. Wisps of mist still floated over the harbor, but the terrible green mountain was sliding back down into the sea. Coughing, the two friends made their way back into town, but there was no one to be seen—only buildings smashed and ravaged by the storm, blood stains on the broken cobbles, and lily petals strewn everywhere.

Holmes straightened his jacket. "Lean on me, Watson. It's a long walk to the train station at St. Ives."

"Just a second," Watson said. He went into the battered looking pub and found his Gladstone bag. Holmes shot him a look as he emerged with it. "I've got my pen and notebook in there," Watson explained. "I don't want to forget anything that happened."

Holmes offered Watson his shoulder. "This time, my friend, I think we should keep the mystery to ourselves."

Watson looked down at the sign for the Sea's Arms, half-submerged in a puddle at his feet. The painted octopus seemed to grin at him with needle-sharp teeth. He touched the base of his throat and wondered if he had ever really seen a woman at the cottage. After all, he hadn't really felt himself since he woke up in that cramped little room.

"Perhaps that's for the best," Watson agreed, and they began walking.

THE FIRST FOOTERS

Stephen Volk

It was not customary for Sherlock Holmes and I to exchange presents at Christmas. To me, the season was pleasantly conducive to commemorating familial bonding, one of marking affection between associates; a time of year when passing ills were forgotten in favor of acts of kindness. My friend shared no such impulse and wished the festival to be over as soon as possible. He did not believe in holidays. He believed in the activity of the mind, not snowballs, decorated pine trees or assorted fripperies.

This Christmas, however, a gift was to be delivered to his door, in the shape of a most peculiar and disturbing case. One that arrived, as they often did, in the most unprepossessing form.

"Please, Watson." Holmes waved a limp hand in the air, wearing the most ridiculously pained expression as we heard a spirited knock from downstairs. Mrs. Hudson having absented herself to a night at the theatre, it fell to me to see off the irritant carol singers, hopefully before a rendition of the inevitable "Good King Wenceslas" assaulted the ears of the great detective.

Imagine my surprise, then, as I opened the door of 221B Baker Street to a fastidiously dressed lone figure whose complexion, above his scarf and below his bowler hat, was as brown as any I had encountered in India.

"Mr. Sherlock Holmes?"

"Not quite," I replied.

"Will . . . Will he see me? I know it is late. I have only just disembarked the train. I know I should have made an appointment, but I am too saturated with worry to sleep in my hotel bed." *Saturated* was a strange choice of word, and he was stammering. "My . . . my mind has not been at rest for months. Without his h-help, I doubt it ever shall be."

I had no hesitation in escorting him upstairs.

"I did not know where to turn."

"Then turn to us. Many do," said Holmes, shaking our visitor's hand vigorously. "Sit." He noticed, as I did, that the man consulted the fob watch in his waistcoat pocket. "Have no concern about the hour. Our time is yours, for as long as you are in our company."

The night was chill and the man needed tea to warm him. His shivering hands surrounded the cup as a beggar holds his bowl. He thanked us profusely, I surmised as a delaying tactic, to avoid voicing the very facts that troubled him.

"Have you come far?" I ventured.

"Birmingham. Good journey. On time." As he said so I observed, in the crackling firelight, that one eye reflected marginally differently than the other. I deduced it was glass. "My name is Dr. Arshad Girai."

"Doctor?"

He laughed nervously. "No, not actually. I'm a dentist. I received my LDS diploma from the Odontological Society of Great Britain. My name is on the *Dentistry Register*, if—"

"We have no reason to dispute your qualifications. Tell us why you are here." Holmes said rather tersely, offering him a cigarette from a case.

"Would you like a snifter, to take the chill off?" I removed the top from a bottle of brandy, pouring a measure for myself.

"No . . . No, sir. Thank you very much. My religion does not permit me to partake of alcohol. I am a Muslim."

I coughed into my hand and sipped my drink gingerly.

"Your English is perfect," said Holmes. "But you have a slight accent. I take it you were not born on these shores?"

He shook his head. "I have family in England, but I was sent here after being wounded at the battle of Maiwand."

"Great Scott!" The very military engagement at which a Jezail bullet had incapacitated me. Such a coincidence was quite extraordinary. I had not met a veteran of the campaign for many years, and one who was not white—well, never. Now at least I had an explanation for the glass eye. The poor devil had no doubt been semi-blinded in the line of duty. My heart swelled with a sense of comradeship.

"I was in the Bombay Sappers and Miners," he said. "One of the brigades under Brigadier Burrows."

A second swig of brandy numbed my mouth. The memories flooded back—and not pleasant ones either. "A terrible defeat for the British and Indian troops by the

Afghans. I myself witnessed unimaginable horror amongst unsurpassable bravery. By Englishman and Indian alike."

"I do not think I was brave," said Dr. Girai with downcast eyes. "I did my duty."

"Which is what every genuinely brave man says, in my experience," opined Holmes, lounging back in his chair, stretching out his legs and making a steeple of his fingers.

By the time the teacup was empty, our guest had furnished us with the basic facts of the case.

His brother Basheer, he said, had been murdered a year ago, on New Year's Eve. Basheer had been living in a small town on the border of Wiltshire and Somerset, working as an accountant to local businesses, quite happily. His body had been found on New Year's Day. Basheer's wife Nusrat had raised questions about the circumstances of his demise, to no avail. Cause of death was declared by the authorities to be accidental—by drowning—but Nusrat believed something far more sinister was afoot and expressed her grievance, in floods of tears, to the rest of Basheer's family, who are mostly resident in the Midlands. She herself had no kin to support her in Britain. This is how Arshad heard of the crime, and having listened to his sister-in-law's concerns first-hand, became convinced that the whole story was not being told. For nearly a twelvemonth he had lived with the rage of knowing someone was responsible for his brother's killing, yet nobody had been found responsible, and no-one seemed to care.

Most intriguingly, Nusrat had reported that her husband had been both excited and secretive about something that he wouldn't share with her. He had dressed up smartly to go out that New Year's Eve to meet someone, but refused to tell her who they were or where they were meeting. He'd simply held her face in his hands, kissed her on the tip of the nose, and told her that everything would be all right from now on. Horrid irony, then, that those were the last words she heard from his lips.

"Where had he been invited, and by whom?" I thought aloud. "It seems to me, if we answer that question, we have solved the case."

Holmes was staring into the fire with hooded eyes, giving every appearance that he was hardly listening. I knew of old he was absorbing every word.

"With a secret agenda to get to the truth, I set up my dental practice in the same town, Compton Lydiard, six months ago." Dr. Girai took an envelope from his inside pocket, unfolding a single sheet of paper from within. "And now I have received the same invitation that I think was extended to my brother."

Holmes shot to his feet and snatched the missive from our visitor's hand. In less than a moment he was holding it back-lit by the nearest gas fitting, his nose almost touching the writing, which I could see was in heavy hand-written capitals, not script. His pupils flitted over the surface voraciously, continuing to flicker as he stared at the blank wall in front of him, handing the letter to me with an outstretched arm.

I read its contents avidly.

> DEAR FRIEND,
> YOU CAN BE ONE OF US.
> AS YOU LOVE GOD AND BRITANNIA, COME TO THE BEEHIVE
> NEW YRS EVE AT MIDNIGHT.
> <u>BURN THIS LETTER</u>.
> THE FIRST FOOTERS

"When I told her I'd received this, Nusrat was horrified. It reminded her that Basheer had received a hand-delivered letter a few days before he died. She had thought nothing of it at the time. He had burned it and when she asked what it was, he said 'Nothing'."

"*You can be one of us,*" repeated Holmes. His nostrils flared with distaste.

"But you did not burn it," said I.

"Why would I destroy evidence? No, I did not. It also contained this." Dr. Girai stood and emptied something out of the envelope into the palm of my hand.

A white feather.

Soon Holmes was hovering over it with his magnifying glass. He then transferred the object with tweezers to the plate of a microscope.

"Is there anything else you can tell us?"

"Only that my brother's body was found floating in the River Avon on New Year's Day. The Coroner pronounced it accidental death, but when my sister-in-law saw the body laid out in the chapel of rest she insists there were marks on his neck. She wrote to the police but her letters were ignored. She also found a number of strange objects in his pockets."

Holmes looked up sharply. "What strange objects?"

"A silver coin, a chunk of coal, and a piece of wood."

Holmes grunted as he sucked on his pipe stem so harshly, I thought he was going to snap it off with his teeth. His eyes were flickering again, catching the light like black pearls.

He paced, and not for the first time did urgency act like fuel to the fire of his intellectual hunger. We had the location;

a sleepy town in rural Wiltshire called Compton Lydiard. But we had mere days to solve this mystery if a second murder on New Year's Eve was to be averted. A morbid advent calendar might be the order of the day.

"You could simply not go," said Holmes, handing back the letter to the doctor. "You could stay at home."

"And never find out what happened to my brother?" A firm resolve showed behind fear in the Muslim's eyes. "That is not something I will contemplate, Mr. Holmes. Nusrat has tried to persuade me to let sleeping dogs lie, but I can't. I shall go to The Beehive alone, if need be, and if I find out the truth with my dying breath, so be it." As he almost choked with emotion on the last syllable, I caught a glimpse of the kind of bravery the man must have shown in the field, and felt humbled by the fact that he was prepared, once again, to put himself in the firing line.

"You shall not be alone," said Sherlock Holmes. "Watson, do you have plans for New Year's Eve?"

"I did, but not anymore."

"Good man." He slapped my shoulder and turned to our new client. "Book us in to a local hostelry, if you will, Doctor, and telegraph me the details. I am sure there is a service from Waterloo on the 31st. I am rather minded to spend New Year's Eve in the country this year."

*

We disembarked the train at Salisbury, and while it continued on its weary way to Exeter, we took a branch line in the direction of Heytesbury, Warminster and Bath. I had been a prisoner of London too long, I realized, because I felt almost elated at the sight of frosted fields stretching and gently undulating. The morning mist had been slow to relinquish its grip on the hillocks and hedges. I often mused if, one day, I might migrate west and settle contentedly, perhaps with a small medical practice in a village far from the taxing, sometimes exhausting, capital. Holmes harbored no such romantic view of the rural counties that existed beyond our metropolitan sprawl. He often expressed the view that the countryside was England "laid raw for good or ill"—full of "salt of the earth" types who were good neighbors, but who could equally harbor deep resentments. They might not enjoy the noise and speed of the machine age, and the song of the lark might enable them to sleep easy, but shotguns and scythes were never far from a self-justified hand.

I joked about seeing woad-covered figures performing ancient ceremonies within stone circles. Without cracking a smile, Holmes insisted we focus on discussing the investigation at hand during our journey. He could be a dry old stick at times. When I'd told my wife I would be absent from the New Year's Eve party of close friends to which she'd RSVP'd, she'd been less than happy, to put it mildly. She'd told me my so-called friendship with 'the detective' counted for a good deal less than that of people who genuinely cared about me. She asserted Holmes treated me as little more than a gun dog and intellectual foil over which he could lord supreme. I said that was unfair. She said she thought I was blind. My temper simmering, I pointed out I'd nevertheless made other arrangements of a more pressing nature. Leaving the room, she said they always were.

As a result of the row, we'd been tetchy, with long periods of silence, over the Christmas period and I was ruminating on this when my companion asked what thinking I had done about what we had heard—if any?

Taking umbrage at the implication I had done none, I said I thought the symbolism of the white feather was painfully obvious.

"Oh, is it?"

"Why, yes. The white feather is delivered as a mark of cowardice."

"You are saying Dr. Girai is a coward?"

"I am saying someone thinks he is, almost certainly." I confess to feeling quite smug in my deduction. "And another thing, while we are at it. I could not see why the devil you asked no questions at all about Basheer, his brother?"

"Such as?"

"Such as whether he had any enemies, for one thing."

"Sometimes, a man has enemies all around him, through no fault of his own."

I could see Holmes was in an elliptical mood, and I had no intention of being maddened by it, so changed the subject to that of the random objects found on the dead man's person— the silver coin, the piece of coal, the piece of wood. What did he make of that? I said I could not easily surmise to what end the materials had been obtained. Wood and coal implied fire, whilst metal fragments can be utilized as shrapnel. Were we talking about the constituent parts of a bomb?

"We are talking about the constituent parts of good fortune, dear fellow," he replied. "There is no chemistry, indeed, no science, to it. They are good luck symbols from pre-Christian times, used when celebrating the turning of the year on the shortest day. I consulted one almanac that informed me the usage is still popular in Fonthill Bishop, not a thousand miles from our destination. The silver coin means one shall not want financially; the coke, that one shall not do without heat and light; and the wood, that one will have no need of a coffin that year."

I huffed. "Merely superstition, then."

"When homicide has occurred, Watson, there is no 'merely' about it." Holmes's eyes narrowed as he pretended to survey the scenery. "I have a feeling that when we lift this particular stone there will be some very unpleasant creatures scurrying for cover. Ones to whom a man's death has become not just a desire but a necessity."

Dr. Girai met us at the station. Beside him stood a woman in a bonnet and fur-trimmed ankle length coat and two bashful but extremely pretty little girls of approximately six and ten years old. We were introduced to their mother, Nusrat, to whom we offered our deepest condolences, which she took with exquisite grace, then to Faiza and Shameena, who shook our hands lightly with a curtsey apiece, which charmed me instantly.

Our dentist suggested we take the path along the riverbank to the town center. I wondered why he avoided the main road, but swiftly had my question answered as he pointed out where his brother's body had been found. Admittedly, the sides of the track looked decidedly slippery. He said the corpse had travelled downstream until it was met with an immovable object—viz. one of the stone struts of the Pack Horse Bridge. "And why would he even be walking this way, when his home was over there?" he said, indicating the highest rank of houses on the other side of the Avon. All this conveyed sotto voce, lest the children hear.

"There's the answer to your feather, Watson." Holmes directed my eye to the sight of a couple of swans gliding along the mirrored surface of the water. "The flank feather of a swan can be up to eight inches long and ours was seven. Someone once concluded that the swan has more feathers than any other bird. I'm not sure that is true, but the most widely reported figure is twenty-four thousand."

Church bells chimed the hour of two o'clock. In the graveyard opposite, amongst hopping squirrels, I could see a portly cleric in his dog-collar and surplice fussing around two women with bunches of flowers. Two spinsters of the parish who commonly gravitated to such tasks, I thought, ungallantly.

"Reverend Kirkbright gave permission for Basheer to be buried here, in the town he had taken to his heart," said Nusrat. "Outside the Christian part of the churchyard, in the part reserved for suicides and unbelievers, naturally. So kind and generous of him."

"How deeply Christian," said Holmes through tight lips, though only I picked up on his sarcasm.

Our next task was to deposit our overnight bags at The Swan Hotel. The florid owner immediately informed us that no children were allowed in the public bar, so the widow and her two girls said they would wait outside while we checked in. Dr. Girai said he would do the same.

"Poor woman," the barkeep mumbled, rubbing an icicle of snot from the end of his nose. "Terrible tragedy. Little wonder her mind . . . well." In so few words he managed to impugn the integrity of the woman he'd just told to stand out in the freezing cold. Why he would do so interested me and no doubt interested Holmes, because he chewed on it like a dog with a bone. Soon we discovered that the publican, Fred Vigar, was also a local flatfoot, and had been, in fact, one of the policemen who had found the body.

"I hear the man was well liked," said Holmes.

"Well enough."

Talk about damning with faint praise. Vigar asked if he could interest us in a couple of pints of the local brew. Without answering, Holmes asked what he imagined had happened to the woman's husband a year ago that very night.

"No great mystery. Fell in the river after going to the pub. He was in his cups, like everyone else on New Year's Eve."

"But why would he be walking towards the Pack Horse Bridge," I interjected, "when his home is on Tory, in the completely opposite direction?"

"That I can't say. Maybe he lost his way. Has been known. Of drunks."

"That's strange too, because Muslims do not drink," said Holmes.

"Then perhaps he wasn't a good Muslim."

The man enquired if we required luncheon. Without consulting me, Holmes answered that we did not. We should appreciate a small repast at teatime. Soup and bread would suffice. The fellow disappeared to inform the kitchen.

"Thank you for thinking of my stomach, Holmes. I am rather peckish, as it happens."

"Ha! Hunger is good for the mind. Besides, we do not wish to be sluggish this evening, should all hell break lose."

All hell . . .? Good grief. Holmes was not normally given to such hyperbole, but I didn't pick him up on it. Perhaps for fear that an elaboration of the phrase might unsettle me all the more. As we left, we heard a parting remark from Vigar, as assured as it was hollow:

"I've nothing against them myself."

Holmes and I gave this the response it deserved. That is to say, nothing at all.

Dr. Girai was folding up his sister-in-law's fur collar to warm her cheeks, but dropped his hands as we appeared. The girls were tugging her sleeve impatiently.

"May we walk you home? We would relish the prospect of stretching our legs after the train journey. Watson?"

"Quite so."

By mid-afternoon it was already beginning to get dark. Such is the way with English winters. No sooner does sunlight emerge than it slinks away again, giving up on a bad job. A far cry from the undaunted sun and heat of India. The sisters trotted ahead and Holmes took the opportunity to probe exactly what Nusrat had seen in the chapel of rest. As much detail as she could summon—given it was a twelvemonth ago—was imperative. She insisted she could remember exactly. There was a dark mark on her husband's neck, a patterned groove—she ran a finger towards the back of one ear—and small scratches in parallel lower on the throat. His face had been swollen and red. Here she became distressed and caught her breath. Dr. Girai supported her elbow but she waved that she was all right.

"Mummy! It's Mr. Pettitt! Mr. Pettitt!"

The children heralded the arrival, in our direction, of a gangly, curly-haired chap in yellow trousers and salmon pink waistcoat under his flapping mackintosh. He seemed almost as delighted to see them as vice versa, and greeted "Mrs. Girai" by placing his hat against his chest. She in turn introduced him as Timothy Pettitt, the girls' teacher. I detected a Morningside twang and made an erroneous leap to the University of Edinburgh. He corrected me, citing a double first at Oxford.

"Humanities?"

"Science." The young man laughed, explaining that before the Christmas holidays he had been trying to educate his class about evolution. "I told them Darwin says we are descended from apes. I don't think they were convinced."

"The evidence for our common ancestor is overwhelming," said Holmes. "Though I believe the religiously-inclined would have it that God put fossils in the ground to test our faith."

Pettitt chuckled heartily. "Faith is a matter of personal preference. Facts are facts, whether you believe in them or not. It is the passion of my life to impart such knowledge to eager brains. They are such sponges at that age."

"Shameena excels in mathematics." Dr. Girai smiled. "And Faiza has a talent for the violin."

"With the violin," said Holmes, "one has to tolerate years of caterwauling before the angel soars."

Laughing again, the teacher wished us all good day and a happy new year, replacing his hat and descending to continue on his way.

We climbed the last fifty or so steps to Tory, Nusrat leading the way to her cottage. From this vantage point I could not resist taking in the panorama of the town below. I enquired as to the central, dominant edifice.

"The rubber factory. Yes. When Basheer and I first came here, you could hear the whistle at 7 a.m. and 5 p.m. when the shifts changed. Now there's barely enough labor for one shift.

So many men have lost their jobs. Cheaper imports from abroad. It used to be busy, thriving, but now the town is dying on its feet."

As Dr. Girai ushered the children indoors, Holmes took her to one side. "Lock all your doors and windows." Even though fear was plain in her eyes—as it possibly was in mine—the woman soon did as she was bid, without question. Minutes after she had entered, I heard keys being turned and bolts being thrown.

"Good Lord, Holmes." As the two of us began our descent to The Swan, I glanced over my shoulder and saw the widow in an upper window. "What is going on?"

"We shall very shortly find out."

*

The Beehive stood on a narrow corner on the rise out of town, and was predictably crowded on this of all evenings. The hubbub indeed reminded me of a swarm of those insects. Gazing over the swarthy faces that surrounded us, indicative of the agricultural history of the area, Holmes mused for some time about the social activity of the hive, and how he would not mind devoting his time to studying such a system. I said it might be a welcome respite from his studies of the human beast. "Oh, the animal kingdom is replete with murder," he murmured. "A newly hatched queen will sting her unhatched rivals, killing them while they are still in their cells." It made mankind sound positively civilized, I said, lifting the pint of Arkell's Mild Amber to my lips. Very fine it was too.

"The linear furrow." He was talking about the widow's description of Basheer Girai's alleged neck wound. "What do you make of it, as a medical man?"

"Well, I'd say pressure abrasion resulting from prolonged compression of the epidermis. Doesn't take much force to produce a pressure abrasion, but a ligature does leave a telltale imprint of the material—the parallel marks would indicate a rope. The redness of the face points to occlusion of the neck veins causing facial congestion—blocked capillaries not enabling blood to return to the heart—and the swelling to oedema. All pointing significantly to hanging as cause of death."

Holmes pondered. "And the smaller scratches?"

"I'm not sure. An imperfection in the rope?"

"Possibly so, but possibly scratches made by the man's fingers as he tried desperately to loosen the noose."

"Of course."

My second mouthful of Mild Amber tasted more bitter.

A peal of laughter went up from a table at the far end of the bar, next to the bay window overlooking the street. The pebble glass was steaming up with the heat and turkey breath of so many bodies enclosed inside. Added to which the fireplace emitted an oven-like blast. We had been shivering walking up from The Swan and now we were warm as toast. I unwound my scarf and coiled it into my hat. Holmes took the muffs from his ears, which looked absurd anyway. I was suddenly aware of the trio of men huddled over the table by the window staring at us. Perhaps in our tweeds we stood out conspicuously, or they had picked up on our London accents.

"Something tells me they don't like strangers round these parts," I whispered behind my moustache, whilst smiling in their direction good-naturedly.

"Imagine if we were a different color, Watson."

I turned to look at Holmes but was distracted as I heard the door open and close. The gust of icy wind brought in Dr. Girai, the removal of his own scarf and hat soon revealing a grin. Only we knew the trepidation that lurked behind it and the inner resolve it took to bring him. He moved through the boisterous crowd, edging between tightly packed chairs. A few people slapped him on the arm or back in greeting, others shook his hand with gusto. Jokes were exchanged—well-wishing in any case—of the most benign and warm-hearted kind. I pulled out a chair for him to sit between us.

"These are my friends." Said as if to convince himself.

Holmes poured him water from a pitcher.

"Nothing can happen in the public glare," I said. "As long as you are here, with us, you can be in no danger."

"Not until the First Footers arrive." Holmes looked at his watch, then squinted at the clock behind the bar.

"You talk as if you know who these dashed First Footers are."

"I know it's an ancient Scots belief imported to England, to do with the first person to step over the threshold on January the first. A wholly benign folk belief, as far as I am aware. Though I am prepared to have that presumption repudiated."

Dr. Girai's hand on his glass of water was trembling. "I feel I am on the battlefield once more."

"Watson has his service revolver, and he has your back."

A cove with the complexion of a butcher stood up and gave a hale rendition of some traditional folk ballad of Merrie Old England whilst swinging a tankard fore and aft. Something about Robin Hood being a forester good, and the merry greenwood, "where the wild deer did follow". Here a number of locals joined in, equally heartily, "none being so bonny and blithe and gay", et cetera, then "Little John with his courage so strong", finishing with the obligatory *Fol the rol the rido, and that's the time of day, O.*

"Time for a tipple," I said, thinking, if there was much more of that to endure, I would need it, and stepped across to the bar. "Same again, please." The publican was a long-nosed Scot who resembled an anguished collie. The booze must have been having an effect in the last three hours because the bottles seemed out of focus and my feet a little less steady than they had been. My eyes sharpened on a glass case with a large pike in it, and a long pole above the bar with a fishing net at one end. "Thank you."

The man stilled my hand as I slid the drinks towards me, advising me and my friends to sup up and absent ourselves. I asked what the deuce he meant, as it was a free country when I last looked. He warned me "as a friend" that it can get rowdy, that's all.

"I like rowdy."

"As may be, but I'd advise you to go home to your bed or I can't be responsible for the consequences."

"I appreciate your concern but I think we will stay. Now is the season to be merry, is it not?"

I reported the barman's dashed impudence when I returned to our table, seeing a faint smile play on Holmes's lips as he tucked his newly-lit pipe in the corner of his mouth.

The pub was heaving with drunkenness by half past eleven, when Holmes squeezed through the noisy throng to order our last round, returning shortly after with two whiskies to "chase away the hoar frost", as he put it.

Our fastidious client, in his immaculate pigeon-gray suit, was now silent, the strain of covering up his sense of fear rendering him mute.

"Courage," said I.

The clock edged towards the hour. All eyes were on it. As the minute hand met the other, not only did the clock itself chime but the bells of Holy Trinity rang out. A cheer went up, the customary exclamation resounding on the air as lips and cheeks were kissed.

"Happy New Year, Holmes."

"Happy New Year, Watson."

We shook hands with each other and with Dr. Girai.

Before we knew it, we were linking arms with complete strangers in the time-honored fashion as we belted out "Auld Lang Syne", after which Holmes uncoupled his elbow from mine as hurriedly as he could without appearing ungentlemanly, staring at his spats for a while before looking at me with a smile and returning to his pipe in the ashtray, which was in danger of extinguishing. The singing continuing around us, I struck a match and he accepted it graciously, blowing it out after it had done its job.

I chinked my glass against Dr. Girai's, but his mood did not appear to be lifted. I remembered the wording on the note and understood why. Holmes stared into mid-air, as intense as I had ever seen him. I opened my mouth to speak but he held up the flat of his hand.

The pub fell silent. My back straightened at the clarity with which I could suddenly hear a hand bell being rung in the street outside, in the manner of an approaching town crier.

"The First Footers are here!"

Noses pressed to the window panes. Excited whispers circulated and were just as quickly hushed. I did not know what to expect but the locals very obviously did. Their anticipation was palpable.

Two characters entered, in buckled shoes and with sleigh bells on their garters, causing a cheer louder than any that preceded it. They wore cloaks made of strips of paper, streamers trailing from their necks and waists. The smaller one, playing a button concertina, I thought to be affecting the appearance of Puck or the Fool. As he twirled, I saw dolls strung over his back in the manner of a rat catcher's haul. The taller, wearing a military tunic over his costume, eschewed the deafening hand bell to blow on a whistle pipe for attention.

"I am Valiant Soldier!"
"I am Little Man Jack!"
"He has nothing
But here is one with riches on his back . . ."

Further ribald cheering accompanied the entrance of Father Christmas—a stout lad of the parish pretending to look old. Bedecked in a long white nightshirt and scruffy top hat, he sported an unconvincing snowy beard and leant on a broomstick with holly and mistletoe coiled around it, his back noticeably humped.

"Here comes I, old Father Christmas
Christmas or Christmas not
I hope old Father Christmas will never be forgot
Roast beef, plum pudding and mince pie
Who do like that better than I?"

Here he turned to the publican, rattling a tambourine.

> *"A jug of your Christmas ale will make us merry, whistle,*
> *dance and sing*
> *Money in our pockets is a very fine thing!"*

Whereupon Valiant Soldier took a bucket from table to table, shaking it with every coin that was cast into it.

> *"Room, room, I say, and let King George come in!"*

Delighted hurrahs greeted the arrival of King George—*Saint* George, as far as I could tell, from the red cross upon his tabard—gold crown atop a plumed helmet with a visor as might befit a knight of yore. His clothes, over knitted chain mail, were sewn all over with different colored cambric slashed into ribands. He swung his wooden sword over the heads of the crowd, missing them by inches, but they found only hilarity in this.

> *"Here comes I, King George, King George, the man of*
> *courage bold*
> *With my sword and buckler I've won three crowns of old*
> *I slew the dragon and brought him to the slaughter*
> *And won a beauteous Queen—the King of Egypt's*
> *daughter."*

An "Oooooo!" from the audience was required, and received. They were enjoying this hugely, as I suspected they had done for decades, if not centuries. *And last year—what about* last *year?*

I stared across my drink at Dr. Girai, detecting that his chest was rising and falling heavily. With good reason.

"I now let old Turkey Snipe clear the way!"

Next to appear, in a rage and blur of tatters, was a man in fez, tin breastplate and cloak, his face daubed with blackface, no doubt created by the plentiful application of boot polish.

Dr. Girai's visage was pasted with a forced rictus. I could not blame him.

Holmes gripped his forearm, urging self-control and patience. I thought: How much patience could you expect from a tethered lamb?

"Here comes I, old Turkey Snipe!
Come from old Turkey land to fight!
I challenge thee, King George, King George, the man of courage bold
And if his blood be hot, I will soon make it cold!"

With gritted teeth I observed the 'Turk' drawing the biggest scimitar one could imagine, swishing it in the air, clashing his blade with that of the knight. A brief, choreographed scrap ensued, their weapons narrowly missing the regulars, who treated it all as great pantomime. Saint George, suddenly crying out in the throes of an extravagant death worthy of the stage at Drury Lane, staggered with the curved sword tucked under his armpit, till he lay dead on the scrubbed floorboards.

"Boo!" the audience roared as one, shaking their fists as the Turk held up his weapon in glory. Father Christmas pleaded:

"Is there no doctor to be found
To cure this man lyin' bleeding on the ground?"

Indeed, there was . . . as the final member of the six-man troupe made his dramatic entrance—a mystery wrapped all in black, his mask comprising of a white goat's skull, its horns curling back from the forehead in twin spirals, seven wooden tassels with beads made of seed hanging like a beard from its jaw.

By now my heart was thudding. I could not imagine what Dr. Girai's heart was doing. I could only think: Which of these players had entertainment in mind, and which had murder?

"I am Beelzebub, a doctor good,
And with my hand I can stop thy blood.
I have cured in England, I have cured in Spain.
And I am come to old England to cure again.
If he's got the itch, stitch, the palsy or the gout,
Or if the Old Man's in him, I'll soon fetch him out.
I cure the sick of ev'ry pain,
And raise the dead to life again."

Holmes leaned forward, paying rapt attention as the sinister figure opened a small doctor's bag—not dissimilar to my own—from which he produced a flask of cure-all medicine.

"This bottle I carries by my side

'Noints the collar bone of the neck, the temple of the eye
Rise up, Sir Knight and fight the Turk again!"

In comedic fashion The Doctor knelt and tried to revive the knight—with no success. Cue exasperation and laughter—but not from me. He peered into the bottle as if to spot something wrong, then hurried to *mein host*, who topped up his elixir with beer from a bottle.

"This calls for hop and stout
To drive the pus and poison out
My head's so big and my wit so small
I'm still the best man amongst ye all!"

Holmes remained inscrutable as The Doctor showed his knuckles to the Turkish Knight, whose sword scribed a figure of eight in the air before coming down, missing its target and instead slapping Father Christmas three times on the back, causing the old man's hump to explode with gifts in silvered paper and gold leaf, at which Valiant Soldier cried:

"Gold, frankincense and myrrh!
To tide you over till this time next year!
Huzzah! Huzzah! Huzzah!"

"Huzzah! Huzzah! Huzzah!" repeated the onlookers as Dr. Beelzebub knelt once more and pressed his bottle to the mouth of Saint George, who miraculously, this time, sprang to his feet, resurrected, and stood to face his enemy, his sword drawn and his dander up.

"So mind thy head and guard thy blow:
Mind thy eyes and face also!
Slasher, Slasher, dossent be too hot,
Before thou knowest who thou'st got!"

I turned my back as a well-rehearsed if clumsy fight was enacted, with a clashing of sticks according to rule, so many strokes above, so many below, more akin to a dance than combat.

I could read nothing into Holmes's expression and he gave no indication to me, or to our companion, as to what to do. I had never needed his direction so keenly. Yet, though my eyes bore into him, response came there none. We seemed to be in the eye of a storm—but *what* wretched storm, and who were we meant to fear?

The mood of the crowd lurched.

The Turkish Knight had dropped his sword, which Father Christmas picked up. The black-faced Turk then seized Saint George's. They twisted it this way and that, each champion gripping it with both hands, until finally Saint George wrenched the sword away and ran his opponent through.

Cheers hit the roof! The foe was vanquished!

Father Christmas delivered the inevitable moral coup de grace:

"Peace on earth, goodwill to men
The heart of Old England hath triumphed again!"

The action having reached its completion, the ragtag company then gave voice to "Here We Come a-Wassailing" which was taken up enthusiastically by the assembled.

Valiant Soldier circulated, rattling his bucket, as the mummers gathered at the bar to slake their thirsts with pints of foaming ale. Whereupon Father Christmas raised his tankard and gave a final toast:

"Hurrah for us, hurrah for you
For every day ahead
May blessings rain down from now henceforth
On every Christian head."

Christian head . . . that hammered a nail into my brain. Not least because of the Muslim sitting next to me.

The company took their bows and left the building to great cheers and applause which echoed long after they were gone and the draught from the door locked out.

Relieved to see the back of them, I clapped like everyone around me, looking over my shoulder at Holmes then Dr. Girai, thinking we had come an awfully long way for some warm beer and a mumming play. "The fun is over."

"The plan is thwarted." Dr. Girai said, rising to take his empty glass to the bar. "If there was a plan. Perhaps we were mad to think it so."

I was feeling the same sentiment when I saw Little Man Jack slip back into the room and hop up onto the bar, light as a feather. He stood erect with arms akimbo, shouting:

"We are six jolly Compton boys
Come to do our play
And when we have done our bit
THE BAD WE'LL TAKE AWAY!"

The last line barely had time to register before he'd reached up and taken down the fishing pole I'd seen earlier. In his fists, combined with the gleam in his eyes, it suddenly took on the aspect of a weapon.

In a split second I was on my feet, but it was already too late.

The pole whipped across the room, its net falling over the head of Dr. Girai, who was immediately yanked away from the bar, almost pulled off his feet, any cry which might have come from his throat curtailed in an instant. His fingers were grappling with the fiber of the netting, attempting to extricate himself from the trap while at the same time Little Man Jack hauled him towards the door where the Valiant Soldier, Saint George and Father Christmas waited eagerly.

My pint glass shattered as it hit the floor.

I rushed forward, but a sour-faced man with parentheses around his mouth as deep as gouge-marks fastened onto my arm and bent it back. Another kicked the legs from under me.

God knows how but I held onto my footing—fixed upon the wide-eyed shock in Dr. Girai's face as he was flown across the room to the exit. It felt as though a hundred people barred my way. The swell was against me. A wall.

The entire pub was chanting in unison.

"Out! Out! Out! Out!"

His body was borne aloft like a flimsy boat on a raging sea, transported at shoulder height towards the costumed mummers, out into the ice-cold of night. Many followed in an exuberant and hideous flow. Those who stayed began thumping on the tables.

"Kill the wren! Kill the wren! Kill the wren!"

I punched my assailant in the jaw. He soon let go of me and found himself half in the fire. The other individual felt his forehead connect with the table top and that put paid to him. Where was Holmes? Not beside me as I would have expected. I spun around.

His chair was empty. Had he given chase already? *Impossible.* He could not have got past me without my noticing. Then I saw a figure sprawled on the floor.

"Holmes!"

I dropped to one knee. Cradled his head. His eyes were closed. He was dead. *God in heaven!*

I told myself to calm down. Quickly took the pulse in his wrist. Though it was erratic, he was alive—but unconscious. My relief was overwhelming. But this was no time for resting on my laurels.

I shot a glance to the door, which lay ajar. My choice was horrible; whether to speed after the mob and do what I could to save the doctor, or tend to my lifelong and closest friend.

In an instant I knew what my decision had to be. Holmes would have taken it unflinchingly. He was unconscious. Dr. Girai, however, was facing the same fate as his murdered brother—of that I was certain. And neither the detective nor I could allow that to pass. I almost heard Holmes in my ear. *Go, now!*

I elbowed past some ineffective men and women whose limbs tried to form some kind of resistance.

The cold wash of night air hit me like a club. Bubbles and baubles seemed to be washing around inside my skull. I blinked away snowflakes and snowballs, but there was nothing in the air but spiky needles of hail.

Was I imagining it or was the hand bell sounding? Yes, it was, and I could hear the trilling of the tambourine and tin whistle in accompaniment, together with the constant repetition of the horrid ululation I had heard in the pub:

"Kill the wren! Kill the wren! Kill the wren!"

I darted glances right and left. The top of the street curved away towards the Hall, and I dimly perceived the last of the stragglers heading in that direction.

My twisted arm felt broken. I was sure it wasn't, but the pain had spread to my shoulder and neck. My fingers could barely close around my pistol, but I was dashed if I was going to allow my body to let me down when an innocent man's life was at stake.

The wrought iron gates to the Hall lay wide. The residents of Compton Lydiard trailed after the mummers, lacking only candles to resemble a pious Easter parade. The flock had already wended their way down the drive and across the lawn towards the woods. Luckily, none of them was looking back, or they would have seen a loping individual dogging their progress.

Within the copse, branches were too overhung and meshed together to enable moonlight to intrude, but ahead I could see it illuminate a clearing—bathed in sea green, cerulean, fluttering teal—seemingly chosen for a purpose. As soon as they reached there, the music abruptly stopped.

So did I. Almost thinking they might hear my breath. Ridiculous thought, because the hate-filled taunting continued undiminished.

"Kill the wren! Kill the wren! Kill the wren!"

I clung to the dank trunk of a wintry oak. It shielded me, should any of them look back, and gave me stability as the earth swung to and fro. The Mild Amber had been more potent—*much* more potent—than I thought. But my perception was not so compromised that I had the luxury of doubting what was happening, though I should have liked to reject it with every fiber of my being.

"Kill the wren! Kill the wren! Kill the wren!"

The townsfolk gathered in a circle, linking arms much the same way as they had done during "Auld Lang Syne". Skipping and dancing, Little Man Jack had relinquished the fishing net. Now another pole stood erect, a roughly hewn tree trunk, its summit hacked into a bifurcated V in the manner of a hazel walking stick. Over this head had been strung a thick rope, at the far end of which Father Christmas, Valiant Soldier and the publican from The Beehive heaved as if in a ghastly game of tug-of-war. At the other end, a weight was lifted.

A man's feet left the ground, kicking madly. The suited figure with shiny shoes and a dangling fob watch was that of Dr. Arshad Girai, a knot under one ear and a noose around his neck. Having manhandled him to the spot, Saint George and The Turk—his pink-rimmed eyes staring out from blackface—gazed up at him.

"Kill the wren! Kill the wren! Kill the wren!"

Dr. Beelzebub, all swathed in black, raised his arms aloft, basking in the obedience of his clan. Here was the ringleader, whose chest was swelling with perverse accomplishment as their victim was hauled higher up the stripped oak.

Even in the gloom I could see in the dentist's bulging eyes the realization that the worst of his imaginings was true—and it might be the last thought he ever had before entering Jannah, the Islamic abode of the righteous.

"Damn you!"

I spoke it before thinking it, and found myself staggering into the clearing with my pistol arm outstretched, the other sweeping branches of thorn and briar from my path.

Some of them turned. Some did not. I could not care about that. My job was to stop them. My first bullet went wide, but at least it caused some to duck, some to bleat or squawk, and for the rope to waver.

Valiant Soldier and Father Christmas clung onto it. The doctor's legs were still shuddering and, as I got closer, I fancied I saw his tongue protruding between his teeth. I let loose another round, knowing my aim was less than accurate as I was moving apace—charging at them, in fact.

A gout of red spurted from Valiant Soldier's bicep. He tottered back into shadows, as did the others, when faced with a loaded revolver and an angry assailant. Father Christmas alone—absurd in his false beard and feathered hat—tried to wrestle with the counterweight, but gave up as my barrel trained squarely on his face, backing away with his hands up.

Even as I heard the dull thud as Dr. Girai landed, crumpled on the ground just feet away from me, I heard a sound to my left and spun around.

The black-faced Turk had drawn his scimitar. There was time only for me to see the oily pinkness of his lips when, to my shock, he hurled the weapon in the air, to be caught by someone behind me. I felt the long, curved blade pressed to my throat.

A piercing whistle cut through the mist.

I took it first of all to be a note from the First Footers' pipe, but its searing persistence soon enabled me to identify it differently.

Policemen burst from the surrounding foliage. In my dazed state I imagined there were thousands but there must've been merely dozens. That was enough.

Bullets flew. I found myself whisked back to the battle of Maiwand.

The lawmen meant business. I was glad of it. How were they there? I had no idea, but I did not want to question it lest they disappear in a puff of smoke. The rest of this business had been like a pantomime, why not they?

Whoever had hold of me dragged me backwards into the surrounding thickets. I tried to dig my heels in the dirt to slow him down. Dragged off my feet and half-throttled, I nevertheless had time to see the fez knocked from the head of The Turk as the police wrestled him to the ground. The pink bald pate above the blackface was unmistakable—Fred Vigar, proprietor of The Swan and local bobby. Behind him I saw Father Christmas, divested of fake beard—the vicar of Holy Trinity, Reverend Kirkbright. And beyond that, Saint George, writhing from the grip of the arresting officers as they clipped him in handcuffs . . . Inspector Lestrade tore the makeshift helmet from the man's head to reveal the tousled head of Timothy Pettitt, the teacher—shaking his curly mane with as defiant an expression of insouciant malice as I ever saw in the dock at the Old Bailey.

Lestrade?

—Could it be? Was I going mad?

Just as I thought this, branches closed over my vision as I was bustled into the undergrowth, my last image being the ill-lit clearing as the coppers rushed about, pinning the rest of the criminals to the ground. Amidst all the chaos—a terrible, still center—the body of Dr. Girai was not moving.

The sight of this lit a fuse in my heart and I whirled upon my opponent, sending the scimitar spinning away into the dark. Suddenly, instead of him having control over me, it was my weight pressing his to the grass, my thighs straddling his hips and the heels of my hands pressing down on his shoulders.

I stared down at the goat-skulled mask of Dr. Beelzebub. Its beaded beard shook from side to side as he squirmed under me. I tore it off.

The face beneath was my own. I first of all thought I had drawn the curtain back from a mirror—but no, these were not my eyes, these were the eyes of a dying thing. And the skin, how could I have thought it *skin*?

The surface before me was rippling as if something, no, several things, were eager to get out. I had seen an infestation in the East when an insect had lain eggs under a soldier's epidermis, and this was the same, the toxicity gathering in taut, hard blisters before bursting and cracking, letting out pus the color of egg yolk. The lips, the eyes, the whole face was malformed by these suppurating buboes, from which centipedes emerged into the light and crawled and scurried.

I could not move.

The human face, if it ever was human, was transformed. Great tusks, duplicating the sweeping goat horns on his head, were now growing from the mouth, twisted and spiraling. And yet the thing laughed . . . *It laughed!*

Sensing my abject terror, the creature lunged out and gripped me by the scruff of the neck, throwing me off, then getting up and hoisting me to my feet. I found myself nose to nose with the unspeakable entity. A cloud of flies formed a corrupt and obscene halo around Dr. Beelzebub's head. The symbol of Resurrection in the mummer's play was now a fetid symbol of death.

"Doctor, heal thyself."

Beelzebub reached inside his cloak and extracted a service revolver not unlike my own. Mirror upon mirror. He pressed the barrel to my forehead. But in the gap he had revealed I could see a checkered waistcoat, and some unfailing part of my brain cogitated: Demons to my knowledge do not wear checkered waistcoats, therefore this was a man. I grabbed said waistcoat. Said gun fired—but its bullet went wide of the mark. If anything, serving only to alert the forces against him.

A volley of police gunfire took chunks out of the bark of a tree inches from us. I instinctively wrapped myself in a ball, and when I had uncoiled, I could see, in a swish of his black cloak, the pantomime devil had disappeared through the trapdoor. I could hear Lestrade dimly—*so dimly*—uttering my name. I felt his reassuring hand on my arm. I pushed him aside, apologizing, as I emptied my stomach contents onto a holly bush. Not the best way to decorate a tree at Christmastide.

Shivering, I looked down into my tightly closed hand. It opened to reveal a button.

"Holmes?" I asked in a dismal croak. "Is Holmes alive?"

I did not like that Lestrade took so very, very long to answer. I think that consolidated my body's decision to collapse in a heap.

*

"The First Footers of Compton Lydiard were simply a gross distortion of an age-old superstition," pronounced Holmes, lighting his pipe from a tautly-screwed stick of newspaper touched to the licking flames in the grate at 221B Baker Street. "You can find the Wren Boys as a tradition in Ireland, England and the Isle of Man. Originally, the hunt for the wren involved a real wren, kept alive in a pitchfork with a net over it until its sacrifice on St Stephen's Day or Twelfth Night. Over the years, this was replaced with a stuffed 'wren' stuck on a tall, decorated pole. Bands and parades became part of the festivities, and money collected by a troop of 'straw boys' would be given to charity or to fund a 'Wren Ball' later in January. To all intents and purposes, it was a midwinter sacrifice, the wren being symbolic of the past year."

"The ancient idea of replenishment by blood," I said. "John Barleycorn is dead, and all that."

"The origin of mummers, on the other hand, is too obscure for anyone to offer a definitive explanation." The detective sank into the cushions arranged on his armchair and crossed his long legs. "No doubt it originated in a solar myth: that is to say, it bears some relation to the astronomical order and the nature of the calendar, but it appears to have come to us from the East. In the Hindi Jatras, or birth tales, we find the counterpart of the English Miracle Play, only older by many centuries. However, once transported to England, it becomes a seasonal opportunity for poorly-paid laborers to make extra income by taking their play around the houses of local farmers and gentry where they habitually receive food, drink and money in return for their efforts.

"There are many elements in mumming-lore, both pagan and Christian, and the narrative and characters have changed little from generation to generation. The Turkish Knight killed by Saint George and revived by the Doctor would seem a constant—though in Compton Lydiard the resurrection was reversed, for reasons a folklorist might be interested to explore.

"At any rate, each village would have its own version, kept alive by ordinary people who had an interest in being able to supplement their wages once a year, with liquor flowing and lots of sore heads in the morning. My research has informed me that in certain places in Wiltshire—" Holmes lifted a small book from the table at his elbow and read from a page singled out with a bookmark. ". . . 'great enjoyment was to be had going from house to house on the morning of Christmas Day, acting out a drama of St George' . . . This in Wooton Bassett, and not dissimilar in Avebury . . . 'we perambulated around the town for all we could get, acted the drama, followed by a hymn'. Always the same script, or variation of. The wooden sword representing the mythic 'good old times' of Olde England that, outside the fabrication of the simple-minded, were never objectively good."

I looked across at Dr. Arshad Girai, his skin reddened by the glow of the firelight. With his scarf tucked under his chin, and his overcoat still on, he looked a different man that night than the one I had seen four weeks previously, swinging from a makeshift gibbet. His stillness and contemplation gave the illusion of recovery, but I knew he could no more be recovered—*resurrected*—from his ordeal than I was. Or Holmes was, for that matter.

On New Year's Day I had woken in a hospital bed, my stomach having been pumped. The hallucinatory delirium had continued to hit me in waves, reality taking a beating every time it tried to assert itself, but sleep in the end won. I drew strength only in the fact that the nurses—sometimes covered in rupturing sores, sometimes horned—never let go of my hand. Nor did my wife. Holmes lay in the bed opposite. Not even he had anticipated the beer would be drugged. Now we could comfort ourselves that both the local pharmacist and the publican of The Beehive were incarcerated—alongside Timothy Pettitt, Fred Vigar, Reverend Kirkbright, and two others we did not recognize; 'Little Man Jack' Harry Hudgell and 'Valiant Soldier' Peter Thirkettle. Dozens of other charges of aiding and abetting were pending.

It had hit me badly, and Holmes himself was uncharacteristically shaken. What disturbed him on a fundamental level was how an educated man like Pettitt had arrived at the cruel and unnatural belief that certain races were inferior to others. It is a truism that such pernicious views are motivated by fear, but the sheer will required by an individual to pervert a longstanding tradition into something that would enable and encourage such hateful violence was nothing short of extraordinary.

"The eradication of an unwanted presence," as Holmes put it bluntly, "with only the flag of tradition to justify it."

"They revere Saint George." I recalled the red cross on the figure's tabard, the insignia of England itself. "Without the slightest knowledge that Saint George himself was a Turk!"

"When fear is at large, people select the details that suit them." Holmes wrapped a shawl around his shoulders, his shivers perhaps the tail-end of his brush with death. "I unearthed a clipping from the Wiltshire Times. Five years ago, the bones of a dog and a sheep were found in a cave behind the factory. In past times the sacrifice was a wren, then more recently an animal, then a man. There was a deep-seated belief in this community that a blood ritual would purge them of ills.

Whether they were faced with a tough winter, a failing crop, dwindling employment, financial hardship . . ."

"The silver coin, the piece of coal, the piece of wood," I remembered. "Though why the killing of a Black man confers good luck, I have no idea."

"It was the way he got the population to do what he wanted," said Dr. Girai with absolute clarity and exemplary restraint. "He told them my presence was what caused everything bad. He didn't even need to say it. They knew. White people know. He just offered them the actions to put it right."

Holmes did not move. For once in our long acquaintanceship, I thought that he could not muster a reply, but after a while he did.

"They can harm you no longer."

"And the town?" I asked.

"Will pay the price," said Holmes. "The name Compton Lydiard will become synonymous with hatred forever. If it shall die because of that, because of the sickness at the root of its soul, perhaps it is fitting."

Without any pleasure, Dr. Girai let his head slump. He examined the fingers of his thick woolen gloves.

"Thank you."

"Not at all. Thank the fellow beside you. Luckily his constitution is more robust than mine, therefore the effect of the drug we were given less pronounced. Come, come, Watson. Don't blush. You saved this man's life."

"Hardly. Lestrade's men had as much to do with it."

"I have written to the Inspector to express my gratitude," said our client, extracting an envelope from his pocket. "And this I would like to give to you, to express the same. To both of you. I . . . I find it easier to express myself in writing."

"So do I." I admitted.

Holmes's grunt reminded me he read every word that appeared in *The Strand*, though he refused to admit it. He rose and placed the envelope on the mantelshelf, weighing it down with a jade Buddha.

"You have been the best of England, but they I cannot forget, nor forgive." The Indian gentleman's sentiments were entirely valid. "She lost her husband. She looks over her shoulder with every step. I desire nothing but to give my fiancée a happy and safe home."

"You are to be wed? To Nusrat?"

"Evidently, Watson. Congratulations."

"She acts as my assistant now, back in Birmingham. I see her studying to become a dentist herself, in time. She has a rare interest in pain-free extraction." He offered a smile and I was very glad to mirror it, slapping my knees.

"Well, I hope to visit you one day."

Dr. Girai bowed his head shyly, then met my eyes with the firmness I knew dwelt there. "With great respect, sir, I know you will not. This must end now, or I fear the wounds will never heal, and I have my future wife and children to consider."

I took the blow on the chin. "It is a matter of immeasurable sadness that you feel like that. But I understand."

"I do not believe you can, sir."

Not wishing to embellish upon that thought, our guest stood up and shook our hands. As he did so, I saw his scarf slip down slightly, giving me a view of the rope burn scar that ran from behind his left ear to the line of his jaw. I guessed it would eventually become a discoloration, easily mistaken for a birthmark, but to use his own words—*never forgotten, never forgiven.*

Dr. Arshad Girai let himself out, but it was minutes after the closing of the front door before either of us spoke, and it was me.

"What a fool I am." I'd spotted the feather still on Holmes's examination table next to the microscope. "It never symbolized cowardice. It symbolized whiteness. The bait, to be as we are. To be accepted."

"You are never a fool, Watson. Far from it. Surely you do not think I would tolerate you if you were?"

"That's true." I crossed the room and stoked the fire from the coal scuttle, encouraging it with a few prods of the poker. "We didn't tell him about the real ringleader. The one that got away."

"I can see no benefit in him knowing the greater truth."

Holmes had already revealed to me that from the moment Dr. Girai had told his story, he'd immediately linked it to other assaults upon and murders of dark-skinned people all across the country. Without my knowledge, he had been working with Lestrade over several months, discovering that in every instance of violent attack, the codename "Beelzebub" had appeared in small advertisements and incendiary literature, yet the person or persons behind it proved impossible to identify; with typical cowardice, such extremists invariably hide their malice behind anonymity. Therefore, Holmes knew all along the scale of the enemy he was up against, and that Dr. Girai's brother was far from an isolated case. With this in mind, he'd arranged for Lestrade and a troop of Scotland

Yard's finest to be at Compton Lydiard in numbers. *When the bugle calls, he answers.*

"I curse that I had that creature in my hands and let him slip away."

"My dear fellow, you are too hard on yourself. When you were found, you were clutching a shank button of an unusual lion and unicorn design. Thanks to that and a plaster cast of a footprint made at the scene, I can safely predict Lestrade will be striding into the House of Lords tomorrow to clap in irons one of our peers of the realm. You may not read about the arrest in the *Pall Mall Gazette* or the *Union Jack*, but rest assured the gentleman will do prison time for the hateful acts he had inculcated. However, the festering poison behind those acts will not be so easy to quell. 'Dr. Beelzebub' may have many faces, many masks. Its evil seethes under the veil of civility, but we must rip away that veil and look it squarely in the face. If we do not, we do our fellow citizens—of whatever creed or color—a disservice. There is a Devil out there in the land, Watson, and we must all be vigilant lest he takes hold."

Observing the time, I solemnly retrieved my hat and coat, urging Holmes to remind Mrs. Hudson I would not be breakfasting at Baker Street, as I had an engagement with my wife's family to watch her cousins playing football. One was, by all accounts, rather fearless at the goal mouth. I could tell he wasn't listening.

"Purity of race is an absurd fallacy." He arranged test tubes in a rack. "I have French blood in my veins and it makes me no less a Briton. William the Conqueror did not destroy the land but built upon it. We are a mongrel nation, always have been, and all the better for it."

Holmes watched me strangely as I buttoned up and pulled on my gloves. I remarked how beautiful it was to see snowflakes dancing outside the window. Without looking, he sat at his desk and said he estimated the temperature to have dropped by two degrees in the last half hour.

"Well. Quite."

He looked up at me intently again with an air of faint examination, then his features broke into an unexpected smile as he chewed on his pipe stem. "Difference is richness, Watson."

"Indeed so, indeed so." I stroked my moustache. "Goodnight, Holmes."

"Goodnight, old chap."

I confess, that night, as I walked home with my walking cane making holes in the layer of precipitation that was thickening, eager to take in the fresh night air and the soft flurry it carried so romantically, and more eager still to return to the bosom of my dearly beloved family, I found, in spite of the unforgiving cold, a contentment within me that made it feel as warm as a summer's day.

EBONSTONE

James A. Moore

The waves crashed against the rocks as they had for as long as anyone could recall, and the sounds thundered along the shoreline, unrelenting and uncaring. From a distance the coastline near Ebonstone was unforgiving, and from closer in it was just as harsh, with the rain pouring down as it had the night before, the week before, seemingly ever and always, cold and unrelenting. It was the time of year when the landscape seemed particularly brutal, and most everyone stayed inside if they could avoid going out into the cold and damp, the merciless winds and the torrential downpours.

Ebonstone, near Barnsleigh, was not a place fit for man nor beast in the autumn months, but both sorts of creatures still lived there, regardless.

The Church of All Saints was the tallest building in the area. Built in the eleven hundreds, it had withstood the test of time for seven long centuries, a dark edifice of locally quarried stone, built to the glory of God Almighty and built to endure, standing in the same spot for those many years with few changes. It still stood, though abandoned for use sometime in the previous century, having been proclaimed unfit for its original purpose. Now, it crouched silently in the dark, a darker shadow, though somehow faded, and very nearly forgotten despite its size.

Still, at certain times, lights were seen to spill from the narrow windows and, on rare occasions, some local would claim it to be haunted. Ghostly illuminations were spotted in the western tower, sickly lights that were too pale in color and flickered wildly. It was on just such a night that the Dodsworth family disappeared from their home at the edge of Ebonstone proper. The Dodsworth family was not wealthy. Father Roger and sons Lewis and Mark all labored in the coal mines, and daughter Lurene, in keeping with local tradition, was preparing to start at the same menial task after her next birthday, although with duties limited to the surface.

All that we knew of the situation was what we were told in the letter from Lucius Ellison, the brother of Winnifred Dodsworth, the wife of the aforementioned Roger. It was his letter that invited the notice of Sherlock Holmes, and it was Holmes, of course, who brought me along on this latest investigation.

*

We arrived in Ebonstone fully two days after the letter reached us, and though he spoke little about the case while underway, I knew Holmes well enough to know that the case presented curious features that had fully engaged his attention.

Six people had been abducted from their home in the middle of the night. There were obvious signs of a struggle but no one had made any demands of any sort regarding the safe return of the missing family. They'd have managed very little by way of recompense in any event, as the family had little by way of a fortune, save the house they lived in, from which they had been taken by force.

Lucius Ellison met us at the train station, prepared to serve as our escort to the scene of the abduction. He was a thin man with the nervous habit of almost constantly wringing his hands together. His graying hair was carefully swept across the top of his head in an effort to hide a growing thin spot, and his clothes, though meticulously repaired, showed signs of long use. The worry lines were etched into his features, and his dark eyes shone with a nearly feverish intensity. "Mister Holmes, Doctor Watson. I'm very pleased to make your acquaintance."

The man had a surprisingly strong grip for a fellow with such a timid expression, and though most would have missed it, I spied the slip of paper he pressed into my friend's hand as they shook in greeting. He got no further than a simple introduction before Holmes expressed his desire to see the residence from which Ellison's sister and her family had been forcibly removed. By the time we clambered onto a waiting dogcart, moments later, the paper had been secreted into Holmes's coat pocket, to be studied at his leisure, with none the wiser.

The cottage in question was small, but well kept, or at least it had been before the abduction. Holmes climbed from the cart with care, and studied the exterior of the structure carefully, not speaking at all as he crouched near the threshold of the front door and then studied the ground at each window.

The glass had been broken in two of the three windows, and the door itself had been forced open, as small chips and scratches showed where something had been used to pry at the stout wood.

"Mister Ellison, do all of the buildings in this area employ such strong locks?" Holmes looked to our host as he spoke, his eyes studying the man's demeanor.

Ellison, for his part, looked surprised by the question. "Strong locks? What do you mean?"

"The door itself is well made, but the locking mechanism on the door is much sturdier than I would expect in an area like this. The mechanism is top of the line, and I'd expect to see it on a manor house rather than a cottage of this size."

Ellison frowned. "I've never given it much consideration. Roger has always had a mind for security, I suppose. There have been occasional thefts, of course. It happens everywhere these days, but I seldom visited my sister and, I have to say, never paid the lock any notice."

Holmes stared at the man for a moment and then looked at the door again. I looked with him, perplexed by his questioning. The lock was, indeed, a very secure-looking piece. Heavy iron with surprising thickness, and the door itself was, as previously mentioned, very stout and durable. Much more suited to defending a larger structure.

"Did your sister or her husband have any enemies that you know of? Had there been threats against them from any of their neighbors?"

"Not that I ever heard of Mister Holmes. And this is a small community, I would have heard of any feuds long before it became necessary for them to defend their home from ruffians."

"It is curious." Holmes looked at the ground and frowned. "How long ago were they taken?"

"It's been five days, I believe. I wrote to you as soon as I heard about the situation."

"Why me? Why not wait for the local authorities to handle their investigation?"

Ellison looked uncomfortable when asked, and he frowned. Not far away a small gathering of locals was doing their very best to appear indifferent to the conversation. They were likely fishermen, as they did not bear the look of miners. One of them, possibly the largest man I had seen in my entire life, stepped nearer and interjected the words, "We aren't like London here, I'm afraid. We have no police force. There's little by way of crime aside from an occasional squabble between neighbors. Most everything has always been handled by a consensus of neighbors, and occasionally by the office of the watchman, but our Nigel Penford, our watchman, disappeared a few months ago and has yet to be replaced."

The man loomed over Holmes, moving closer while the fellows with him remained a short distance away. He had heavily wind-weathered skin and hair that had been bleached by long exposure to the sun. His gray eyes studied Holmes with the same sort of alertness I usually saw from the master detective himself, offering a quick, hard scrutiny before he decided to offer a warm smile. That he was the leader of this group would have been evident even if he had not spoken. He had a presence about him that was the sort to draw the eye. Though he was brutish in form, he walked with the rolling gait of a man accustomed to long hours on turbulent water, a sort of uncanny grace that always made me think of cats and their ability to land on their feet.

"Indeed?" Holmes offered a quick appraisal and smile of his own.

That he recognized Sherlock Holmes was evident, and the smile he offered was also rather like a cat's, neutral and bordering on predatory. "I'm afraid so. I expect we were all hoping he'd simply come back to us. There's hardly any crime out here aside from an occasional fight between neighbors. We've coal miners and fishermen and little else in Ebonstone." The man frowned and shook his head. "What is there to see?"

Holmes remained calm and pointed to the ground at his feet. "By the looks of things quite a bit. I know you've had rain for a few days now, and much of the exterior evidence I'd have liked to see was washed away, but shall we look inside the cottage for a moment?"

Curiosity aroused, the large man stepped aside and gestured for Holmes to continue. If my friend found the man at all threatening, he hid it well. Ellison did not. He was worried about the stranger, and it was evident in the man's every move.

Despite the damage to the front door, it seemed as if no one had been inside since the night of the break in. A large collection of muddied prints marred the small rug at the threshold of the cottage, and Holmes moved into the small home carefully, examining every detail as he went. His eyes seemed to be everywhere at once, and he touched different surfaces carefully, even stopping to sniff at a few areas, seeking clues that even after years as his associate I would have missed easily.

"There are footprints from no less than ten people here," he remarked. "Different shoes, different boots, and all of them tracking in mud from the poor weather. It was very obviously raining the night your family was abducted." Holmes spoke to Ellison, ignoring the larger man's presence with astonishing ease. If the stranger was offended, he hid it well. He also remained outside of the cottage.

Holmes moved to the window to the right of the front door and pointed without touching. "At least two people climbed through this window." He paused and very carefully examined several strands of fabric caught on the edge of the windowsill. He looked at them without speaking, and then plucked them from the sill before placing them in a clean handkerchief, that he then folded and replaced in his coat pocket. "Once again there is mud and a print from a boot heel. There are several more tracks under the window, and evidence of at least one person bleeding." He pointed to a small droplet on the hardwood floor. "Judging by the way the blood fell, I believe the wound must have occurred inside the cottage and bled as someone was either leaving or being forcibly removed."

Holmes frowned and grew silent as he continued looking. He spent an additional ten minutes examining each of the small rooms in the house before moving back outside. By then the rest of the strangers had gathered again and the large man had retreated a distance, but all of them remained near enough to listen, if they were so inclined.

"There is no doubt that your family was taken by force, Mister Ellison." Holmes frowned and looked around the area, but there was little to see beyond a small garden that had been trampled thoroughly, very likely on the night when the Dodsworths were stolen away. Beyond the garden patch there was a small copse of trees, a hedge and, in the distance, the Church of All Saints.

The weather threatened rain, with dark clouds moving in on a strong breeze from the shoreline scarcely a half mile distant. Ellison frowned as he looked at the church's silhouette against the gathering gloom.

When I looked again, the fishermen, if they were fishermen, were headed off on their own, and the big man was laughing at a comment I did not overhear.

"Who is your friend, Mister Ellison?"

Ellison stared after the departing group and frowned. He looked worried. "Captain Arthur Wade. He owns the fishing fleet around here, and runs the wharf besides. In his time, he's hunted whales and served in the Royal Navy." The man frowned and shook his head. "We barely know each other," he confessed.

"Are you a churchgoing man, Mister Ellison?" Holmes nodded towards the dark tower, and my eyes were drawn there as well.

"I attend services, Mister Holmes, but not in that old pile. It's been derelict for as long as I can remember."

Holmes nodded and asked, "And does your Captain Wade attend your church?"

"I've never seen him in attendance."

"Do you know why the church was shut down?"

"I can't say for certain. All I know is that the old church is sealed tight and not used any longer."

Holmes said nothing, but he nodded, his gaze intently fixed on the church in the distance.

Ellison took us to an inn, where we were to stay, an establishment offering rooms and meals adjoined to a pub called the Eel and Gull. Holmes and Ellison settled on a time to meet the next day and we parted company from the anxious man with little else said. My friend was already thinking his way through all of the details he had absorbed since our arrival in Ebonstone. It was not until we'd settled down to a meal of roast mutton that Holmes finally decided to confide in me.

"He's nervous, our Mister Ellison." Holmes spoke softly, so as not to catch the unwanted attention of the other patrons around us. There were only a few, but most everyone in the room had eyed us with great curiosity as we seemed the only strangers in town at the time. The people around us were not coal miners, and despite the appearance of Wade and his followers, the fishing boats had only begun coming in when we settled down to our meal.

"What makes you say so?"

"He constantly wrings his hands, and his demeanor is not that of a man comfortable with his surroundings. Whatever happened at his sister's house, he is very worried about something similar taking place again."

"A nervous habit, to be sure, Holmes, but hardly indicative of more than a bad case of anxiety over his sister's disappearance, is it?"

Holmes cut another slice of the meat on his plate and contemplated his words carefully.

"It's more than that, I think. Did you see the way he studied the church?"

"Not particularly, no. If I'm being honest, I was too busy noting the way you were looking at it."

"Ellison said it's shuttered and has been for a long time, but I think we shall need a closer look all the same, should we get a chance. Our guide was not looking at the building as one studies a closed and abandoned structure, but rather with a worried intensity that something might well be amiss." He paused long enough to chew on a bit of roast. We'd had a long journey up and the meal was a welcome respite. Finally, he said, "The many footprints leaving the cottage moved through the small garden, I'm sure you noticed that."

"Yes, I did."

"The only thing of note in that direction is the church. I observed that much when we arrived. There were no other houses or buildings nearby. While I expect Ellison is right, and the church has long been closed down, the signs of struggle point to all parties heading in that direction. There wasn't much to go on. The rain had washed most of the telltale evidence from the scene, but there was enough damage to the garden; and the small fence around it, at the relevant side, had been thoroughly trampled." I had not noticed the fence at all, but I've no doubt if Holmes said there was a fence, it was there, and that it had been crushed down by a small mob's worth of people inarguable. "All of the signs remaining told me the family had been taken in that direction. Perhaps to the church itself or to a waiting conveyance. In any event, we need a closer look."

The rains were harsh, and the weather did not look like it would be getting better during the night. Though there was little by way of lightning or thunder, a proper storm was brewing. Regardless, shortly after we finished our meal we headed out, hats lowered and collars raised against the downpour. Acquiring a lantern was easy enough, we borrowed one from the innkeeper, and made our way to the church.

At the church, all was quiet and dark. There was no one about that we could see, and the doors were firmly locked and chained shut. I did my best to keep an eye out for possible trouble while Holmes made his investigations. Within a few minutes of our arrival, he had managed to pick the lock on the door leading to the vestibule and we slipped inside the old building. I didn't ask Holmes why he decided to gain entry. I merely had to see the condition of the lock to understand that we were not the first to find a way inside. The evidence of previous efforts to bypass the need for a key were obvious.

The silence within was very nearly oppressive. I don't say it lightly, but there was a presence to the building that did not sit well with me. It wasn't merely the darkness or the storm. It was a pressure within the structure, like gathering clouds before nature vents her fury. The air was damp. And the smell of mildew was prevalent. Though I have no doubt that religious icons had once been present on the walls, it was a church after all, there were no symbols of Christianity to be found within the darkened halls and any furnishings that might once have rested within the place had long since been removed.

Holmes examined the floors carefully. Heavy scuff marks and trails of mud were obvious on the old sandstone floors of the great structure. Though there were patterns carved into the floor, they were obscured by shadows and hidden beneath layers of mud and dust accumulated over decades, or possibly even centuries of neglect.

In the farthest western corner of the church, lost in shadows and placed almost as an afterthought, it seemed, there was a carved altar. It was the only furnishing that we could see. Holmes said nothing as he approached it, and I followed along in silence, our footsteps echoing in the darkness.

The altar was wide and long, rising some three feet from the floor, and obviously heavy enough that several people would be required to bring it inside the building. Holmes seemed to read my mind. He said, "This was built here, Watson. It's too wide to pass through the doors of the church." He added "Hornbeam, near as solid as a stone wall." As we got closer Holmes gestured me forward and indicated where he wanted me to hold the lantern I carried. I obliged, of course, letting the light wash over the altar's surface. The wood was carefully, skillfully carved, and put together with obvious craftsmanship, though since the times when it was built it seemed the piece had been neglected. Dark stains washed the wooden surface, having long since discolored any finish there might have been on the heavy surface.

Neither of us spoke, both fully aware that this altar has been used for blood sacrifices and more than once over the years. Then Holmes added, "I see no symbols here, and that's rather telling."

"It is?"

"Most religions have symbols, Watson. A cross, or the Star of David, something to honor the deity in question, but there is nothing here." He pointed to a hole at the far end of the altar, where one might rest the head or feet of one of the sacrifices. "There is a spot here, where something might well be added along those lines, but if that's the case they've been careful to remove the symbol in order to honor their god and perhaps keep the god's name hidden from the likes of us, or any other prying eyes."

"I've never heard of such a thing before."

"It's most peculiar." Holmes paused a moment and then added, "It's also pure speculation. There simply might not be any adornments at all. That blood has been spilled on this altar is a given. I expect human blood, as I see no signs of animals

239

having been led inside." Holmes still spoke softly, and his eyes examined the darkness around us, seeking possible clues he might have missed. I left the lantern pointed at the altar, first to illuminate the only real sign of foul play, and also to keep the light from possibly alerting passersby to our presence.

"What sort of madness are we dealing with here?"

"The sort that fascinates me, Watson. It's horrible, of course, but so far from the norm that I can't help speculating on the nature of the crimes. The sort that challenges my mind. Why would anyone ever see fit to take a life in such a fashion?"

Holmes paused then and took the lantern from my hand as he looked at the altar. He moved carefully, examining every aspect of the surface, until he nodded and then pointed at a small marking. It seemed insignificant until I looked closer. I could not have said what the marking meant but it was delicate and beautiful in its way. It was also unsettling. I could not have said precisely why, but the simple collection of thin lines crossing over each other, and the seven-pointed star above them left me disturbed.

"What does it mean, Holmes?"

"That's the question here, isn't it?" He had that tone of voice I knew so well. Whatever the symbol, it had caught his attention and I suspected he'd seen it somewhere before, perhaps in one of his many books or articles. Sherlock Holmes collected knowledge as voraciously as a miser gathers wealth, and hoarded that knowledge in his mind to the point where, sometimes, he needed to sit in silence and sort through his memories to catch the one trinket of information he sought.

We left the dark church not long after that, none the wiser.

That night I slept deeply and had odd dreams of a turbulent sea and a shoreline that moved violently enough to shame the ocean's waves. I awoke from my fitful slumber to find Holmes in the same chair where he had placed himself before I went to sleep. The air around him was clouded with tobacco smoke but otherwise he seemed not to have moved from his previous position. He might well have been a statue if not for the evidence that he had been smoking. He saw me, nodded a greeting, but otherwise remained still.

The sun was just rising as I stirred. Holmes had likely not slept at all, but I knew he'd rested just the same. His body was relaxed, it was his mind that stormed furiously seeking an answer to the riddle of that odd marking on an otherwise unmarked sacrificial altar.

I did not disturb him. Instead, I left him to his musings and began my day.

Near noon he finally let out a sigh and extinguished his latest cigarette, looking pointedly my way. "Let us eat, Watson. I'm famished." He stood and stretched silently, blinking eyes that had been looking inward for the last few hours. He seemed more rested than me, despite having been awake the whole night and most of the previous day and a half.

We removed ourselves from the hotel room and returned to the very same table where we'd taken our last meal. We ordered and ate in comfortable silence. When the meal was almost finished, and we were merely dawdling over coffee, he looked at me and said, "The mark is an obscure one. The only similar reference I could think to make looked markedly different, but similar enough to catch my attention. If it is meant to be from the same point of origin, then it belongs to a cult, one I had understood to be long dispatched."

"What sort of cult?" I gave in to temptation and pulled pipe and tobacco from my pocket, preparing my smoke even as my companion considered his answer carefully.

"I'll not say the name here, not aloud. The group has always been secretive, and I'll not risk anyone hearing their name uttered in a public place. It's said the followers of this obscure belief would kill anyone who discovered them. I fear that might well be what happened to the Dodsworths. If they discovered the followers and tried to report them to the local authorities, such as they were, it would explain both the disappearance of the watchman and the abductions."

The notion seemed outrageous. But as my friend had pointed out, more than once, what seemed improbable was sometimes the answer to seemingly preposterous situations.

"In any event, it seems that we have stumbled across a conspiracy that might have any number of members." Holmes paused long enough to find and prepare his own pipe before speaking further, and then paused even longer as the waiter replenished our cups, cleared away the plates, and replaced them with teacakes. "But we'll discuss that in more detail after we've finished our meal."

We chatted about a dozen mundane events while we completed the repast, and then left the establishment and the curious who might have sought to listen in on our discussion.

"What do you expect is going on here?" I was extremely curious as to what notions had come into his mind. Sherlock Holmes had the sharpest abilities to see beyond what might be easily seen, and he was alert and his curiosity piqued that day, despite the long hours without sleep.

"The markings we saw, Watson." Holmes looked around carefully, his eyes seeking any possible hiding place large enough to hold a person. "They come from a group without a true name that I can find. There are a dozen variations of the name Hrolgathir that I have run across. Deviations in spelling and pronunciation, but all leading to the same thing, a being that allegedly feasts on the formless, or the unformed. Or possibly," he leaned in closer to me and whispered softly, "the unborn."

"Unborn?"

"Not yet born. Sacrifices of a most unusual and extreme nature, Watson. The most innocent of all, those for whom life has not yet begun."

Once convinced there was no one around us, Holmes directed me into a more open area near the water's edge. Here, with the waves crashing along the shoreline, our voices would be obscured from being overheard. We could speak with less caution. It was a small thing, to be sure, and most would not have noticed it, but it was clear to me that Holmes was being extremely cautious. When he spoke again, I was reminded of my old teachers in medical school, their voices set to lecture and offering an inordinate amount of detail to be absorbed in short order.

"They have no proper name that I can find. They are not a brotherhood, nor an order, nor a proper church. They are merely followers of a different form of religion, I suppose." Holmes cleared his throat and looked out at the sea.

"The formless, the nameless, the unformed, the unborn, the undead. All of these names and more have been used with this cult. Near as I can tell the point of origin seems to be from the era of the Viking invasion, or possibly even the earlier Romans. It's that uncertain. It's hard to pinpoint an origin, Watson. The little information available speaks of all of the things I've mentioned in association with Hrolgathir, a deity of some sort, one supposes, often worshipped or reviled, or feared. It remains completely uncertain. What is known is that this creature, be it deity or demon of some sort, accepts the unformed or unborn as its sacrifices."

"What does that even mean, Holmes?"

Holmes stared at me as the waves crashed nearby, sending a thunderous roar through the air. The rocks along the shore were uneven, and reminded me of teeth rising from the coarse sand. "I expect it prefers the deaths of children still within the bodies of their mothers, Watson. I believe it prefers the sacrifices be as yet unborn. Of course, I've read of such things, but never actually believed anyone, certainly not in this day and age, could ever delude themselves into taking up such dreadful practices."

"But why take the Dodsworths?"

"Did you not notice, Watson?" Holmes looked at me, a slight frown on his face. "Ellison said there were six members of the family taken, but he only named husband, wife and three children. Mrs. Dodsworth, his sister, was pregnant. She was expecting another child."

My skin crawled at the very notion. A family sacrificed because of an unborn child. "Dear Lord, Holmes."

"I expect no sane god has anything to do with this, Watson. This is a gathering of the mad and depraved, out to please a god that demands the unborn as sacrificial lambs."

"But why here?"

"That requires more investigation, my dear fellow, but I expect a bit of digging will reveal that several women who were with child have died or disappeared in this area. We are in a town where scandals can be hidden with ease. The most common cause of death on record hereabouts appears to be accidents in the mines. Notably, several of those occurred to younger women. The sort where an accident could well be used to hide an otherwise scandalous situation. Last night, while you slept, I took a walk in the cemetery. I was contemplating the list of names Ellison had slipped to me on arriving in Ebonstone. I'm certain you noticed the somewhat clumsy transfer of paper. In any case, I found them all clustered together, each listed with dates for birth and death in a small section of the yard set aside for the victims of mining accidents. No less than twelve young women in the last year and a half. Though I doubt we'll find evidence that all of them were expecting, I wouldn't be at all surprised to discover that they were, in fact, with child when they died. The Dodsworth abduction, Watson, is merely the latest link in a chain. I think this is something that has been covered over for some time now. Someone is killing expectant mothers to placate the forces they believe are in control of Ebonstone."

We still walked the shoreline, though in the distance we could see the docks looming closer. The ships and boats for fishing were absent, out on the water at the moment, and I wondered how long they would be out in the growing stormy weather. The rain had stopped for the moment, but it would be back soon, I was certain.

"So, who are these people? Where are they hiding?" I looked back toward Ebonstone to see if anyone was following us, but we were alone,

"Captain Wade is certainly among them."

"Is he?"

Holmes nodded. "Either he was at the scene of the Dodsworth abductions, or someone wearing his very large boots was there. Rain and all, I saw the prints distinctly both outside and inside the cottage." He turned to look at the crashing waves. "We will need to learn a great deal more about the curious Captain Wade, and I think our friend Ellison is trying to hide something from us, or perhaps from himself."

That was our plan, of course, but the best plans often fall through. Sometime during the night somebody had broken into the home of our guide and taken him by force. There was no investigation, so we took the matter into our own hands.

There was little obvious to see, but Holmes found evidence just the same. Muddy boot prints including, as he pointed out to me, what was surely the heavy tread of our Captain Wade.

"There's been no attempt at secrecy. None at all." Holmes shook his head, as astonished as I was by the very notion. "They fear nothing."

"There is no law here, Holmes."

"It's worse than that. They might well be the law here. I don't know who allegedly runs this town, but I expect the real decisions are handled by Wade and his associates."

In the harbor the boats were coming in, driven home by the weather, perhaps, or by some other burning need. I expect many other men would have considered retreating to London, the better to find assistance, but I don't believe Sherlock Holmes considered the idea for even a moment. He wanted to know what was happening and he wanted to find Ellison if it wasn't already too late for the man.

We left Ellison's house and set off for the inn, but as we walked we considered what we knew.

"There are no religious consistencies, Watson."

"What do you mean?"

"Most often if there are ceremonies and sacrifices, they take place at the same time over and over, Christmas, for instance. Easter. These celebrations take place on the same date, or at the same point of significance. I have found no consistency or pattern to the dates on the grave markers in the cemetery. If the sacrifices are scheduled, they are using a different reference than our modern calendar."

"So we've no idea what they have planned?"

"These people are too bold in their actions." Holmes looked around our room for signs that anyone had been in the chambers, but there was nothing. The bed remained unmade from earlier, which in and of itself seemed unusual. "They don't care if they're caught in the act. They seem to feel they are untouchable."

"So, what are we going to do here?"

"Prove them wrong, of course. What else is there for it?"

"And how do you plan to do that?"

"We may know little, but we do know from whence they operate. It is time to rectify the situation to the best of our ability. One thing seems universal. Desecration of the sacred is a deterrent. We may not completely stop what is happening, but I believe we can at least slow it down if we are quick about it."

I knew then what he meant to do and, without another word, we made our way back to the Church of All Saints.

The great edifice stood as it had before, silent and ominous, and where the first time around it had taken him minutes to gain entry, it took less than thirty seconds for Holmes to master the lock.

Everything looked the same in the light of a stormy day as it had at night. We saw no new tracks, and the muddied trails that had been prevalent before were now dried into the accumulated soil covering the floors of the grand old church. The atmosphere was just as dark as before, and I felt the hairs on my neck and arms rise in protest to some presence that seemed to linger in the darkest corners of what had once been a holy place.

The wood of the old altar was well-seasoned and quickly caught ablaze. We retreated as the fire devoured the evidence of more human sacrifices than I wanted to consider. Neither of us spoke, but instead we retreated from the hot blaze and waited to see what would happen.

"I can't yet say what they've done with Ellison, but I don't believe they brought him here, not yet at least." Holmes examined the area again. "It's always possible that there's more to see than we have observed yet." To make his point he nodded at the burning wood and the smoke rising from it, which blew to the west in what was an area closed off from the outside winds. The smoke should have risen straight up, but instead a breeze from somewhere caught it and pushed the plume of acrid fumes along the stone wall, and as he pointed, I could make out faint lines where smoke had done the same thing from previous visits and fires, most likely from torches brought with the followers of Hrolgathir in the past.

"You think they'll come here?"

"I believe they'll be here soon. I expect they've had someone following us from a distance, Watson. I don't believe they'd take a chance on us simply leaving and reporting our findings elsewhere, unless their plans are so far along, they do not fear interference."

"Yes, but what are their plans?"

"Transformation, I expect. The Unformed are trying to become something different. I think their sacrifices are their catalyst, as it were, the fire that allows them their metamorphosis."

"I don't understand."

"My apologies, Watson. It's simple enough to me because I've read about them before, but I often forget to share knowledge properly." He shook his head. "These people seek something, of course. What I think they want is some sort of change, either in themselves or in their deity, Hrolgathir."

"Close, Mister Holmes."

The voice of Captain Wade came as a complete surprise to me. As I watched, he stepped out of a tunnel on the far side of the burning altar, an access point that must surely have been in place for long years. It was nearly impossible to see, and honestly, I had never looked for such a thing on our previous visit. I never considered that the muddy tracks might well be used to hide signs of a hidden method of gaining entry to the abandoned church. Holmes, of course, showed not the slightest degree of surprise.

Wade's eyes focused on the ruined altar for only a moment. "A loss, but not insurmountable." He shook his head and then shrugged his broad shoulders. "You made mention of Hrolgathir. The stories your chronicler has told of your skills," he glanced momentarily at me, "do you a rare justice, Mr. Holmes."

As he spoke, others stepped out of the passage, crawling up from wherever their tunnel led.

"You've hardly been secretive."

"There's no reason for it now. It's too late to stop what is happening. Too late to turn back the tide of change coming for us. We have made the requisite sacrifices and Hrolgathir will join with us soon."

"Join with you?"

"Years of secrecy and practice, Doctor." Wade stared at me, a slight smile on his face. "We have performed the rituals and we have offered the requisite sacrifices. Tonight, we will become one with our god. We don't seek anything as nebulous as a wonderful afterlife. We seek godhood."

To make his point clearer, the man held up his right arm and rolled up his sleeve. The skin of that arm was mottled. It looked bruised and angry, but beneath those dark markings, the flesh shifted in ways that made my eyes hurt to see. The skin twisted and moved as if it were a part of the ocean, small waves rippled across his flesh.

"We discussed killing you. We thought about it, but why? Instead of dying you will bear witness to the greatest transformation anyone has ever seen."

I stared at his arm, fascinated. As I watched, something bulged under the skin, pushing and straining for a moment, before receding back into the heavy flesh.

"You worked out more than I would have thought from almost nothing. I think you've earned this knowledge, Mister Holmes."

Captain Wade stepped closer to us and winced as his arm suddenly spasmed heavily. Behind him, several of his companions let out groans and one fell to the ground, his hand clutching at the leg of another.

"What are we supposed to see?" Holmes watched with shining eyes, absorbing the minutiae of every action, of every feverish twitch.

Captain Wade did not scream, even when I knew the pain must have been enough to cripple his self-control. I have been a doctor for a long time, and a soldier for a short time, and have seen battlefield surgeries in wartime that left me with nightmares about pain. Wade's arm split open in front of me, and I stared on, mesmerized, as something grew from the rift in his arm. It blossomed in the blood and split meat, growing at an impossible speed. While Captain Wade did not scream, his arm let out an impossible shriek and whatever grew there snapped teeth in my direction.

All around him his followers bucked and writhed as their flesh contorted and reformed, hurtling through a changing wave of different shapes that rippled and fell apart before flowing back together. That is the only way I can describe what happened. One moment they were different, individual people and, a few heartbeats later, those people dissolved then came together in a new and horrifying unified shape. Arms and other, stranger limbs swam to the surface of the shifting mass. Wade himself fell backward, dissolved almost instantly into that roiling mass of ruination, his eyes remaining locked on Sherlock Holmes until they too were absorbed into the malignancy. Shreds of his clothing remained adrift for a moment, then were pulled into and vanished beneath the surface of that reeking collection of gelatinous semi fluids.

I had thought Captain Wade a large man, but when new limbs, of horrifying configuration, erupted from the heaving, shuddering growth, they were of a scale nearly impossible for me to comprehend. I simply stared, too astonished to understand what it was I looked upon.

Sherlock Holmes saved my life before one of those clawed appendages could crash down on me and tear me asunder.

251

What could have been a head began to rise from the mass, but it was not even slightly human in shape. There was a muzzle, like that of a wolf or bear, perhaps, with large, uneven teeth and two eyes of different shapes placed in unbalanced locations under a heavy, bestial brow. One arm was long and thin, reaching more than ten feet from the growing, swirling blob of crimson and gray fluids. Another two arms, smaller, rose straight up toward the church's spire as if seeking heaven.

Whatever was growing from the unformed mass, it sought to be born into our world, and it cried out as it bled forth. Smoke filled the air from the burnt remains of the unholy altar. Holmes pulled me away as I stood staring mutely at the horror creeping into our world.

"Move, Watson! Run, you fool! Run!" I stumbled backward and then caught my balance as Holmes roared his orders at me. The thing that had been Wade and his men simply screamed as it was born into the world.

Sherlock Holmes pushed me toward the open door of the church. I fell out that door as surely as a drunken sailor might stumble down the walkway of a lurching ship on a turbulent dock.

I could not feel my legs beneath me.

I caught myself as I fell to the ground, scraping my palms in the dirt of the abandoned church's yard.

By the time I had pushed myself back to a standing position, Holmes had gone back inside with the nightmare abomination, I heard him scream unintelligible words past the horrid noises of the twisted, growing mass I knew he now faced alone.

Before I could make my way back in, the door slammed shut before me. Not because of anything Holmes had done, but because that creature had shifted itself towards my best friend in the world.

There was only one way out of the church at that point, the same passage that had allowed Wade access earlier.

When I could finally force open the door and regain entry, both Sherlock Holmes and what had been the followers of Hrolgathir were gone. When I tried to reach the passage, heavy flames and smoke barred my way. Somehow the tunnel beneath the church had caught fire.

There was no way to reach my friend.

I wept, certain that Sherlock Holmes was dead. After nearly an hour I made my way from the churchyard and headed toward Ebonstone.

I spent most of the night and early morning hours pacing frantically in our room, trying to absorb everything that had happened to me, pondering what must have happened to Holmes and what I should do now. When the sun was just rising, there came a sudden thud and a scratching at the door. Had there been more followers? Had the creature come for me? Before I could move, the door opened. Holmes slumped against the door frame, his eyes wide and his lean face drawn and haggard.

Oh, my joy at seeing the man alive!

I rushed to him and felt the feverish heat coming from him, smelled the scent of singed fabric on his person and despite the impropriety, I hugged the man close to me and silently thanked God almighty that my best friend was alive.

"Carefully, John," he cautioned me. "I've a desperate need to rest."

He clearly suffered from smoke inhalation, but after a quick examination that I insisted on performing, I found the man otherwise uninjured. Putting him to bed, I took up a position in the chair. The both of us slept then, exhausted and somehow, miraculously it seemed to me, alive.

In the late morning when Holmes finally awoke, he said the last he would ever speak to me on the subject of Hrolgathir and Ebonstone. There have been few cases he would not speak of, and few I have not arranged for the world to read, but this case was both. I have written this down solely for my own benefit.

"It was luck and luck alone that saved me, Watson. The hidden passage, a tunnel really, running from the Church of All Saints to an old shaft, had been carved from the local stone, you see, and that stone is rife with veins of a curiously compressed coal. Once I understood the nature of the surrounding rock, my plan of action was simplicity itself. I set it alight with a flaming piece of the altar. Had the creature been as godlike as Wade believed, I think I'd be dead. We might all be dead in this wretched place, but Hrolgathir, or whatever it was, was not itself intelligent. It was a beast of pure instinct. When the coal truly began to burn it turned back on itself and tried to retreat, but the coal caught at a frightening pace, Watson."

I think there was more to the tale than he told me. It is even possible, though I expect he would deny it, that Sherlock Holmes performed some ritual of his own to save himself and the people of Ebonstone from the nightmare he faced in that tunnel.

He never volunteered the information and I refused to ask him. What happened to Lucius Ellison remains a mystery to this day. One that Sherlock Holmes has no desire to solve.

I learned later that the colliery in Ebonstone was shut down and an effort made to seal all shafts, and any radiating tunnels, undertaken. Apparently, however, the threads of coal beneath the ground there continues somehow to burn.

Whatever the case, the best man I know is still alive, and that's enough for me.

FOR FEAR…

Mark Morris

"Mr. Holmes! It's an honor to meet you, sir! A veritable honor!"

Dr. Cornelius Layton, a pathologist of my acquaintance, bustled across the dour little room that comprised the entrance vestibule of Spitalfields Mortuary with his hand outstretched. The junior assistant, who had opened the door to us, appeared equally overawed by the presence of my friend, the great detective, but unlike his superior, he was clearly too intimidated to speak.

Holmes, for his part, retained his customary, somewhat aloof demeanor, though I knew him well enough to discern that he was flattered by Layton's ebullient display of esteem. He allowed the red-faced and luxuriantly bewhiskered fellow to grasp his long, white hand and pump it like a bellows for several seconds, before murmuring, "Dr. Watson informs me you possess an interesting corpse that you wish us to view."

"Indeed, sir! Indeed!" Layton relinquished Holmes's now somewhat crumpled hand, and indicated the door at the back of the room. "If you would be so kind as to follow me?"

The noxious stench which emanated from Spitalfields' overpopulated streets, and which had pursued us even through the doors of the Mortuary, finally began to dissipate as we plunged deeper into the building. Or, more accurately, it was superseded by other, marginally less noisome odors – those of scorched lamp oil, damp plaster and moldering wood.

Layton led us along several corridors and finally down a set of stone steps into the basement room where he carried out his post mortems. It was noticeably colder here than on the floor above, our collective breath, as we exhaled, emerging as white curls of vapor.

Despite the frigid conditions, the dank smell of death was all about, the cause of which was immediately apparent. On a stone table in the center of the room lay the naked corpse of a heavily-built, middle-aged woman. It was clear she had been dead for several days, her flesh bloating and marbling, her extremities black with rot.

Flourishing at the corpse in the manner of a chef presenting a banquet, Layton said, "Pray, gentlemen, tell me what you make of these wounds."

Holmes and I bent over the earthly remains of the deceased. The stench of corruption that rose from her was not pleasant, but the two of us were possessed of strong stomachs, having become accustomed to death in its many forms during our long acquaintance.

The wounds to which Layton referred were curious. Around the woman's throat, wrists and ankles were marks that might have been made by tightened ropes, were it not for the fact that *within* the encircling abrasions were what appeared to be myriad small puncture wounds. Examining the corpse's throat, it struck me that these wounds were like the marks made by spines or thorns, and that it was as if the woman had been strangled (for I had no doubt that strangulation was the cause of death, judging by her bulging, blood-suffused eyes and protruding, blackened tongue) not by a rope but by the thick stem of a thorny plant, such as a rambling rose.

I voiced this observation to Holmes, who nodded curtly. "I am of a similar mind, Watson. It is most baffling. But observe this wound here, which is the most baffling of all."

He indicated the right-hand side of the woman's belly, just beneath her rib cage, then stood back to allow me access. What at first glance I had taken to be a wound made by a knife, or some similar instrument, I now realized was nothing of the sort. At some point I surmised that a great deal of blood must have crusted around the rim of the wound, but Layton had cleared this away to reveal an aperture in the woman's flesh, some four inches in diameter, that was perfectly circular, like a 'bore-hole' in wood or earth made by a spiraling drill.

I further observed that at the 'twelve o'clock' position of the 'bore-hole' was a neat, vertical incision some six inches long, which from the lack of swelling or other bodily trauma I surmised to have been inflicted post-mortem.

Glancing up at Layton, he nodded as if to confirm this. "Yes, the incision is my work. I wanted to ascertain the depth of the wound."

"And what were your findings?" Holmes asked.

"The woman's liver has gone." Layton acknowledged my look of surprise. "I do not exaggerate, Dr. Watson. Every trace of the organ has been removed, or dissolved, or..." He tailed off with a shake of his head, at a loss to explain the phenomenon.

Holmes looked thoughtful, absently tapping his chin with the tip of his forefinger. "Who was this poor unfortunate?"

"Her name was Nelly White. She lived in lodgings close to the market with her husband and four children, and worked in a nearby tobacco factory."

"And where was she found?"

"In a yard between a tavern she frequented called The Red Crown and her lodging-house. She was last seen drinking in the tavern five nights ago. Her remains were discovered this morning."

Layton hesitated for only a second, but Holmes was quick to spot it. "There is more to tell."

The pathologist nodded. "There is, Mr. Holmes. Deaths of a bizarre and gruesome nature are not uncommon in the poorer areas of London, and if this was a singular occurrence, I would not have been so quick to bring the matter to your attention. But the fact is, this is the second such murder in as many weeks. And that is still not the entirety of it..."

All at once Layton, who despite his bluff ways had dedicated his life to aiding the poor and needy rather than attending to the minor ailments of the cosseted rich, looked troubled and weary.

"Do not hesitate to tell all," said Holmes gently.

In a quiet voice Layton said, "For some time now – I do not recall precisely how long, but I should say I first became aware of the peculiarity five or six years ago – cadavers have, on occasion, been delivered to these premises with their livers removed. In all cases the deceased were the victims of violent assaults. Many had been stabbed; some had had their throats slashed open; yet others had been bludgeoned to death, or strangled. Some had been fished from the Thames, some found in the streets, some discovered in lodging houses. The victims were of all ages and of both sexes. There was no discernible pattern to the slayings."

"Aside from the missing livers," said I.

"Yes – although with such disparity between the victims and their causes of death, I discovered the phenomenon almost by accident."

"Which suggests that the practice may have been prevalent before you yourself became aware of it?"

"Indeed, Mr. Holmes."

"Did you inform the police of your findings?" I asked.

"Of course."

"And what was their response?"

Holmes gave a snort. "One hardly need ask the question, Watson. The victims were poor and unconnected. The removal of their livers was neither the primary cause of their deaths, nor readily explained. Naturally, the police gave little regard to the matter."

"You are correct, Mr. Holmes," said Layton. "The most common suggestion was that killers were removing their victims' organs in emulation of Jolly Jack. It was even suggested to me that the poor of London were oft-times hungry enough to resort to desperate measures…"

I shook my head in disgust. Holmes regarded Layton with narrowed eyes.

"Aside from the common factor of the missing livers, the earlier killings were not as these latter two, I take it? If they had been, the police would have given the matter more attention, due to the singular nature of the victims' wounds. Either that, or you would have called Watson and I in sooner."

"Correct again, Mr. Holmes," Layton said.

"My guess," continued Holmes, "is that the earlier murders were more 'commonplace', shall we say, the livers of the victims removed by force from their bodies, their attackers wielding conventional tools."

This time the pathologist only nodded.

"What does it all mean, Holmes?" I asked. "Are you saying that the killer or killers of these disparate victims is the same in every instance? And that he, or they, have now discovered a more... efficient, but mysterious, method of achieving their aims?"

"Not at all, Watson," said Holmes, "although I do believe that the missing organs were all put to the same purpose." Rather than elaborate further, he whirled to face Layton and swiftly shook his hand. "Thank you, Dr. Layton, for bringing this matter to my attention. I bid you good day. Come, Watson."

With that, he turned and strode away, all at once a dervish of energy. Glancing apologetically at my friend, and swiftly raising a hand in lieu of a proper farewell, I hurried after Holmes.

*

Like any East End establishment where the poor congregated to imbibe strong, cheap alcohol, The Red Crown was a low, filthy place, full of ill-lit corners, redolent with a stench of unwashed humanity that was only slightly less malodorous than had been the rotting remains of Nelly White. We had barely crossed the threshold before I sensed the hostile scrutiny of many eyes, and I was glad of the reassuring weight of my Webley inside my jacket.

Holmes, too, I am certain, was aware of the simmering threat of violence, but he is a man who possesses the uncanny ability to adopt, when required, a persona full of charm and bonhomie that more often than not serves to disarm any would-be malefactor. Within ten minutes of entering The Red Crown, we were seated at a table with two of the most fearsome-looking fellows in the place, who, after Holmes had bought them each a glass of brandy, introduced themselves to us as Bill Gideon and Ernie Summers.

"So what's a couple o' toffs like you doin' in 'ere?" Gideon asked. "Come for the ladies, 'ave yer?"

He was a big man with bushy eyebrows and a tangled black beard flecked with gray. His companion, Summers, sinewy and pockmarked, stretched his mouth wide as he sniggered, displaying a shocking array of brown and broken teeth.

Holmes barked a laugh, as if delighted by the man's wit. "In a manner of speaking, though our intentions are not as you suppose." He leaned forward in a manner that encouraged the men to do the same, the four of us drawing together like a den of thieves. "My colleague and I heard tell of the appalling murder of Mrs. Nelly White, not far from here, several nights ago – a murder of which the police appear inclined to do nothing. It is our intention to solve that murder and bring the perpetrators to justice."

I felt that Holmes was playing a dangerous game here. What if these men were the perpetrators in question? Unless it was his intention to rattle them?

Gideon, however, did not behave as a guilty party might. He scoffed, regarding Holmes with pitying contempt. "You? What can you do?"

"A great deal, I believe," said Holmes. "But to pursue my investigations, I require information. What are people saying about Mrs. White's death?"

I tensed, aware that this direct approach by Holmes could go either way. Even though he had employed the full weight of his authoritative personality, it would not have surprised me if the natives suddenly decided we were privileged busybodies with nothing better to do than indulge our whims in a little amateur detective work.

Our companions, though, seemed impressed by Holmes's bearing, not to say convinced by his sincerity.

"They're saying she was not the first to go the way she did," Gideon muttered.

"They're saying she was taken by the little men," offered Summers.

Holmes glanced sharply at him. "The little men?"

Summers nodded grimly. "There's plenty as 'ave seen 'em." He glanced around, then stabbed a finger in the direction of an old man with long white whiskers, who was smoking a pipe beside the fire. "Old Barney, fer one."

"Would Barney speak to us, do you suppose?" Holmes enquired.

"Fer a tot o' gin he'd speak to anyone," Summers said, cackling.

And so it proved. No more than two minutes later, gin in hand, Old Barney was seated at our table, peering at us with small, wet eyes. The stove pipe hat perched atop his head was as crooked as a witch's chimney pot, and his clothes were little more than thick layers of rags.

Prompted by Summers, he nodded slowly, and in a cracked, surprisingly high voice he said, "Aye, I seen 'em, misters. And I ain't the only one. Whenever they appear, someone's fer the chop."

"And what are they like, these 'little men'?" I asked.

"They ain't like you and me, mister," Old Barney said. "No, they ain't like you and me at all. I ain't sure they're even men as such, if you know what I mean. They're little, like I said, and sorta... hunched over. First off, I thought they was children. But then I seen the face o' one of 'em, and I seen they weren't children at all."

"What were they?" I enquired.

Old Barney fixed me with his little, wet eyes. "Demons," he said solemnly. "Demons with the faces o' rats."

*

"What do you make of what we heard back there?" I asked Holmes as we strode together through a squalid alley. "Were they playing us for rich and gullible fools?"

A twitch of a smile played on Holmes's lips. "I think not, Watson. The sightings I believe to be genuine. It is their interpretation which is perhaps open to question."

"But the girl who accosted us on our way out. You cannot deny she was deep in her cups."

"But her eagerness to tell her tale, coupled with her genuine fear at the memory of it..." Holmes shook his head. "She saw what she saw, Watson. Of that I have no doubt."

I rolled my eyes in exasperation. "But damn it all, Holmes! Pint-sized demons! And snakes the color of blood! It is like something from the feverish imagination of Hieronymus Bosch!"

"Let us keep an open mind, Watson. I am sure an explanation will present itself in due course."

The blood-red snake to which I referred had been sighted – or so she claimed – by Peggy, a girl of perhaps eighteen years, who had overheard at least part of our conversation with Old Barney and had been keen to add her own contribution. Peggy told us that she had been 'out for a walk' one night, close to the docks, when a snake the color of blood had reared up out of nowhere and chased her along the street.

"Horrible it was, sirs! I thought my end had come!" she related breathlessly.

I regarded her cynically, and was about to ask how much gin she had consumed that night, when Holmes said gently, "How did you escape from the creature?"

"I ran as fast as I could, sir. And I didn't stop until I reached Fisher Street. When I looked behind me, the thing had gone. But it was there, sir! I swear it was!"

"I believe you," Holmes said, and the conviction in his voice caused relief to spread across Peggy's face like sunshine across dull ground. Holmes reached out and briefly clasped Peggy's hands in his own. "Thank you for sharing the details of your ordeal with us. It is much appreciated."

*

"What a terrible place to die," I said.

Holmes and I had reached Hobb's Yard, where Nelly White had met her end. Situated some two hundred yards off the main thoroughfare, it was a vile, stinking place, surrounded on three sides by the high, scabrous walls of what I took to be dwelling houses, although feeble candlelight glowed behind only a few of the dozens of otherwise black windows that overlooked us. In lieu of gas lighting, Holmes and I were examining the place by the flickering illumination of Lucifers, from my friend's plentiful supply. What we saw, however, was not encouraging. Scattered liberally across the inch-high detritus underfoot, which smeared the cobblestones and made me grateful for my stout boots, was a plethora of broken and useless everyday objects – wooden pallets, furniture, buckets, and dozens of other items, the majority of which were now nothing but shattered shards and splintered remnants.

Holmes was striding about, kicking the discarded miscellany aside, much to the chagrin of a sizeable population of rats, who had made their home among the debris and now fled, squealing in indignation. I followed his lead, but in a more desultory fashion.

"We are wasting our time, Holmes," said I eventually. "There is nothing to be found here."

As I finished speaking, Holmes squatted down and struck another match. The yellow glare illuminated his ascetic features, which were all at once avid.

"Nothing, you say, Watson? I beg to differ. Look here."

I plodded across to where he was examining the ground, the black slime squelching around my boots. I half-expected him to have found some keepsake of the victim's, or a personal item dropped by her killer. Instead, he was keenly examining a metal manhole cover, its surface caked with more of the black grime.

"What of it?" I said, unable to mask my lack of enthusiasm.

Holmes offered me a wolfish grin. "Observe the edges of this metal cover, Watson. There is a break in the filth all the way around, which suggests that it has been raised recently."

"By sewerage workers, no doubt," I said.

Holmes shook his head. "Nelly White disappeared several nights ago, and her body was discovered only this morning. Unless the cover was raised just a day or two before our unfortunate victim was slain, the break we see would have closed again, the two edges of filth oozing together like a closing wound."

"But it is possible that sewerage workers were here just a day before the murder," I insisted, "if not on the day itself."

"Possible, yes, but not likely." Holmes's match went out and he lit another. "It is certainly worthy of further investigation, wouldn't you say?"

*

Five minutes later, Holmes and I were descending into the sewer, having used our combined strength to lift the manhole cover aside. With only the light of our Lucifers to see by, conditions were not ideal.

Not unexpectedly, the place stank to high Heaven, and I bemoaned the fact that I had not worn an older suit, one I could consign straight to the dustbin once our night's endeavors were done. The tunnel in which we found ourselves, once we had descended the metal ladder inset into the wall, was cylindrical in shape, with a narrow walkway running alongside a gushing channel of evil-looking effluent. The brick walls ran with moisture, and water – at least, I hoped it was water – dripped from the ceiling onto our shoulders and our mercifully covered heads. When Holmes raised his Lucifer, gimlet eyes caught the light and reflected it back at us. More rats.

With Holmes leading the way, we moved forward, pausing every now and again to strike more matches. Although my friend had plenty in the capacious pockets of his overcoat, I could only suppose that at the rate we were using them, his supply must be dwindling rapidly.

After five minutes, Holmes halted to examine the wall beside him. The walkway was too narrow for me to see what had taken his attention, and so I asked, somewhat irritably, "Why on earth have you stopped, Holmes?"

He glanced at me, then flicked his dying Lucifer into the flow of effluent, before moving two steps forward. Striking another match, he held it close to the wall.

"What is your medical assessment of this substance, Watson?" he asked.

At first glance, the wall appeared wet and lumpen, nothing more. And then I realized that what I had supposed to be swollen or distorted brickwork was a thick band of jelly-like substance, mostly clear, but with yellowish-gray streaks within it. As far as I could tell the substance was odorless – or at least, its odor was not enough to cut through the already noxious fumes that swaddled us like a thick blanket. I leaned forward to examine the 'jelly' more closely, though I felt loath to touch it.

"I'm dashed if I know, Holmes."

"I think it's mucus of some kind."

"Mucus!" My cry of surprise echoed around the tunnel walls. "Do you realize what you're saying?"

Holmes smiled thinly. "When have you ever known me to speak idly, old friend? I think it is akin to the substance one would find secreted by a mollusk, or a gastropod."

"A gastropod? But a snail that left a trail like that would be the size of a... a brougham!"

"I am only speculating, Watson. Further analysis will prove or disprove my theory." And so saying, Holmes tossed away his match, then took a tobacco tin from his pocket and emptied its contents into the sluggish river beside us. He scraped some of the glutinous substance off the wall and into the tin, before firmly replacing the lid and slipping the tin back into his pocket.

He was in the process of striking another match when, above the gurgling of effluent and the scurrying and squeaking of rats, we heard a sound ahead of us. We turned and, as one, raised our matches above our heads. By our combined light, which did not extend very far into the tunnel, we saw two figures standing on the periphery between illumination and darkness. Mostly in silhouette, they were small and squat, like portly children. They may have been wearing hoods, for their heads seemed to rise like mounds direct from their hunched shoulders.

Uncertainly, I called out, "Halloa. Who–"

Before I could say more, Holmes leaped at me, seized my lapels and slammed me hard against the tunnel wall!

Although my friend is thin and wiry, he possesses a surprising strength, added to which I was so taken aback by his sudden attack that I had no defense against it. He must have already discarded his Lucifer to grasp me with both hands, and as my body hit the wall, knocking the breath from me, I dropped the match I was holding too, plunging us into darkness.

Barely a second after the painful impact and the expulsion of air from my lungs, I heard a sound beside us. It was the swift scraping of metal on stone, followed by a splash.

Although I could see nothing, I understood immediately what had happened. One of the small figures had hurled some form of projectile at us, and Holmes had reacted on the instant, thrusting me out of its path.

Now, just as quickly, he pulled me back to my feet. "I feel a tactical withdrawal is the best policy in this instance, Watson," he muttered. "Hold on to my coat and follow me directly."

I did as he asked without question, tightly clutching the tail of the overcoat which he thrust into my hand and matching the swift clack of his footsteps, as best I could, with my own. I knew that Holmes's sensory faculties were finely attuned, and that he had an excellent nose for direction, but even so it was a nightmarish minute or two, racing at full pelt through the pitch blackness, little knowing whether, at any moment, I might slip off the narrow pathway and into the river of human filth beside us, or else be felled by an arrow in the back.

As it was, we made it safely back to our starting point of the iron ladder, and scrambled up it with all haste. Once we were out of the sewer, we dropped the manhole cover back into place, and then Holmes stood upon it for good measure as we strove to recover our breath.

Finally, I felt able to speak. "Who were those devils, Holmes?" But immediately it struck me. "The murderers we seek, no doubt!"

Holmes pursed his lips. "You are partly right, Watson. They, or others of their acquaintance, may have been responsible for the commonplace murders that your friend, Dr. Layton, informed us about. Mrs. Nelly White's death, however, was another matter entirely."

"How can you be so certain?"

"Our attackers in the tunnels were armed with crude implements. The item that was hurled at us was a length of sharpened metal, or perhaps a spiked iron railing – I did not have time to examine it closely. The killing of Nelly White, however, was an altogether more sophisticated affair."

"I would not have termed it sophisticated."

"And yet it was so. Unlike the earlier victims, her liver was not hacked out with crude blades, but removed with great neatness and efficiency. It is interesting, is it not? A series of murders whose primary motivation was the removal of a particular organ, and yet all at once the method of extraction has become considerably more refined." Abruptly he clapped his hands. "The matter is intriguing. But our night's work is done."

"What will our next move be, Holmes?" I asked.

"We return here tomorrow – but better equipped for battle!"

He grinned widely, as if already relishing the prospect.

*

Holmes spent the majority of the next day ensconced in his laboratory. After breakfasting with him, I took myself home, where I apologized to my long-suffering wife Mary for the appalling state of my apparel, and then retired to my bed to acquire some much-needed rest in preparation for what I felt sure would be the further travails of the night ahead.

By 10 pm I was back at 221B Baker Street, on this occasion wearing my oldest and most expendable suit. At Holmes's request, I was this time armed not only with my Webley, but also with a Bullseye police lantern that had been given to me during a previous investigation by our acquaintance, and sometimes colleague, Inspector Tobias Gregson.

As always, at the prospect of danger, Holmes was effervescent with energy, whereas my only wish was that we would make it safely through the night, and that my darling Mary would not be a widow come the morning. During our carriage ride back to Hobb's Yard in Spitalfields, Holmes apprised me of what he had discovered that day.

"The substance that I found on the tunnel wall is, biologically speaking, wholly unknown to me," he said glibly, "although I surmise it, as I said at the time, to be mostly akin to the acidic mucus exuded by common mollusks, such as slugs and snails, albeit allied to some by-product of digestion." He smiled. "As I subsequently discovered by accident, it also has hallucinogenic properties – or perhaps it is even more than that."

Here he paused, and I looked at him curiously. My friend was frowning, as if struggling to express himself, a hitherto unheard-of phenomenon.

"More than that?" I prompted. "In what way, Holmes?"

"I am not sure the language exists to explain it," Holmes said. "But the substance seems to possess the ability to... bend reality in some way." Before I could comment, he said quickly, "Tell me, Watson, how did you feel last night in the tunnel?"

I considered the question. "Uncomfortable," I said at last. "And somewhat disorientated by the stench and the darkness."

"And by something else perhaps?" mused Holmes. "Did you not feel a tugging on your thoughts? A sense that perhaps what you were experiencing was akin to a dream?"

"I'm… I'm not sure." His words disturbed me. There *was* something in what he said, but I could not put my finger on it.

Abruptly Holmes waved a hand. "Oh, well, it is of no matter. But once we are below ground, keep your wits about you, Watson. Make an especial attempt to do so."

"I shall," I said.

*

I assured myself that the disquiet I experienced upon entering Hobb's Yard for the second time was caused by the prospect of what lay ahead of us, and was not due to any extraneous influence. By the strong glow from our lamps, which Holmes and I lit immediately upon alighting from our carriage, the yard did not appear altered in any way from our visit the previous evening.

Nevertheless, there was movement all around us, the strewn detritus rustling and trembling as rats scampered to and fro beneath it. Holmes looked around keenly and then crossed to the manhole cover. Putting his lantern down on the ground, he said, "Come, Watson, help me with this."

I too put down my lantern, and for the second time in as many nights helped him lift the manhole cover aside. Instantly we were assailed by the familiar, though no less noxious, fumes from below. Holmes glanced at me, as if assessing my response.

"Remember, Watson, hold tight to your wits," he said, and then, lantern in hand, swung his long legs into the circular opening and on to the rungs of the iron ladder.

Once we had climbed down, and were once again standing on the narrow stone walkway beside the rushing river of evil-smelling effluent, Holmes said, "Have your revolver at the ready, Watson. Quick reactions may be required tonight."

Alarming though his words may have been, I felt reassured with a strong and steady light in one hand and my trusted Webley in the other. Thus equipped, with Holmes in the lead, holding his own lantern high, we once more proceeded into the depths of the London sewerage system.

After a few minutes we came to the section of tunnel where Holmes had discovered the mucus-like substance on the wall. It was still there, quivering, a great streak of it, and I concede (although I did not admit as much to Holmes) that the sight of it made my head swim a little, my thoughts seeming to detach themselves momentarily from my mind. Taking a firmer grip on my lantern and revolver, I tore my gaze from the unprepossessing sight, and admonished myself for succumbing to the foibles of my own imagination. Keeping my breath shallow to reduce the pernicious effects of the miasma that pressed upon us like fog, I focused firmly on the way ahead.

Shortly thereafter we came to the point in the tunnel where the two figures had stood yesterday, positioned at the very limit of what had then been our meagre source of illumination. Tonight was a different story, the light from our lanterns shining out strong and bright, and we saw now what we had not seen previously, which was that the tunnel branched off, one juncture curving to the right, the other to the left. We walked forward until we reached the junction point, whereupon we saw that access to the right-hand tunnel was obstructed by a pair of sawhorses, with a sign attached to them that read: DANGER. NO ENTRY. UNSAFE PASSAGE.

I glanced at Holmes. "What do you think?"

Holmes raised his lantern high, directing its beam into the 'unsafe' tunnel.

"Observe the wall, Watson," said he.

I did so, and immediately saw the light shimmering on a wide streak of the mucus-like substance. The streak was some five feet long, and it curved in an arc, reaching almost to the ceiling, before petering out. Deeper into the tunnel, almost at the furthest limit of Holmes's lantern light, another patch of mucus could be seen, glimmering faintly.

"So the warning is a ruse," I said hopefully.

"Possibly, although that is not primarily what interests me. Look again at the substance on the wall, Watson. What are your observations?"

I did as Holmes asked, wondering what he had seen that was not immediately apparent to me. I thought of what he had said about the substance equating to the secretions of a mollusk or gastropod. And all at once I had it.

"The substance on the wall does not form a consistent line. It is broken in places. There are streaks here and there, with bare patches between."

"Precisely, Watson. Which suggests that the trail does not tally with consistent movement, but rather with intermittent contact."

"Meaning what, Holmes?" I asked. "That our monstrous gastropod can fly?"

Holmes smiled thinly. "That is certainly one theory. But perhaps the answer will reveal itself before long."

So saying, he marched into the right-hand tunnel, lifting the sawhorses aside when he reached them and leaning them against the wall. I followed warily, my finger resting on the trigger of my revolver.

Despite the warning sign, there was no evidence that the tunnel was unsafe. Its construction seemed as steadfast as the section we had recently walked through. Ahead, the walkway curved to the left, the light from Holmes's lantern ballooning around the corner, though naturally fading at the extent of its stretch. In the shadows beyond, the watchful eyes of rats glowed briefly like corpse-candles before the creatures fled at our approach. One pair of eyes, however, remained fixed on us, and then the twin pinpoints suddenly rose like sparks from a fire, coming to rest approximately three feet above the level of the walkway.

This pair of eyes was swiftly followed by another, and then another, and then, to my alarm, several more. They seemed to come from our left as we faced them, and then to move across to the right, rising up as they did so. As Holmes took two further steps forward, the light from his lantern leaped ahead of him and illuminated the darkness occupied by these hovering white specks. I gasped and took a firmer grip on my revolver, but Holmes remained calm. Raising his free hand in a placatory gesture, he said, "Good evening, gentlemen. We mean you no harm."

His words were directed at a group of seven or eight squat figures, the tallest no more than three feet high, clad in layers of rags, hoods pulled up over their heads. What could be seen of their faces, which were partially obscured by shadow, was alarming, if not monstrous. Their features were gnarled, bent out of true, additional to which they seemed peculiarly rodent-like, their mouths pulled forward into snouts, their front teeth protruding and jagged. Frightful though their appearance was, however, what in some ways was the most disquieting thing about them was the realization, judging by their dripping, slime-caked garments, that they had crawled up out of the channel of human waste that ran alongside us.

Holmes's words rang around the tunnel walls with both reassurance and authority – albeit in vain. Whether the creatures failed to understand his greeting or simply chose to disregard it, I cannot say, but the next moment they expelled a series of hideous, ear-splitting screeches and charged towards us!

As they approached, they produced various weapons from beneath their filthy robes – makeshift spears and long blades. One of the spear carriers raised his weapon above his head, clearly intending to hurl it in our direction.

By now, I was already stepping forward, my revolver raised. Reluctant to shoot the creatures, despite their murderous intentions, I aimed the gun at the roof above their heads and pulled the trigger.

The gunshot in the enclosed space was like an explosion. There was a spark of light as the bullet struck the curved roof, gouging out a plethora of brick splinters, which flew in all directions, and raising a sizeable quantity of dust.

My intention had been to give our attackers pause for thought, but the effect upon them was altogether more dramatic. Having presumably never encountered firearms and their effects, they squealed in terror, the two at the front of the group prostrating themselves upon the ground, while several at the back turned tail and fled. The remaining two hurled themselves, without hesitation, into the fast-flowing channel of human filth, whereupon they plunged beneath the surface, only to re-appear further 'downstream', their heads emerging like those of seals or turtles.

As I watched this spectacle with repugnance, Holmes dropped to one knee. His eyes roved keenly over the two prone figures, taking in every detail of their vile appearance. Then, as the echoes of my gunshot died away, he said, "Can you speak? Do you understand what I am saying?"

One of the rat-men, as I now thought of them, responded by leaping to his feet and scurrying away into the deeper darkness of the tunnel. The other, and the only one now remaining, raised his head and hissed in a venomous manner, before, with a bizarre, slithering motion, flipping sideways off the walkway and plunging into the river of effluent, whereupon he swam away like an otter, his foreshortened body rippling sinuously before sliding beneath the surface.

Feeling all at once weak and light-headed, I staggered, putting my gun hand out to the wall to steady myself.

Holmes rose to his feet. "Are you all right, Watson?"

"In all honesty, Holmes, I don't know that I am," I admitted. "You know me for a rational man, and yet there is such a pressure in my head that I can barely think straight. I cannot help but feel that the sewer entrance in Hobb's Yard has led us not beneath London's streets, but directly into Hell itself. Tell me, Holmes, were those creatures I saw even real? Did you see them also?"

"I did, old friend. And it is my belief that there is some influence down here that is affecting not only our thoughts, but our very physiognomy. For now, I hope the effects are so slight as to be negligible, if not reversible, though I fear the poor wretches we just encountered are the living embodiment of lengthy exposure."

Unable to take deep breaths of fresh air, I shook my head in an attempt to clear it. "Do you mean to say that those creatures were once human?"

"And still are to some extent, although the internal workings of their bodies have been altered, remade. Not by surgery but by some more subtle and insidious process. Via that process, I believe the bodies of men have become augmented with certain characteristics of the rodent population, perhaps in order to make them more adaptable to the subterranean conditions."

I gaped at him, barely able to take in what he was saying. "But that's... *monstrous*, Holmes! Not to say a scientific impossibility!"

"And yet we have the evidence of our own eyes to rely upon. Shall we proceed?"

I admit, I did not want to, and yet I could hardly say no. Holmes clapped me on the shoulder, then turned and strode deeper into the tunnel, his lantern held high. Renewing my grip on my revolver, I plodded after him, shaking my head in an attempt to dislodge the pressure from my mind. This part of our journey seemed to me interminable, but I was losing the ability to judge the passage of time by this stage, and so it is probable that only minutes passed before we happened upon the child.

It was his voice I heard first, clear and sweet, and so plaintive that tears sprang immediately to my eyes. "Help me!" he cried. "Oh, please help me!"

It was only when I looked up that it occurred to me, I had been walking with my eyes downcast and my mind elsewhere. Realizing that if the rat-men had returned for a renewed attack, I would not have been ready for them made me feel shocked and ashamed. Wondering how I could have been so careless, I glanced at Holmes, but thankfully he was facing ahead and seemed oblivious to my shortcomings. Determined not to fail my friend again, I peered through the gap created by his upraised arm. Sure enough, a small child was sitting in the center of the walkway ahead of us, arms held out beseechingly.

It was a boy of perhaps six or seven, blond-haired and bare of feet, dressed in rags, emaciated, and evidently very frightened. He called out again, "Oh, sirs! Please help me!" His voice was like the purest crystal, ringing around the tunnel walls and resounding in my head.

His desperate plea raised such a swell of emotion within me that my heart felt on the verge of bursting. I had to help this child, I had to save him. Suddenly there was no mission more important in the world than to offer him succor. Barging Holmes aside, I rushed forward, slipping my revolver into my pocket almost unconsciously as I approached the helpless infant. Vaguely I was aware of Holmes calling out behind me, but his words went unheard, my mind focused wholly on my philanthropic duty.

I was no more than five steps from the child, and readying myself to reach down and scoop him up into my arms, when I heard rapid footsteps behind me, and then felt a hand upon my shoulder. The hand tightened, first arresting my progress and then spinning me around. I felt only outrage as I looked into Holmes's face, barely registering the frantic expression thereon.

"Go no further, Watson! It is a trap!" I heard him shout.

It was only rarely that Holmes ever gave me reason to doubt him, but on this occasion his words evoked nothing but an unreasoning rage within me. A trap? This tiny child a trap? His words defied logic to such a degree that the proclamation was almost an obscenity!

My fury transferred itself to action, and I drew back my fist with the avowed intention of punching my best friend squarely on the nose. Holmes's reflexes were far quicker than mine, however, and enclosing my upraised wrist in an iron grip, he used his other hand to thrust something into my face – which I swiftly realized, from the sharply pungent stench, was a bottle of smelling salts!

The stench overrode all else, and I reeled back, my eyes watering, my senses and thoughts overwhelmed. I was aware only peripherally of Holmes holding me upright, and then turning me back around, so that I was once again facing the child.

"Look again, Watson!" he shouted directly into my ear. "Look again and see the truth of it!"

For several moments my watering eyes caused the tunnel to shimmer and blur, with nothing registering in my vision but a throng of dark shapes, bleeding one into the other. I blinked rapidly, and gradually the shapes before me acquired definition. Immediately I wished that they had not, for what was revealed to me was worse than the product of even my most terrible nightmares.

I have seen hell on the battlefield, but the sight of men torn open, limbless, yet still alive and screaming in agony, is at least a horror that I can understand. The horror in that tunnel, however, is one that defied nature and rationality. Stretching from one side of the tunnel to the other, in place of the child that I had previously seen, was a creature that I can only liken to a vast, pulsating starfish. Its flesh, oozing with slime and covered all over with tiny, upraised spines, was a deep blood-red, and at its center was a puckered orifice, like the wrinkled, toothless mouth of a crone, from the 'lips' of which multiple thin red fronds quivered and writhed, like blind snakes testing the air.

I think I gasped, or perhaps even moaned. Certainly, I made some sound that alerted the creature, although it is entirely likely that it was already aware of our presence.

All I know is that my first instinct was to reach for my revolver, which I had put into my pocket. Before I could do so, however, several of the red fronds suddenly lashed out like whips, one of which entwined itself around my right arm, another around my left, and a third around my throat.

The fronds were cold and wet, and although in circumference they were no thicker than a woman's finger, they possessed a tensile strength that was impossible to struggle against. Instantly I found myself unable to move, the frond that had wound itself around my neck tightening remorselessly, stinging my flesh as it latched on to me with tiny teeth-like spines, and causing my head to pound as my supply of air was slowly reduced.

Pinioned and helpless, I could only watch as the puckered orifice in the center of the creature's body gaped open, and another snake-like appendage emerged from it, this one colored black, dripping with slime, and considerably thicker in girth than the red fronds. The thing reared up above us, and to my utter horror I saw that its entire 'head' comprised a circular, lamprey-like mouth that was lined all around with row upon row of bristling, razor-sharp teeth.

Then, like a striking cobra, the thing swooped downwards, clamping itself to my stomach directly above my liver. I felt its teeth moving, shredding the material of my thick overcoat, and although I was grateful for the garment, I knew it would be only a matter of seconds before it managed to burrow its way through to my flesh.

Panic gripped me, but I could do nothing. My consciousness fading, and my vision along with it, I dimly perceived Holmes running forward, pulling something from the pocket of his Ulster. As the undulating length of the black tentacle that was clamped to me slammed against the tunnel wall, leaving a thick smear of colorless slime on the brickwork, I saw Holmes at first leap back, and then duck beneath it, emerging on the other side to hurl whatever he was holding at the spiny, pulsating body.

Through the pounding in my ears, I heard glass break, followed instantly by a fierce hissing, as if the brakes were being applied on a vast steam engine. The next second, the fronds that were wrapped tightly around my wrists and throat began to loosen, and then, to my immense relief, the circular maw that was burrowing through the thick tweed of my overcoat unclamped itself from my body.

As the fronds retracted, my legs, weakened by lack of oxygen, gave way, and I collapsed to the ground. Aware that to lose consciousness might be my undoing, I raised my head to see what was happening. Even in my dazed state, I realized that whatever Holmes had thrown at the creature had had some catastrophic effect upon it. The red fronds and the larger, lamprey-like appendage were now thrashing wildly back and forth, as though in acute agony. The central bulk of the creature, against which Holmes had dashed his glass beaker or vessel, was bubbling and melting, tendrils of vapor rising from the suppurating wound just above its puckered orifice, and amassing like mist beneath the ceiling. The creature's flesh was now not simply hissing but *sizzling*, like bacon dropped into hot fat, as the wound blackened and expanded.

It took only minutes for the creature to die. First its fronds shuddered and hung limp, then its lamprey-like appendage slumped to the ground. Finally it collapsed in upon itself, like a piece of rotting fruit.

Holmes helped me back to my feet, though our combined gaze remained fixed on the rapidly putrefying mass of now black and stinking flesh heaped upon the walkway before us. I was barely beginning to regain my strength when my friend murmured, "We have company, old man."

Peering beyond the abomination's steaming remains, I saw, reflected in Holmes's lantern light, the lambent eyes of the stunted creatures that had first attacked us, and that I now realized must have been guardians or servants, or perhaps both, of the monstrous foe we – or rather, Holmes – had vanquished. As the creatures crept closer, I heard a peculiar high keening sound echoing from the tunnel walls, and realized that they were mourning their hideous companion.

"They are emboldened by grief," Holmes said, "which I suspect may soon turn to rage. How are your legs, old friend?"

"Becoming stronger by the moment," I replied, willing it to be so.

"Then let us beat a hasty retreat."

We began to back away, and then, after several moments we turned and ran back the way we had come. Whether the little men pursued us I know not. All I could hear as we fled was the echoing clatter of footsteps, that I hoped were our own, and the rushing of blood in my ears. It seemed to take an age to reach the iron ladder situated beneath the opening in Hobb's Yard, but reach it we eventually did. The London that existed above us might have been a filthy, dangerous, often mean-spirited place, but as we clambered towards its still-pungent but infinitely fresher air, I had never been more grateful for it, nor more affectionately inclined to call it 'home'.

*

"It is an outlandish story, to be sure," Dr. Cornelius Layton said, "and yet if you, Mr. Holmes, and you, Dr. Watson, assert that it is true, then what recourse do I have but to believe you?"

It was a little over a week after our subterranean adventure, and Dr. Layton had invited us to dine with him at his club. The day following our ordeal, I had felt it incumbent upon me to inform him that Holmes and I had solved the case of the stolen livers, and that the killer would no longer plague the streets of East London. Naturally enough, the good doctor had been eager to hear the full details of our investigation.

At Layton's words, Holmes sat back in his chair, his food, excellent though it was, no more than nibbled at. I sipped my glass of wine and said, "It will perhaps not surprise you to know, Dr. Layton, that your ears will be among the very few to hear this particular tale. Write it up I shall, but it will not be for public consumption – not until Holmes and I are long in our graves, at any rate."

"Very wise," Layton said with a smile, and stared thoughtfully at the morsel of venison upon his fork. He chewed thoughtfully, and swallowed, and finally said with some reticence, "If I may… I am replete with questions…"

"Ask away," Holmes said.

The pathologist pursed his lips, as if, now that Holmes had given him leave to proceed, he was uncertain how to do so. Then he said, "What are your thoughts, Mr. Holmes, on what this creature may have been, and where it may have come from?"

Holmes and I had discussed this matter at length, and although he answered the question in a lazy drawl, I knew that my friend relished the presence of an attentive audience.

"The origin of the creature will forever be a mystery," he said, "though I am inclined to believe, given its singular properties, that it may have come from beyond the stars. My particular theory is that it arrived here as an infant, and that its journey to physical maturity has been a slow process, taking many years, perhaps even many decades."

"And its guardians came with it, I suppose?" Layton said eagerly. "To care for it, I mean?"

Holmes shook his head.

"On the contrary, its guardians, as you call them, are as human as you and I – or at least, they once were. As Dr. Watson and I experienced, the creature generated what can perhaps best be described as a wave of psychical energy, which altered not only the minds of those unfortunate enough to find themselves within its range of influence, but also the physiognomy of those exposed to it over a protracted period.

My belief is that when the creature first arrived here, it transmitted a summons of sorts to its would-be protectors, who may have seen it – as did Dr. Watson here – as a vulnerable child in need of nurture and sustenance. Perhaps these protectors were originally local inhabitants who happened to be unfortunate enough to live directly above the creature's lair, and so proved susceptible to its influence. Over many years, they transformed to become a protective cult – apostles who took up residence in the sewer, and were physically altered to better adapt to their surroundings. It was these apostles, I surmise, that initially ventured above ground to seek sustenance for the creature, butchering their victims and procuring livers for the beast to consume."

"Why livers in particular, Mr. Holmes?" Layton ventured.

Holmes smiled. "As a pathologist, I am sure you are aware of their value as one of the most nutritionally dense foods in the world. My theory is that the creature feasted on them, perhaps only intermittently at first, but as it grew it began to require a greater number – to the extent that eventually the frequency of their removal from the cadavers of murder victims alerted you to the peculiarity, Dr. Layton, in spite of the apostles' attempts to conceal their true intentions by dispatching their victims in a variety of ways."

"An act of vigilance for which you should be congratulated, Dr. Layton," I added, glancing at Holmes, who nodded.

"Yes, indeed. Dr. Watson is quite correct."

The portly pathologist blushed. "Why, thank you, Mr. Holmes, Dr. Watson. Your praise is valued, indeed. But if I may ask, the more... shall we say, *efficient* killing of the unfortunate Mrs. White..."

"...was perpetrated by the creature itself," Holmes said. "Either the beast had finally achieved a level of maturity that enabled it to venture from its lair and commit its own crimes, or Mrs. White had unwittingly stumbled into an area – namely Hobb's Yard – whereby the creature could launch an attack by way of the sewer entrance, the metal manhole cover to which, you recall, Watson, had been recently removed."

Layton shook his head sadly. "I need hardly wonder why the wretch found herself in such a vile place at that hour of the night. The poor must earn a penny howsoever they can."

With a sharp glance at their host, Holmes retorted a little waspishly, "Your insinuations do the blameless woman a disservice, Dr. Layton. The greater likelihood is that she was targeted while upon her homeward journey, and subsequently pursued into Hobb's Yard by the apostles, whereupon the creature rose up from below – the manhole cover having already been removed for the purpose – and did its ghastly work."

"Like chasing a mouse into the jaws of a snake," said I, my analogy causing Holmes to wince slightly.

"How horrible!" exclaimed Layton, to his credit looking as if he truly meant it. "And was the creature fully grown, would you say, Mr. Holmes? Or might it yet have extended its foul influence still further?"

"Who is to say?" Holmes replied.

"Who indeed?" said Layton with a shudder.

Layton and I each cut a slice of meat and chewed in silence for a moment, while Holmes idly pushed his vegetables around his plate with a fork. Replenishing our glasses, the pathologist said, "I am intrigued by this solution that you developed in your home laboratory, Mr. Holmes, and that you used to vanquish the creature. What did it consist of, may I ask?"

"It was a concentrated saline solution, nothing more," Holmes said. "Upon analyzing the mucus exuded by the creature, it was clear to me that the flesh of the beast would be highly permeable, and that, just as will happen to a slug, a liberal dose of salt will draw moisture from the skin and cause rapid dehydration, followed by cellular collapse." He paused, looking momentarily pained. "In many ways I regret the creature's demise. It was a unique and extraordinary specimen. Under controlled conditions, we may have learned much from it."

"You did the right thing, Holmes," I assured him, not for the first time. "The world is a far better place without such horrors in it."

"Dr. Watson is right," said Layton. "Of that I have no doubt. And what of the little men? The apostles? The cult that served this abomination? Have any of them yet been found?"

"Not yet," said I, "but I'm certain it will be only a matter of time before they are rooted out."

"I am glad to hear it. What say you, Mr. Holmes? Is Dr. Watson right?"

"Perhaps," said Holmes, and then all at once he smiled. "Pass the salt, would you?"

THE FIVE SYMBOLS

Simon Kurt Unsworth

The boy was lying on his back, arms spread wide as though to embrace the sky above him, and there were nails in his eyes.

Not one or two, but maybe twenty or more in each eye, so that the sockets were crammed with them. I couldn't see anything of the eyes themselves and thought that probably the birds had had them. A little blood had run across the poor little bleeder's face, soaking down to the collar of his shirt and staining his hair. There was dry eye-jelly slathered down both his cheeks.

"Jesus," said one of the constables, Neary I think, new to the job and not as used to this as his colleagues.

"If you plan to spew, do it somewhere else," I said without looking around. "And don't look for Jesus anywhere near this mess."

He was a street boy, or at least, he had been. His clothes were old, restitched and torn, filthy with mud and stinking of the docks. That probably made him a wharf rat, one of the beggars who hung around trying to roll drunken sailors at night and scavenging for dropped things during the day. The weak sun reflecting off the dried blood and eye slime made it look as though he was scaled, at least part fish, adapting to his environment.

I took out my notebook and sketched him, writing details down so that I might not forget them later. Then, using the tip of my pencil, I pushed at the nails. They didn't shift, instead I was forcing the boy's head sideways. They must have been deep inside his skull. Leaning over him I forced myself to count, focusing only on the number of nail heads that I could see. There were 23 in each eye socket and that little detail went in my notebook too.

"Sir," said another voice, "the porters are here."

I looked at the boy for another moment, then stood, wincing at the ache in my knees. I've got better at being a detective as I've grown older, but the improvement in my thinking and deducing are counterbalanced by the weaknesses I'm beginning to feel in my joints— and a weariness I've started to feel for the work. It grinds at you, the constant litany of it, and there's only so many times you can look at the torn, abused flesh of your dead fellow men and women and children before it starts to gain a weight that sits heavy and cumbersome on your shoulders, after all.

"See if any of the other rats know him," I told Neary, who impressively hadn't vomited.

"Sir," he said. I nodded to the porters and they moved in to take the body. Neither of them reacted to his face, I saw, and I wondered if they somehow avoided feeling the weight of his death and if so, how they did it.

"Leave that body alone!" said a voice I knew well.

"Hello, Holmes," I said without turning and then, to the porters, "leave it a moment."

I hadn't seen Holmes or Watson for several weeks. They'd been called away on some case or other and my evening visits to 221B hadn't resumed on their return. I hadn't called on them, or worried about it, because I knew we were bound to run into each other again. It's impossible to wade through the rivers of crime the way we do and not find each other. Kindred spirits, I suppose, call and attract.

He stepped forward, to my side, and looked at the corpse. Holmes didn't look well. His usual gauntness had peeled back to something almost skeletal and there were shadows under his eyes, dark and punchmark deep. Gossip had reached me through the other detectives that their interactions with Holmes had been even more fraught than usual, with him seeming distracted and even less sociable than ever before. Was it possible, I wondered, that he was also feeling the weight of the dead? That even the great Sherlock Holmes was capable of feeling something the way normal humans did?

I was being unfair, of course. Holmes has a mind set to a different speed than most of us and he may seem aloof and cold, but he's driven by a desire to see truth and justice served. He's also capable of friendship as Watson and, recently, myself know. It was the dead, the burden of their gaze and their need and their hands clutching at my ankles making me angry.

"What have you got, Lestrade?" asked Holmes, taking another step towards the body.

"A dead child," I said, keeping my voice flat as though discussing what I'd bought from the butcher. Holmes crouched by the dead tyke and studied him for a long moment. "He's a wharf rat," he said finally.

"I thought so," I replied and was gratified that Holmes glanced over his shoulder at me and smiled, a tired, there-and-gone glimpse of the man I'd been getting to know during my times at 221B.

"It's easy to forget that you've proved yourself over and over to be good at this," he said, turning back to the child, "but have you seen the other clues he's left you?"

I didn't say anything. Holmes would tell me anyway; of this I was certain.

"He's been dead a good few hours now, probably dying sometime last night." I wrote 'April 1' in my book. The Fool's Day. "He'd eaten recently, not that long before his death, there are fresh food spills on his jacket," said Holmes, pointing out the stains. "That's gravy, thick, so someone bought him a pie, or perhaps he stole one. He wasn't killed here. There's no blood on the ground beneath his head. He was put here afterward. There are no wounds other than the damage to the face, the eyes in particular. I've heard recently about this kind of thing, it's a form of punishment for debts unpaid. 'Look at this' the assailant is saying, 'look and see what happens when you don't pay your dues'."

This was new to me and I noted it.

"You're looking for a new gang," Holmes went on, "or at least, an adapted version of an old one. New leaders, maybe, or a new enforcer." He stood, holding his face for a moment in both hands, as though worried his head might topple

293

forwards. I thought again that he may be ill, or weary in his heart.

"Do you think he's been posed? Put this way deliberately?" I asked, holding my own arms out in demonstration. "It seems very...I don't know...theatrical?"

"No," said Holmes. "That's the way a body would fall if carried face down over a shoulder and then flung to the ground." He demonstrated, miming throwing an imaginary load off his shoulder and then turning, miming the body falling, its arms opening wide. "The legs stay together because they're still in, or have only just left, the assailant's arms."

It made sense. Everything Sherlock Holmes said made sense. It always did.

"I suppose there are no witnesses?"

"None as yet," I said, and couldn't get the slightly defensive tone out of my voice. It's hard not to think of Holmes as always being critical, because most of the time, he is.

"I suspect you won't find many. The eclipse had everybody staring upwards. A whole moon nearly vanishing must be more interesting than some poor child's time on earth ending, after all." He sounded sick, sick and tired and disgusted and it was all I could do to prevent myself reaching out and placing a hand on his shoulder.

"I know," I said, and hoped my friend knew I was talking about more than the death.

Holmes turned, nodded at me and left without another word. I watched him go, an exclamation point of a man in a world where most of us are mere questions, and then I turned back to the body. The porters were already moving back in and my constables were already moving out among the waifs and strays and drunks and working men arriving at the Borough Market dock for their day's labors. As tarnished and warped as it was, all was as right as it ever got in my world.

*

We spent a couple of days trying to find out about the new gang Holmes had mentioned but nothing turned up. The dead boy became one of many and fell from the top of my pile to the bottom as new atrocities were committed and new crimes came to light. No one knew anything, no one saw anything, no one heard anyone, everyone was one of the wise monkeys.

Somewhere out in the cold oceans hundreds of people were reportedly drowned when the Titanic went down. The talk about the disaster was split between sorrow and how the rich nobs deserved it but I thought then and I think now that those people saying that had never had to truly deal with death, because if they had they wouldn't have wished it on anyone. Death went on, as did life. Barnsley won the FA cup, which pleased those that liked that kind of thing but did little for me, and the streets of London continued full of swill and mud and violence.

And then we had another child.

It was another urchin, some dirty, scruffy little sod from one of the orphanages. I vaguely knew his face because he begged around the Victoria Embankment just down from the Yard and we had to keep having constables run him and his friends off. I had a feeling he was supposed to attend one of the church schools near the embankment but as we mostly saw him in the daytime, I suppose he'd decided education wasn't for him.

I didn't make the connection at first, because the young die as easily and often as the old in the city, but when I looked at him closely, I realized that he might be linked to the earlier boy.

Like the first body, he was lying on his back, although not at a dock. Instead, he was in one of the ginnels that warrened the backstreets of my city. Arms spread wide, palms to the sky as though asking for benediction. So far, so similar, but there were differences as well. His eyes were unmarked, but his ears had been completely filled with thick black tar so that his ears were plugged. I saw that the skin around the edges of the tar was reddened and burned. The tar had been heated when it was poured in. There was more tar in his greasy hair but none on the ground below him. When I tapped at it with a pencil it was fairly hard, which meant it was hours since it had been poured. I looked at the totality of the scene as my constables went around the houses so that they could be told no one had seen nothing and sod off copper and thought again how theatrical it looked. I knew what Holmes had said, but I couldn't shake the feeling that in his assertions about this he might be wrong. I wanted to talk to him but he didn't come to see this dead child, and I found I missed his and Watson's insights and help. Hell, I missed *them*. However we had started, we had become friends over the last years and I valued their perspectives on my cases even when, as now, they didn't quite square with my instincts. I'd heard Holmes was on a case in the Midlands and wouldn't be back for a few more days, but I resolved to speak to him on his return.

That afternoon, with the promise of payment and a meal, I got another urchin to come to the police gym with me, and then spent a few hours slinging him from off my shoulder and onto matting, ignoring his *oofs* and gasps and demands for more money. I found that I could get him to fall the way the two dead boys had fallen, but it took some time and didn't happen accidentally. Usually, momentum would bounce the child from his back over onto his side when dropped from any kind of height. Of course, the matting may have contributed to that, and the fact that the body I was using would constantly tense and wriggle, but I didn't think it would make that much difference.

The splayed positions of the corpses, I was sure, was deliberate.

After I'd paid my debt and bought the boy food from a street vendor, I went back to my office. I've learned to ignore the noise of the station around me, and the smells of sweat and shit and piss and cheap meat that seems to hang in the air around the cells unless it's bad, which it was that day, so I rolled a coffin nail and smoked it while looking between two sets of notes. Two dead boys, two identical body positions. It stretched my credulity that they had both landed like that randomly, which meant...what? A killer who'd learned, as I had today, the very particular twist and turn you had to do to get the body to stay that way when dropped from a shoulder? Or two bodies that hadn't been dropped but positioned?

By who? And if they hadn't died where they'd been found, why had no one seen them being brought. Hell, why had no one seen a figure carrying a child on its shoulder near the crime scene either time? Although, I suppose, if Jack the Ripper can do what he did those six times and nobody saw a dickybird, then maybe I shouldn't have been surprised. I was doodling on a piece of paper, drawing eyes with nails in them when Neary appeared at my door. "Sir," he said, "there's a

German bloke been beaten by two Irish blokes and he's demanding to speak to a detective. You free?"

I looked at my notes and the cigarette I held, now burned to almost nothing, and said, "Not free, maybe, but I can come and talk to the Kraut. Have we got the two he says did him?"

"In the cells, sir. Both pissed and one's puking."

"Get the other one to clean it up and tell them I'll be speaking to them soon." I stood. The dead boys would have to wait, and my doodling could wait with them.

*

We had a fortnight's gap, then there was another.

This one was lying on his back, arms outstretched, on the shore of Long Water near Serpentine Bridge, and his nose was broken, although 'broken' doesn't really do justice to what had been done to him. It looked as though someone had put the poor bastard's nose in a clamp and twisted, and twisted hard, so that the bone had splintered and torn through the skin and the nostrils were now distorted into new, angry shapes and had moved position so that they were lying to the side. There was no blood except for a dark scrub of it around both misshapen nostril rims.

The weeks had been frustrating ones. Feelers I'd sent out about the possible gang link to the first murder continued to come up empty and there were no new leads for either of the previous deaths. The coroner had concluded that both boys had likely been poisoned, and that both had eaten well before their deaths: steak and kidney pie for one and fish for the other. Both were malnourished but apart from the obvious signs of a life lived out past the margins neither had injuries that would have caused their deaths. The nails and the tar, it seemed, had been applied post-mortem. "Poison," he'd said to me. "God knows what sort and I haven't got time or the resources to check, but I'm confident it was poison." Why in the holy hell would anyone want to poison little kids?

And now I had a third, linked by the positioning of the body and the strangeness of the violence done to the bodies. Reluctantly, I sent for Sherlock Holmes.

Reluctantly, because I'd heard he'd returned from wherever he'd been sometime earlier in the week but he'd still made no contact with me. A couple of my constables had bumped into him a night or so back, and Watson had been sniffing around the station to see if anything interesting had come in, but still hadn't seen either of them myself, and I didn't want to intrude if he was feeling less sociable than usual. Needs must, though, and didn't feel I had much choice. This was, at least for now, beyond me.

While we waited for the constable to get to 221B and return, hopefully with Holmes in tow, I inspected the body more closely. It was clear straight away that this one had been a runner for one of London's backstreet bookies. His pockets were full of betting slips and promissory notes. He had no money, as kids weren't ever allowed to handle the actual cash, but runners sometimes got tips and gifts from the winners and it showed in his stature and appearance. His clothes were slightly cleaner, slightly better fitting, slightly less foul-smelling, and he was a little better fed and healthier looking than the other two. He didn't look unhealthy at all, not really. Apart from the nose, of course.

That damage aside, there were no other obvious injuries. On a hunch I used my pencil to push back one of the lapels of the jacket he was wearing to reveal the shirt beneath. It was stained and old but showed signs of being cared for, repaired and washed at some infrequent points in the past. The poor thing had spent his days and nights working in this ugly city's back streets and ginnels and yards and lanes, trying to survive, trying to stay well and warm, and where had it got him? On his back by the Long Water where any passer-by crossing Serpentine Bridge could gawk down at him in this, his last undignified pose on the earth.

There were stains on his shirt that looked fresh. I leaned in and sniffed and caught of a scent, something like gravy. Not long before he died, he'd eaten. It wasn't much but it gave us somewhere to start. The slips in his pocket were all headed by the bookie's mark and although it wasn't one that was familiar to me, I was confident one of the constables would recognize it. I detailed them to find the man, get the boy's name from him, work out his base of operations the previous night and then fan out and speak to every food vendor they could find and see if any of them had served the boy, with or without a companion.

That done, I carried on studying him.

There was nothing else. Nothing to help, to give me a clue or a hint or even a fucking hunch to work on.

"Another one?" asked Holmes from behind me. He'd approached as silent as ever and was studying the corpse over my shoulder.

"Another one," I said. "I need help, Holmes. Please."

"You're sure they're linked?" I didn't answer. I didn't see how they *couldn't* be linked, and couldn't see how Holmes could think that either. "Yes, you're probably right. He's eaten? Recently?"

"Yes. The others were poisoned so I think this one may have been too."

"Poison's a woman's tool, Lestrade," said Holmes. "Perhaps a street mother gone odd? Have you checked the local hospitals for recently bereaved females, especially any who lost a child at, or just after, birth and didn't seem to be carrying the weight of that well?"

It was as good a plan as any I'd had and I sent another couple of constables to check with the local hospitals, doctors and midwives. "I can't see a logic to it," I said. "Most killers do the same thing, use the same method, but even if poison's the commonality, why the butchery after? And why different butchery?"

"There's a doctor in Canada, Ogden. She and a detective have dealt with this kind of thing a time or two and have written about it. I've read their work, and it's interesting. In one of their monographs they call this the work of a 'sequential killer'. They mean a killer whose methods mean little from the outside because they run on some internal logic and their motives aren't the usual ones of money, sex, revenge or anger. They have compulsions they have to act upon, and the deaths are a result of this rather than any more usual cause. The trick is to identify the similarities because that's how they say you can find your way to the center. Focus on the poison, Lestrade, the poison and the food. That's how you'll crack this."

"Focus on them how?" I asked, but when I turned, Holmes had already started walking away.

It was a frustrating few days. We found a name for this one, the first time we'd managed to get that far. The poor mite was called Coaldust for some reason, and he ran for a master called Benoit Twoknuckles. Twoknuckles was a decent enough bookie, apparently, fair to pay up and not too quick to use his fist on punter or runner. Once he realized he wasn't in trouble, at least in relation to Coaldust's death, he was fairly open with the constables and seemed to be genuinely upset by the boy's passing. Coaldust, he said, had been sent to take bets and pass messages in the areas around Kensington, where Twoknuckles boasted he had many gentlemen clients.

Kensington didn't have many food hawkers, and although one or two of them had seen Coaldust, all were positive that they had not served him food or served anyone food that was then passed to him. None had ongoing disagreements with Twoknuckles and we couldn't find any link between them and the other dead boys.

The hospitals and midwives gave us the opposite, a surfeit of women who'd lost children, and my constables' time was taken trying to track them all down and see if they were mad or not. Most were miserable, poor, worn down, but none looked good for the killing of Coaldust or the others.

The coroner, meantime, had got no further with identifying a poison despite my verbal boot up his arse. All he could tell me was that it was something naturally occurring as there had been nothing obviously foreign in any of the bloodstreams of the corpses. As an aside, he did tell me that the first of the boys, the wharf rat, had congested lungs and would likely have been dead within a few months and that the second was malnourished to the point that he was almost starving to death. He'd not mentioned it before because it was common.

More dead ends, more non-starters, and the dead were heavier and heavier on my back and their breath was on my neck, cold and dank and smelling of failure and loss. In desperation, I cleared everything else off my desk, convinced now that the solving of these three cases, these sequential killings, was of an importance beyond the rest of my cases. So far, because of the longer gaps between the deaths, no one in the press had linked them and I wanted it to stay that way, to keep the panic that could thread its way along London's packed streets like wildfire, at bay. Jack had shown us what happened when the angels of death held more sway than the questionable angels of order and it hadn't been pleasant. Panic, mob rule, accusation, intimidation and fear made for uneasy streets, and uneasy streets made for a city impossible to keep within the twin lines of law and morality. I needed a break, a thread, anything, something to pull and receive some answering tug. On my desk's surface I put every piece of paper, every sketch, every note I had about the cases and swirled them with my hand, hoping that the chaos of papers would reveal some new order, but before I could get to looking my office door opened and Neary, like some bleak messenger of darkness, said, "We've another, sir."

*

On her back, arms outstretched, unmarked except for her tongue, which had been drawn out from her mouth and run through with a set of crossed skewers, so that it could not retreat back behind her rotten and bent teeth.

She was, I thought, maybe fourteen, older than the others, but slighter. I made a note in my book wondering if she had looked younger in the darkness because of her slimness and short stature but really, what did it matter? What would it help, knowing that?

It'd help because it might narrow down how the murderer picked the buggers he killed, I told myself angrily. I'd had cases that hadn't moved before, plenty of them. Hell, there were case files aplenty in my cabinets that showed no gains in momentum, were open now years after the crimes had been committed and which I knew would never be solved. What was so different about these, that were getting under my skin so?

Because, I realized, of something I'd said to Holmes whilst stood over that first body. Most crimes were sordid, ugly, small things, brutal and shocking, yes, for reasons that were unimaginative and predictable, but these? There was a theatricality to the way the bodies had been left that showed the murderer had a purpose beyond the average, that they wanted these bodies to be found and to be seen and to be recognized.

But recognized for *what*? Recognized by who?

I had nothing. I sent the body to the coroner with strict instructions he was to check if the girl had eaten in the hours before her death, and if poison was the likely cause of it, and then wandered around, disconsolate, looking for clues. I needed help.

I needed Sherlock Holmes.

He wasn't at 221B, so I left a message with Mrs. Hudson, who eyed me with her normal suspicion, as though I might try and nick the silverware, and returned to the office. The swirl of papers yielded no hints but remained resolutely mute, and I gathered them back into order. As I finished a voice said from the doorway, "He's outside, mate."

'Mate'? The speaker was a boy slightly younger than the jacket I wore, who was leaning against the doorjamb smoking a cigarette. "How did you get in here?" I asked. "The public aren't supposed to come back here."

"S'easy," he said, shrugging, "when you know what to do and where to go."

"You're one of his, aren't you? He's outside?"

"That's what I said. Never took you as a deaf, mate."

"Don't be cheeky," I said. I glanced over my now-tidy desk, wrote a note for whoever might come looking for me, and went over to the Irregular.

"He says you 'ave to tip me," the boy said and I cuffed him on the side of the head, although only gently. "Does he, bollocks," I replied, "he pays you well for your services and I damn well know it. Now, take me to him and we'll say no more about your attempt to steal from a poor, near-deaf copper."

Grumbling, he led me from the office to where Holmes was waiting for me in a hansom.

*

"Lestrade," Holmes said, when I was settled in the cab and it had started to move.

"Holmes."

"You've needed my help recently and I haven't been here to provide it." It was a statement, not a question, and I did not reply. "I apologize."

My first thought was that his illness, if he had one, was worse. He had lost, if possible, more weight and his face now appeared as shrunken and lined as one of those heads explorers sometimes brought back from Africa. Worse, maybe, was that he was unsettled and nervous, his head constantly turning so that he could peer out of the hansom's windows. His hands fluttered up and down like birds whose nest had been raided by a snake and whose eggs were now a meal.

"I can't offer you help now, friend, but maybe I can offer you an explanation. It may not make sense to you, but I owe it to you. Friends, after all, do not treat friends as badly I have done you, do they? You'll know that I've been away a lot recently but not, I think, where I've been?"

"No."

"Let me show you, and while we travel let me try to explain." I settled back. Holmes was rarely expansive and I was determined to luxuriate in this unexpected opportunity, no matter what the circumstances.

"I'm getting old, old friend, and do me the courtesy of not trying to state otherwise because we both know it'd make a liar of you, and in aging I have found myself unsure. I am a creature of logic, Lestrade, of the step-by-step solution, of pieces of a puzzle being found and fitted to form a picture that creates a solution. Sometimes the puzzles might be fiendish, yes, or outlandish, but there is always a logic to them that I can find. I walk into a place and I see its elements, I smell the polishes and tobaccos and hair pomades, I hear its creaks and feel the hollows and solids of its walls and I can tell you who has been there, when, why, how long ago. You know this, yes?"

I did.

"But these last years something has been happening. There are crimes that fail logic, whose patterns I simply can't read. The Ripper made no sense to me, Lestrade. It's not logical, do you understand?"

The cab jolted and my body jerked, head nodding because I did know what he meant. "And since then there have been more, Chapman and the Lambeth strangler and others, people whose crimes speak to a set of rules I cannot fathom."

"Sequential killers?"

"Yes! But the sequences they work to are warped somehow, not like the cold elegance of maths or chemistry or physics, which you can map out, predict. Oh, I know people have tried to look backwards along the paths of the crimes to try to elicit some kind of graspable form like poor Thomas Bond's attempt to study the bodies left by the Ripper to discern who the Ripper might be, but it doesn't work. Or at least, I can't make it work."

I'd never seen Holmes like this, so vulnerable, admitting so much of his own ignorance. He was usually the very model of arrogance and self-belief, and I didn't know what to say. Oddly, and for the first and only time, I wanted to put my arms around him and simply hold him, to try and give him comfort and strength that way. I didn't.

"For a number of years I wasn't sure what to do about it," Holmes continued. "How do you learn about a new type of crime, a new type of *criminal*, when they are by their very nature almost impossible to track and trail? So I tried to think about what made them, what their structures must be. That they evade capture means there must be some level of intelligence, of planning and structured reaction to events, even at the height of their frenzies. Look at Jack, how he was never seen. His crimes are surely the work of a madman, yet his absence from the courts means he must have been able to plan and adapt, because it cannot have been simple luck." Again, I nodded because he was right.

"Madness. As a word, we think it means a single thing, but what I've come to realize, Lestrade, is that it encompasses a vast range of differing conditions, or differing experiences or perceptions. Some madness is savage and bitter and howling, yes, but other madness is calculating and sharp, and that's what I've been trying to do.

"I've been allying myself with the mad."

The hansom stopped and we were at Bedlam or, more accurately, the St Mary Bethlem hospital in Southwark.

I'm sure Holmes would have made an excellent showman because he finished his speech perfectly to coincide with the cab stopping by Bedlam's gates. He opened the door and stepped down, motioning me to follow. I did, wondering what we were doing here. It was dark now, and the hospital would surely be closed to public visitation, although if needed I could try to police the doors open with my badge and the invocation of some law or other.

I didn't need to. Holmes and I were waved through the gates, waved through the reception and waved into a side room without so much as a query. "They let you in?"

"I'm well known," Holmes replied. "I think they've enjoyed my visiting here."

"How long have you been coming?"

"Several years now. They're kind enough to let me look at the patient notes and sometimes talk to the patients. I've made some suggestions to help, although not many. Logic, as I've said, doesn't have a great foothold here."

"Holmes, what are we doing here? What has this to do with my cases?"

"Patience, Lestrade. I will explain, as best I can.

"There used to be two statues at the entrance to the hospital called Melancholy and Raving Madness. They were life-sized reclining human figures but entirely different. Melancholy was slack-faced, disengaged, whereas Raving Madness was angry, raging, chained to prevent escape or damage, and they represented the two extremes of insanity."

I put my head in my hands and groaned. "Holmes," I said, "how is this helping? It's fascinating, surely, but how is this helping *me?*"

"Because to solve crimes like this, Lestrade, we need to be able to understand the language of melancholy and raving, but their language is not yet one you know. Here, look at these." He rose and went to the cabinet in the corner of the office and took out a folder which he passed to me. When I opened it, I found it was full of pieces of art, intricately detailed sketches of fae creatures against dark woodland backgrounds, their faces beauteous yet somehow turned and tortured. Some of the backgrounds contained detailing that might have been eyes peering from shadows and hands reaching out to grasp the foreground figures. The pieces were quietly beautiful and terribly ominous all at once.

"Beautiful, aren't they? They're the work of a former patient here called Richard Dadd. He was struck with a brain fever early in life and came to think his father was the devil. He eventually killed him, and then tried to kill another fellow whilst fleeing. From the outside, a clear case of insanity, yet to Dadd his act had rational purpose: to murder the great evil, Satan.

"Dadd couldn't tell people that he was mad but he tried to draw it out. Look at the art, you can feel the tension and desperation in every piece. Dadd was searching for a way to communicate his difference to the usual, to the normal. Can't you see?"

"No." I stood. This was getting me nowhere. I had come to Holmes for help and all I was getting was history and madness. "Thank you," I said, "but I have to go. There's a killer out there."

"Who you'll never catch unless you understand *why* they're doing what they're doing. Jack didn't get caught because there was no rationale for his acts, so no way to predict them from the outside, but to him they may well have seemed like utterly necessary, rational reasons. Jack's acts, Dadd's acts, this killer's acts, they're symbols, they have meaning outside of themselves. To understand them, you have to make sense of them, you must find the senses in the symbols. Don't you see?"

"No," I said again. "I'm sorry, Holmes, I don't." I'd never seen him like this, and I didn't like it. This Holmes was unsure, grasping at something, but unable to clearly explain what he was grasping for, an arch rationalist, perhaps *the* arch rationalist, talking about symbols and senses.

"I'm sorry," said Holmes, "I've not explained myself well. Maybe I won't ever be able to. Please, Lestrade, take my hansom and use it to return to your office. Follow the poison, follow the mothers, try to understand the symbolic elements of the deaths. Good luck. Call upon me soon?"

"I'd like that," I said, and meant it.

*

It was the early hours when I got back from Southwark and my odd meeting with Holmes. The station, although not quiet, was at least quieter. I rested for a while on the couch in my

310

office but found myself unable to sleep and eventually rose to sit at my desk again. My head ached and my eyes felt like dry weights in a skull that was too big for the skin covering it. "What am I missing?" I asked out loud, but the files merely stared back at me, mute and dull.

I tried to look at the cases as Holmes had urged, to see the deaths as symbols, but I didn't understand their...what had he called it? Their language. How could crimes like this, like Jack's, make any sense to anyone but their perpetrator? I had a dull thud somewhere behind my eyes from thinking, from concentrating, and still, I could go nowhere with it, simply turning in circles and circles and...

...circles. I grabbed a map from in my desk and unfolded it, putting my inkpot on the first murder site, my pen on the second, notebook on third and an ashtray on the fourth. It was a little rough and ready but I saw straight away that the four could be joined by lines to form the base and sides of a pentangle, but if you looked at it another way, they were also equidistant points on the circumference of an incomplete circle. And if they were a circle then there was a fifth point needed to complete it.

Yes.

And what had Holmes said? Make sense of the symbols? And then I saw it, and I cursed myself for an idiot and a stupid addle-pated fool. Not 'sense' in the way Holmes had meant but *senses,* sight and hearing and smell and taste, four of the five. Things were crashing together now, twisting about each other and forming new strands and my mind was haring after them hither and yon. The deaths were symbolic of senses, but symbolic of what exactly? A call for them? An exultation of them? Four bodies, four senses, making a near complete circle with only a fifth needed – touch.

And there was a thread, a logical one, that ran through these killings, only it was a thread of things not there and that should have been and that, maybe, was why I missed it.

Symbols. Something that had been said at the scene of the first murder popped like a bubble of air in mud within my head and I dove into the papers for my notes from that day. Something about why the killer hadn't been seen, about all eyes being upwards. Jesus, yes, there'd been an eclipse that night, a partial one of the moon, and wasn't that a symbol, a sign of forces greater than all of us, impartial and implacable?

First boy killed during an eclipse. I looked out of the window and saw that the moon was again being sliced away and knew that I had to move fast to try to prevent a murder. I looked at the map, running a finger up from the existing line to the next evenly spaced point, the place of the fifth symbol.

I had to get to Primrose Hill.

*

The police carriage clattered up to the park gates, which were locked. I didn't have time to find the keeper to get them open so I scrambled up and over, dropping to the other side and disappearing into the shadowy depths of the park with a shouted instruction back to the driver to gather more constables and follow when they could.

I followed the path, reasoning that the killer would too, as they would have a burden. If I was right, if this was about the symbolic rather than the prosaic, I didn't have to search because I knew where the killer would be. There was only really one place, one symbolic center. The top of the hill, looking down on the whole of London. I hoped I was wrong but I knew in my copper's gut that I was awfully, terribly right.

Up I went, emerging from the shadows of the trees into the corrupting moonlight, and saw a figure ahead of me on the hill's crest. They were kneeling over something and I shouted "No!" as I ran, panting. Grass whipped at my ankles and water soaked my trouser cuffs. I had my truncheon, a holdover from my uniformed days, which I always had stuffed in my overcoat pocket, and was holding it before me as I ran. I wished I'd thought to bring a torch, but even with the moon being eaten out of the night's sky there was enough light to see by.

Enough light to see the body.

I'd forgot, damn me, forgot that the deaths weren't at the places the bodies were found. Maybe they happened at the center of the circle, maybe I should have realized earlier, gone there sooner. Maybe. I roared as I ran, raised the truncheon and sped up. The kneeling figure rose, dropping something as it did so.

"Lestrade. You're too late," said Holmes, and the expression on his face was one of mingled triumph and relief.

I swung the truncheon and, to my surprise, he didn't move fast enough to avoid it. The Holmes I had known, had thought I'd known, all these years was nimble, calculating, aware and a canny fighter, and should have dodged the blow easily. Instead, his reaction was slow and although I missed his head because he jerked back, I caught him on the shoulder, knocking him sideways and back down to one knee. I stood over him, panting, betrayed, head filled with things that needed to be said and to be asked and to be screamed but all I could think of, the only word that escaped, was, "Why?"

"Because I realized that this was the only way." He might have been talking about deciding which shirt to wear. I glanced at the body; another boy, young and dead, arms outstretched. All of his fingers had been removed and placed on his chest, pale worms against his dark jacket. There was not a lot of blood around the severed edges.

"They're my symbols, Lestrade. The language of the crimes we used to investigate wasn't enough, I needed something more. I needed the language of crimes so terrible that understanding them is beyond most people." He didn't look mad, but he must be.

"Symbols to achieve what? What do you want, Holmes? Why this? To hold onto your senses as you get older? Hold back the years? Keep your skills? To stop losing them?"

He stood, carefully. His arm hung motionless and he rubbed at his injured shoulder with his other hand. "Have you any idea what it's like to be me, Lestrade? I walk into a room and every detail leaps out at me whether I want it to or not. I know where people come from, where they're going, what they planned and schemed and carried out. I can see and hear where secret panels lead to secret passages and where marks on benches lead to dead men and lost riches and all manner of things. I can know the tobacco a man smokes from the smell lingering on his clothes and food he ate from the stains on his weskit.

"It's hateful. It's exhausting. I'm not asking the universe to give me more of this, Lestrade. I'm asking it to take it away."

I looked at Holmes and he looked back at me. "I'm worn thin," he said simply. "I'm exhausted. Everywhere I go I know *everything*, and the clamor of it in my head is constant. I can't turn it off and I realized that this must be what it's like to be mad, to have the voices of Melancholy and Raving in your head, but I looked at Dadd and the others, and they found peace through their actions. They found a way to balance Raving and Melancholy. That's all I want, Lestrade, to have some well-earned rest. To retire to Sussex and keep bees and to not have to think about crime again.

"I didn't hurt the children. They were all dying anyway. Ill and malnourished in their turn, none of them was long for this world. I gave them companionship, a good meal and when they fell to slumber... I used them to try and find peace."

"You led me wrong all the way through," I said. "With the nonsense about gangs and then mad women. Even tonight, you sent me away hoping I'd keep chasing phantoms."

"Yes. But I'd forgotten, Lestrade, how tenacious you are."

"You didn't forget, you under-estimated me. Again."

"Yes. I'm sorry."

In the distance we both heard a clank of gates opening and the shrill blast of police whistles. I reached for my cuffs, not taking my eyes off Holmes's face.

"Please," he said. "I'm done. If it works or if it doesn't, there's no more. Don't tarnish my reputation. Let me retire. I have the letter of withdrawal in my pocket. Take it and let it go. I've earned it. Please."

I wanted to hit him again. Tarnish his reputation? I raised my truncheon high and although I could feel my hand shaking, I knew I would kill him if I hit him hard enough.

"It'd destroy John," said Holmes quietly. "You have my word they didn't suffer. What I did to them later, well, I'll carry that with me ever after, you know that, but I had to do something. I'll go mad if I carry on the way I am."

"You could have put the tar in your own ears or the nails in your own eyes," I said, and I could hear the bitterness in my voice.

"I couldn't," he said. "I'm not able to. I won't tell you I tried but I did consider it for a long time. Please, Lestrade, we were friends and if that counts for anything please let me just retire."

The whistles were closer now, spreading out across the park as they searched for us. I had only to call out and they'd be on us in moments. I didn't know what to do. How many people were alive, were free, because of Sherlock Holmes? How many injustices had been righted by him, how many international and national incidents averted or settled?

And there was the other thing. Before, I'd had what he described, the sudden explosion of information that comes at you like a roaring wall and there's no way to keep up and you can't write it all as fast as your mind is grasping it. I was lucky enough to get it during most cases, that moment where the dominos fall and where the trails suddenly become obvious. It lasted a minute, maybe more, and it was dizzying. *Imagine being like that every minute of wakefulness*, I thought, *that's what it must be like for Holmes. Jesus. Imagine the sheer pressure of it!*

"Do you think it'll work?"

"I don't know. I hope so. If it doesn't, I'll end up in Bedlam myself," he said. The truncheon wavered in the air, the cuffs dangling from my other hand. He was looking at me and I think if he'd spoken again things may have turned out very differently, but he didn't. Holmes stayed silent and after a long moment I dropped my truncheon and, gazing up at the diminishing moon, called out, "We're here."

We waited, Holmes still staring at me, brow wrinkled. When the first constables arrived, I said, "We saw someone run that way. You and you, after him, you and you get a cordon set up around this poor bastard's body, you call the porters, then go and wake the coroner," and then we stood and watched as the machinery of the constabulary took over. Constables fanned out across the park while others set up lights and called the porters and swept the ground for clues.

"Thank you," said Holmes. I didn't reply. What was there to say?

Holmes started off down the hill and then stopped, turning back to me. "Lestrade, as this is, I presume, the last time we'll see each other, can I ask one last thing? What's your first name. I've never heard anyone use it, only ever call you 'Lestrade'?"

"I don't have one. My parents left that part of the registration blank, so I'm simply Lestrade."

"I see. Thank you again, friend Lestrade." And with that, he was gone. I never saw him again.

Later, after the porters had taken the body, I walked back to the gates and the dead were on my shoulders, the five new members of the congregation sitting at their head, and the weight of them was like the drag of chains fixed to an anchor.

A KILLING THOUGHT

Josh Reynolds

It is not often that Sherlock Holmes can be said to be distressed. In fact, I can count on one hand the number of times I have seen my friend's equanimity broken. Yet, when I called round to the Baker Street lodgings we had shared, prior to my marriage, on that particular day, I found him in a state of most unusual agitation. Were he anyone else I would have called it fear, but I had never known Holmes to be afraid.

It was a grisly autumn day when I made my visit. I had not heard from Holmes in some months, so when Mrs. Hudson contacted me and asked me to pay a call on my old friend, I braved the inclement weather and the foggy streets and made my way to Baker Street. I arrived to find Mrs. Hudson in a state of some anxiety. I put her at ease as best I was able, and made my way upstairs to confront the dragon in his lair.

I found Holmes huddled in his favorite armchair, which he had at some point dragged from its usual spot by the fire to face the window. There, he crouched in his threadbare dressing gown, staring down at the street with an air of what I could only call unsettled anticipation. "Watson," he said, as Mrs. Hudson closed the door behind me. "You have chosen a most inauspicious time to visit, I fear."

"Oh?" I asked. "Am I interrupting something?" I spoke lightly, for I could see that a dark mood was on him. It was not the first time I had seen him in such a state, and initially, I suspected that he was suffering from that old and familiar malady – ennui.

As the most preeminent of that now sadly common breed of consulting detective, my friend had his pick of cases to investigate. Like any gourmet, he chose them carefully; he disdained the commonplace in favor of more outré offerings. Sadly, such matters of interest were often few and far between. Or so he insisted.

"My imminent demise," he said, flatly.

I stopped. "What?"

"Take a seat, Watson. There's tea on the table." He gestured towards the nearby table, but did not take his eyes from the window. The tea was there, but had long since gone cold. His breakfast was still on the table, untouched. I took my usual seat.

"What do you mean, your imminent demise?" I asked.

"I should think the phrase self-explanatory, Watson."

I bristled a bit at this, I admit. Since moving from Baker Street, I had lost some of the toughness of feeling that living with Holmes required. But I knew better than to rise to the bait. "Forgive me, Holmes. You are right, of course. Shall I leave you to it, then? Perhaps I can ring round later and tidy up after your inevitable messy end."

Holmes gave a bark of laughter. "That would be most kind of you, Watson. But I fear that if you attempt to leave, you may not make it home to Mary."

"Someone is watching, I take it," I said.

"Always. But in this instance, our observer is decidedly hostile." His gaze returned to the window and he gave a hiss of dismay. "Gone! Curse my inattentiveness." He rose from his chair, and I saw a telltale bulge in the pocket of his dressing gown. It was rare that Holmes felt the need to arm himself while in Baker Street. That single element told me that Holmes was truly in fear for his life, in a way I had seldom seen before.

"Who's out there, Holmes? Some assassin?"

"An assassin? Yes, one might call it that." Holmes retreated to the fireplace, where he lit a cigarette and began to furiously puff away. "A most singular assassin indeed. It is unlike any member of that dubious fraternity we have ever encountered."

"It," I repeated, in confusion. "Surely you mean he – or even she?"

"I always choose my words with care, Watson. It is neither man nor woman, brute nor human, as the American fantasist Poe might have it." He turned to me, his eyes burning with feverish intent. "Rather, it is something…inconceivable." Seeing my expression, he added quickly, "Note that I do not say impossible, Watson. Merely incredible."

"Tell me," I said.

Holmes gave a small shake of his head and turned back to the fire, one lean hand pressed to the mantle. He stood that way for long moments, smoking his cigarette in contemplative silence. Well-used to these displays of reticence, I said nothing. In another lifetime, Holmes might have been one of the finest actors to ever have trod the boards. He knew well how to command an audience's attention and hold it, even in silence.

After a time, he cleared his throat and began. "You have read, I trust, of the recent death of the honorable Sir Mortimer Pakenham. The circumstances were splashed across the front page of every Fleet Street publication, so you can hardly have missed it."

I nodded. Pakenham had been a shipping magnate of no small reputation. He'd been found dead in his locked study, with the appearance of having fallen from a great height. It was exactly the sort of case that would interest Holmes. "Were you asked to help the police with their inquiries?"

Holmes, still watching the fire, nodded. "Hopkins caught the case. He brought it to me the very same night. He's a bright fellow, and will go far, circumstances allowing."

I hid a smile. It was rare that any Scotland Yard inspector impressed Holmes. It helped that Hopkins was an eager student of Holmes's methodology. And unlike the ambitious Gregson, or even poor Lestrade, he was more than willing to acknowledge Holmes's contributions to his arrests. "I assume you made short work of it," I said.

Holmes frowned and glanced at the window. "Regrettably, my investigation was interrupted." He took a last pull on his cigarette, and tossed it into the fire. Then, his hand darted into the pocket of his dressing gown and emerged clasped about a revolver. Before I could so much as speak, he spun and levelled the weapon at the window – but he did not fire immediately. Instead, in a low voice, he said, "Come away from the window, Watson. Quickly, if you please, there's a good fellow."

I did as he asked with as much haste as I could muster. My hand itched for the feel of my own service weapon, still tucked safely in a drawer of my writing desk at home. I suddenly wished that I had thought to bring it, but I had not imagined needing it. "What is it, Holmes? What's out there?"

"What is it, indeed," he murmured, never taking his eyes from the window. "A good question, Watson. One I have, as yet, been unable to answer. Perhaps we shall find out together, if it proves more courageous this time."

"This time?" I asked. I could see nothing on the other side of the window save the yellowish fog which characterized autumn in London.

"It has been stalking me for several days. Just out of sight, but always there nonetheless – and getting closer with every passing day. I believe it is a game, of sorts; like a cat, stalking a mouse. It is not a feeling I care for."

At that moment, I felt a prickling sensation on my neck, as if some unseen individual were breathing down my collar. I turned and saw the door opening. I thought Mrs. Hudson had returned, but there was no one there. "Holmes," I murmured. "The door – look!"

Holmes acted as soon as the words left my lips. He turned, hauled me aside and fired. The bark of the revolver nearly deafened me. The door slammed shut and I heard what could only be the sound of someone fleeing downstairs. It was not Mrs. Hudson, of that I was certain. She would not have fled in silence.

My friend turned immediately back to the window and stopped. I followed his gaze and froze. For there, pressed to the glass, was a most hideous countenance. A face unlike any I had ever had the misfortune to see, at once bestial and calculating. The face of a lunatic, or a devil. Perhaps both. It glared at us, mouthing what I took to be silent threats or recriminations, and then vanished in an instant, swallowed up by the fog.

I felt sick to my stomach and collapsed at once onto the couch. Holmes raced to the window and flung it open, as if to pursue our ghastly visitor into the fog. He peered down at the street for long moments, but finally turned back and closed the window, a look of frustration on his face. He glanced at me and said, "The sensation will pass in a few moments. If it is any consolation, the first time is by far the worst, or so I have found."

"What was that – that apparition?"

"My constant companion for the past few days," Holmes said, as he dropped himself into his chair. "Hence my somewhat disturbed equilibrium. This is not the first time it has made itself known so boldly either. It tried to throttle me a few nights ago as I was walking back to Baker Street. It is an ambush predator; of that much I am sure."

"You speak of it as if it's not human."

"It is not. What man can be in two places at once? What man can appear before one's eyes, only to attempt to strangle one from behind?"

"Twins?" I said. It sounded ridiculous, even to me. The look on Holmes's face was enough to make me drop the suggestion.

"I have considered all possibilities, Watson. And one by one, I have marked a line through them. No, the only possibility which remains to me, however impossible-seeming, is that the entity which stalks me is not of earthly origin." Holmes sounded weary; disgruntled. I was not surprised. He preferred his investigations to take place with both feet on the ground.

We had encountered improbable situations before, of course. I have written of some of them, such as the dreadful curse of the Baskerville line. Others, like the tale of the giant Sumatran rat, or the macabre final performance of the puppeteer, Lazare, will not see the light of day until after the passing of all those involved – including myself. But even the strangest of these affairs, such as our ill-fated encounter with the murderous Fellowship of Herne, had, in the end, some rational explanation. Thus, I cannot say which I found more disturbing in that moment – the apparition itself, or Holmes's admission of its unearthly nature.

I pushed myself to my feet. The nausea I'd felt was fading, thankfully. "Holmes, is this related in some way to your investigation into Sir Mortimer's death?"

Holmes steepled his fingers, but did not turn from the window. "An astute observation, Watson. Tell me, have you ever made the acquaintance of a gentleman named Absalom Holywell?"

The name was familiar to me, though it did not have pleasant connotations. "Holywell…a spiritualist, isn't he? Had something to do with that bad business in Barbary Downs last year, didn't he?"

"If by bad business you mean the fraudulent haunting that he investigated, which resulted in the near-deaths of twelve children from over-exposure to *salvia divinorum,* a plant found only in the cloud forests of Oaxaca, Mexico, then yes. He was never charged, of course. Holywell has some influence among the great and the good. Indeed, he has of late turned his attentions to building upon that influence, after the manner of Messieurs Woodman, Westcott and Manners."

I frowned. "He's a Mason?"

"Oh, our Mr. Holywell is a good many things, though I doubt there is a lodge in the entire country which would admit to having him." Holmes looked at me. "Since the Barbary Downs business, Holywell has come up in the world. He is now the head of his own fraternal order, called somewhat grandly the *Ordo Hermeticus Cogitationis Unitae.*"

I frowned. It was a poor doctor who didn't know Latin, but the name made little sense to me. "The Hermetic Order of…Thought?"

"Unified Thought," Holmes corrected. "And that thought is Holywell's."

"Of course. I can't imagine its membership rolls are very large."

Holmes gave a bark of laughter. "Not as yet. Perhaps that is why he chose to make an example of the unfortunate Sir Mortimer."

I paused. "Sir Mortimer was a member?"

"Oh, yes," Holmes said, as if this revelation were no more than a trifle. "But not a happy one, I fear. It seems the order, though nascent, has already got the makings of good doctrinal schism." He pushed himself to his feet, and set his revolver on the table. "I do not think it will return tonight. But we had best get a move on. Speed is our greatest ally."

I looked at him in bewilderment. "Where are we going?"

325

"Devon, Watson. Dartmoor, to be exact."

"Dartmoor?" I said, my confusion growing by the moment.

"Yes, Watson. Earlier today I sent a telegram to Sir Henry Baskerville, beseeching him for the use of Baskerville Hall at the weekend. He was only too glad to indulge my rather impolite request – the mark of a true gentleman."

"And why are we going to Baskerville Hall?"

"To trap a tiger, one must first set the bait." Holmes gestured to himself, with a self-deprecating smile. "But then, one must set the scene, so as not to alert the tiger to the trap." He went into his room, still talking. "We flee, and so our tiger will follow – far from its territory, and into ours."

"Holmes, what are you talking about?" I hesitated, as a sudden thought occurred to me. "Did you ask Mrs. Hudson to send for me? After all your talk about inauspicious timing, you wanted me here – why?"

"Why, I needed your eyes, of course," Holmes said. He returned fully dressed, with an untidily packed carpet bag in one hand. "Now I know for certain that our foe is not simply a trick played upon my senses." He paused and met my gaze. "Thank you for coming, Watson. I know it is an inconvenience, to both you and Mary."

I waved this aside, though it was an inconvenience, and one I dreaded explaining to the ever-patient Mary. "Always, Holmes. You know that."

Holmes smiled. "Good. Come. The train for Dartmoor leaves on the hour."

I insisted on stopping by my home to procure my own bag, of course. Holmes waited impatiently as I said goodbye to Mary, though to his credit he said nothing. Mary wished us well, even taking Holmes's hand in hers; a gesture which I knew never failed to discomfit him, though he had never admitted such in my hearing.

We were soon at London Victoria, awaiting the next train to Dartmoor. But as we waited in the cozy confines of the traveler's lounge I felt a curious sensation, as of a cold breath on the nape of my neck. I glanced at Holmes, and saw that his expression was one of the utmost alertness. "Yes," he murmured, as if sensing my sudden unease. "I feel it as well. We are being watched."

"Have you felt this before?"

"Yes. Not a subtle hunter, our friend. It cannot resist letting us know that it is on our trail. That overweening hubris will be its downfall, and by extension, the downfall of the one who created it." Holmes leaned on his walking stick, his keen gaze flitting across the faces of our fellow passengers in waiting.

"Holywell," I said. Holmes nodded, clearly pleased by my show of acuity.

"The very same, Watson. The thing even wears his face." Holmes relaxed. "That was his first mistake – fashioning it in his own image. Perhaps he intends that his features should be the last its victims see. It is the sort of grisly jest that would appeal to such a man."

"You speak as if he made it out of clay."

Holmes snorted. "Hardly."

"You said it was his first mistake...what was his second?"

"He made an enemy of Sir Mortimer." Holmes looked at me. "I told you, there is a schism brewing in the brotherhood. Sir Mortimer was part of that – and, I fear, it is why he had to die. Nor, I believe, was he the first."

"This thing that's hunting you – hunting us – it killed Sir Mortimer?"

Holmes nodded. "The evidence seems to point that way." He pulled out his pocket watch and checked it. "We should go. But not too quickly. Let it see where we go, what train we take." He snapped his watch shut and stood. I followed his example.

The cold sensation had faded, which I took to mean that our unseen observer had retreated for the moment. But as we left the lounge and made for our train, I noticed a familiar face watching us from a nearby table – the face I had seen at the window, albeit not contorted in elemental fury. "Holmes," I murmured, a chill stealing through me.

"I see him," he replied, without slowing. "It is as I hoped. Holywell has his hound on a tight leash. That will be to our benefit, I think. Come. Before he realizes that we've noticed him. The trap beckons, and I do not wish to spook our quarry now."

When we had at last taken our seats safely in our berth aboard the overnight to Dartmoor, I said, "It had his face. Why?"

"Why does a child resemble its parents?" Holmes said, leaning back in his seat. "Now, if you will excuse me, Watson, I have not slept in some days." He tipped the brim of his hat down over his eyes and crossed his arms and was soon asleep.

I forbore to bother Holmes for further explanation as the train carried us to Dartmoor. Not because I was not curious, but because I knew that Holmes preferred to reveal such things in his own time. If he chose not to share the rest of his theory, it was because he had not yet fixed it in his mind to his own satisfaction.

So, instead, while he slept, I occupied myself with watching the landscape roll along through the window. The journey would be a swift one; the industrial sprawl of London gave way grudgingly but inescapably to the damp greenery of Devon.

The train had not long left the station, however, when I saw something odd. At first, I thought it no more than a trick of the murky afternoon light. The sun was but a faded echo, hidden by clouds and fog and a slanting rain that left curious patterns on the glass of the window. But even so, there was light enough to spy something moving. As I said, I at first thought it an optical illusion. But as I peered more closely at it, I realized that it was no illusion. Rather, it was something…running. Keeping pace with the train.

It bounded over hedges and scuttled over rooftops. It loped along the empty stretches. I lost sight of it once or twice, but it never swerved from its route. I could not perceive its shape, for there was an unhealthy malleability to it – like a wisp of smoke caught in a flue, it bent and twisted all out of joint as the situation demanded. Sometimes it resembled a great serpent, slithering along. Other times, a hound, racing along on great paws. Once, I even imagined it to be a horse and rider, hideously conjoined so that I could not tell where one ended and the other began.

I lost sight of it for good at a crossing. Had we lost it – or had it merely chosen a different route? I almost gave in to the temptation to wake Holmes and inform him of our fellow traveler. Instead, I rose and left the berth in search of the drinks car. I felt badly in need of something to settle my nerves.

As I made my way to the drinks car, I felt as if something – someone – were walking on my shadow. I wondered if perhaps the reason I had lost sight of our pursuer was because it had managed to board the train. I hesitated at the door to the drinks car, wondering if I should return to the berth. But I pushed the thought aside and went in.

The car was quite crowded. There were few seats available, and I had resigned myself to standing at the bar when an unfamiliar voice called my name. Startled, I turned to see Absalom Holywell sitting in a chair in the corner. I knew it could be none other than he, for I recognized the man I'd glimpsed earlier at the station. I paused, uncertain as to how to proceed and Holywell gestured to a chair opposite him. "Here, Doctor Watson. I've saved you a seat."

"You know who I am," I said, in some bewilderment – and not a little unease. I studied him, and found him to be remarkably unremarkable. There was something unfinished about him; his face, his build, but none of it called attention to itself. The only startling thing about him was his gaze – a thing at once so flat and vivid, it was as if two polished stones rested where his eyes ought to have been.

Holywell nodded. "I know who you are, Doctor. Indeed, I doubt there are few who do not. The redoubtable Watson, chronicler of the Great Detective himself." He looked me up and down with a slight smile. "You do yourself little justice in those tales of yours. A man of your obvious talents, reduced to a proxy for a Scotland Yard jack-in-office." He gestured to the empty chair again. "Sit. Please. Would you care for a drink?"

"No," I said, somewhat stiffly. "Thank you." I found I was suddenly no longer in the mood for a drink. Indeed, I wanted nothing more than to be away from there.

Holywell shrugged. "Have it your way. But do sit. I cannot stand talking to someone while they loom over me." His smile widened. "Please. We have much to discuss, you and I."

I sat, but reluctantly. If Holywell had something to say, I thought it best to hear it so that I could report it to Holmes later. Holywell leaned towards me, and tapped my knee in a familiar manner. "I bear you no malice, Doctor. I want you to know that. It is your friend who has put you in this position."

"You are not the first to tell me that. Nor, I expect, will you be the last."

Holywell chuckled and sat back. "It does not have to be this way, you know. As I said, I have no ill feeling towards you. You are a bystander. My quarrel is with your friend. And even that I am willing to overlook, if he would but relent."

"You wish him to cease his investigation of Sir Mortimer's murder."

Holywell spread his hands. "What you call murder, I call suicide. Pakenham did not believe in my power – but one does not have to believe in gravity, to become its victim. He attempted to take what was mine, and sealed his own fate. As your friend has done." He frowned and fixed me with a serpent's eye. "I am not a man to be challenged, Doctor. And I am prone to teaching harsh lessons to those who try my patience."

"Is that what happened to the children in Barbary Downs? Did they try your patience, Mr. Holywell?" I spoke without thinking. I was angry – and not a little unnerved.

Holywell grunted, as if I'd struck him. "Not the children, no. Their parents." He rubbed his face. "The children were the first test of my theories on unified thought. They created something – something wonderful. But unformed. Weak. I took it, fed it, made it strong. Strong enough to break a man in half." He paused and gave me a sly look. "Strong enough to, say, push a woman —left alone at home by her neglectful husband— down the stairs. A tragedy, and an avoidable one. If only someone had been there…"

"Mary," I whispered. I half-rose from my seat. "If you've harmed her I will – "

"I have done nothing," Holywell said. "Yet. But if you insist on setting yourself in my path, I will destroy you. I must, to maintain what is mine." He ran a hand over his bald head. "Do not follow Holmes into the abyss, Doctor. There is no glory in such a death. And I would hate to see such a fine author perish, before he crafts his masterwork."

"I will not abandon my friend," I said, softly, and I cursed myself even as I said it. Holywell sighed and nodded.

"I expected no less of you. Still, I thought I owed it to you to try. But if you will insist on such a foolish course, well – so be it." With those words, he clapped his hands. As if that were a signal, the lights in the car flickered. A sudden premonition gripped me. I shot to my feet and raced out of the car, back towards our berth, Holywell's laughter dogging my steps.

Holmes was still asleep when I flung our door open – but he was not alone. Someone – *something* – sat opposite him. It had Holywell's face, but there the resemblance ended. Its form writhed, as if it had not settled yet on what it was. I have no words to describe it, save that it could easily pass for a devil out of Blake's most fevered imaginings.

I knew only that I was in the presence of something utterly malign – and utterly deadly. Slowly it turned towards me, its mockery of a face twisting into an almost gleeful expression. My hand fell to the pocket of my coat, where my service revolver rested. As if it knew what I was planning, it rose and came at me in a rush. I found myself borne back, out of the compartment and against the far wall of the carriage. I was helpless to resist. It was cold – wet – my senses were overwhelmed by the stink of it. Like the worst peasouper; all the industrial foulness of the city, mingled and redoubled. It was as if I was confronted by the smog of London, fashioned into the likeness of a man.

It lifted me from my feet and I felt its grip on my throat. I clawed at its hands, and my fingers sank into them. It was like fighting a stream – a river. I smelled damp stones, and felt as if I were being crushed beneath a pile of fallen brick. I heard a shrill titter, as if my flailing efforts were no more than an amusement. Its grip tightened and my world shrank to a black halo around a pinpoint of red. Would it break me, as it had Sir Mortimer? Or would it settle for throttling me?

Then – a sudden, sharp shock as something collided with my breastbone. I fell to the floor of the carriage, and heard a frustrated susurrus, as of hundreds of angry wasps. An instant later, I heard Holmes's voice. "Up, Watson. Up!" He helped me to my feet. He held his cane before him, like a sword, and I realized that it was what had struck me – Holmes had obviously thrust his walking stick into our foe, somehow forcing it to release me. My attacker stood now at the far end of the carriage, glaring at us with bulging eyes. Its mouth contorted, as if it were spewing silent obscenities. Then it was gone, with a slam of the carriage door.

Holmes helped me into our berth and closed the door. "How did you get it to release me?" I panted, as he sat me down.

"It is easily startled, perhaps due to its somewhat atavistic state. Had it been more observant, my tactic would have achieved little." He frowned at me, as he sat down opposite. "That was foolish of you, Watson. Provoking it, in that manner, I mean."

"You – you knew it was there?"

"Of course. Impossible to miss such a thing. But I wished for a chance to observe it at rest, as it were. It is hard to note detail, when one is being throttled."

I rubbed my throat. It ached, but there seemed to be no real damage. Nonetheless, my flesh felt scraped raw, as if I had fallen in the street. "Why didn't it attack you?"

"It was waiting for me to wake up, I believe. Or maybe it was simply curious. No way to tell, really. Not without a more thorough observation of its habits." He paused. "You saw Holywell, then?"

I blinked. "You know?"

"I told you. He keeps his hound on a short leash. Where it goes, he goes. What did he say, then? I assume he wishes me to drop my investigation?"

"I believe so." I did not mention Holywell's threat to harm Mary. "Though he does not seem confident in your acquiescence."

Holmes laughed sharply. "Nor should he be! War has been declared, and I have no intention of quitting the field."

"Yet decamping to Dartmoor feels very much like retreat, Holmes."

334

"Retreat is not synonymous with surrender, Watson. We are engaged in a strategic withdrawal, the better to draw our foe in. No doubt Holywell believes he has us running scared. We shall disabuse him of that notion once we reach Dartmoor."

"But why there, Holmes?" I asked. "I cannot think of a less welcoming place to make our stand. Unless the isolation is somehow part of your plan." I paused. "A plan you have not yet fully explained, I might add."

"Have I not?" Holmes said, in that manner that I found at once comforting and aggravating in equal measure. He tapped his walking stick on the floor. "Simply put, Baskerville Hall is not our final destination. Rather, I intend to meet our foe on the open field of Grimpen Mire."

He fell silent after this revelation, and we spent the rest of the trip in relative silence. Holmes was lost in thought, as was I. I thought about the cold grip on my throat, the savage strength of it – what use a revolver against that? I had seen much that was strange in my time, both alongside Holmes, and prior to meeting him. Things I couldn't explain.

These events did not haunt my dreams, save on rare nights when my old wound played up, or when I heard or saw something that put me in mind of an old case. So it was that our return to Dartmoor prompted me to recall the case that had first introduced us to our host, Sir Henry Baskerville. And, of course, Stapleton and his bogie-hound. The latter was on my mind as we arrived to the familiar features of the Devon scenery. It was impossible to forget such a brute – half-starved, slathered in phosphorous and trained to kill.

We didn't see Holywell as we stepped down from the train, a fact for which I was grateful. Holmes paused as the train whistled, and steam billowed like a shroud about us. I fancied I saw something in the gray-white envelope, a vague suggestion of movement that made me tense, and my hand stray towards my revolver. But then it was gone and Holmes led me out of the station, where the familiar, tall, thin form of Dr. James Mortimer awaited us with a dog-cart.

Mortimer had changed little in the years and months since we'd last seen one another. He still dressed shabbily, in frayed frock coat and trousers. But his expression was as benevolent as ever, and he greeted us with every visible sign of pleasure. "Sir Henry is most looking forward to your visit, as am I."

"He is recovered then," I said, as we shook hands. Sir Henry had suffered an acute attack of nerves in the aftermath of the Stapleton affair. Mortimer had been obliged to take him on a trip around the world in order to restore his vigor. He nodded.

"Oh yes, quite so. Hale and hearty as he was when first we met."

"Excellent," Holmes said, a trifle impatiently. "Shall we go? It has been a tiring journey, as I'm sure Dr. Watson can attest."

Mortimer hastily bundled us into the dog-cart and we were away in moments. I chatted amiably with Mortimer as we rode, inquiring after the health of his spaniel. Holmes remained silent, almost taciturn. He withdrew into himself, as if husbanding his resources for the fight ahead. Thankfully, Mortimer did not seem to take offense.

When we arrived at Baskerville Hall, Sir Henry was waiting for us at the door. He greeted us with open arms and a wide smile. He was much as I remembered – a small, dark-eyed man, alert and weather-beaten. He shook hands with me, and then with Holmes, and ushered all of us inside. The hall was not much changed since our last visit, though I could already see that its new tenant was intent on marking it as his own.

We arrived just as evening fell, and a fire had been stoked in the great apartment, with its lofty rafter of aged oak. A light repast was provided, and we fell to talking over old times and the adventures Mortimer and Sir Henry had had on their travels. Holmes listened, and ventured the occasional comment, but largely remained silent. He stared into the fire, hands clasped on his chest, his gaze alert but fixed on vistas invisible to the rest of us.

Mortimer departed after an aperitif, trundling home in his dog-cart. Holmes remained by the fire, while Sir Henry and I took in the evening air on the hall's newly built Andalusian patio, overlooking the Yew Alley and the edge of Grimpen Mire.

"You've started to put your stamp on the place," I said, approvingly.

"That I have. And I hope to do more in the coming months. But I don't want to talk about that." Sir Henry fetched a cigarette case out of his jacket pocket and opened it. "Mister Holmes's telegram was a trifle terse. I know you two didn't come out here just to take in the Devon air, but not much beyond that." After selecting a cigarette for himself, he proffered the case to me.

"You know as much as I do, I fear," I said, as I gratefully accepted the offer of a cigarette. "One of Holmes's few defects of character is his refusal to divulge his full plans until the moment of their fulfillment."

Sir Henry nodded. "I remember, believe me." We laughed at that, and watched the moon rise over the moor. There was a beauty to it, but it was a beauty without pity or mercy. I remembered well the screams of an unfortunate moor pony as it sank into the mire…and those of the wretched Stapleton, as he suffered a similar fate. Sir Henry looked at me. "Still, I'm happy to come with you, if you'd like. I owe you both plenty."

"That will not be necessary, Sir Henry," Holmes said as he joined us. "Better the danger is confined to we two. Watson agrees."

"Another gun might come in handy," I began. Holmes gestured sharply.

"A third firearm is not a useful multiplier of force in this instance. Our foe has no fear of firearms. Indeed, I doubt there is anything of this world which could harm it." Holmes accepted a cigarette from Sir Henry with a nod of thanks. "Force will not win us this fight. Instead, we must out-think our opponent." He tapped his brow for emphasis.

Sir Henry nodded reluctantly. "I trust you to know your business, Mr. Holmes. But if you need me, I am at your service."

Suddenly, from out on the moor, there came a wild scream as of an animal in pain. All three of us froze in shock, our heads turning to follow the sound. We saw nothing, of course. The cry came again, but louder. A third time, and louder still. It was as if the screamer were drawing closer to us with every utterance. But when it seemed as if the howler were no more than a few steps from us, it fell silent.

Sir Henry opened his mouth to speak, but Holmes motioned for him to be quiet. We stood, waiting, but the sound didn't come again. Instead, eerie laughter rose up from the night. It seemed to come from all directions, as if a chorus of hecklers were making sport of us. Then it too ceased. Holmes peered into the night, but if he spied anything, he gave no sign. Instead, he turned away from the moor and said, "I think we had best go inside for the night. There is a chill on the air."

We spoke little after that. Sir Henry retired for the night, leaving Holmes and myself alone before the fire. Eventually Holmes bestirred himself. "Do you recall the last time we were here?" he asked, softly.

"I most certainly do," I said. "It is hard to forget such a thing. And I have tried, believe me." Being back here had brought the memories back full force. I remembered our mad pell-mell race across the moor, following the screams of the man we'd thought at the time to be Sir Henry, and the sight of the great, savage wounds upon his crumpled body; the lonely, eerie cries of the hound in its underground cage; the sight of its glowing form hurtling towards us out of the murk, jaws wide and slavering, eyes like burning coals.

Holmes gave a small smile. "I am sure your readers appreciated every grisly detail."

"Perhaps." I sat back in my chair. "Do you ever think about it?"

"The case? Yes."

"What about the hound?"

Holmes looked away, his gaze straying once more to the fire. "No."

"I find that hard to believe," I said.

"Nonetheless, it is true." Holmes took a pull on his cigarette. "I have, at times, noted that I suffer a paucity of imagination – or, rather, what I possess is a precise instrument. It is a scalpel, useful in the correct situation, but otherwise lacking in utility. I can assess variables, predict outcomes and consider alternatives. But I must have clay to build these bricks." He glanced at me. "You, on the other hand…"

I raised an eyebrow. "What about me?"

Holmes smiled and turned his attentions once more to the fire. "You should go to bed, Watson. There will be no sleep for us tomorrow night."

"What about you?"

"I will sit up for a while. I must think."

I hesitated, but only for a few moments. Holmes was not simply being kind. He meant what he said. But even so, I found sleep evasive. When I managed to find it, I would invariably wake suddenly, heart thudding, certain I had heard or felt something. Once, I thought I detected the stealthy tread of something outside my room. Another time, I glimpsed a fluttering shape – too large to be a bat or bird – outside my window, and thought I heard Mary cry out, though I knew it to be impossible.

The times when I didn't wake were even worse, for my dreams were not reassuring things. Rather, they were full of sound and fury. Perhaps dream is the wrong word, for they were more like memories. I relived our encounter with Stapleton's foul pet – the awful baying, the sound of its snarl as it sprang for us out of the fog. Again and again, I experienced that incandescent jolt of purest horror.

When at last I awoke the next morning, my person ached, as if I had spent the night fleeing for my life; my head throbbed. I made my ablutions, dressed and went downstairs to find Holmes where I had left him, his eyes on the smoldering ashes in the fireplace. I cleared my throat, and he turned. "Ah, Watson. I trust you slept well."

"Not in the least," I said. "And it's all your fault."

"My fault?"

"Yes, I spent the entire night dreaming about that damnable hound of Stapleton's. When I wasn't hearing things, that is."

"Yes, Holywell's pet was prowling the grounds last night. I daresay it invited itself in, once or twice."

I stared at him in bewilderment. "And you didn't think to wake me?"

"I told you Watson – I wished to observe it. It never provided me the opportunity to do so in London, but it has become bolder away from its natural environment, and thus less wary. Or perhaps Holywell is the one who has become less wary. Either way, I took advantage of its boldness and made a thorough study of it."

"And?" I asked.

Holmes rose. "Let us see what Baskerville Hall has in the way of breakfast, shall we?" he said, neatly avoiding my question. "We have a long day, and an even longer night, ahead of us."

We breakfasted well, thanks to Sir Henry's kind indulgence, and spent the rest of the morning making our preparations. When our repast was finished, and the dishes cleared, Holmes spread out a survey map of the area across the table and indicated a tor some distance from Baskerville Hall. According to Sir Henry there was a cairn at its top suitable to keep any inclement weather off of us. "I made a night of it there myself, once. Not particularly comfortable, but I don't think you're looking for comfort, are you, Mr. Holmes?"

"Not as such," Holmes said, with a grim smile. Our destination identified, we packed bags and set out at midday. I took my service revolver, of course, and Holmes carried his as well. In addition, we both armed ourselves with stout walking sticks.

I will not bore you with the details of our trek through Grimpen Mire, or up the steep, rough slope of the tor. Suffice it to say, it took us longer than I imagined, and we were muddy and sore by the time we reached Sir Henry's promised cairn. Upon spotting the curious tumble of stones I felt an immediate sense of relief, for the sky had turned a foreboding hue, and the air smelled of incipient rain.

We quickly situated ourselves and made a fire beneath an overhang of rock. As I stoked the fire, I said to Holmes, "How long do you think we will have to wait?"

"It will not come before nightfall," Holmes said, scanning the slate-colored horizon.

"How will it even know where we are?"

Holmes looked at me. "It followed us, of course. Surely you noticed."

I frowned, about to reply when I realized that he was right – I had noticed something. It had been a sensation, rather than anything overt. A premonition of being watched. I had unconsciously chalked it up to the events of the previous day. "Then why did it not attack us?" I asked. "It could have fallen on us at any moment as we crossed the moor."

"Holywell is a showman, Watson. He cannot help himself. It is why he chose this method, rather than something more commonplace."

"You still haven't explained how you came to learn of all this, Holmes." I poked the fire with a stick, watching it crackle and rise. Smoke pulsed upwards, through a natural flue in the rock above. "I feel I've been rather patient, but seeing as we have some time yet until nightfall, perhaps you could finally finish telling me about your investigation into Sir Mortimer's death."

Holmes sat back against the rock face and watched the fire. "I suspected Holywell's involvement in the affair the instant I learned of Sir Mortimer's membership in the Hermetic Order of Unified Thought. My investigation revealed that Sir Mortimer and several other well-heeled members were growing unhappy with Holywell's style of leadership and the emptiness of his promises; unhappy enough to create their own rival sect."

"Yes, but how did you come to believe – to know – about this…thing? That is what you have yet to explain, and frankly, it is the part I find most curious."

"Ah. Well, my suspicions on the nature of my stalker were founded in an understanding as to the purpose of Holywell's brotherhood – nothing less than the creation of a thoughtform; one capable of accomplishing whatever task they set it to."

"A thoughtform?"

"You may have heard it referred to as a tulpa, though I doubt that word is yet in common utterance." Holmes gestured as he spoke, as if trying to shape the very air. "Imagine it, Watson…an entity crafted from one's own thoughts. A thing roused to life by the will and belief of a single man, or, as in this case, men. What deeds might such a creature be able to accomplish – it's strength and knowledge, its power, limited only by the imagination of its creators?"

I stared at him. "And that is what we face?"

343

Holmes nodded, and pulled a cigarette case from within his overcoat. "I have made a study of a number of esoteric practices, particularly those found among certain Tibetan sects, as well as those recorded in the Bardo Thodol." He lit a cigarette and tossed the spent match into the fire. It flared weirdly for a moment, and I slid back from it, despite the creeping chill of dusk. Holmes went on. "While these rituals and methodologies have not yet achieved notability among western occultists, I have no doubt that they will, in time. Men like Holywell are magpies of the first order. They take what they like, and ignore what does not fit – or is not of immediate use."

"Then this thing – this tulpa – is akin to an astral emanation?" I asked. Holmes looked at me in some surprise. I smiled. "You are not the only one who has read up on such matters."

"Don't tell me you've become a closet spiritualist in your dotage, Watson?" he asked, as if scandalized by the very thought. "What will Mary say?"

"I assure you it was only a passing curiosity," I said, with a chuckle. "But they are similar, yes? That is why you think Holywell followed us."

"Quite the contrary, Watson." Holmes puffed on his cigarette. "A tulpa is a thing unto itself; it no more requires a guiding hand than a mortal assassin. No, Holywell is here for one reason – he fears that he is losing control of his pet."

I felt a chill at his words. "What do you mean?"

"A tulpa can only grow in strength, and independence. Or so I have read. If, as I suspect, Holywell has read the same texts, then he may well be worried that his creation is growing too strong, too quickly. But necessity has compelled him to unleash it."

"On us," I said, faintly. Holmes nodded.

"I am sorry, Watson. If there had been any other way…"

From outside came the clatter of falling rock. We both fell quiet, listening. But no further sounds came. Holmes broke the silence first. "You are possibly wondering why I have chosen to meet this threat here, rather than in Baker Street."

"I assumed it had something to do with protecting our loved ones," I said. "We have done so before, after all. And from what I know of him, Holywell is very much the sort of man to go after someone like Mrs. Hudson, or even Mary, if the thought occurred to him." My heart raced as I said it, and in that moment, I wanted nothing more than to be home.

Holmes sat back. "That was one of my considerations, yes." He paused, then fixed me with an unsettling look. There was something anticipatory about it – almost predatory. "You see, I quickly deduced that no mere force of arms would win us this day. So I had to come up with another plan."

"Oh?" I shook my head. There was a particular smell on the air – pungent and curiously familiar. But I could not bring to mind what it reminded me of. "And what does this plan entail?"

"Have you ever thought about this place, Watson? About these moors. They have a weight of place quite unlike any other. Even the smoke of London pales in comparison." Holmes puffed on his cigarette. He had not offered me one, I noticed. I said nothing, however. "It gathers in on itself, like a shadow deepening towards twilight. That is why Stapleton's plan almost worked, you see – the weight of place. What seems merest hokum in London becomes all too real in this haunted landscape."

"That's very interesting, Holmes, but what does any of that have to do with why we're here?" I was beginning to feel slightly dizzy, as if I had not had enough to drink.

"A tulpa is not drawn whole cloth from the underside of the mind; it is born from the experiences of its creator, their biases and beliefs. It is shaped by the events and places that shaped its creator. Holywell's tulpa was made in London, by a Londoner. It is the veritable tiger in the Smoke, to borrow a phrase. It is every unsolved murder, every shadow in an alleyway." Holmes blew a plume of smoke in my direction. "It would not be remiss to call it the specter of Crime itself."

I rubbed my face, feeling somewhat out of sorts. "Holmes…" I began.

"Tell me about the hound, Watson," Holmes said. For some reason, his voice sounded as if it were coming to me across a great distance. I shook my head again, but could not clear it of the strange sensation now plaguing me. I wondered if I were more tired than I'd first thought. Perhaps I had taken ill.

"Why?" I asked, dully.

"Describe it," Holmes said, his voice seeming to echo through the rocks. I wanted to argue with him, to ask why. But even as I made to protest, the image of the hound was there in my mind, as big and as baleful as it had been in life.

"Black," I said. "Coal-black; the size of a lioness; gaunt and savage. Fire dripped from its mouth; it's eyes…glowed. Outlined in flickering flame. Infernal and terrible…" As I spoke, I felt a curious pressure in my head. The world spun, and I felt sick, but I could not stop the flow of either words or memories. I saw the hound race towards me out of a roiling fog. I heard its panting snarl, and the click of nails on the rock. My heart raced. Sweat beaded on my skin. I felt cold and hot at once, and a detached part of my mind idly calculated the odds of my succumbing to a nervous fit.

I fell away from myself. I saw us sitting before the fire. I was talking, and Holmes looked as if he were asleep, and – and there, at the edge of the cairn, something with the face of Absalom Holywell leered at us in cruel satisfaction. Its form had achieved a remarkable, if monstrous solidity since I had last seen it. It resembled a man in its outline, but there any resemblance ended. There was something detestably simian about it – a devilish atavism, wrought from the deepest pits of a man's psyche.

It crept towards us, eyes blazing with an inhuman malignity, and though I attempted to cry out, I could not. My voice faltered – failed. I could only stare at Holywell's tulpa as it loomed over us. But, before it could so much as ready its great fists, it paused, head cocked. The smile slipped from its brute countenance, and it took a hesitant step back – as if something had startled it.

A moment later, I saw what that something was. It crouched where the shadows pooled deepest, its eyes flickering like the very embers of Hell. A deep, rumbling growl echoed out from the darkness and it rose from its crouch and took a step into the light.

It was not Stapleton's bogie-hound. That poor brute had succumbed to our revolvers, after a lifetime of deprivation and misery. But if such a beast could be said to have a ghost, then what I saw was surely it. A phantom, conjured out of the recesses of my nightmares. It padded slowly towards the fire, slavering in anticipation. Holywell's tulpa stared at this newcomer with incomprehension. I wondered if it was the tulpa itself that was bewildered, or the man controlling it.

Things happened very quickly after that. The hound hurled itself over the fire, at the throat of the tulpa. The impact was deafening, and the momentum carried the two creatures away from the fire, onto the slope of the tor.

Overhead, thunder rumbled and rain began to pelt down. I watched, helpless to move, as the two entities fought with a savage abandon. At first, it seemed Holywell's tulpa had the advantage in strength and size, but little by little, the hound drove it back. Finally, with a blood-curdling howl, the hound seized the tulpa's throat in its jaws and gave a great, heaving shake. There was a sound like tearing paper, or falling water – and something else…a faint, far-off cry, as of a man in pain.

Holywell's tulpa, the thing that had so remorselessly pursued us from London, staggered back, its eyes bulging, its hand clutching at its mangled jugular. Slowly, surely, it collapsed in on itself, like a deflating pig's bladder, and came apart. What was left of it splashed onto the rocks and was swiftly washed away by the rain.

The hound turned, and Holmes stood between us. He met its blazing eyes and nodded, once. As if in reply, the hound raised its head and gave voice to a booming bay of triumph. Then it too was gone, loping away into the darkness.

I collapsed then, like a puppet with cut strings. I do not know how long I lay insensate; minutes, or perhaps longer. At some point, I slept and dreamt darkling dreams.

I awoke some time later to find Holmes at my side and gray sunlight streaming across the tor. "I apologize, Watson," he said. "I can only hope you will forgive me my desperation."

"What do you mean?" I gasped. Holmes helped me sit up, one hand on my back. "What happened – I remember Holywell's creature and – and the hound. But surely that's impossible!" I looked at him for explanation.

"Improbable," Holmes corrected. "Your grogginess is due to a derivative of *salvia divinorum* in my cigarettes. There's some mixed in the fire, as well."

"You – you drugged me?" I asked, in disbelief.

To his credit, Holmes looked away in obvious regret. "It was necessary, I assure you. I needed your mind to be open, so that you could achieve the proper concentration of thought required for the endeavor I'd planned. I calculated the dosage exactly."

I looked up at him, though even that slight movement made the throbbing in my head even more unbearable. "That is scant comfort, Holmes."

Holmes stood. "It is done now, in any event. We have taken Holywell's weapon from him, and with it, his hold over his brotherhood. It should be easy enough to apprehend him now, especially if Sir Henry has done as I asked, and alerted the local constabulary to Holywell's presence in town."

"What do you mean? What happened here? I saw – but it couldn't have been. Could it?" I pushed myself shakily to my feet. I felt wrung out and empty. Somewhere, birds were singing. Holmes nodded.

"The hound, yes. You saw it, as I did."

"But how…?"

"I told you, Watson. I have made a study of such practices – though, I admit, never with the intent of putting them to use myself. Once I realized what it was that we faced, I knew there could be only one defense. If it is any consolation, I could not have accomplished it myself." He paused and then tapped his temple. "Indeed, I tried – but failed to summon the needed force of imagination." He smiled ruefully. "It seemed what was required was a writer's touch."

"That's why you kept going on about the last time we were here," I said, in understanding. "About the hound. That's why you brought us here – away from Holywell's place of power."

Holmes nodded, pleased. "Bravo, Watson. Yes, I theorized that the weight of place here would be enough to counterbalance that which Holywell had crafted. I was correct, thankfully. Our hound proved stronger than Holywell's enforcer."

"What now?" I asked. "The hound – is it…?"

"It will fade, in time," Holmes said, looking out at the new day. "Until then, perhaps, we had best stay off Grimpen Mire."

I was only too happy to comply with this advice. We left for London that afternoon, after paying a final call on Sir Henry, and I was glad of it, for I dearly wanted to see Mary again. For himself, Holmes wished to confer with Hopkins on the matter of Sir Mortimer's death. I do not know for certain how he explained it to the police, but it was put down as murder in the end and laid squarely on Absalom Holywell's doorstep.

Yet I must note with some regret that Holywell avoided arrest. To all appearances, he escaped the village and fled for parts unknown that same evening. Warrants for his capture were soon issued, though I doubt anything will come of them.

I look back on it now, and wonder if he will ever be found. I wonder too what strange communication passed between Holmes and the hound that night. I think back to that night, and to my dreams, for the memory of them is as vivid now as it was that gray morning.

I dreamt of a great, horrid panting in my ears, and Grimpen Mire streaking past, as if I were moving at great speed. I was a passenger within something that pelted through the village, searching for…what? Something.

Or perhaps someone.

I saw a face – white, staring, oddly unfinished – pressed to a window, and heard, or perhaps felt a low, evil growl. I awoke then, but the dream came again periodically over the weeks that followed our adventure on Grimpen Mire. Always different, but somehow the same. The village gave way to a city, a ferry, a countryside – as if my quarry were fleeing great distances, to no avail. But always the dream consisted of the same panting, the same unfinished face with its vivid eyes – eyes wide in terror at what they beheld. Always, I awoke with a vague sense of unease, of dissatisfaction and savage desire unfulfilled.

Of guilt.

Until, finally, one morning many months later, I did not. And I knew then what we had done. What Holmes had done. Often, my friend has taken the side of justice over that of the law. Holywell had friends enough that he might have avoided the noose, might have come seeking revenge. Perhaps he would have conjured a new horror, with which to kill other innocents – like my Mary. Or even Holmes himself.

It is for that reason that I did not tell Holmes of my dreams, though I suspect he knows that something is wrong. It is why I did not tell him all of what I saw that night. I wish, even now, that I had not seen it. I wish that I had not witnessed that monstrous countenance, at once that of an animal and of a man

– the man I call friend. For as Holywell's tulpa resembled its creator, so too did ours.

I wish too that the dreams had ended with what I hope to be Holywell's death. But instead, they have continued. I dream now of something padding in the dark, coming closer with every passing evening. The faithful hound returns to its master, job done.

And I cannot help but wonder, when we see it again...whose face will it have?

SONG FROM DARK ANNIE'S BOWER

Angela Slatter

"Well, that's going to leave a stain," said the voice, its flippant tone let down by a distinct tremor.

Kit Caswell, ex-police officer and current private investigator of London's weird and often-less-than-wonderful, lay flat on her back, staring at the clouds. The breath had been knocked out of her, and the hat jarred from her head, and she was covered in green goop that spurted when she'd stabbed the Hob's End Abomination. At least, Kit thought, it wasn't acid and it didn't smell especially awful, which admittedly was a very low bar. The new tweed suit was ruined and Mrs. Kittredge, her long-suffering housekeeper, was not going to be happy if asked to clean it. Better Kit find a barrel and burn it. Slowly, she sat up. Nothing felt broken, though she'd certainly be bruised in the morning.

"Hello, Dr. Watson. How long have you been standing there?"

"Good afternoon, Miss Caswell. I arrived just as that thing flew out of the crypt at you." The man was a brown smudge a few feet away in the failing light.

"Didn't feel an inclination to help me at all? To put that lovely cane and the blade it conceals to good use?"

"You seemed to be handling it quite effectively on your own." He tried to sound hearty; however, Kit could tell he was well and truly rattled. The good doctor closed the distance between them and offered his hand, which she took, rather enjoying his expression as his natural urge to chivalry warred with the sensation of goop on his palm. To his credit, he didn't let go until she did and only then made a show of reaching for a handkerchief.

"Thank you, Doctor." Kit dusted herself off, examined the mess; on closer inspection, the worst of it was concentrated on her coat and waistcoat. The shirt was surprisingly pristine, the trousers clean, grass-stains notwithstanding. Salvageable. Mrs. Kittredge would be pleased. "Now, how may I help you? Assuming you weren't simply taking a stroll through the cemetery for the good of your health?"

"I wish I could say that was it, but alas: I must ask a favor. Holmes and I must. In fact, Holmes has specifically requested your presence."

Kit raised an eyebrow. "Good Lord, straits must be dire."

"You've been making quite the name for yourself in matters arcane and eldritch, m'dear. Holmes acknowledges your expertise."

Kit hid a grin. "That's big of him."

Watson paused. "If I say "appreciates", does that sound any better?"

"Only marginally, but do go on."

"An old friend of Holmes has requested our aid. Some of the details are … unpleasant and very strange indeed. You were such a help with the Harrington case last year. We thought it best to call you in at the start rather than after we'd, errr, run into a wall of things with which we've less experience."

"And where is Mr. Holmes at this very minute?" Kit asked, looking around at the trees and undergrowth as if they might conceal the very man himself.

"Ah, Holmes has already departed …"

"How long ago?"

"Four days," admitted the good doctor.

"So, one may reasonably assume he's already run into a wall of things?"

"Correct," admitted Watson, then added slyly, "You'll come, won't you? Surely you wouldn't pass up a chance to correct the great Sherlock Holmes? Show him what he's missed?"

Kit grinned. "Well, yes. That is irresistible. But I'll need to go home and change, pack a bag. Shall we reconvene tomorrow?"

"Ah, well, that's the thing: time is of the essence, Miss Caswell—a life is at stake." Watson looked pleased with himself. "Your Mrs. Kittredge was kind enough to prepare a suitcase for you. Everything you need is waiting in a hansom cab at the gates of this quite pleasant graveyard." He pointed to her outfit. "Clean and more appropriate attire."

"You mean dresses and skirts?" She raised a brow once more. With her hair tucked under a hat she could pass for a soft-faced boy and had often found it more convenient to go forth incognito.

He held up his palms. "And another suit. Mrs. K seemed to think something like this"—he gestured at the goop—"might happen."

Kit sighed, then bent to retrieve her hat from the patch of grass into which it had rolled. "It generally does. Honestly, I'm keeping at least three tailors in profits."

Watson stepped aside and motioned that they should walk. "Holmes will meet us upon arrival at our destination. Shall we hurry? You know what he's like when left too long to his own devices."

"It is the very stuff of legend." Kit looked at the ground for the remains of the Abomination – but there was nothing left. The body had deflated and dissipated upon being punctured, as if it was little more than an ill-natured balloon. Everything else appeared to have soaked into the earth. Nothing to tidy. Or hide.

"What was that thing?" asked Watson as they moved towards the black metal gates of the entrance.

"No idea, really. I think it used to be a man—clearly, no longer. There's been talk for some while of haunts in this place, though no attacks. But in the past month, eight young women have been injured. The last one was hospitalized. I couldn't find any history or lore about it, which is unusual in itself, so that made me think it was a recent inhabitant, or simply something that no longer knew itself."

"And that dagger you stabbed it with? Ancient and sacred?"

Kit pulled it from her pocket: slim, with a glinting mother-of-pearl handle. "A sterling silver folding fruit knife. I convinced a priest to bless it so it's just right for jobs like these."

"Death by fruit knife? Bit undignified."

"Indeed."

Up ahead waited the cab, its lanterns lit; the driver did not bother to pretend disinterest, and stared directly at the unlikely pair: a tall young woman in a man's suit and the middle-aged gentleman swinging a mahogany cane as if it was no more than an affectation. Kit gave the driver a nod. "Sturdy and easy to conceal, Dr. Watson. Unexpected." They reached the vehicle and Watson opened the door.

"Are you planning on telling me why you need my help?" she asked. "Whose life is in danger?"

Watson shook his head. "I wouldn't dare. You know how Holmes loves to do his reveals. Suffice to say young men are being horribly murdered in Leicestershire."

"Oh. That makes a nice change." Kit swung up into the conveyance.

"Miss Caswell! Young men are being horribly murdered!"

"Well, yes. In Leicestershire. You said. But surely you must admit that's a change from all the women's bodies that scatter this city?"

Watson opened his mouth, but nothing came out. Kit could see his mind working behind his gentle eyes. In the end, he shrugged, and got in beside her, his hands resting on the cane. They were silent as the driver geed up the horses; Watson, his thoughts his own, and Kit planning how best to extract information from him.

*

The first-class carriage made a difference, thought Kit. She'd been poor or poor-adjacent most of her life, and even though she was now more than well-off due to a confluence of strange circumstances and some light blackmail, not-poor was infinitely better. She was vaguely ashamed of how quickly she'd acclimatized.

"Will you tell me at least where we're going, Dr. Watson?" Kit tapped at the newspaper the older man had raised in front of himself. "You'd surely not want my curiosity to kill me."

Watson paused, peered over the edge of *The Times* and considered her.

"I promise I won't tattle to Holmes," she coaxed. "Come along, something a little more precise than simply *Leicestershire*."

"A small village in the Dane Hills," he said quietly.

"Black Annis!" Kit cried. "Dark Annie. The Blue Dame. The Skinner Goddess. The Dane Demoness."

Watson looked taken aback, possibly more at the volume of her comment than her knowledge. "You've heard of her?"

"I've done a lot of research, Dr. Watson, since I began dealing with the otherworldly and the unusual. Not simply about London's weird things, but across the country and beyond. Every little bit helps."

"Well, as you know, we tend to deal in facts and what we can see, not ghosties and ghoulies that go bump in the night." He grumbled a little.

Kit smiled. "Black Annis with her blue face and iron claws, hunting children and lambs. Living in a bower close dug by her very own hands into the sandstone cliffs. They say she has such long arms that cottage windows were made tiny so she could only fit one hand in when she tried to snatch away a child—and folk would never look outside for to see her was to be cursed. She'd howl and grind her teeth when she went a'hunting so you'd know she was coming—which seems counterintuitive in my humble opinion."

Watson snorted with laughter. "Nothing more than a bogeyman then."

"There are always things to threaten children with, ways and means to make them behave. *If you don't eat your dinner, Black Annis will come for you.* It doesn't mean they're not real or that they weren't once. Didn't your own mother try such tactics? Mine did." The doctor grunted agreement, and Kit continued: "She—Black Annis, not my mother—would tan the skins of children and hang them from the branches of the oak tree outside her grotto, or tuck them in her belt as a fetching skirt."

Kit tilted her head, looked at the darkness beyond the windowpane. "But it rather begs the question: if Black Annis' preferred prey is children—and lambs when the other is lacking—then why have young men been dying?"

"Why indeed, Miss Caswell? Why indeed." Watson settled back into his seat. "I'd suggest you try to get a few hours rest while you can. I've no doubt Holmes will be abuzz with energy and there'll be no respite until we solve the mystery."

*

But when they arrived at the tiny station of Black Bower, there was no sign of Holmes at all. Both Kit and Watson spent some minutes examining their fellow passengers and those greeting them, just in case the Detective had indulged in his taste for disguise and subterfuge. But very quickly the platform cleared and even the station master locked his office and ambled off into the gloom. Watson and Kit exchanged a glance, and continued to wait.

It was only as Kit gave in and opened her mouth to speak that the most awful noise tore through the night. A combination of a screech and a scrape, like metal on metal, but somehow not like it, something that issued from a set of lungs and tapered off—eventually—as the breath ran out. Then started up again as those lungs filled once more. The sound seemed to be some distance away, although Kit felt it increased in volume ever-so-slightly with each new iteration, as if the source was moving closer.

"Miss Caswell, I must say that I do not like the idea of being outside at this hour, with whatever's making that racket, and with no sort of cover between it and us." Watson applied his hat more firmly to his head as if that might make his point stick.

"Dr. Watson, I do agree. And I'm not ashamed to admit that I'm disinclined to investigate in the darkness armed only with a fruit knife." Kit took long strides towards the station master's office while Watson hefted their cases—fortunately both travelled light. Kit flipped a small set of silver lockpicks from her pocket and set to work. With a speed that would have made the locksmith who'd taught her proud, she'd ushered Watson inside. She reset the lock, and then the good doctor helped her to drag a rather heavy oak desk over to bolster the door in case of … something.

The shrieking was definitely coming nearer. Kit backed away until she was standing beside Watson, the wall behind them, and they both slid slowly and silently down it to sit on the floor in the shadows.

Hiding was no bloody help whatsoever, thought Kit, *if Black Annis—or whatever it was—had a finely-tuned sense of smell. Sure as a bloodhound.* She really hoped the door would hold. By an unarticulated consensus, neither she nor Watson spoke. Kit listened so hard her ears began to ache, which seemed ridiculous. The howling was very close, rising and falling in pitch, then dropping to nothing until they heard the dragging of, perhaps, feet with clawed toes, and perhaps arms so long they straggled on the concrete of the platform outside.

And then: the sniffing.

Deep inhalations, held far too long, released in a great rush. Growls. Scratches. Gnashes of teeth. Finally, a thud that made the door and desk shudder, but nothing else. At last: a grunt, a noise of resignation that said it was all too hard for too little reward—or they were simply of no interest whatsoever. And then the shuffle-slide of feet and hands got quieter and further away, the howling starting up again, but decreasing in volume as the distance between it and the train station grew. Finally, it was no more than a periodic shattering of the night.

Kit realized that Watson had reached for her hand at some point, and she'd not let it go, sweaty palms and all. The doctor muttered, "Do you think it's gone? Or trying to trick us?"

Before Kit could answer, there was a thump, a violent knocking, and a man's voice shouting, "Watson! Watson! Are you there? Miss Caswell?!"

Kit scrambled to her feet, releasing the doctor's hand, and they shifted the desk back into roughly its original position. She threw the door open just as Holmes was poised to resume his hammering. Kit swayed back to avoid his raised fist, then forward again, yelling, "Was that you? Did you think it funny?"

Her own rage surprised her, but she knew it was powered by fear. She'd been attacked by the Abomination that very afternoon—and while she'd become somewhat accustomed to the preternatural, she did have her limits. Two eldritch horrors in one day was definitely a bit much. This was precisely the sort of thing Holmes would think hilarious: dragging her here on the pretext of seeking help only to make fun of her. They'd parted well enough after the Harrington case, but before that the Detective had not been one of her supporters—indeed had been a vocal critic. It was possible he'd reverted to type. *Except*, the voice in her head said, *except Watson was utterly terrified too. And Holmes does have a care for Watson.*

The tall man with a beaky nose, looking a little more cadaverous than the last time she'd seen him, appeared shocked. Silently, he pointed to the door. Deep grooves had been carved into the wood. They'd not been there when Kit and Watson first entered the office. Kit sagged, then caught herself, straightened up even though her legs did not want to hold her. It was one thing to believe in such creatures; one thing to have fought them; another entirely to have such surprise first meetings. And usually she was the hunter, not the prey.

"I was on my way to meet you and Watson, but the howling began and the driver would not leave until it had passed by. He insisted she comes out only on the full moon." He gestured to the sky where the silver disk hung. "My apologies, I left it too late to get here before your train arrived. I had faith, however, in your combined resources, Miss

Caswell, which seems perfectly placed." He smiled, then looked past her. "All well, Watson?"

"Well enough, Holmes, but I prescribe the judicious application of a hot meal and some medicinal alcohol."

"Seconded," said Kit.

"Come on then. I'm assured Black Annis doesn't tend to do more than one sweep, however, there's a first time for everything." Holmes shepherded them along the platform and towards a fine black carriage and four.

*

They reached their destination a little after midnight: Latimore Manor, looming large but most of its detail was lost to the night. In the carriage Holmes had been tight-lipped, only sharing the fact that Sir Horace Latimore was the client and his son Narcisse the subject of all the concern. Kit had been too wrung out to extract any further information. The Detective, bordering on uncharacteristically solicitous, insisted they immediately get some rest. The threat, he said, was over for the moment. They would reconvene refreshed in the morning and strategize.

Sir Horace having long since retired, they were met by Mrs. Ardelia Demeter, the housekeeper. She was small and bird-boned, once very beautiful, and now differently so, like a marble sculpture worn away by the elements, but no less lovely for it. Her black hair was shot through with gray and Kit put her age around fifty. The woman was polite and pleasant, smiling as if the late appearance of guests was no trouble whatsoever. She escorted Kit, while Holmes showed Watson to his chamber, explaining there was a meal waiting in the suite for Kit if she was hungry.

Up the staircase to the first floor, along a corridor lined with busts and paintings of Latimores long-past, Mrs. Demeter led her, until suddenly she stopped and flung open a door, smiling. "It's hard to be away from home, so I do hope you find this comfortable—it's the prettiest room, I think."

Kit crossed the threshold to be met by shades of blue and gold, an enormous canopied four-poster bed, an armoire, a velvet-covered duchesse and a free-standing gilt mirror. The walls were covered with a turquoise silk, and the ceiling was a mural: angels and harps and clouds. A fire crackled in the hearth. It really was beautiful and Kit was grateful for the consideration. She turned to the housekeeper. "Oh, my. Mrs Demeter, it looks fit for a queen. Thank you so much."

"Well, we've been a stop on many a royal progress over the years."

"Have you been with the family long?"

"Oh yes. Twenty-two years, if I remember correctly. A couple of years before young Master Narcisse was born and his poor mother died." She looked contrite. "But you're not here for gossip! Miss Caswell, I do hope you sleep well—no doubt you're in need after meeting Dark Annie."

Holmes had recounted their adventure to the housekeeper, who'd shown no surprise; Kit had been slightly taken aback that the matter had been mentioned so openly. Then again, it wasn't London where it was still quite unfashionable to believe in such things. "It was … unexpected, I must say."

"Nothing for adults to fear." Her smile was tender.

Kit felt dubious; she'd not have wagered anything of value on the good nature of whatever had clawed at the station door. She paused, then asked, "Have you *seen* her?"

"Oh, yes. Live around here long enough it'll happen."

"Everything I've read says that it's a curse, to see and be seen by her."

"Not everything's written down, Miss Caswell." That smile again, not superior, just gentle. She touched Kit's arm softly, explaining, "She's like any goddess, she gives and she takes—and only takes what she's owed."

"What ... does she look like?" Kit couldn't help but ask.

"Like Dark Annie, of course." Mrs. Demeter laughed.

Dark Annie again, thought Kit. Not Black Annis. No, something more familiar and fond, as if discussing an old friend or a family pet. Something *known*. And 'goddess', not 'monster'.

"Blue skin, long arms, teeth that grind like millwheels," continued Mrs. Demeter. "Now, put it from your mind. If you need anything in the night, don't hesitate to use the bellpull by the fireplace. Someone will attend as soon as possible."

And with that, she was swiftly gone.

*

Kit found it impossible to sleep. She'd bathed, eaten and slid between crisp sheets, but she'd napped on the train and her mind continued to pick at the railway station encounter. She was both exhausted and alert. Her ears felt sharp, attuned for any trace of Black Annis's grating shriek—not merely outside in the grounds, but inside the house, the entry hall, along the corridors, perhaps echoing down the chimney. She'd locked the door and propped a heavy chair behind it, however after perhaps an hour of tossing and turning, she rose and set off in search of a glass of warm milk to tranquilize her scampering brain. She had no intention of disturbing any servants, and the full moon lit her way quite sufficiently.

Big houses, Kit'd concluded some time ago, had basically the same layout; or at least there were enough similarities that one could navigate effectively in most cases. Mainly because although rich folk didn't particularly like to *see* their servants, they also didn't like their food arriving cold, so the kitchen was never too far away. She located the entrance to the Latimore one on the ground floor, down a short set of stone steps and hidden behind a door that could be easily bumped open with a hip or shoulder, if hands and arms were full, and well-oiled to swing silently closed. Inside, her feet chilled by the flagstones, she heard the whispers.

At first, came a rush of adrenaline, but then she realized the tone was entirely different. Not only that, there were words, a soft crooning lullaby, not the guttural growling and groaning of the dark dame of the hills with her grinding teeth. As her eyes grew accustomed to the dimness, Kit made out a faint glow in a far corner, and tiptoed forward, her curiosity propelling her before she could think better of it.

Lit by the last of the flames in the hearth, Mrs. Demeter rocked back and forth in a chair that gave only the slightest squeak. Her hair was loose across her shoulders, and on her lap, wrapped in her arms, was a child. The housekeeper appeared to be breastfeeding, the front of her white nightgown open. Kit, retraced her steps silently, not daring to breathe until she was out in the entry hall once more. She'd not wished to embarrass the woman at such a private moment, that was certainly part of her strategic retreat.

The other element had been the child itself. She'd caught no sight of a face, curled as it was against the mother; could not have recognized anything apart from its bright copper hair. But it had not been a baby, not an infant. No. Considerably larger, perhaps the size of a ten-year-old; even that may not have been entirely unusual, for some women nursed their offspring a much longer while than others.

Whatever the housekeeper did in her dark hours was her own business; she'd been kind to Kit, who would not judge her. And Mrs. Demeter had been calm and content, clearly awake and willing at her task. Yet Kit could have sworn there'd been blood on the front of the woman's nightgown, as if she was bleeding from the chest area.

*

"Good morning, Miss Caswell. May I offer you tea or coffee?"

Alone, Holmes had made himself at home at the dining table in a small duck egg blue breakfast room; a sideboard held tureens and platters with a variety of foodstuffs. The tall windows showed a wild garden, and a slight slope leading down to an impressively large lake. The sky was gray, and the landscape looked still, as if it held its breath. Kit rubbed her tired eyes, and chose a seat across from Holmes, smoothing her daffodil skirts.

"Coffee and details, forthwith." She'd chosen one of the dresses Mrs. Kittredge had packed. The more feminine of her outfits tended to disarm men before she opened her mouth and began asking impertinent questions. It wasn't for Holmes's benefit—he knew enough by now not to underestimate her—but she would speak to Sir Horace at some point today and it wouldn't hurt for him to think her harmless for a while at least. "No sign of Dr. Watson?"

"I fear Watson may have over-medicated his nerves after last night. We'll not see him until lunch."

"Can't say I blame him," muttered Kit; a headache from disturbed slumber sat at the crown of her head. The Detective pushed a delicate bone china cup towards her. She added neither milk nor sugar, but sipped at the steaming liquid, then sighed. "Thank you, Mr. Holmes. Now: dead young men, horribly murdered."

"Watson told you?" He looked displeased.

"No. Nothing more than the barest hint, just enough to get me onto a train. Stop being a child, no one's spoiled your surprise. Dead young men, horribly murdered. Leicestershire. Etcetera. How many? Where and precisely how? Who found them? When did this all start?"

"You really do take the fun out of things, Kit Caswell."

"I'm not your audience to applaud how clever you are, *Sherlock*. Watson said you needed my help. Or was that a lie? Do you have some scheme to make me look like a credulous fool?"

Holmes put both elbows on the table, dropped his head into his hands, then ran stiff fingers through his hair. "You're a frustrating child. I imagine the sort I'd have fathered."

"No need to insult both of us," she said. After a pause, they laughed. "But really, Holmes. What's going on? What has Black Annis got to do with all of this?"

"I don't know, but let me begin at the beginning. Four young men have been found murdered—"

"—horribly—"

"—in the village in the last two weeks."

"But if Dark Annie only hunts on the full moon …"

"Exactly. And youthful though they are, at almost twenty, these victims are most definitely not children. And Black Annis only eats the tenderest and youngest."

Kit steepled her fingers. "So, what makes you think this is an eldritch matter? Surely they could be perfectly ordinary murders?"

Holmes shook his head. "All four had been found drowned—"

"—surely—"

"—in their own beds."

"Oh." She scratched her head. "Dark Annie's not a creature of water. She's not Jenny Greenteeth or Peg Powler. Nor a storm hag."

Holmes smiled, self-satisfied. "I knew it was a good idea to bring you along."

"Oh, hush. Who are the victims?" Kit rose and went to the sideboard for a piece of bread, which she returned to the table and to which she applied generous smears of butter and jam. Then she gestured for the Great Detective to refill her coffee cup.

As he carefully poured, Holmes said: "Local lads, friends of Horace's son, Narcisse."

"And where's Narcisse been when his friends were drowning in their beds?" She crunched thoughtfully on her breakfast. A movement caught in the corner of her eye— outside the window a willowy young man and a heavy-set older one walked beside the lake. Kit turned to take them in better; well-dressed, deep in discussion, wearing identical worried expressions and the same bright red hair. She jerked her chin towards them.

Holmes nodded. "That's Sir Horace and Narcisse. Who, by the by, was at home with his father when the boys died."

"There's a solid alibi," murmured Kit.

Holmes rolled his eyes. "And he was with Sir Horace *and* myself when the fourth lad shuffled off his mortal coil. Unless you suspect me of bearing false witness to protect someone's vain, rather witless son? Really, Miss Caswell."

Kit grinned around a last bite of bread. "Probably not."

"I'm deeply relieved to be off your list of suspects."

"When did Sir Horace begin to fear for his son? I'm assuming that's why you were called here? To prevent the untimely death of what is likely the sole heir?"

Holmes nodded, refilled his own cup. "Where is Mrs. Demeter? She promised me three-minute eggs twenty minutes ago."

The idea of a runny three-minute egg turned Kit's stomach, but she supposed it was the least of Holmes's perversities.

"Perhaps she has other matters to attend to," said Kit mildly, thinking of the child in her lap the night before, of the song the woman had been singing. "There were no witnesses to these dry land drownings?"

"Found in the morning by a distressed parent when their sons failed to come down to breakfast. No sign of forced entry into their homes."

"And none taken on a full moon when Annie roams."

"Not a one."

"And Narcisse safe after last night's excursion by the Dane Demoness."

"So far. A brawny footman's been sitting up, watching over him as he sleeps—two of them, in fact, to make sure neither of them drops off." He nodded towards the father and son outside; they'd paused in their walk, and not far off Kit could see two liveried menservants, yawning as they trailed their lord and master and his cub.

"And no one's concerned for any other young men, except these ones connected to Narcisse?" Holmes shook his head. "Why did anyone think it was Black Annis?"

"I didn't. But an interesting creature to be lurking about, no?"

Kit realized *she* was the one who'd leapt to the conclusion that Dark Annie was involved—Watson had mentioned the Dane Hills, her mind looking for a monster, had flown to the local legend. But no one had *said* Black Annis was to blame. She sighed, irritated at herself; she'd not be admitting her assumption to Holmes anytime soon. He'd probably already figured it, she thought morosely. "And how long have you known Sir Horace?"

Holmes sighed. "I'm beginning to understand why Watson complains when I jump around like this."

"Well?"

"A year."

"So, when Watson said "an old friend" he was exaggerating."

Holmes laughed. "Well, knowing Watson he probably felt it would add an impetus to your decision to come. An old friend sounds far better than 'some chap Holmes met at his club a year ago who's got himself into a spot of bother.' He's not as obtuse as he appears ..."

Before Kit could reply with exactly what she thought Watson was, a flustered Mrs. Demeter burst in carrying a tray. Strands of hair were loose from her otherwise neat bun. The lace on one side of her collar was invisible, caught inside the neck of her dress, as if she'd dressed carelessly.

"Eggs! Mr. Holmes, I'm so sorry. There was an incident in the kitchen and I've been distracted. Freshly boiled three-minute eggs, sir, as requested." She slid the plate in front of Holmes, and gave Kit a bright smile. Her gaze veered, however, to the window and the two Latimores on the lawn. Kit imagined how concerned the woman must have been for the young man she'd helped raise.

"Is everything alright, Mrs. Demeter?"

"Oh. Yes. One of the maids burned her hand, silly girl. She's sitting with a salve on it. It will heal well enough." A brief smile, not quite attached to her lips. "And for you, Miss Caswell? Eggs? Bacon? Kippers?"

As if Kit wasn't perfectly capable of helping herself to the food on the sideboard. "Nothing, thank you." Kit smiled, but the woman's eyes were again tracking the men outside. Then the housekeeper shook her head, as if returning to the room. "But of course, Miss Caswell, no trouble at all."

When Mrs. Demeter had gone, Holmes said, "Poor woman. The strain's showing."   Kit nodded.

"Have you spoken to Narcisse about the problem?"

"I have."

"Have you spoken to him without his father present?"

"I have not."

"I see."

"I thought you might." Holmes leaned forward, elbows on the table in his enthusiasm. "I wondered if you might like to take a run at the lad."

Kit leaned forward, mirroring his pose. "Certainly. But first, Mr. Holmes, I rather think I'd like to chat to his papa."

"Really? I've questioned him and he genuinely doesn't seem to know why this is happening to his son's friends—his main desire is to stop it from happening to Narcisse." His voice grew thin. "Do you think I missed something in my conversation with Horace?"

Kit didn't move, remained hunched forward, and tapped a finger on the table. "I think you asked different questions to the ones I'm going to ask." She sat back. "Eat your egg, Sherlock, it'll get cold."

*

"Don't go too near the water."

Kit, waiting for a terribly busy Sir Horace to find a gap in his schedule, had taken a walk down to the lake. She turned to see a pale and weary-looking Watson coming towards her, leaning on his walking stick more than he was wont. She'd always thought him the better adjusted of the Baker Street residents, but perhaps age was taking more of a toll than anyone realized. And being faced with the world being considerably different to what he'd expected and experienced for most of his life. When Watson reached her side, she linked an arm with his. He looked surprised but didn't pull away. She couldn't have said why she did it, only that there were times she missed her own father so much that it was a physical ache, and there was something about the good doctor that reminded her of the Reverend Caswell. As they continued on, they passed a slim jetty with two small boats moored there, each big enough for two people.

"A pleasant enough way to spend a few hours, don't you think?"

"Rather, but the water's very deep by all accounts," said Watson. "So. Any brilliant ideas, Miss Caswell?"

"You sound hopeful, Dr. Watson."

"I would very much like, I think, to go back to London."
He stared at the lake with a troubled expression. "Can't you
feel it? There's something … not right"—he threw his hand
out to the glassy surface broken only by the occasional lily
pad— "*there*. Am I being a foolish old man?"

Kit shook her head. "Not so old and certainly not foolish.
Something's definitely not right. It's not Black Annis, though,
I'm quite sure of that. She does exist and I've no desire to
encounter her again." She narrowed her eyes. "Something else
…"

Watson sighed. "Don't suppose you could speed things
up? Get an old man back home to the comfort of a filthy city?
All this clean countryside and its monsters is a bit much."

He sounded so put-upon she couldn't help but laugh. "I'll
do my best. I have ideas. I need some more answers, however.
Now, you and your fib about Holmes being old friends with
Sir Horace?"

He blushed, looked a little ashamed. "Ah yes."

"Do you know anything about him, really? Latimore?"

He shook his head. "This is the first time I've met him to
be honest. I'd say he's not much different to most men of his
position and financial status. He's not the worst, I suppose.
Widower, never remarried, brought the lad up on his own,
gave the very best of everything. Probably too much of it."

"And your opinion of the son?"

"Spoilt. I'm unsure how much of his concern is for his
departed friends. Mostly for himself, I suspect." He shrugged,
cleared his throat. "Perhaps I'm being unfair. But I ministered
to Narcisse not an hour ago, gave him something for his
nerves, and there was no word of thanks. Perhaps the young
have simply dispensed with manners nowadays."

"Perhaps," she said, then stopped and turned, pulling him around with her. A shout from the house drew their attention. Holmes hung from one of the lower windows, waving. "It appears Sir Horace has cleared a space in his diary, Dr. Watson. Shall we?"

*

The library was cavernous, brightly lit, and those walls not covered with shelves wore hunter green silk flecked with gold. Kit would have dearly loved to spend several weeks in here, but it was not the time to nose through tomes. Sir Horace remained seated behind an enormous desk, ledgers and documents in front of him, giving the impression of a man being interrupted against his will. Nevertheless, Kit pinned on a smile, and took one of the seats on the opposite side of the desk. Watson folded himself onto the sofa to watch proceedings. Holmes took up position by the hearth, one elbow resting on the mantle, pipe between his teeth as he dipped a taper into the flames of the fireplace, then touched it to the tobacco and puff-puff-puffed.

When he had a good halo of smoke around his head he said, "Horace, old man, this is the investigator I was telling you about."

"Hello, Sir Horace. I have only a few questions for you, then I would like to speak with your son."

"Is this really necessary, Holmes?" complained the man, ignoring Kit. Up close, his skin was coarse and rosy around the nose, his red hair at the temples was turning white, as was his moustache. The extra flesh under his chin wobbled in preparation for outrage.

Kit didn't wait for Holmes to answer. "If you wish your son to survive, I would advise being open and honest. The longer you stall and obfuscate, the lower his chances are of living through the day."

Sir Horace stared at her.

"Now." Kit carefully placed her hands in her lap, fingers intertwined. "Did Narcisse know that Mrs. Demeter's child was his half-sibling?"

Sir Horace blustered, his face turning a bright cherry. Kit had wondered ever since seeing father and son this morning whether there was a photograph somewhere in Mrs. Demeter's quarters: herself, Sir Horace and the illegitimate child between them. The child a father could not publicly recognize, but who'd been raised in his home nonetheless. Kit remained calm, her gaze steady, and waited. In the end, he shook his head but said, "We never told him, but he might have suspected."

"And Mrs. Demeter's son?"

"No. We'd agreed, Ardelia and I."

Kit wondered if Mrs. Demeter had *actually* agreed or merely pretended to. "And how old is Mrs. Demeter's child?"

"Freddie was almost eleven. Terrible shame about what happened. Awful tragedy. I didn't think she'd recover ... I don't know how she ... came to terms with it ..."

"What happened, Sir Horace?" Kit frowned, a chill dancing up her spine.

"The boy drowned, about a month ago. In the lake. His poor mother found him."

Kit's fingers knotted and unknotted with each other as she thought furiously. Without a word, she rose and left the room, the three men following, tripping a little to keep up.

Through the silently swinging door and into the kitchen.

Mrs. Demeter was alone, folding sheets. The rocking chair was where it had been last night, but no sign of a child or anything else. The housekeeper looked up and smiled at Kit, but her expression wavered when she saw the others.

"Everything alright, Miss Caswell?"

"I have some questions, if you don't mind, Mrs. Demeter."

"For me? More about Dark Annie? Are you going to write it all down?" The woman's smile turned a little, something malign fluttering beneath it so quickly Kit thought she'd imagined it.

"First, tell me about Freddie," Kit said, and the woman looked as if she'd been struck.

"Horace," she said, and the tone was all reproach. "Why would you let them speak to me like this? Why would you want me hurt again?"

Holmes broke in, "Please answer the questions, Mrs. Demeter. Miss Caswell is only trying to help."

"I've no wish to distress you, Mrs. Demeter. There are simply things I must find out."

The woman leaned against the table, as if her weight had become too much, and Sir Horace helped her into a chair. Kit stood by, waiting. Implacable.

"He was a good boy and then he drowned. And I'm alone." Her tone was sulky, hurt.

"But, Mrs. Demeter, I saw you feeding him last night. Here."

The woman's gaze turned black, just for a second, and then she shrank into herself. She hung her head, and seemed older when she finally looked up again. Not at any of the men, but at Kit alone as if it were only they two in the kitchen. "He was such a good boy. From the time he could walk, he would wander after Narcisse—as if he knew they were blood. He just wanted to be around him. Narcisse was so much older and he wasn't interested. Why would he be interested in a servant's child?" Her tone was bitter. "He had his friends, his father gave him everything, except a reason to be kind."

"Ardelia," began Sir Horace, but Kit held up a hand to silence him. The woman went on as if he'd not spoken.

"Freddie would follow them. He just wanted to play, but I know they were mean. He didn't complain how badly they treated him even though I saw the bruises, when I bathed him—not big ones, but enough to know they were rough with my little lad. He just wanted to play with his brother!" She was sobbing now, the last sentence shrieked at Sir Horace.

"What happened, Mrs. Demeter? I'm so sorry, but what happened to Freddie?" Kit knelt in front of the housekeeper and took her hands.

"And then ... then he drowned." Mrs. Demeter's gaze shot over Kit's shoulder as if to look through time. "They said they didn't know he'd followed them, when they took the boats out on the lake ... but he always followed them, didn't he? Had since he could toddle. He swam after them or tried to, but that water's too cold, too deep, and they didn't see or just didn't stop. By the time they returned ... it was too late."

The sheer devastation on the woman's face made tears heat Kit's eyes, but she pressed on. She had to. "And what did you do, Mrs. Demeter?"

"The only option open to me, of course. I brought him to Dark Annie's bower and I asked for him back. She hadn't taken him, but she's a goddess, isn't she? She could do *something*. I needed her to do something. I told her that whatever she would return of him, I didn't care what it was." Her voice dropped low, rasping, and she clutched painfully at Kit's hands. "Only, I think, she gave me something of herself too. He had her tastes in him. And I ... didn't really care. He didn't want just anyone, did he? He wanted *them*. Wanted them to die the way he did, nothing but the water. And didn't he deserve that at least? That tiny justice."

Kit thought he probably did, but Sir Horace was unlikely to agree. She was about to continue when Holmes interrupted: "Why are those footmen in the kitchen? Aren't they the ones watching your son, Sir Horace?"

"Oh, I called them for lunch. Told them there was no need to watch during the day. Let Master Narcisse sleep peacefully after Dr. Watson gave him his medicine." And Mrs. Demeter smiled, a terrible smile, and Kit bolted from the kitchen. Pausing only as she realized she had no idea where Narcisse's room was.

"Holmes?" she yelled and that was all that was needed. He led the way, Kit and Watson close behind, Sir Horace and Mrs. Demeter bringing up the rear, the housekeeper screaming all the way, almost like Black Annis, only a little more human.

Up to the second floor and a locked door, which Holmes disposed of with a swift kick. The noise resounded like a gunshot. Kit and the Detective were first in.

On the bed lay Narcisse Latimore, and on his chest perched something the size of a child, bright copper hair covering its face, but Kit could clearly see the stream of water falling from its mouth into that of the Latimore heir. A torrent, really, a cataract.

"No!" Kit heard her shout echoed by Sir Horace. The child on the bed turned, snarling. There was barely a face, only slits for eyes and a mouth filled with teeth—the maw of a leech, the thing that fed on Mrs. Demeter. Kit leapt forward, intending to pull it away, but the thing jumped to meet her and, with an unpleasant sense of déjà vu, she was flat on her back for the second time in two days.

A wave of water hit her, poured into her mouth, down her throat. Dank and mildewy, tasting of the lake bottom, of mud and rotten vegetation. The child's strong, clawed little hands grabbed her ears to stop her from turning away; intent upon drowning her. Kit struggled to locate the opening of her pocket, to find the weight of the fruit knife in it. Her fingers felt stiff and slow; just as they touched the mother-of-pearl handle, searched for the release, the creature made an awful choking sound, and suddenly the deluge was gone.

Kit blinked the liquid from her eyes, gasping for breath. The thing sitting atop her was still, the tip of a sword-cane protruding from its chest. What had been Freddie Demeter squealed horribly, fell and was motionless. Mrs. Demeter's scream was awful. Holmes knelt beside Kit and held her steady; she coughed and coughed trying to get the taste from her mouth; soon she forgot trying not to throw up and vomited spectacularly on an expensive silk rug.

When she was finally fit to pay attention again, Holmes helped her to her feet. Watson had revived the damp Narcisse, and the young man was sitting, coughing explosively. Sir Horace stood by the bed, patting his son's back.

"Are you quite well, Miss Caswell?" asked Holmes and managed not to wither as she breathed out "Delightful."

"Holmes?"

"Yes?"

"Where's Mrs. Demeter?"

380

The child's body was gone too.

*

The initial search of the grounds showed no sign of Ardelia and Freddie Demeter. But Sir Horace finally had the waters of the lake dragged and they were found. Mrs. Demeter's arms were wrapped around her son even in death. She'd taken the time to fill her pockets with stones from the garden to make sure there would be no salvation.

*

The train carried them inexorably back towards London and its own peculiar strangenesses. Dr. Watson's large hip flask was offered around as if they were soldiers in a trench, rather than two middle-aged men and a young woman. Even Kit had to admit that the burn of the whisky seemed to put some life back inside her chest, which had felt quite, quite hollow.

Holmes shook his head slowly and admitted: "I would never have thought it of a child."

"Most men wouldn't, Mr. Holmes," said Kit.

"But you did. You knew, somehow."

"But not soon enough. I didn't think it might be Mrs. Demeter's child or that he might be dead."

"But it wasn't quite a child anymore, Holmes," said Watson, hands clasped firmly about the walking stick that once again appeared nothing more than an affectation.

"And thank you for your swift action, Dr. Watson." Kit reached for the flask again. "Not a child anymore. Part monster."

"Yet his mother protected him," Holmes pondered

"He was still her child. Mothers protect their monsters as fiercely as their children." She shook her head. "I don't know. Perhaps it's simply love that makes them do it. Women have so much taken from them so easily—perhaps their children are where they draw the line, no matter what that child does."

"What a strange thing to say," Watson observed. "And yet, you might be right. Poor woman."

"Poor woman," Holmes echoed.

Kit stared off into the mirror of night formed by the window glass. After a while, the rocking of the train lulled her to sleep.

ABOUT THE CONTRIBUTORS

EDITORS

J.R. CAMPBELL is a Calgary based writer and editor. His short fiction has appeared in numerous anthologies including *A Study in Lavender* and *Challenger Unbound*. With Shannon Allen he has edited the anthologies *By the Light of Camelot* and *The Astronaut Always Rings Twice* and with his brother in arms, Charles Prepolec, he has edited the anthologies *Gaslight Grimoire: Fantastic Tales of Sherlock Holmes*, *Gaslight Grotesque: Nightmare Tales of Sherlock Holmes*, *Gaslight Arcanum: Uncanny Tales of Sherlock Holmes*, *Professor Challenger: New Worlds, Lost Places*, and *Gaslight Gothic: Strange Tales of Sherlock Holmes*. A new collection of his short fiction, *Improbable Remains: The Bizarre and Unconventional Adventures of Sherlock Holmes* is now available from Weird House Press.

CHARLES PREPOLEC MBt, BSI ("The Man with the Twisted Lip") is co-editor of four previous Sherlock Holmes fiction anthologies (with J. R. Campbell) for EDGE SF & F - *Gaslight Grimoire: Fantastic Tales of Sherlock Holmes* (2008), *Gaslight Grotesque: Nightmare Tales of Sherlock Holmes* (2009), *Gaslight Arcanum: Uncanny Tales of*

Sherlock Holmes (2011) and *Gaslight Gothic: Strange Tales of Sherlock Holmes* (2018), plus *Professor Challenger: New Worlds, Lost Places* (2015); as well as co-editor (with Paul Kane) of *Beyond Rue Morgue: Further Tales of Edgar Allan Poe's 1st Detective* (2013) for Titan Books. At the turn of the century, he served as news editor for late actor Christopher Lee's official website. A speaker and frequent contributor to Sherlock Holmes related non-fiction books, journals, etc... *Gaslight Ghouls: New Tales of Sherlock Holmes, Monsters and Madmen* (2022) is his first anthology for Belanger Books. He resides with his patient wife, Kris, and a yet more patient cat, in Calgary, AB, Canada. Twitter: @sherlockeditor

AUTHORS

Stoker and World Fantasy Award nominee, winner of British Fantasy and International Horror Guild Awards for his short fiction, **STEPHEN GALLAGHER** is the author of fifteen novels including *Valley of Lights*, *Down River*, *Rain*, and *Nightmare, With Angel*. He's the creator of Sebastian Becker, Special Investigator to the Lord Chancellor's Visitor in Lunacy, in a series of novels that includes *The Kingdom of Bones*, *The Bedlam Detective*, and *The Authentic William James*. Screen credits include a BBC *Murder Rooms* drama in which he speculated on the possible inspiration behind *The Lost World*, with Charles Edwards as the young Conan Doyle and Ian Richardson as his mentor Joseph Bell. In 2022 he received the inaugural fiction honour from the Arthur Conan

Doyle Society for his story *The Governess.*
www.stephengallagher.com

MARK A. LATHAM is a writer, editor, history nerd, proud dogfather, frustrated grunge singer and amateur baker from Staffordshire, UK. An immigrant to rural Nottinghamshire, he lives in a very old house (sadly not haunted), and is still regarded in the village as a foreigner.

Formerly the editor of Games Workshop's *White Dwarf* magazine, Mark still dabbles in tabletop games design while writing strange, fantastical and macabre tales. His long-form fiction includes two Sherlock Holmes novels, *A Betrayal in Blood* and *The Red Tower,* available now from Titan Books.

Visit Mark's website at mark-latham.com or follow him on Twitter: @aLostVictorian

ALISON LITTLEWOOD'S first book, *A Cold Season,* was selected for the Richard and Judy Book Club and described as 'perfect reading for a dark winter's night.' Other titles include *Mistletoe, The Hidden People, The Crow Garden, Path of Needles* and *The Unquiet House.* She also wrote *The Cottingley Cuckoo,* as A. J. Elwood.

Alison's short stories have been picked for a number of year's best anthologies and published in her collections *Quieter*

Paths and *Five Feathered Tales*. She has won the Shirley Jackson Award for Short Fiction.

Alison lives in Yorkshire, England, in a house of creaking doors and crooked walls. She loves exploring the hills and dales with her two hugely enthusiastic Dalmatians and has a penchant for books on folklore and weird history, Earl Grey tea, fountain pens and semicolons.

JONATHAN MABERRY is a NY Times bestselling author, 5-time Bram Stoker Award-winner, 3-time Scribe Award winner, Inkpot Award winner, and comic book writer. His vampire apocalypse book series, V-WARS, was a Netflix original series. He writes in multiple genres including suspense, thriller, horror, science fiction, fantasy, and action; for adults, teens and middle grade. His novels include the *Joe Ledger* thriller series, the *Kagen the Damned* novels, *Bewilderness, Ink,* the *Pine Deep Trilogy*, the *Rot & Ruin* series, the *Dead of Night* series, *Mars One, Ghostwalkers: A Deadlands Novel.* etc. He's the editor of many anthologies including *The X-Files, Aliens: Bug Hunt, Don't Turn Out the Lights, Aliens vs Predator, Nights of the Living Dead* (co-edited with George A. Romero), and others. His comics include *Black Panther: DoomWar, Captain America, Pandemica, The Punisher* and *Bad Blood.* He's the president of the International Association of Media Tie-in Writers, and the editor of Weird Tales Magazine. He was a featured expert on the History Channel's *Zombies: A Living History* and *True Monsters.* www.jonathanmaberry.com

JAMES A. MOORE is the award-winning, best-selling author of over forty novel length works mixing the horror, fantasy, science fiction, crime and western genres. His titles include the *Blood Red* series, the *Seven Forges* books, the *Tides of War* trilogy and many books with his immortal monster hunter Jonathan Crowley, including the *Serenity Falls* trilogy, *Cherry Hill*, *Under the Overtree* and several short story collections like *Where The Sun Goes To Die* and *One Bad Week*. He has written over a hundred short story and novella length pieces, and has been published by Marvel comics and in multiple magazines over the last thirty odd years.

MARK MORRIS has written and edited around forty novels, novellas, short story collections and anthologies, and his script work includes audio dramas for *Doctor Who*, *Jago & Litefoot* and the *Hammer Chillers* series. His most recent work includes the *Obsidian Heart* trilogy (*The Wolves of London*, *The Society of Blood* and *The Wraiths of War*), the original Predator novel *Stalking Shadows* (co-written with James A. Moore), new audio adaptations of the classic 1971 horror movie *Blood on Satan's Claw* and the M.R. James ghost story *A View From a Hill*, a 30th anniversary short story collection *Warts And All*, and, as editor, the anthologies *After Sundown* and *Beyond the Veil*. *Blood on Satan's Claw* won the New York Festival Radio Award for Best Drama Special, and *A*

View From a Hill won the New York Festival Radio Award for Best Digital Drama Program, and was also awarded Silver at the 2020 Audio & Radio Industry Awards. Mark has won two British Fantasy Awards, and has also been nominated for several Stokers and Shirley Jackson Awards.

JOSH REYNOLDS has been a professional author since 2007, and has over thirty novels to his name, as well as numerous short stories, novellas and audio scripts. In addition to his own work, he has contributed to numerous popular franchises, including *Warhammer 40,000*, *Arkham Horror* and *Legend of the Five Rings*. Born and raised in South Carolina, he now resides in Sheffield with his wife and daughter, as well as a highly excitable dog and something he hopes is a cat. A complete list of his work can be found at https://joshuamreynolds.co.uk/.

CHARLES R. RUTLEDGE is the author of *Dracula's Return*, and the co-author of three novels in the *Griffin & Price* series, written with James A. Moore. His short stories have appeared in over 30 anthologies. He has also co-edited Horror anthologies for Pavane Press and Twisted Publishing. Charles owns entirely too may editions of Dracula, keeps actual soil from Transylvania in an envelope on his desk, and is seldom seen in daylight.

ANGELA SLATTER is the author of five novels, including *All the Murmuring Bones* and *The Path of Thorns*, and eleven short story collections, including *The Bitterwood Bible* and *The Tallow-Wife and Other Tales*. She's won a World Fantasy Award, a British Fantasy Award, a Ditmar, two Australian Shadows Awards and seven Aurealis Awards. Her work has been translated into multiple languages. She has an MA and a PhD in Creative Writing, teaches for the Australian Writers' Centre, and occasionally mentors new authors. She can be located on the internet at www.angelaslatter.com, @AngelaSlatter (Twitter) and angelaslatter (Instagram). Dark Horse Comics has recently announced her Hellboy Universe collaboration with Mike Mignola, *Castle Full of Blackbirds*.

SIMON KURT UNSWORTH was born in the north of England in 1972 on a day when, he can confirm, there were mysterious power cuts across the region. He always knew the universe would note his arrival in some way... He is the author of two novels set in Hell (*The Devil's Detective* and *The Devil's Evidence*), 4 collections of stories set in places that might be close to Hell, a mini-collection set in a version of the town where he grew up and, with his son, a mini-collection set all over the place. He now lives in the Lake District with his wife, some fish, some children sometimes, a tortoise, a brace of dogs and cats and too many books and movies. When not working (as a bookseller) he writes a bit, swims in the lakes and rivers and dreams about sharks.

389

STEPHEN VOLK is best known as the award-winning writer of the BBC's notorious "Halloween hoax" *Ghostwatch* and the ITV paranormal drama series *Afterlife* starring Andrew Lincoln and Lesley Sharp. His screenplays include *The Awakening* starring Rebecca Hall, the miniseries adaptation of Phil Rickman's *Midwinter of the Spirit* starring Anna Maxwell Martin and David Threlfall, and Ken Russell's *Gothic* starring Natasha Richardson as Mary Shelley and Gabriel Byrne as Lord Byron. He is the author of four collections – *Dark Corners, Monsters in the Heart* (which won the British Fantasy Award), *The Parts We Play* and his most recent, *Lies of Tenderness.* His acclaimed *Dark Masters Trilogy* features Peter Cushing, Alfred Hitchcock and Dennis Wheatley as central characters, while the seven stories in *Under a Raven's Wing* (2021) team up a young, Pre-Watson, Sherlock Holmes with Edgar Allan Poe's master detective C. Auguste Dupin to solve grotesque and inexplicable crimes in 1870s Paris. More information and news can be found at: www.stephenvolk.net

WENDY N. WAGNER is the editor-in-chief of *Nightmare Magazine* and the managing/senior editor of *Lightspeed.* Her short stories, essays, and poems run the gamut from horror to environmental literature. Her longer work includes the novella *The Secret Skin* (one of *The Washington Post's* best SF/F/H books of 2021), the horror novel *The Deer Kings,* the Locus bestselling SF eco-thriller *An Oath of Dogs*, and two novels for the Pathfinder role-playing game. She lives in Oregon with her very understanding family, two large cats, and a Muppet disguised as a dog. You can find her at winniewoohoo.com.

COVER ARTIST

DAVE ELSEY is an Academy and Saturn Award Winning creator of special characters and creatures using special Makeup Effects and Animatronics. He is known for his work in movies such as *X-Men: First Class*, *Ghost Rider*, *Star Wars*, *Hellraiser*, *Alien 3*, *The Wolfman*, and *Mr. Holmes*. A keen Sherlock Holmes enthusiast, he has provided cover art for the comic book series *Sherlock Holmes: The Dark Detective*, as well as the books *Gaslight Arcanum: Uncanny Tales of Sherlock Holmes* and *Professor Challenger: New Worlds, Lost Places* and *Gaslight Gothic: Strange Tales of Sherlock Holmes*.

AUTHOR INTERVIEWS

A series of brief Q and As with the authors and editors were published as part of the *Gaslight Ghouls* Kickstarter campaign. For your reading pleasure, we include the interviews as a bonus section of the anthology.

JONATHAN MABERRY

Q: How were you first introduced to Sherlock Holmes?

JM: When I was a kid back in the sixties the old Basil Rathbone and Nigel Bruce films were playing quite often on TV. They were compelling, fun, and weird for someone from inner-city Philadelphia. They were actually my first real introduction to British culture, albeit the version filtered through cinema. Around that time the Scholastic Book Fair offered a couple of inexpensive volumes –*The Adventures of Sherlock Holmes* and *The Hound of the Baskervilles.* And I found that the stories were generally far more entertaining, detailed, nuanced, and interesting than the films. By the time I was twelve I'd read every single tale.

Q: Do you have a favorite Sherlock Holmes story?

JM: I've always liked the rural or country tales. *The Adventure of the Copper Beeches, The Engineer's Thumb, The Speckled Band,* and, of course, *The Hound of the Baskervilles.* However, my favorite all-times Holmes tale is *The Blue Carbuncle*, set in London.

Q: Have you written previous Sherlock Holmes adventures?

JM: This is my third Holmes story, but my fourth involved Holmes's creator. The first short story I ever wrote was *The Adventure of the Greenbrier Ghost* for an anthology called *Legends of the Mountain State Vol II,* in which I embroiled

Holmes and Watson in a weird bit of absolutely true American history in which the second-hand testimony of a ghost was admitted as evidence in a court case and led to a murder conviction. I checked the Holmes records online and found that he was actually supposed to be in America at the same time as that case. Lucky timing for me. And it's one of my most frequently reprinted stories.

I did a story called *The Adventure of the Empty Grave* for the anthology, *Echoes of Sherlock Holmes,* where a grieving Watson is startled to meet Poe's Auguste Dupin at the graveside of the great detective. It's set the day before Holmes reveals that he is alive (*The Empty House*).

More recently I wrote a time travel story in which H. G. Wells takes Sir Arthur Conan Doyle to the future to meet crime writer Ed McBain (author of the brilliant 87th precent police procedurals).

I also used the Holmes-Watson dynamic for a fantasy story (*"The Hammer of God"*) in which an investigator for the Office of Miracles and her assistant are looking into a possible miracle, but which is actually a clever crime. Those characters have since been folded into my new epic fantasy novel series, *Kagen the Damned.*

Q: What do you feel is the most underappreciated aspect to Holmes?

JM: There is a sense of play in Holmes at times. Sure, it frequently misfires like the way he revealed to Watson that he was still alive; but he clearly loves what he's doing. He's wildly dramatic, loves playing dress-up, thrives on attention, and digs the big reveal. All that can either be a charming eccentricity –hinting at not enough time to be a child when growing up; or it can be hugely irritating (mostly to poor old Watson). And…Holmes has a heart, which the end of *The Blue Carbuncle* clearly shows.

Q: Do you have a favorite film/television/theatre actor to play Holmes? What attracted you to the performance?

JM: There are so many talented actors who have brought unique interpretations to Holmes that it's hard to choose. Of course, I grew up with Basil Rathbone's Holmes, and also Peter Cushing's. And I really dig the quirky Robert Downey, Jr. version and the dynamic revisionist Benedict Cumberbatch take. But my favorite, and will likely always be, Jeremy Brett. His Holmes is the version that has been in my imagination since I first read the books as a kid, and when those episodes first launched on TV I was enthralled. *This* was Holmes, done to a T. And the second Watson on that series, Edward Hardwicke, was letter perfect. I always disliked Watson portrayed as a buffoon. And, frankly, I doubt the *Sherlock* actors' takes on Holmes and Watson might not have come to pass had Brett and Hardwicke not set the bar so high in such exciting and fascinating ways.

ALISON LITTLEWOOD

Q: How were you first introduced to Sherlock Holmes?

AL: My first introduction was probably the Granada TV series starring Jeremy Brett, which started in the 80s when I was thirteen. He was a delightfully sneery and rather handsome Holmes, and of course we all fancied him rotten - almost as much as Avon on *Blake's 7*.

Q: Do you have a favorite Sherlock Holmes story?

AL: It's an obvious choice, but it has to be *The Hound of the Baskervilles*. Grimpen Mire is such a moody, atmospheric setting, and the suggestion of the supernatural hanging over the story definitely appeals to my dark side.

Q: Have you written previous Sherlock Holmes adventures?

AL: My first foray was with the Simon Clark edited anthology, *The Mammoth Book of Sherlock Holmes Abroad*. My initial thought, on reading the invitation to submit, was that it was impossible: it demanded a greater knowledge of Holmes than I had at the time, by nature it required a historical piece and it had to have an overseas setting. Then I decided that I like a challenge – surprising things can happen when you push yourself – so I said yes. I embarked on a mountain of research and not only fell in love with Holmes all over again (for rather better reasons this time), but gained a fascination with writing historical fiction that led to my writing several novels set in the Victorian era.

Q: Do you have a favorite film/television/theatre actor to play Holmes? What attracted you to the performance?

AL: It still has to be Jeremy Brett, mainly because he's 'my' Holmes, rather in the way that Tom Baker is 'my' Doctor Who. I guess the ones you grow up with tend to stick!

MARK LATHAM

Q: How were you first introduced to Sherlock Holmes?

ML: My first memory of encountering Sherlock Holmes as a young lad was watching the Granada Television series with Jeremy Brett. It hooked me very early, not just on Holmes, but on Victoriana in general. I think it was very soon after the first series was aired in the UK that the *Young Sherlock Holmes* movie came out – I'm not ashamed to say that I still love it, perhaps more from childhood nostalgia than anything else. It was a few years before I was old enough to read Doyle's stories, but when I did that was it – I've been a fan ever since.

Q: Do you have a favorite Sherlock Holmes story?

ML: I'll be very cliché here and say *The Hound of the Baskervilles* – but honestly, it's not just my favorite Holmes story, but one of my favorite novels. Of the short stories, it's a close-run thing between the *Blue Carbuncle* and the *Solitary Cyclist*. Carbuncle probably edges it, because it's not just a great story, but one of my go-to 'comfort reads' every Christmas.

Q: Have you written previous Sherlock Holmes adventures?

ML: Several. In fact, I've probably written Holmes more times than any of my own characters by now. This is my fourth Sherlock Holmes anthology, whilst my two novels – *A*

Betrayal in Blood and *The Red Tower* – are both available from Titan Books.

Q: What do you feel is the most underappreciated aspect to Holmes?

ML: I think something that Sherlockians all know, but that isn't really appreciated by the casual reader/viewer, is just how fond Holmes is of Watson (and vice-versa). It's why I never really gelled with the old Rathbone/Bruce partnership, because Watson *always* seemed like an idiot and Holmes was *always* condescending. Canonically, Holmes's barbs at Watson's expense are part defence mechanism, part very-British-bonding (something that might sometimes be lost in translation). It's something I always try to capture in my stories.

Q: Do you have a favorite film/television/theatre actor to play Holmes? What attracted you to the performance?

ML: For me, Jeremy Brett is Holmes. The nuanced expressions, the sudden outbursts of enthusiasm, the portrayal of troubled genius, the relationship with Watson, the playful sparring with Mrs Hudson... I just think he 'got' the role better than anyone else (really helped by the fact he had not one, but two excellent Watsons during the run). Whenever I'm stuck writing a character-driven scene in a Holmes story, I find myself asking 'What would Brett have done?' On saying all that, a close second for me is actually Peter Cushing. It's a different interpretation, a more confident and commanding

Holmes perhaps, but his versions of *Hound* and *Carbuncle* are my very favorite adaptations.

CHARLES RUTLEDGE

Q: How were you first introduced to Sherlock Holmes?

CR: I read one or two stories as a kid but didn't really become interested in Holmes and Doyle until the early 1990s when I caught an episode of the Granada Sherlock Holmes on PBS. It was *Thor Bridge* and I enjoyed it so much I went to the library and checked out *The Complete Sherlock Holmes* and read it straight through. I've been fascinated by the character ever since. I made my first trip to London specifically to visit Baker Street.

Q: Do you have a favorite Sherlock Holmes story?

CR: I'm very fond of *The Copper Beeches* because it's so Gothic.

Q: Have you written previous Sherlock Holmes adventures?

CR: I started one or two adventures, but they ended up as fragments. This was the first one completed. It's also the first story of mine to be published that was written in the first person point of view. All my novels and other short stories were writing in third person pov. I wanted to follow Doyle's pattern, though I made no attempt to imitate his voice.

Q: What do you feel is the most underappreciated aspect to Holmes?

CR: Conan Doyle's prose. He writes well and has an ear for dialogue. I think people get so caught up in the plots and in the character of Holmes himself, they don't notice what a solid writer Sir Arthur was.

Q: Do you have a favorite film/television/theatre actor to play Holmes? What attracted you to the performance?

CR: Jeremy Brett, hands down. He is so much the character to me that I see him as Holmes when I read Doyle's stories. I was imagining him saying all my dialogue as I was writing my tale for this book.

STEPHEN GALLAGHER

Q: How were you first introduced to Sherlock Holmes?

SG: Almost certainly through some anthology borrowed from the children's section of my local library, which would have led me to acquiring the John Murray volume of complete short stories. I read that one end to end and still have it today.

Q: Do you have a favorite Sherlock Holmes story?

SG: I've a special affection for *The Adventure of the Six Napoleons*, for its bizarre setup masking the elegant simplicity of its premise.

Q: Have you written previous Sherlock Holmes adventures?

SG: No, this is my first; otherwise, I have my own line of novels and stories to scratch that itch. I did write one of the *Murder Rooms* TV movies with Joseph Bell and the young Conan Doyle in a Holmes/Watson partnership, but that's as close as I've been.

Q: What do you feel is the most underappreciated aspect to Holmes?

SG: People often don't pick up on Doyle's humour, but it's there.

Q: Do you have a favorite film/television/theatre actor to play Holmes? What attracted you to the performance?

SG: Douglas Wilmer was my first, and first impressions are hard to beat, but I thought Christopher Plummer brought a rare warmth to the character. Jonny Lee Miller nailed the depth and complexity of an addict's broken soul growing back together, and then there's Robert Stephens in *The Private Life of,* which I thought was terrific.

WENDY WAGNER

Q: How were you first introduced to Sherlock Holmes?

WW: The first exposure to Sherlock Holmes was actually the wonderfully fun board game *221B Baker Street*. My sister bought it for us when I was seven or eight, and I loved the artwork and mechanics. There was something incredibly satisfying about collecting all the evidence and solving cases, and it turned me into a little mystery junkie.

The first Holmes story I ever read was *The Hound of the Baskervilles*, which I found in my parents' enormous Doyle collection at about age eight. As a life-long animal lover, I was interested in *any* story about dogs, so of course the title was like catnip to me. But the story more than lived up to its title, with all its atmosphere and adventure. Plus, I loved the blend of science fact and mystery fiction! Those two genres are still my favorites, and *Baskervilles* remains my favorite Sherlockian tale.

Q: Have you written previous Sherlock Holmes adventures?

WW: This is actually the first time I've ever written one! I've actually been terrified to work in his realm. I got to write about Professor Challenger once, which was intimidating enough. Needless to say, when I was invited to write for this book, I alternated between excitement and absolute terror.

Q: What do you feel is the most underappreciated aspect to Holmes?

WW: Dr. Watson! He is one of my favorite characters in all of literature. He's the Samwise Gamgee of mystery fiction.

STEPHEN VOLK

Q: How were you first introduced to Sherlock Holmes?

SV: It must have been at the age of six or seven. I was staying over at my cousin's house in Cardiff. Geoff was a year or two younger than me. His father switched on the radio – the "wireless" as we called it in those days – and we listened, enraptured, to a dramatization of *The Hound of the Baskervilles*. It scared us to death! To the extent my uncle had to explain to us afterwards that the blood-freezing howls were not the product of an enormous hound but just a little man in glasses standing at a microphone at the BBC. The thrill of the story and of being terrified never left me, and I have loved the character ever since.

Q: Do you have a favorite Sherlock Holmes story?

SV: It has to be *The Hound of the Baskervilles*, partly because, as I said above, it was my formative experience. And I adore the Hammer film as I adore many Hammer films. I am not a sucker for all crime fiction and I particularly dislike "cozy" crime, but if you have a detective versus the supernatural, I'm in. The clash between cold logic and the unexplained is an intoxicating one, to me.

Q: Have you written previous Sherlock Holmes adventures?

SV: I have. I wrote "Hounded" for the anthology *Gaslight Grotesque* and "The Comfort of the Seine" for *Gaslight*

Arcanum, both edited by Charles Prepolec and Jeff Campbell. The latter was a story about the pre-Watson Sherlock meeting Edgar Allan Poe's famous detective Dupin in 1870s Paris. I went on to write more tales featuring this pair investigating bizarre and seemingly impossible cases. My complete Holmes/Dupin stories are collected in my book *Under a Raven's Wing* (PS Publishing, 2021).

Q: What do you feel is the most underappreciated aspect to Holmes?

SV: His innate sense of justice, and applying his craft to help the underdog. With his great brain he does not hide away in a laboratory or write text books – he wants to help people. It's possible to overwrite his autistic qualities. In my opinion it's important to balance that with his sense of fairness and good versus evil.

Q: Do you have a favorite film/TV/theatre actor to play Holmes? What attracted you to the performance?

SV: It has to be Peter Cushing. I grew up with Douglas Wilmer on BBC TV in the sixties, but I was aware, of course, of the immaculate Basil Rathbone – my dad's favorite - but for me Cushing (who took over from Wilmer) had a quality apart, and still does. I know fans rave about Jeremy Brett (and perhaps it is to do with at what age you encounter these performances) but to me all others are actors: all very good, undeniably, but they are acting Holmes whereas Cushing really felt like he was Holmes. I think it is the combination of studied fastidiousness with a sense of inner, steely morality.

Q: Can you tell us about your story in Gaslight Ghouls?

SV: Since experiencing New Year's Eve in a local pub in the town where I live in the county of Wiltshire many years ago, I have always wanted to write a story about mummers. The tradition is fascinating and complex. I saw the brief for *Gaslight Ghouls* as an opportunity to weave a piece that edges into folk horror as well as detective mystery, but one in which the victim reflects the modern world we are living in. I always like to put something of now in my Holmes stories, something for the pastiche quality to bite against, or to reveal, in a sense. That is why it is great fun and a great honor writing these wonderful archetypal heroes like Holmes and Watson. I really wondered what Holmes might say about our "mongrel" nation and what threatens it.

JAMES A. MOORE

Q: Do you have a favorite Sherlock Holmes story?

JAM: *Hound of the Baskervilles*. It had a delicious, creepy edge to it.

Q: Have you written previous Sherlock Holmes adventures?

JAM: Only for *Gaslight Grotesque*, and I loved it. I had so much fun!

Q: What do you feel is the most underappreciated aspect to Holmes?

JAM: That he is an adventurer, not just an amazing detective. In a lot of ways, he's like Batman, minus the cowl. He's physically able and a strong fighter, proficient in multiple forms of combat.

Q: Do you have a favorite film/television/theatre actor to play Holmes? What attracted you to the performance?

JAM: I really love the Benedict Cumberbatch version, because the chemistry between the actors is flawless to me, which is odd because allegedly they really don't like each other very much. Still, I think they play off each other beautifully.

MARK MORRIS

Q: How were you first introduced to Sherlock Holmes?

MM: Sherlock Holmes is embedded in British culture, so I'm pretty sure I knew roughly who he was from a very early age, even before encountering him in fiction. I'm almost certain that my first exposure to an actual Holmes story was the 1959 Hammer movie adaptation of *Hound of the Baskervilles* with Peter Cushing and Christopher Lee, which I must have seen when I was around ten years old, and remember finding incredibly thrilling.

Q: Do you have a favorite Sherlock Holmes story?

MM: There are so many that I love, but my knee-jerk reaction is to say *The Red-Headed League*, simply because I remember thinking how brilliantly clever it was the first time I read it. I have to give a special shout-out, though, to the phrase 'The Grimpen Mire', which of course is from 'Hound'. *Such* an evocative phrase, and a pairing of words which still send a delicious little shiver through me to this day.

Q: Have you written previous Sherlock Holmes adventures?

MM: Yes, I've written three previous Holmes stories, which have appeared in three different anthologies: "The Affair of the Heart" in *Gaslight Grotesque*, and "The Lizard Lady of Pemberton Grange" in *Gaslight Gothic*, both of which were edited by J.R. Campbell and Charles Prepolec, and "The

Crimson Devil" in *The Mammoth Book of Sherlock Holmes Abroad*, edited by Simon Clark.

Q: What do you feel is the most underappreciated aspect to Holmes?

MM: I'm not sure whether it's underappreciated, but I'm always struck by how fast-moving and incredibly readable the Holmes stories are, considering the age in which they were written. I like Victorian ghost stories, and I mostly like Dickens, but the style employed in Victorian fiction is often wordy and ponderous, and needs some mental adjusting to. Not Conan Doyle's work, though. His Holmes stories, and his supernatural fiction, have a pace and an immediacy, which I think new readers would find both refreshing and surprising.

Q: Do you have a favorite film/television/theatre actor to play Holmes? What attracted you to the performance?

MM: I have two – Peter Cushing and Jeremy Brett. Peter Cushing is my favorite actor of all time; he's a joy to watch in everything he does. The word 'consummate' might have been invented for him. Jeremy Brett, though, is the actor who I feel has embodied the character most completely. Whenever I read any Holmes fiction now, be it the original Conan Doyle stories or work by other authors, it's always Brett I envisage as Holmes.

SIMON KURT UNSWORTH

Q: How were you first introduced to Sherlock Holmes?

SKU: Like a lot of authors, I came to Holmes via film. The old Basil Rathbone movies used to play fairly frequently so although I don't have any specific memories of thinking "Ah! A Sherlock Holmes movie!" they form part of the general tapestry of my childhood. Not long after that my grandparents bought me a large hardback collected works with a weird pale brown tartan-esque cover and that, I suppose, was that.

Q: Do you have a favorite Sherlock Holmes story?

SKU: Honestly, no. I watch and read a lot of crime what I'm in some ways more interested in how Holmes (and indeed, Doyle) are used in other places or interpreted by other creators, for example in the TV series *Murdoch Mysteries* (whose characters appear peripherally in my story). In that extended universe, I like the Hammer *Hound of the Baskervilles*, the aforementioned *Murdoch Mysteries* (whose central character, the Toronto detective William Murdoch, is clearly modelled on Holmes – as, I suppose, are probably thousands of other detective characters), the Granada Brett series, *Elementary* and Meyer's *The Seven Percent Solution*…amongst lots of others.

Q: Have you written previous Sherlock Holmes adventures?

SKU: Just two, both short stories and both horror. Both, also, like this story aren't exactly Holmes stories – two are narrated by other characters and one…well…one does a terrible thing to Holmes.

Q: What do you feel is the most underappreciated aspect to Holmes?

SKU: I'm not sure there's anything underappreciated!! There's so much Holmes material out there that I think almost every aspect of him has been investigated. I suppose, if there's one thing in terms of the stories themselves, it's how much of a friend he is without every really being friendly or making overt displays of companionship.

Q: Do you have a favorite film/television/theatre actor to play Holmes? What attracted you to the performance?

SKU: I love Nicol Williamson's manic but oddly delicate performance in *The Seven-Percent Solution* and, for nostalgia's sake, Rathbone's spiky, austere marvel. But really, for me, there's only one: Peter Cushing in Hammer's Hound adaptation. Why? Because it's Peter Cushing, he's with Christopher Lee and the film is a gothic delight.

JOSH REYNOLDS

Q: How were you first introduced to Sherlock Holmes?

JR: By way of *The Hound of the Baskervilles*, courtesy of my school library. It had a great cover, with the titular hound leaping out of the fog towards a pair of crouching figures. I must have checked it out 2-3 times a year before someone thought to mention there were more Holmes stories available.

Q: Do you have a favorite Sherlock Holmes story?

JR: Obviously, *The Hound of the Baskervilles*, since it was my first. But I've always been partial to *The Red Headed League* as well. Though I think *The Adventure of the Creeping Man* is the one I've reread the most, just because it's such a weird turn for the characters.

Q: Have you written previous Sherlock Holmes adventures?

JR: A few times now. I always look forward to an opportunity to play with Conan Doyle's characters. I hope I do them justice!

Q: What do you feel is the most underappreciated aspect to Holmes?

JR: His kindness. It's one of the reasons I love Jeremy Brett's take on the character - he always shows Holmes' basic decency and kindness, even at his most acerbic.

Q: Do you have a favorite film/television/theatre actor to play Holmes? What attracted you to the performance?

JR: Oh Brett, definitely. He managed to capture all of the facets of the character like no one else. When I write Holmes, I'm really writing Brett-as-Holmes. I like the Rathbone Holmes as well, because I can easily imagine him facing off with Claude Rains' Invisible Man or Bela Lugosi's Dracula, and Clive Merrison's take for the BBC radio dramatizations is just fantastic. Those'd be my top three, I think.

ANGELA SLATTER

Q: How were you first introduced to Sherlock Holmes?

AS: I suspect it was actually via a movie, *Murder by Decree*. When I was a kid, if you mixed Jack the Ripper with anything, I would pay attention. And to be honest nothing's really changed since then!

Q: Have you written previous Sherlock Holmes adventures?

AS: I wrote a story called "A Matter of Light" for the *Gaslight Gothic* anthology. It's the first meeting of my character Kit Caswell (from the novella *Ripper*) and Holmes and Watson. I really enjoyed writing that one, and *Gaslight Ghouls* presented the perfect opportunity to get the band back together so they could snipe at each other again.

Q: Do you have a favorite film/television/theatre actor to play Holmes? What attracted you to the performance?

AS: I actually adore *Murder Rooms* by David Pirie, about Drs Bell and Doyle. I think Charles Edwards' Doyle had the right mix of vulnerability and trusting for a good Watson character without being the stereotypical sort of dolt we too often see. And Ian Richardson's Joseph Bell was the sort of Holmes I would have loved to meet – very clever, acerbic but also very kind. He's definitely my favorite 'Holmes'.

J. R. CAMPBELL

Q: How were you first introduced to Sherlock Holmes?

JRC: There is a phrase, 'Everyone thinks they know Sherlock Holmes but they are wrong', and that described me pretty well. I was aware of Sherlock from an early age, I'd seen him here and there, read him a couple of times, and he appeared to me an interesting but rather flat classic detective. It wasn't until I read through *The Adventures of Sherlock Holmes* that Holmes became a more rounded, more impactful character. He really is addictive but, for me at least, it wasn't until I'd a few of his investigations under my belt that he started to emerge from the shadows.

Q: Do you have a favorite Sherlock Holmes story?

JRC: In general, I prefer the short stories. They add to more than the sum of their parts. My favorite? I'll go with *Silver Blaze*, it has everything. Deductions based not just clues uncovered but on the absence of evidence, some great quotes, and I adore the independence Holmes shows by waiting until after he has cashed in his winnings before presenting the solution to the case.

Q: Have you written previous Sherlock Holmes adventures?

JRC: I have and I've enjoyed it. I've contributed to prior Gaslight anthologies, other anthologies, and radio scripts to Imagination Theatre's *The Further Adventures of Sherlock*

Holmes. I'm looking forward to the release of *Improbable Remains: The Bizarre and Unconventional Adventures of Sherlock Holmes*, a collection of my Sherlock Holmes short stories.

Q: What do you feel is the most underappreciated aspect to Holmes?

JRC: I'm always fascinated with who Holmes is willing to trust and who he doesn't. In *Thor Bridge* when Gibson denies any wrong-doing, while everyone insists he's had an improper relationship outside his marriage, Holmes is willing to at least entertain the notion that Gibson is telling the truth. In *Blue Carbuncle* when he accepts Ryder's pledge not to steal again and lets him go. I always expect his prior investigations, the terrible things he has seen, will render him unwilling to trust others but that's not the case.

Q: Do you have a favorite film/TV/theatre actor to play Holmes? What attracted you to the performance?

JRC: Enjoyed the way the Benedict Cumberbatch portrayed the detective in BBC's Sherlock, the analytical way in he seemed to observe the world as if he were not a part of it. That said, I always enjoyed the Robert Downey Jr. films, presenting a Holmes who was more a part of the world. There were times when Jeremy Brett's performance was amazing and Basil Rathbone's voice is often the Holmes voice I hear (even though I know it is not as correct as Brett's was). My guilty pleasure remains the Michael Caine comedy Without a Clue/My Friend Sherlock Holmes.

CHARLES PREPOLEC

Q: How were you first introduced to Sherlock Holmes?

CP: I'd read *The Hound of the Baskervilles* when I was about 10 years old and disliked it thoroughly as I found the absence of Holmes for much of it rather unsatisfying. Close to a decade later I found myself picking up *The Cases of Sherlock Holmes* comics, as I was a fan of the artists (Dan and David Day), and found myself getting into the text, which was entirely ACD's original text, not adapted. From there it was a short step to buying a copy of *The Adventures of Sherlock Holmes* and I've been hooked ever since.

Q: Do you have a favorite Sherlock Holmes story?

CP: As much as I go on about the short stories being the best, my favorite remains *The Sign of Four*, the second appearance of Sherlock Holmes. It's pretty much a perfect late Victorian adventure novel, with romance, flashbacks to exotic locales, creepy and bizarre characters and a more fully-formed version of our hero than the proto-Holmes of *A Study in Scarlet*. Of the short stories, I rate *The Speckled Band*, with all it's Gothic-revival elements as one of Doyle's absolute best, but when push comes to shove, my heart belongs to SIGN.

Q: Have you written previous Sherlock Holmes adventures?

CP: No. I've never written any, ever, but have edited five Sherlock Holmes anthologies and written a good number of published non-fiction pieces. I'm simply not imaginative enough to come up with clever ideas and plots on my own, but am analytical enough to recognize, appreciate and finesse the work of others who do.

Q: What do you feel is the most underappreciated aspect to Holmes?

CP: That he's as human as the rest of us, with all the idiosyncratic foibles and personality traits, both positive and negative, that go along with being one. There is that moment in *The Norwood Builder* when McFarlane announces he expects to be arrested and Holmes replies "This is really most grati—most interesting" and Watson notes "My companion's expressive face showed a sympathy which was not, I am afraid, entirely unmixed with satisfaction." The mask slips and Holmes's innate human selfishness stands clearly revealed and we are reminded to take him seriously when he said in *The Red Headed League* that "My life is spent in one long effort to escape from the commonplaces of existence. These little problems help me to do so." We forget that he isn't some super-human altruistic servant of justice, but rather a somewhat too-clever guy who does what he does simply to avoid going mad from boredom, regardless of Watson's hero-worshipping efforts to convince us otherwise.

Q: Do you have a favorite film/television/theatre actor to play Holmes? What attracted you to the performance?

CP: Peter Cushing usually tops my list. His waspish energy and a certain ever-present intelligence in those piercing blue eyes make for a very convincing Holmes, plus I just love him in most anything. And, given his 'Hammer Horror' associations, I can't imagine a more perfectly representative Holmes for the stories we have in our books.

BELANGERBOOKS.COM

CPSIA information can be obtained
at www.ICGtesting.com
Printed in the USA
BVHW092328181122
652274BV00036B/769